ONSET
TO SERVE AND PROTECT

BOOK ONE
OF THE ONSET SERIES

ONSET
TO SERVE AND PROTECT

BOOK ONE
OF THE ONSET SERIES

GLYNN STEWART

**FAOLAN'S PEN
PUBLISHING**
faolanspen.com

This edition published in 2018 by:

Faolan's Pen Publishing Inc.

22 King St. S, Suite 300

Waterloo, Ontario

N2J 1N8 Canada

ISBN-13: 978-1-988035-41-3 (print)

A record of this book is available from Library and Archives Canada.

Printed in the United States of America

2 3 4 5 6 7 8 9 10

Second edition

First printing: January 2018

Illustration © 2018 Shen Fei

Read more books from Glynn Stewart at faolanspen.com

[1]

THE POLICE CRUISER RADIO CRACKLING UNEXPECTEDLY TO LIFE SHOCKED David, resulting in boiling hot coffee spilling across his uniformed legs. The rookie in the seat next to him started to pass him Kleenex, freezing as Dispatch's words sank in.

"All units, all channels. Armed robbery at three six five Center Street, witnesses report at least four entering the building, shots fired, at least one staff down. All units respond immediately. Repeat, armed robbery at three six five Center Street, multiple offenders, at least one down. All units respond immediately."

Ignoring the burning sensation dripping down his legs, the dark-haired police officer grabbed the radio. They were only a few blocks away, and he threw the cruiser into gear as he thumbed the transmitter on.

"This is Lieutenant White," he radioed quickly. "En route from five six zero Center."

He slammed on the gas as he spoke, the old cruiser's engine whining as it shot off down the street, siren blazing to life as it moved through the night. Dispatch's lack of response was a silent editorial on the night shift's commanding officer being on the street at all—let alone responding to calls!

As the cruiser approached the store, David clicked the safety off on the massive .44 magnum Desert Eagle he carried. Charlesville had grown from a small town to a large one some years back, and the police force had traded in for the larger guns in a somewhat illogical attempt to be ready for larger crimes.

He offered the slender young officer in the other seat of the car what he hoped was a reassuring smile. Aaron Keller was the Charlesville Police Department's newest, rawest recruit, barely six days out of the state's training academy. This was his first night patrol, so the Lieutenant had decided to take him out himself and keep an eye on him.

It was turning out more exciting than expected.

The tires screeched as he spun the cruiser around to a stop just outside the door of the 7-Eleven at 365 Center Street. A massive glass front in the old brick building announced SODAS. ICE CREAM. SLUSHIES. Several streetlights illuminated the entire area in stark white light.

"Watch the back door," David told Keller. With the front door blocked by the police car, the lieutenant threw his door open and lunged out, hoping that Keller would be able to get around back on his own.

The stockily built Lieutenant charged through the half-open door, turning to face the counter while he covered the room with his gun. A moment later, he had the weapon trained on the figure standing over a body slumped against the counter. A second body in a staff uniform sprawled across a collapsed set of potato chip racking mere feet away from the perp.

"Police! Freeze!" he barked.

The figure blurred around to face David and snarled, exposing a pair of elongated, fang-like canines that contrasted sharply with his torn black jeans and shirt.

"Holy shit," David breathed, and the scene seemed to freeze for a moment. A single drop of blood fell off one fang to plink onto the floor, the youth's bloody mouth causing the officer's brain to completely freeze.

Then the punk moved, leaping over the rack of shelves and

charged for David. Reflex and training took over, and the *crack-crack* of the Desert Eagle double-tapping rang through the small store.

Two holes, easily large as a man's fist, blossomed in the perp's chest and he crumpled backward, sending a candy bar rack crashing to the ground in a clatter of metal and plastic. David stepped forward, desperate to check on the boy sprawled across the racking.

Before he made it another step, however, the punk rose, suddenly —*impossibly*—back on his feet and charging forward. His fangs glistened with blood, and his fingers reached out like claws.

David barely had time to think before he opened fire. He kept firing as the monster—he couldn't call it a person anymore—stumbled but kept coming. Desperately, he kept firing until he'd emptied the magazine into the *thing* and it collapsed to the linoleum floor and lay still, the body now little more than gobbets of flesh held together with lengths of skin.

Swallowing back bile with an effort, David stepped over to the fallen clerk, his hands half-unconsciously reloading the heavy pistol as he went. The young girl on the floor amidst the wreckage of the store's shelving's flesh showed multiple wounds—fang wounds. The mess of blood where her throat should have been confirmed his fear. She was dead.

Fearing the worst, he turned to check over the boy. More fang wounds marked his arms and neck, but David found a pulse amongst the blood. The boy was alive.

"Dispatch, this is Lieutenant White," he reported into his radio, then paused to spit out the sick taste in his mouth. It didn't help. "Need an ambulance ASAP," he ordered, his voice calm for a moment before breaking as he continued. "I've got an injured boy here, one of the staff. Perp and a customer, both dead. He *bit* the poor girl. My god," he said, his voice pitching higher with panic, "he just wouldn't go down. He took a full mag from the Eagle before he...came apart."

"We have an ambulance en route," the dispatcher confirmed, and paused for a moment. "Are you okay, boss?" He paused again, but David said nothing. "The guy was probably wired on steroids or some shit—they can take a lot of damage if they are."

"I'm okay," David said slowly as he nodded and swallowed, then jerked his head up at the sound of an engine behind the building—where he'd told Keller to watch!

He charged through the back door of the convenience store, into the loading area behind the building. A group of youths scattered away from the door as he flung it open, leaving Officer Aaron Keller's corpse abandoned in the middle of the shadow. The young policeman was very clearly dead, half of his throat missing and a rapidly expanding pool of blood surrounding him.

The six youths, clad in torn black clothing similar to the perp in the store, ran out the alley toward the street. One of them laughed as he ran, and the light reflected off two shiny and far-too-long canines.

The laugher looked back at David and flipped him the bird as he leapt into the back of a car parked on the brand-new cobblestone-style surface of the main street. Even as David realized that the car's window had been smashed in, the massive blue Oldsmobile, overburdened with the six punks, took off.

"Officer down, I repeat, officer down. Keller is dead," David said into his radio in a calm voice he barely recognized as his own. "I have six apparent perps taking off in a stolen car," he continued as he bolted for his car. "I am pursuing."

———

OTHER EARS than the dispatcher's were listening to David's panicked transmission. Like most other transmissions made in the public service, it was recorded in a database for future review. At the same moment the call was being recorded into that database, a quiet program no one at Charlesville's police station knew about streamed it across a dedicated line onto the internet, to an automated site no human *could* visit.

Moments later, it was downloaded to a server that officially didn't exist, and a data-matching program analyzed it. Ten thousand such transmissions hit its filters every minute, but most passed by and were deleted without raising a flag.

Lieutenant David White's description of the man he'd killed, however, raised flags. A *lot* of flags. Nothing living in the world could take a full magazine from a Desert Eagle to kill. At least, nothing *mundane* could.

It took sixty seconds for an analyst from the Office of Supernatural Policing and Investigation to see the flag. Thirty seconds more for him to realize just what he was seeing and grab David's next transmission.

Two minutes after David told his dispatcher he was in pursuit, that analyst was radioing someone else.

———

THE FIRST THOUGHT through Michael O'Brien's head as the radio in the chopper's cockpit suddenly started paging him was that this was only supposed to be a transport flight.

With a grunt, the massive, bear-like team Commander flicked the radio on.

"This is ONSET Nine Actual," he answered calmly.

"Commander O'Brien, this is Analyst McGill at OSPI," the radio blurted out. "We have a confirmed Omicron One incident in Charlesville, Maine. We have definite confirmation on one dead civilian and one dead police officer, as well as a possible vampire kill by local law enforcement. The surviving officer is pursuing six individuals that are associates of the possible."

"Where the fuck is Charlesville?" O'Brien responded genially. Over the years, he'd ended up protecting innocents in some of the weirdest corners of the mainland United States, but he had *no* idea where this Charlesville was. Or, perhaps more accurately, *which* Charlesville it was.

"I've already transferred the coordinates to the chopper's computer," McGill responded, and a quick glance confirmed it. A nav point icon now blinked on the chopper's HUD. "I'm also linking you to the GPS transceiver in the pursuing cruiser."

The analyst paused. "Do a thermal sweep before you go in hot," he suggested. "It's possible they're not vamps, in which case, leave it to local law enforcement."

"And if they're vamps?" O'Brien asked.

"Then the poor bastard chasing them probably won't be a survivor for very long."

———

THE ENGINE of David's poor old police cruiser whined in his ears as he slammed the car into high gear. Old and tired as the cruiser was, it leapt forward as if possessed with a desire for revenge as David spun it around to follow the stolen Oldsmobile down Center Street.

The moment was almost surreal, with only the brand-new gas-lamp-imitation streetlights shining onto the deserted streets as the two cars tore across the expensively cobblestone-styled pavement of Charlesville's touristy downtown, their engines and David's sirens ripping apart the peaceful night.

"Dispatch, this is Lieutenant White," David said, hitting the radio with a single finger, his hands white on the steering wheel. "Have whoever is in position move to blockade the south end of Center Street; we're maybe two minutes out."

"Bairns and McClaren are pretty much there," Dispatch told him. "They'll be ready."

The night shift Commander took a deep breath and said the words he'd never expected to say in his life.

"Make it clear," he said quietly, "that they are to shoot to kill. These guys have already killed one cop tonight."

It was almost as if the punks were listening in on his radio. Moments after he ordered the blockade, the Oldsmobile swerved in a wide arc around a chunk of road construction onto a side street.

David made up precious seconds going around the corner after them, his smaller and older—but better maintained—car making the turn in a smaller arc. He quickly reacquired the stolen car as it blazed toward the industrial park.

Slowly, ever so slowly, the police cruiser gained ground on the heavier and more loaded car. As the pair swung into the deserted industrial park with its brand-new warehouses and factories, David's anger over Keller's murder caused him to risk taking his full attention off the wheel for a moment. He leaned out the window and aimed the Desert Eagle at the Oldsmobile's tires.

The recoil of the pistol firing threw him off, dragging his whole body sideways and throwing the steering wheel over. For a few seconds, the cruiser pointed straight at the wall of one of those shining new warehouses. His heart pounding, David grabbed the wheel, yanking it over to bring the car back in line with the road.

His shot appeared to have had no effect whatsoever, and he looked up just in time to watch the stolen car scream into a turn behind another brick-and-steel warehouse. With a desperate jerk, he spun the wheel of the cruiser and followed them around.

The stolen car carrying Keller's murderers had disappeared. The road they'd turned onto continued out of the industrial park across the railroad tracks, but there was no sign of the Oldsmobile.

David slowed down, looking around to see where they would have gone. There couldn't have been more than five seconds between them turning the corner and him following them around. They couldn't have made it far.

Charlesville's industrial park was very young, all built within the last twenty years. Where the rest of the town was either picturesque old stone and wood construction or intentional imitations thereof, the industrial park was modern to a fault. A very different esthetic had ruled its construction—one of efficiency and chrome, not postcards and stones.

That chrome caught a flicker of light in one of the alleys between warehouses—a flicker like a car's lights turning on as a door opened, and David stopped the cruiser next to the road. There wouldn't be any other cars here halfway through the night.

He grabbed his radio and thumbed it on. "Dispatch, this is Lieutenant White," he reported. "Stolen vehicle appears to have stopped between 14 and 18 Warehouse Boulevard. Suspects may be proceeding on foot or into the warehouses. I'm following them in. Send backup," he ordered.

Unfortunately, Charlesville only had a part-time tactical team. As the town's third most senior officer, David led the team—and he was the only member on duty tonight. Any backup would be a long time coming—time in which Keller's murderers could get away.

With a long, deep breath, David picked up his flashlight and stepped out of his car, the Desert Eagle once more in his hand.

———

HE WALKED SOFTLY into the alley between the two multi-story-tall warehouses, scanning from side to side with his heavy flashlight, looking for any sign of the punks he'd followed in. A nerve twinged in the back of his head, and everything seemed just a little sharper than usual. All the sights, sounds and smells of the dimly lit industrial park were clear.

As expected, David found the stolen blue car empty. Both front side windows were shattered, and blood slowly dripped from the jagged remnants of the glass. He realized that the original thief must have punched through the window with a bare hand. Somehow, after the events of the night, that didn't even faze the cop. It all fit together; it was just that it fit together in a way that terrified him almost as much as Keller's death had enraged him.

The only light other than his was the streetlights' reflection from the car, and David slowly surveyed it in the silence. No motion showed in the alley. For a moment, it seemed as if the six people crammed into the Oldsmobile had just disappeared.

Then a quiet noise caught his attention and he turned to shine his light on a side entrance into one of the warehouses. A breeze had caught the open door and pulled it out before allowing it to thump back against the wall. This late at night, no door on an industrial building should have been unlocked, let alone open.

David quietly crossed over to the door, keeping the heavy semiautomatic pointed at it. Drawing closer, it became clear that someone—or some*thing*—had ripped the entire security lock assembly clean out of the door by brute force. The door swung loose because nothing held it shut.

With a deep breath, the police officer kicked the door open and swung around to point the flashlight and pistol in through it.

"Freeze! Police!"

Only silence and the deep darkness of the warehouse's entrance answered him, and he smiled mirthlessly. Whoever these idiots were, they were obviously intending to play games. A back portion of his brain gibbered in fear of the idea of intentionally wading into a fight with a lethal weapon, but his training and the memory of the junior officer, brand-new, utterly earnest, and now viciously torn apart in an alley his first week on the job, drove him forward.

He stepped forward into the dark of the warehouse, sweeping from left to right with the flashlight and pistol as he slowly moved through the small security checkpoint inside the door. No guard occupied the bulletproof glass booth, and shadows obscured its insides. The single security camera in the corner glinted, its tiny light marking the only life in the room.

The only way into the warehouse was through a metal detector between the two concrete half-walls splitting the room. The detector was off, a silent metal archway leading deeper into the dark building.

Passing through the silent metal detector, David realized that the door into the warehouse proper had been torn from its hinges. His quarry had given up subtlety by the time they'd made it there.

The main floor of the warehouse seemed silent and infinitely large as he entered, the beam from his flashlight picking out scattered details of the rows of skids and boxes, and the metal stairs that led up to the offices. The only sound was the thump of his feet on the concrete floor as he walked into the vast concrete cavern, the flashlight beam questing along the aisles.

The attack came unnaturally silently and scarily fast. Two of the black-clad and silver-studded punks seemed to materialize out of the shadows and lunged toward him. They charged toward him like enraged wolves.

Somehow, David got the Desert Eagle between him and the monsters. The doubled report of its firing echoed in the warehouse, and one of the *things* went down in a heap in front of the cop, two slugs through the upper chest. Then the second creature leapt on him.

The kid ripped the pistol out of his hand in the first second and threw it across the warehouse to clatter to the ground somewhere. The next, David's arm twisted aside in one of the youth's hands while the other hand rained a series of impossibly fast, unimaginably strong blows into David's chest.

David White was a short but heavily built man. He took his duties as a police officer seriously and worked out religiously. No weedy teenager who looked like he was made out of twigs and black duct tape should have been able to outmuscle him. That, however, was exactly what this skinny, unhealthy-looking youth did.

For all his training, David could *not* seem to stop any of the blows. Each time he tried to block, he was too slow. One of his ribs cracked, and then, as fear and *pain* filled him, he *was* fast enough, his hand snapping into place to stop the next blow, almost as if he could see it coming. Without thinking, he blocked the next blow, and then the next series of blows, his free hand matching the vampire—for his mind had finally accepted that label for what had killed Keller—motion for motion.

Then the first vampire—the one he'd shot and hadn't seen get back up—joined the fray. Somehow, David bent out of the path of his new opponent's first blow, allowing it to slam into the other vampire. Both the vampires were stunned for a moment, and David tore his arm from the first one's grip, stepping back to buy space.

No sooner had he done so, however, then a third vampire arrived out of shadows and swung at his head. Now the liquid-lightning speed of their motions and strikes were so slow. He caught each of the third vampire's blows easily, his training moving him smoothly from block to block. Finally, he shifted from defense to offense. The vampires' motions were sluggish, and David calmly, easily evaded his target's blocks to throw the black-and-silver-clad punk backward into a stack of crates.

Footsteps echoed behind him, and he dodged as the first two vampires lunged at him again as though stuck in molasses. White easily grabbed one of each of their arms and spun the pair forward, using their own sickening strength to propel them into the same pile of crates as the third.

For a moment, calm reigned in the dark room; the only motion the twitching of the three stunned vampires, half-lit by the flickering light of the flashlight on the floor. David took a deep breath, and the world seemed to slowly speed up, as if everything around him had been in slow motion.

Then motion at the top of the stairs caught David's eye. He saw the girl there—saw her jump off the balcony fifteen feet up and thirty feet away from him and almost fly across the room to hit David in the chest.

In any other circumstance, the tight leather bodysuit the girl was wearing would have been highly distracting, especially with her sitting on his chest. But the impact drove any notice of her gender from his mind, as did the fangs she drove toward his neck with blinding speed.

He managed to get up his hands and fend off her teeth despite his shock, but then two more vampires showed up. Shockingly swift kicks shattered both of his forearms, and then sickeningly strong hands pinned him to the floor. He had just enough time to understand how they'd killed Keller so quickly before the vampire on top of him sank her fangs into his neck.

For a moment, all he could perceive was pain. The next moment, he thought the pain was making him hallucinate as the roof vanished. Not collapsed, not exploded—vanished.

Figures dropped down from a helicopter hovering above the missing roof. The first let go of the rope halfway down and turned into a giant wolf as he dropped down. Another spun on the rope, showing an athletic female figure he was sure he shouldn't have been noticing at a time like this, and launched tiny darts of fire from her fingers into the just-recovering heap of vampires he'd originally fought.

The world around him blurred, and he heard rushing footsteps before a massive paw swung across his vision, massive claws smashing into the vampire at his neck. He *felt* the fangs jerk out of his neck as the crashing sound of gunfire began to echo through the starlit warehouse.

David barely comprehended the sound before finally, mercifully blacking out.

———

THE HACKER WOULD NEVER REMEMBER what she'd been looking for in the warehouse's computer system. She hadn't even been in the surveillance feed intentionally—she'd been trying to get into the inventory files or something like that. But she had been in the security camera feeds when the first bunch of psychos burst in and ripped the door off its hinges in a casual manner.

She'd spent the next twenty minutes fixated on the feeds, flipping from camera to camera to follow the ensuing fight. It was like something from a bad action movie—vampires and a supposedly normal cop fighting like they were on wires and the tape had been sped up.

Then the Men—and Woman—in Black had shown up through—dropping through the roof as if it weren't even there. The vampires had been quickly and efficiently annihilated and they'd loaded the cop up on a stretcher. Then one of them headed toward the warehouse's server, and the hacker realized they were going to wipe the tapes.

It was the work of only moments to copy the video files from the surveillance system for the entire time frame. Moments more erased the hacker's presence as her programs retracted into the rest of cyberspace, their owner wondering just what the *hell* she'd stumbled across.

O'BRIEN WATCHED CALMLY AS THE FORENSICS TEAM REMOVED THE SIX black body bags they'd stuffed the sliced, bullet-ridden or crisped corpses of the vampires into from the helicopter's storage bay. At the edge of the helicopter landing pad, a med team was already rushing the unconscious body of the cop who'd got there first across the grass toward the nearby hospital facility.

The hospital was one of the four major structures inside the walled "corporate" campus that was ONSET Headquarters. All four were apparently stumpy office buildings from the outside, but Michael knew that the glass was a step *up* from bulletproof, and the rest of the buildings were made of reinforced concrete. Even with that, a good half of HQ's facilities were underground, hardened to withstand anything short of a direct nuclear hit and concealed beneath the carefully sculpted grounds of the hidden base. Dozens of small structures, three or four stories tall, provided residences for strike teams like his, as well as hangars for the Office of the National Supernatural Enforcement Teams fleet of specialized aircraft and other vehicles.

"Why'd you bring the cop here?" a voice asked him quietly, and O'Brien turned to look at the slight form of his commanding officer, Major Traci Warner. The Mage made *maybe* three quarters of O'Brien's seven-foot frame, but he knew better than to think of the redhead as frail.

"Two reasons," Michael rumbled. "First, he was bitten by a vampire. Now, that's not as much of a 'you're dead' as some pop culture would have us believe, but it's still something we have to be wary of."

"No go, Michael," Warner told him firmly. "The poor kid at the store this whole mess started at was bitten too, and we left that to the OSPI cleanup team."

"How is that kid, anyway?" O'Brien asked.

"OSPI has a team on site now. They got him tanked on the antivenom and bagged the fang and the two victims' bodies. Diplomatically," she added.

"Which means they lied and said they were from the Center for Disease Control and Prevention, I imagine," Michael replied, a touch of bitterness in his voice. "Diplomacy in our job means we lied our teeth out, deceived them some, and then lied some more."

"Yes, it does. Now stop doing it to *me* and tell me why I have a small-town Maine police Lieutenant in one of the highest-security and most classified hospitals on the planet," Warner snapped.

"All right. Two *more* reasons," Michael promised. "Reason two-A: that poor bastard went into the warehouse ten minutes before we did, and was still alive and conscious when we arrived. That's impressive, and it *also* means he's going to remember a lot of it—including an ONSET strike team coming in hell for leather. Reason two-B: Morgen!" the team Commander bellowed.

One of his team members looked up at the bellow and wandered over across the concrete pad in the middle of the grass. With his helmet —its visor modified to work as prescription lenses—removed, Morgen Dilsner had put his glasses back on. This made the fair-haired Mage look like the hacker nerd he had been before stumbling on a hidden site with spells that had actually *worked* for him.

"You called, bossman?" the Mage asked.

"Grab that hotwired iPad of yours and show the Major what you showed me," O'Brien ordered.

"It's not an *iPad*," Morgen told him pointedly as he pulled the

handheld computer from inside his half-removed gear. He looked at
Traci as he plugged it into the suit's built-in computers.

"The warehouse had security cameras," he told Traci. "Night
vision–equipped ones, actually—so that even if the lights were down,
security would know something was going on. Of course, nobody was
watching them last night, but they recorded everything anyway."

"You deleted the recordings, of course?" Warner queried.

"Of course," Morgen confirmed. "And I threw a quick splice of
quiet time from before we showed up in there to cover everything, too.
But before I did that, I downloaded the original files."

"And?" the Major demanded impatiently.

"Well, sir, ma'am...watch," Morgen told her, and then hit play.

Warner watched the video clip of the appropriate moment from the
fight in the warehouse, all the eerier for being shown only in green, in
silence. A moment in which a supposedly mundane cop made three
vampires look like they were stuck in molasses and then beat the shit
out of them.

"I see," she said finally. "Your recommendation, Commander
O'Brien?" she asked.

"Even if he walks out of here, we'll need to keep him under
surveillance," the team leader told her quietly. "We may as well be
honest enough to tell him what the *hell* is going on and give him the
choice. I recommend recruitment, sir."

"Well, he'll have the best care in the world until he wakes up," Traci
said. "In the one hospital in the world that knows *exactly* how to
handle vampire bites."

———

THE WORLD SEEMED fuzzy for a very long time. That was about all
David remembered afterward. It wasn't the total blank of normal
unconsciousness, but if there were dreams, he couldn't remember
them. It just seemed...fuzzy. Like a sheet of gray fluff stretched over
the unconscious blank.

When he finally woke up, it took him a minute to realize it. The
sounds coming in from the outside world were still blurred, but they

existed. He couldn't say how long he lay there with the feeling slowly returning to his body. He recognized that he was on a bed and covered with blankets. Eventually, his brain finally identified the sound of machinery quietly beeping in the background, and the soft rustle of someone turning pages.

Finally, he opened his eyes. Like his hearing and sense of feel, they were confused at first, and by the time they cleared, the woman who'd been reading had put the book down and stood next to his bed. The uniform was definitely "nurse", but it was more military in cut than anything he'd expect in Charlesville, and the woman wore a set of insignia David didn't recognize. The uniform somehow fit with the stark white of the room around him and what he recognized from previous hospital stays as an extraordinarily well-equipped recovery ward.

"Lieutenant. You're awake," she said softly, but David still winced as the words echoed inside his head. He nodded. "How do you feel?" she asked.

"Fuzzy," he croaked. "I got...bitten..." His voice trailed off as his mind rebelled against the idea of voicing what his memory—somehow much less fuzzy than his physical senses—insisted had happened.

"You were bitten by a vampire, yes," the black-haired nurse said in a businesslike tone. "The fuzziness is normal—a side effect of the antivenom. It will wear off in a day or so now you've woken up."

"Antivenom?" David repeated, somewhat disturbed by her matter-of-fact approach to the idea of his being gnawed on by a vampire.

"Yes," she confirmed briskly. "A vampire's bite injects a high-powered supernatural infection that attempts to transform the victim into a vampire. One bite usually isn't enough to cause the effect, but we prefer not to take chances." She looked at him for a moment, as if remembering something. "Just so you know, this information is classi-fied Omicron-Bravo, but that won't matter until you leave the Campus."

"Campus?" David asked. "What campus?"

"You're at ONSET Headquarters," she told him. "And that's prob-ably more than I should be telling you. Your body is still recovering, and I have some tests I want to run. Can you sit up?"

David slowly nodded, and the nurse came over to help him up. Both of his arms were wrapped in casts, so he found himself needing the help. Once he was upright, she pulled a somewhat sinister-looking array of equipment out from under the bed.

"Now," she said calmly, pulling out a small shaped hammer, "let me know if this hurts."

———

IT TURNED OUT, as the nurse told him after she'd finished her battery of tests, that David had been unconscious for two full days since being brought back to this "Campus"—wherever that was! He didn't know what or where the Campus was, but the capital C was pretty clear when the nurse spoke about it.

With David still weak from the aftereffects of the vampire's venom, the nurse refused to let him leave the bed, other than for a short trip to the bathroom. For two more full days, this situation continued, with David's movements still sharply curtailed even as he began to recover. He recovered quickly—far faster than he should have.

On the third morning, after having his casts removed, David had had enough. "Am I a prisoner?" he demanded roughly as the nurse entered his room with his breakfast—the first meal he'd been able to eat without help. "I am a police Lieutenant; I have duties and subordinates who rely on me. Why am I being held here?"

"You are not a prisoner, Lieutenant White," she replied firmly. "You are weaker than you think. It is not safe for you to be wandering the Campus alone."

"Bullshit," he snarled. "You haven't even let me out of this damned room in two days!"

"Do you have any idea what the possible side effects of a vampire bite are?" the nurse snapped back. "Or of the magic that is healing your arms?"

"Well, I sure as hell am not turning into a vampire!" he replied harshly, his memories of the vampires he'd met *very* clear in his mind now. Even with that fresh in his mind, his thoughts avoided her mention of magic.

"Only because of our treatment," she told him flatly. "We had to keep you quarantined in case it didn't work!"

"Oh, right. And if I'm a good little boy, you'll let me out?" he snapped.

A hard female voice interjected. "Not exactly, Lieutenant White," it told him calmly.

Still angry, David turned to face the speaker. A short redheaded woman in an unfamiliar black uniform stood just inside the door. The uniform was a jacket over what looked like a full-length bodysuit, all in black except for a long blue stripe down each arm of the jacket and an odd rank insignia of two silver bars vertically crossing a diagonal lightning bolt in a circle.

"Who are you?" David demanded, still angry.

"I am Major Traci Warner, commanding officer of this base and executive officer for the entirety of ONSET," she responded smartly. "That young lady you are busy berating saved your life. You could show her a little more appreciation."

The last of David's frustration slowly drained away, and he looked over at the nurse. "I'm sorry," he said quietly. "It's just frustrating to be cooped up in here."

He realized, as he apologized, that he was probably angrier about having his entire worldview shattered into a million pieces than at being locked up in the hospital room. *That* wasn't the fault of anyone here. The...*things* whose fault that was were dead.

"That was mostly at my orders," Major Warner told him. "This facility's *existence* is classified Top Secret Omicron-Alpha. What Nurse Sheldon told you, which is admittedly an unusually low amount of information to give a patient, is *all* classified at a similar level."

"Top Secret Omicron-Alpha?" David repeated. "And what does *that* mean?" According to his—undeniably limited—knowledge of the United States classification scheme, it ended at "Top Secret".

"That's classified Top Secret," Warner told him dryly. "For the duration of your stay at this facility, I've been authorized to grant you temporary limited Omicron-Alpha clearance. The lack of that clearance was why you were restricted to this ward, as well as the quarantine concern."

"Does that mean I'm now allowed to leave?" David asked, wondering about the rest of his department. "And how long am I going to be staying here? I have a job back home."

"You are currently on medical leave due to injuries incurred in the line of duty," Warner informed him. "Your PD was advised that you'd been taken to a state-level facility due to infectious disease concerns. This also helped us cover up the aid we had to give the poor boy they attacked and our sweep of Charlesville to check for more vampires."

"You lied to my people," David accused. Now he was angry again. If there were vampires everywhere, then people *needed* to know.

"Our *job* is to lie to people, Lieutenant White," the woman informed him. "You have brushed the edge of a much larger picture— one that, if you would like, I am now authorized to explain to you in somewhat more detail. Interested?"

"In what?" he asked.

"The truth," she said simply. "You'll be here for one more day before we send you home. Feel like taking a walk and getting some fresh air?"

David considered for a long moment, looking at the oddly dressed woman and considering everything he'd seen so far. He was still stunned by how fast his injuries had been fixed. He was still angry about these people's lies and secrets, but he *needed* to understand. He needed to understand the way the world actually worked—what was being hidden...and why. A cop couldn't serve and protect without knowing everything he had to protect against.

"All right," he agreed slowly.

———

THE TRIP out of the hospital itself was silent. Major Warner didn't speak, and David didn't feel up to asking any questions. The hospital was well equipped and they ran into a small number of staff, but it otherwise seemed unusually empty. The entire hospital was painted an institutional white, and discreet signs led to all the usual departments —and to odd ones like the LYCANTHROPY NATURALIZATION WARD.

Finally, they reached the bottom floor, where a concrete-walled security checkpoint marked the exit from the building. Two armed guards, in the same black-jacket-over-bodysuit uniform as the Major were behind a glass pane, and David saw a nasty-looking multi-barrel minigun pointing outwards from the security checkpoint, toward the main doors of the hospital.

David eyed the ugly weapon and the guards' sleek and odd-looking sidearms, and wondered just what they expected to be showing up at the front door of this hospital.

"Afternoon, Major Warner," a third guard, in front of the glass, greeted the Major while holding out his hand for her ID. He took the card and ran it through a reader, then gestured her toward a pad. "Thumbprint, please."

The diminutive woman pressed her thumb against the pad and it beeped confirmation of her identity.

The guard looked at David. "ID, please, sir?"

David half-panicked for a moment. He was sure he had no identification they'd accept, and these guards didn't look like the type to accept that as an excuse.

"He's with me, Sergeant Kells," Warner told the guard, and David remembered who he was with. "Can you boys run him up an Alpha-grade pass with class-three limitations?"

"How soon do you need it?" Sergeant Kells asked immediately.

"By the time we get back," she told him. "Should be an hour at least."

"Can do, ma'am!"

Warner led David out of the hospital into the sunlight and looked at him carefully. "Until we get you that pass, don't go wandering off on your own," she told him. "ONSET runs with extremely tight security."

David nodded his acceptance of that obvious fact. Sunlight on his face was enough reason for him to remain quiet as they walked away from the hospital to the neat paved path leading across the perfect greenery.

"Who *are* you people?" David finally asked, as they passed out of the field of fire of the minigun in the hospital entrance along the path. The grounds of this "Campus" wouldn't have looked out of place at a corporate R&D or university facility, except for the twenty-foot-high concrete wall he could see surrounding the four large and several dozen smaller buildings.

"ONSET is the Office for the National Supernatural Enforcement Teams," Warner told him grimly. "We are basically the nation's SWAT teams as far as supernatural affairs go. Where the police don't know what's going on and OSPI doesn't pack enough heat, we are the United States' answer to supernatural crime, violence and major incursions."

"Supernatural," David said softly. "Like what? Are we talking vampires and wizards and werewolves and the bloody boogeyman?" Part of him still didn't believe, even after all he'd seen. The part of him that had seen Keller and the girl in the convenience store with their throats ripped out, however, believed all too well.

"Bluntly, yes," she replied. "Vampires are real. Unlike most super-naturals, they are solely our responsibility. OSPI may *find* the fangs, but we deal with them. We decided a long time ago to regard them as a disease. We treat those we can and kill the rest. Werewolves can be OK, but we keep an eye on them anyway. Wizards are very real—we call them Mages." She smiled. "As a matter of fact, I am one."

"You're a Mage?" David asked disbelievingly. Somehow, this small but very military woman did not look like a wielder of strange and arcane powers to him.

In answer, Warner made a blue flame appear above the palm of her hand. It rapidly expanded to encase her entire body, but while he could feel the heat of it from where he stood, her uniform and hair were untouched. A moment later, the flame was gone.

"Believe me now?" she asked.

He nodded slowly as he controlled the sudden surge of fear at the inexplicable fire. That casual demonstration and the spark of fear it inspired hinted at why these people kept this secret.

"ONSET supports the operations of OSPI," she continued calmly, as if her demonstration had been perfectly normal. "That's the Office of Supernatural Policing and Investigation. They keep an eye on known supernaturals and investigate and punish most crimes, remanding criminals to the Special Supernatural Courts in Washington for trial."

"OSPI is also our primary information source and keeps an eye on all government communications to catch any burgeoning supernatural activity before it becomes an issue. That's how we knew to send a team into Charlesville."

"Just in time to save my ass," David said softly. "I still don't understand—why have I never heard of any of this?"

"ONSET and OSPI are the two biggest components of the Omicron Branch, a subsection of the executive, judicial, and legislative branches of the United States government," Warner told him. "Outside of Omicron-rated documentation, they are only ever referred to as the Omicron Offices. Even in Top Secret documentation, both enforcement Offices are supposedly subdivisions of the FBI, while other Omicron groups are subdivisions of their own portions of the government. In practice, Omicron is an independent branch of the United States government, and we and OSPI recruit personnel from wherever we need to—usually the FBI or the military."

"Why all the secrecy?" He finally asked the question that was eating at him. "Why keep it all classified at that sort of level?

"To avoid public panic," she told him. "We keep all supernatural activity very quiet. You were the third-ranking officer of your town police department; you've seen some of the best and worst of humanity." It was a statement on the nature of his job, David realized, not a question. "How do you honestly think," the ONSET major continued, "people would react to realizing that their neighbor is a werewolf and they might get eaten by a vampire on their way home?"

David thought about it for a very long time as the pair entered a small orchard of apple trees hidden in one corner of the campus. He wanted very much to insist that people had to know. He knew better. Few could understand people's reaction to fear better than a veteran police officer.

"They'd react badly," he admitted finally. "They'd either completely disbelieve or riot." He stopped, taking a long breath of the smell of the ripening apples under the late summer sun.

"If secrecy is so important to you, why are you telling me this?" he asked.

Warner looked away, surveying the campus they'd been slowly

walking along. "Lieutenant David White, you walked into a pitch-black room with six vampires," she said quietly. "You lived long enough for our team to arrive. You shouldn't have. You should have been dead in the first thirty seconds."

"So?" David replied, turning away from her and studying an apple tree so she couldn't see his face as the memories flashed through his mind.

"Mundanes don't do that," she told him bluntly after a few moments. "You have now moved yourself into a special category—the Empowered—a human with supernatural powers."

"I'm not a supernatural!" he snapped. "I was just lucky."

The idea of the supernatural even *existing* was causing his brain to run in circles. He couldn't possibly accept that he *was* supernatural. The idea made his hindbrain cringe, with memories of his father and his distaste for "weirdos".

Major Warner shrugged. "That may be the case, but even if it is, we can use you," she told him. "You know what's going on—you already knew; I just gave you some more details. You're a fully trained veteran police officer, with investigative and tactical training and ten years in the service, which is nothing to sneer at, even for us. Even if it turns out you *are* just a lucky mundane, OSPI could use you."

It was clear from her voice that she didn't believe that at all, and David turned back from the apple tree to meet the strange woman's gaze.

"What do you mean, *can use me*?" he asked.

"Haven't you figured it out yet?" she asked. "This is a recruiting pitch, David. We want you to join ONSET."

[3]

AT LEAST THEY GAVE HIM TIME TO MAKE UP HIS MIND, DAVID REFLECTED AS the strange black helicopter swept away from the ONSET Campus. They'd agreed to take him to an airport—they hadn't said which one or how far away—where he'd be flown back to Charlesville. This wasn't a decision he could make right away, and Major Warner had respected that. She'd sent him away with a phone number to call when he'd made his decision.

They'd blackened the windows in the back part of the helicopter, so David couldn't see where ONSET HQ was situated. This meant that the four-hour flight was uninterrupted by scenery beyond the utilitarian interior of the chopper, only by his quiet reading of the book Warner had given him: *The Cracking of the Seal*. An ugly strip of tape across the front cover of the book advised the reader that the contents of the book were CLASSIFIED TOP SECRET OMICRON-ALPHA.

The book delved into the history of something called the Seal of Solomon. Supposedly, the Israeli king from the Bible had made a deal with incredibly powerful supernatural entities and created a spell to seal the supernatural away from the world. For whatever reason, his seal had not held and throughout history had slowly degraded. Every so often, the Seal was restored to complete strength. The book gave the last date for such a restoration as "around the end of the twelfth century CE" but gave no details as to how it had been done. Apparently, the Seal had started to crack again in the late nineteenth century. The cracking had supposedly accelerated in the fifties—when OSPI was founded—and again in the nineties, leading to the foundation of ONSET to deal with the bigger nasties.

Details on the various known supernaturals filled the book's pages. Vampires, werewolves, Mages and other odd creatures of legend, mixed with the grab-bag of supernatural humans the author referred to as "Empowered". Perhaps the scariest part of the book was that there was what looked to have been a thirty-page chapter on "demons"—that had been cut out and replaced with a single page stating, "This material is classified Omicron-Charlie."

Apparently, there were even worse things out there than Warner and her people were willing to tell him about yet. They'd told him about worse things than he'd seen, and what he'd seen had been horrific enough.

Reading the section on vampires, he kept having the image of the punk in the convenience store, lunging toward David even as heavy slugs ripped away chunks of his body.

For all his distaste with Omicron's secrecy, he wondered, reading the book, if there even *was* another way.

———

THE REST of his journey home passed in an almost eerily ordinary manner. Once he was off the black helicopter at the Salt Lake airport, he was handed an ordinary plane ticket and left to his own devices. The flight back to Maine and then the taxi ride home were normal. Part of him was looking around in the airport and on the street, wondering who in the crowd was actually a supernatural creature.

No vampires leapt out at him on his way home, and the prepaid taxi driver dropped him off at his front door and then took off, heading for another client. He lived in a small subdivision of Charlesville, with about two hundred or so houses. They'd all been built to the traditional stone-and-wood pattern, and only the similarities between the houses gave away the fact that these homes hadn't been there for hundreds of years like the town's core.

The small two-bedroom house he called home blended in amongst those other houses. He lived alone, and the house was as empty as ever. He didn't even bother to check his email before falling into bed.

Even if he'd had the training, he would have been far too tired to notice the electronic bug that had appeared in his front hallway.

———

THE NEXT MORNING, David arrived at the Charlesville Police Station rested and, as far as he was concerned, fit to do his duty. Smiles and 'hi Boss's greeted him as he walked through the doors. A week had passed since the last time he'd entered the building, and while the world seemed to have changed for David, nothing had changed here.

He made it about halfway to his office—one of only four private offices in the tiny station house—the familiar sounds and sights of the smoothly functioning police department soothing the troubles in his heart and mind, before a bellow across the office interrupted him.

"WHITE! Get in here!"

Police Chief Darryl Hanson had the voice of the drill sergeant he'd once been, and David paused in mid-step to turn toward the Chief's office. Hanson stood in the door of his office, thick-bodied, broad-shouldered and a good six inches taller than David.

Wordlessly, David changed direction and walked over to Hanson's office, where the Chief gestured him in and to sit down. David obeyed, and the door slid closed behind him with a thunk.

"As far as I am concerned, Lieutenant," Hanson, who was easily twice David's age, told the younger man gruffly as he crossed back to his own desk, "you are still on medical leave. CDC told me you'd be flying back in last night. I should have known you'd be here in the morning."

"I feel fine, sir," David insisted. Part of him had expected this. The rest of him just wanted to get back to work, to try and forget what he'd seen.

"*Aside from* the fact that an officer under your command died in front of you, you just spent six days in a fine government-run hospital," Hanson responded, "and I *watched* CDC burn the body of the bastard you took down. That's not standard procedure."

David twitched at the mention of the vampire he'd killed and opened his mouth, but the Chief waved him to silence and spoke more quietly. "I know a cover-up when I see one, David," he told the younger man bluntly. "I'm also old enough to know when I don't want or need to know what's under it. I *do* know that whatever went down, you got hit hard. So, you are off duty until Monday, no ifs or buts about it. That's three days. Understood?"

"Yes, sir," David finally said, surprised at the Chief's candor.

"I also wrote the letter to Aaron's family," the chief said gently. "It couldn't wait for you to get out of the hospital."

"Yes, sir," David said quietly. "Thank you, sir." He hadn't quite forgotten about that tradition, but he'd spent more time wondering if he could have saved Aaron than thinking about how to tell his family.

"How was your treatment?" Hanson asked. "I'll light a fire under someone's ass if it wasn't the best they can provide."

"I...don't think it gets any better, sir," David told him, thinking back to the nurse's comments on the antivenom. Antivenom he doubted was in common supply in the world's hospitals. And then there was the incredible speed with which his shattered forearms and rib had healed. "They took good care of me."

"Good to hear," the Chief replied.

"Sir," David began, but then trailed off. How could he tell this man, his boss and friend, what had happened? Even if he could find the words, Hanson wouldn't believe him. He hadn't seen what David had seen.

"What is it, son?" Hanson asked.

"They offered me a job," David blurted out, then blinked at his own words. That hadn't been what he'd wanted to talk to Hanson about.

The Chief looked at David in silence for a moment. "I'm not going to ask who 'they' are," he finally replied. "I'm going to say one word, and you're either going to nod, or stare at me in confusion."

David stared at his boss in confusion for a moment, and the Chief said his one word: "Omicron."

For a moment, David continued to stare at his boss in confusion, and then it struck home. *Hanson knew.* Omicron was the code designation for the branch of government that included ONSET and OSPI. Warner had referred to it as the "Omicron Offices". Finally, after a moment or two, he slowly nodded, and Hanson breathed a massive sigh.

"This isn't the place, David," he said quietly. "The walls aren't thick enough. Go home," he instructed, "take your medical leave. But come over for dinner tonight. Marge will love to have you. And then you and I can talk."

———

DAVID WALKED AWAY from the station to his car in a daze. How did Hanson know *anything* about Omicron and the supernatural? Nothing about the old chief suggested anything about an involvement with boogeymen and magic.

It was comforting nonetheless. Scared as David was about the world he'd stumbled into, and Warner's offer, that Hanson knew about it offered a hope. A hope that someone he trusted could let him know where he stood.

The world was a lot scarier than it had been a week before, but David White was a police officer. "To serve and protect," he'd sworn. That oath meant more to him than he could ever explain.

It meant the same, he knew, to Chief Hanson. As David reached his beaten-up old pickup truck, he realized that he was looking forward to dinner.

———

DAVID FOLLOWED the chief's directions to the letter, pulling up to the Hansons' old country home shortly after seven. Stepping out of the car, the short police officer inhaled the scent of the spruce and the smell of someone barbecuing in the early autumn chill.

The Hansons' house was several miles outside the town and buried in the trees. David hadn't seen another car on the drive out. If Darryl wanted to talk in private, his home was a good place to do so.

A couple of centuries or so before, the house had begun as a midsized farmhouse built mainly out of pine. A century or so ago, the old wood had been reinforced with fresher wood and stone. More recently, it had been refitted with modern amenities, adding several sets of large bay windows, as well as internet and indoor plumbing.

As David stepped up to the ancient door in the original core of the sprawling house, it swung open to reveal the tall old police chief standing there with a smile on his face.

"Good to see you, David," Hanson greeted him. "How are you feeling?"

"Like I told you earlier, I feel fine," David insisted.

"David, I can put two and two together," Hanson told him. "And unless I miss my guess, you were bitten by a vampire. Am I right?"

David looked at his boss in shock and then nodded slowly. The intellectual realization that his boss knew about the supernatural had only barely prepared him to actually *hear* his Chief mention the word *vampire* so calmly.

"Thought so," Hanson replied in a satisfied manner. "Come in; have a seat."

Hanson led David, still stunned by his boss's matter-of-fact conclusion, through to a sunken living room and gestured to a leather couch.

"How do you know about all this, boss?" David finally asked. He'd worked for Hanson for ten years, the last three as one of his senior officers. "They gave me the impression that this was all classified beyond Top Secret?"

"It is," Darryl told him grimly. "Marge knows as well as I, so we don't need to worry too much about talking about it here. I technically still hold Omicron-Alpha clearance, though no one is really supposed to keep me in the loop anymore beyond the normal Outreach updates. Fortunately, I still have friends who let me know a bit more than I'm supposed to."

"How?" David repeated, and Darryl grinned at him.

"I wasn't always a small-town police chief," he told David. "Once upon a time, I was a Marine Sergeant with more balls than brains.

Rumor went around the base of some kind of covert op taking place in a closed hangar. I, being an idiot, took the bet to see what was going on.

"The 'covert op' was actually a trio of vampires and some military flunkies setting up for…well, something. I never did work out what," the police chief admitted wryly. "I made my peek just after the vamps had woken up…and were feeding on a girl their flunkies had bought them.

"Marines are as Marines do," he continued, "so I charged in, gun blazing."

"Against three vampires," David observed. "According to the book they gave me, that would be only slightly more survivable than what *I* did."

Darryl nodded. "I had somewhat better timing that you did," he admitted. "You had people diverted to save your ass. *I* charged into a vamp nest that OSPI—Office of Supernatural etc., you've heard the name right?"

"The acronym was explained," David replied slowly, looking at his Chief with new eyes. He'd known Hanson had been a Marine. The image of him as a young glory hound was still…new.

"Heh. This was in the late seventies," Hanson explained. "OSPI was *it*—the heavy strike force wasn't even a pipe dream. In any case, OSPI had the nest under surveillance, and their agent was about as ready to stand by and watch vamps feed as I was. I had an M1911 sidearm. *He* was a werewolf with an M4 rifle loaded with silver bullets.

"When the dust settled, three vamps and twelve US military personnel who'd been working with them were dead," Darryl said quietly. "And one junior Marine drill sergeant had moved into the elite category of folks 'in the know' about the supernatural.

"The agent offered me a job on the spot. Before I knew it, I'd been transferred out of the Marines and was now an OSPI Inspector."

For a moment, David simply looked at the Chief he'd worked with for five years. In all those years, he'd heard Darryl's time as a Marine mentioned a dozen or so times, but he'd never heard even the slightest hint of what had followed them.

"I didn't know," he said finally, the words seeming inadequate. He wondered if anyone else in the town knew. Probably not, he realized, as secrets were hard to keep in small towns, and small towns always had men with ready prejudices and loaded guns. Men like David's father had been...

"No one's supposed to," Darryl told him. "If I wasn't able to keep a secret, I wouldn't have *made* Inspector. But..." He shook his head.

"I made it five years," he said finally. "The average field work life of an OSPI Inspector before being grounded by the psychs is less than four. The supernaturals take it better for some reason, but normal mundanes can't hack it for much longer. We saw too much, and the supernatural has a weird effect on the brain."

"When the psychs told me I wouldn't be allowed back into the field, they gave me two choices," Hanson continued. "I could take a desk job in the Office, analyzing intelligence and giving advice and training to the new Inspectors, or I could go Outreach.

"Outreach's goal was to put at least one 'in the know' officer in every police department in the US—*without* actually going out and training anybody," Darryl explained. "I'd met Marge on a mission out here—she's a Mage—and decided to take Outreach. Joined the Charlesville PD twenty-five years ago, and that's all she wrote."

"So, you know exactly what I went through," David said quietly. "That vampire...I've never seen anything like it." He paused. "Chief, I've served ten years. I lead our tactical team. I've had all the training and psych warnings about how to handle it, but I've *never* killed anyone before, and he...it was like killing him five times over."

"Don't think of vampires as people," Hanson said softly. "Some of them are very intelligent and very scary. Most are little better than junkies, driven by the need for their next drink of blood. They are horrendously dangerous, but they aren't human anymore."

The younger officer slowly nodded. It didn't make the images in his head go away, but it jived with the book they'd given him. Once a vampire had fed, it was too late for the vaccine. The only remaining cure was death.

"Four years, huh?" David said finally. "That's all they expect from an Inspector?"

It was less than half the time he'd already given to service. It seemed too little time for the kind of sacrifice they were asking of him. If a man were to delve that deeply into darkness and magic to protect others, he should do it for more than a few measly years.

"We saw too much," Darryl repeated. "You learn to deal—you *will* learn to deal, David, hard as it seems right now," he assured the younger man. "Some things...you just can't deal with. More than anything else, mundanes can't get used to dealing with magic. It scares us, somewhere deep down inside that we can't teach any better."

David remembered his reaction when Warner had demonstrated magic to him, and nodded slowly.

"The rumors I got said they'd classified you as Empowered," Darryl continued gently. "I won't nay or yea that, but if you are, it'll be easier. Empowered *can* get used to magic—they have to. It's inside them.

"I also heard they offered you a position with the new strike force —which I honestly don't *know* the name of," Darryl finished, and looked at David expectantly.

"What do you think?" David asked quietly. He wasn't sure himself yet. There were too many things he needed to think about. Too much he had to accept. He felt a lot younger than he was, facing something he really wasn't sure he fully grasped.

Darryl shook his head. "I can't tell you what to think," he replied. "It's a dirty job, David. It gets worse every year. But if nobody does it, people get hurt."

"My father would not approve," David said quietly. His father had been a racist and openly disapproving of anyone outside the normal. The idea of his son being some kind of "freak", as he would have called it, probably had the man turning over in his grave. But...

"I took an oath to serve and protect," he continued. Those were the words ringing through his head now, drowning out his memories of his father. The ball and chain that dragged him toward something he really didn't want to think about.

"It's up to you to decide whether that means the people of Charlesville or everybody," the Chief told him.

Footsteps alerted David to the arrival of Darryl's buxom wife. She bustled in, her blond-and-silver braids swinging around her head, and like Major Warner, she looked *nothing* like David's image of a Mage.

"There's as much need for those who know the truth here as there are with the Offices," she told David abruptly, as if she'd been listening to the conversation all along. "But there's also a need for those who can stand and fight to be able to be everywhere. Like Darryl says, the choice is yours. *Unlike* the choice of whether or not you're going to eat my dinner," she said calmly. "That is ready now."

———

DAVID STOOD on the back porch of the country house, staring off into the darkness of the woods with a forgotten beer in his hands. He ignored the cushioned wooden chairs behind him and leaned against the railing, looking into the shadows.

If ONSET was right, he was more than human. He didn't really believe it—but part of him reminded him that they were probably better qualified to judge. Even if he didn't admit that, there were memories of that night in the warehouse that pushed his incredulity.

In amongst the horror of what he'd dealt with, were the flashes of moments at which six vampires *hadn't been a threat*. David remembered that very clearly. Amidst the horror, there'd been a few points when he had not been afraid. According to the book they'd given him, that was something very few supernaturals—let alone mundanes—should have been able to do.

He was sad to find a small part of him was glad that his father was dead—that the old man who'd despised anything out of the ordinary wasn't here to face this. Yet, for his father's narrow mind, he'd taught other things as well. He'd taught David responsibility, and to be true to his word.

If he was what they said he was—if he was everything that night in the warehouse implied—did he have the right to deny people the protection he'd sworn? "To serve and protect." It meant more than just the populace of one town, he realized.

He hadn't sworn that oath only with Charlesville in mind. It was just that as one ordinary man, one smallish town was all he could help protect. He'd done well at that—his rank and responsibilities proved that. Now…it was possible that he could help make sure they never *had* to fear the menaces that stalked the night.

"I have something for you," Darryl said from behind him. "Whether you decide to go or not, you'll need it."

David turned around and Darryl held out a matte black metal case, thicker though otherwise smaller than a regular briefcase. Wordlessly, David took it and opened it.

Nestled in the gray packing foam were a familiar-looking pistol and four magazines. The glint of the lamplight off the exposed bullets in the magazines showed their silver sheen.

David's reading had already brought up the fact that silver was antithetical to the supernatural. No one knew why, but no supernatural could use their abilities with silver touching them. For this reason, OSPI and ONSET both carried and used solely silver ammunition.

"The Colt Model 1911A1 was the standard pistol of the US military for years," Darryl said quietly. "The FBI Hostage Rescue Team used it as well. When OSPI needed to adapt a pistol for its own use, it was the obvious choice. The gun was modified over time to take into account years of OSPI experience with the difference in bullet dynamics between traditional rounds and OSPI's silver bullets. Our cartridges have higher muzzle velocity and the rounds foul the barrel like crazy if you don't watch it, but it's still the same gun, with all the reliability of the model."

"A gun for silver bullets," David said quietly.

"They gave me two when I went Outreach," Darryl told him. "I want you to keep this one, regardless of what happens."

David closed the case and turned to look at the man he'd worked with for the last ten years. Everything he'd been thinking about, the oath he'd sworn, the loyalty he felt to the people around him, and the dogged determination to protect that had driven him to be a police officer in the first place—even his own father's teachings—crystallized at last, into one final decision.

"I'm going," he said simply.

[4]

MICHAEL WAS TAKING ADVANTAGE OF A RESPITE FROM TEAM MEETINGS AND training to actually get some of the stack of paperwork ONSET required done when his phone rang. The ONSET Team Commander looked at the black phone, as unmarked and unremarkable as the wooden desk it rested on, the green steel filing cabinets along one wall, or the white walls that were the rest of the tiny office, for a long moment. Then he answered it.

"O'Brien," he said into it gruffly.

"This is Warner, Michael," the Base Commander's voice said from the speaker. "Your police lieutenant, White, just called in." She paused. "He's volunteered. You're the designated contact officer. Meet me in my office ASAP and I'll give you the rundown. Busy?"

Michael looked at the over-three-inch-high stack of paper in his inbox. "Not really," he responded, glad for an excuse to avoid that stack. "I'll be right down."

———

O'BRIEN ENTERED Warner's office to find the Base Commander on the phone. She nodded to him as he came in and gestured to a seat. The

Base Commander's office wasn't much more adorned than his. She had the same green filing cabinets along one wall, and the opposing wall was lined with low bookshelves. Above the bookshelves was an assortment of pictures and awards from Warner's time in the Army before she'd bounced into OSPI.

Behind the Major's heavy oak desk, the only real affectation in the office, a pair of flags rested on the wall: the stars and stripes of the United States of America, and the blue flag with the Omicron Office's lightning-crossed *O* police badge. The two flags flanked a medium-sized portrait of a dark-furred wolf.

"I understand, sir," she said into the phone after a moment. "I am aware of the President's concerns. But we lost three entire teams last year—we *have* to recruit aggressively to keep pace with our losses." She paused. "I know he understands that intellectually, sir," she continued into the phone. "But the stink he's raising about *any* visibility is starting to risk our people—and I will *not* allow that to happen." A moment of silence followed. "No, I am not talking about disobeying the specific directives of our President," she said calmly. "Dealing with the politicians is *your* job, sir. I'm just telling you what those of us who have to do the job this organization was created for think."

The next pause was long, and Michael began to get the feeling that this was probably not a conversation he should be listening to.

"Sir, *every* incidence of the paranormal is up across the board," Warner said into the phone. "They've been increasing for as long as we've known about them—that's why ONSET was created. Our recruiting efforts aren't affecting that trend. That trend—and the *deaths*, Colonel, it's causing our people—is *why* we need to recruit."

A very long pause followed. Finally, Warner nodded. "I agree completely, sir. But talking to the President is your job. I have recruiting to arrange." Pause. "Yes, sir. Good luck, sir."

With that, she hung up the phone and turned to Michael.

"Sorry about that," she told him. "The Colonel called just after I got off the phone with you."

"No worries," Michael replied. "Anything I should worry about?"

"No," Warner said flatly. "Our current President is having heebie-jeebies about anything supernatural. He wants the entire Omicron Branch to run completely black, make sure *nobody* knows about us."

"Difficult," Michael responded thoughtfully. "Not without accepting a higher level of civilian and Omicron casualties than we *already* have. And it's not like anybody will *believe* anything that leaks."

"That's what I told Colonel Ardent," she replied. "Of course, he knows that, and he'd already told the President that. I am very glad I do not have his job," Warner said fervently.

"Agreed," her subordinate echoed.

Warner snorted. "For me, that's a rhetorical statement," she said dryly. "You could have *had* Ardent's job if you'd wanted it. Or my job. Or any position in the Omicron Branch you wanted."

Michael shrugged uncomfortably. Before OSPI's High Threat Response teams had been spun off to form ONSET, he'd been the Brigadier, their commanding officer, the only Omicron officer to *ever* hold that rank. When HTR had become ONSET, however, he'd refused the Commander's role and gone back to leading a team. He was the longest-serving supernatural in the ranks, and had made a lot of both friends and enemies along the way.

"You called me here about the recruit?" he said finally.

"Yes," Warner said slowly, and glanced at her computer, then slid a blue paper file across the desk. "He called in this morning. We contacted his PD and spoke to the Chief. He's an Outreach officer, former OSPI Field Inspector First Class."

"Which makes our life a *lot* easier," Michael observed.

"Exactly," the Major agreed. "I got an earful, by the way, about poaching his 'right-hand man'—White apparently led his tactical squad as well as being his third-ranking officer, and he's not overly enthused with losing him."

"If he's Outreach, he knows the need," Michael replied simply.

"Which was basically what Chief Hanson said," Warner told him. "White has technically not returned from medical leave, so the Chief has agreed to let him transfer immediately. As of an hour ago, David White is enrolled on ONSET's book as an Agent-Trainee, with clearance Omicron-Bravo."

"I'm assigning you the pickup since you recommended recruitment," she continued. "We told him he'd be met at his house at nine in the morning tomorrow."

"Pendragon or normal flight?" Michael asked.

"It's not an emergency, so you just get government-paid flights once you're out of here," she told him. "To speed things up and keep with the normal obfuscation, you'll be lifted by Pendragon to Salt Lake, and from there you'll take civilian transport. Bring him back the same way."

"All right. How much of a bug do I put in his ear along the way?" Michael asked.

"Public transport," Warner replied, which was a reasonably complete answer in itself. "Give him a briefing at his house and help him close it up—you know how long training takes."

"Understood," Michael confirmed. "I'll be on my way, then."

"Fly safe," Warner told him.

———

THE HACKER HAD SPENT days tracking down the identity of *anyone* she'd had in that insane tape from the Charlesville warehouse. Finally, she'd managed to ID the cop as a senior local officer: Lieutenant David White.

She'd called in a quick favor, and she soon had a bug quietly planted in the cop's front hallway. Barely in time, too—the cop came home the very next day, though he apparently had been gone for a while.

The next couple of days had passed quietly. White had puttered around the house. Today, however, he'd started packing for a trip, and the hacker was keeping an eye on the bug in a side window on her computer screen.

Curiosity may have killed the cat, but the hacker hadn't found it fatal yet. This meant she was watching the door to David White's house when the large man in the black suit came calling.

———

DAVID ANSWERED the knock on his door with a feeling of trepidation. His quiet, small townhome had been disassembled over the course of the day. Not sure how long he'd be gone, he'd packed several weeks' worth of clothes and covered all of his furniture with dust cloths. He had no close family and had never really been willing to deal with pets, so there was not much else to worry about.

He opened the door slowly to see an immensely large man in a perfectly tailored suit on the other side. Despite the suit and the careful combing of the man's short blond hair, there was a sense of feralness around the six-foot-plus man.

"David White?" he asked.

"I am," David responded. "You are?" Something about this man twinged a warning sense deep in the back of his head. His size didn't intimidate David, but that didn't stop the police officer wanting to take a step backward.

"I'm Commander Michael O'Brien," the man responded. "We've met before, but I doubt you remember it. I was with the team last week."

"You're from ONSET?" David somehow doubted anyone else would know about last week, but he wondered about this man.

"I'm your pickup," Michael replied wryly.

"Come on in," David said finally, stepping away from the door and allowing the larger man to step through.

The ONSET agent moved with brisk efficiency, stepping inside and closing the door behind him. David eyed him carefully, wondering just what to expect of a full ONSET Commander. This was a man who not merely knew about the supernatural but did battle and commanded others in battle against its darker side on as a day job.

"Nice place," he commented, glancing around the sparse furniture and decorations. "Very 'young bachelor.'"

David wasn't sure how to respond to that, so he gestured for O'Brien to sit. "You were in the warehouse?" he finally asked.

"Yes," O'Brien confirmed. "I lead ONSET Nine—one of twenty-one teams operational across the country. We're currently on a down week, so Warner asked me to come pick you up and answer any questions you had."

"Are you...supernatural?" David asked carefully, not sure if the question was offensive or not.

O'Brien chuckled. "Don't say it like it's a dirty word, kid," he told David. "All of ONSET's field agents are supernatural. But, since you ask, I'm a werewolf. Like that gives you any more peace of mind," he finished with a wink.

"I don't even know where to start with questions," David admitted, trying not to lean away from the man who'd just admitted he was a creature from myth and legend. "I'm not even sure how long I'll be gone from here."

"A while," O'Brien said bluntly. "Once you hit the Campus, you'll be locked in for four weeks of training. Then we clear you to actually know where the base *is*, and allow you to go home." He shrugged. "Our teams work on a schedule of two weeks on duty followed by one week on leave. Most of us just live on the base, but transport is certainly possible if you want to come back here that third week."

"I'm...not sure yet," David told him. The thought surprised him, but he knew it was true. He was comfortable there. It was home. On the other hand, he was moving into a new life he *wasn't* comfortable with yet, and he wasn't sure how much he'd change.

"Good choice," O'Brien assured him. "You can't know how you'll adapt to the realities of ONSET until you've had a chance—it's like no other job in the world. Most of us find it difficult to hide ourselves among mundanes once we've lived among supernaturals."

"What happens if I'm not actually supernatural?" the younger man asked, voicing another of his many worries at this change in his life. "What if I go through your four weeks of training and flunk it?"

The werewolf looked at him appraisingly for a long moment. "Kid, I saw the tape from the warehouse," he said finally, and David found himself horrified at the thought that there was a tape of that night. The thought of someone like his father—or worse, someone who'd *known* his father—seeing that scared him. "You don't have much to worry about. If, somehow, we're all wrong and you're really a mundane—or if you aren't empowered *enough* to keep up with an ONSET team— you'll still be one of the few in the know, and there's always a shortage of those."

"So, what? You find me odd jobs around the office?" David asked. Somehow, the thought of being the paper-pushing desk clerk at somewhere like ONSET didn't appeal, compared to helping run the slowly expanding police department of a booming small town.

O'Brien barked a laugh. "Not really," he replied. "Most likely, with your experience, we'd send you over to OSPI to join the Inspectors and deal with the less violent or outright evil of the things that come through the Seal."

"I see," the cop said quietly. Even as the werewolf made him nervous, he also somehow felt that he could trust the larger man. For all the feral air around him, the man was calm, collected and determined to make sure David made this transition as easily as possible. It was reassuring.

For a long moment, the two men sat in the cop's living room in silence. Eventually, O'Brien huffed.

"Warner told me to help you pack up and get ready to go," he said into the silence. "Anything left you need to set up?"

"No," David told him, with a shake of his head. "I've packed a few weeks' worth of clothes, and most of the furniture is covered in dust cloths."

"I've got a government car outside," O'Brien told him. "Let's cover what's left for you, and then get your stuff out. The sooner we get you to the Campus, the sooner you'll get adjusted to the world as it *really* is," he said kindly.

THE TRIP BACK TO THE TWIN CITIES AIRPORT AT SALT LAKE WAS AS prosaic and boring as the trip from there back home had been. David hadn't been much inclined to talk, and Michael had been even less inclined to answer questions about ONSET in public.

Finally, the last plane came to a landing in the middle of a thunderstorm, and the two men disembarked to the smell of stormy air. Before even leaving the arrivals area, Michael calmly told David that his bags were being taken care of, and headed over to a security door.

"Where are we going?" David asked.

"Secured helicopter pad," Michael told him. "We have a Pendragon waiting to take us to the Campus."

"Do I dare ask what a Pendragon is?" David inquired dryly as they reached the door and Michael opened it with a swipe card.

"You rode in one before," Michael told him. "I'll tell you more later."

The arrival of a security guard into the unmarked corridor behind the security door had distracted the werewolf from his answer.

"This is a secured area," the guard said bluntly, his hand resting on his sidearm. "I need to see your IDs."

Michael pulled a black travel folio from his trouser pocket and looked the guard over. The guard looked back at him calmly, his hand tapping the grip of the pistol at his hip.

"Today, please," the guard snapped, and David wondered just what was going on with Michael.

Michael opened the folio and removed a single piece of plastic, handing it to the guard. "These are classified IDs," he said calmly. "Can I see your authorization?"

The guard took one look at the piece of plastic and slowly nodded. His hand moved away from his gun and into a half-salute.

"OSPI Security Detail 4, Salt Lake," he reported crisply. "Sergeant John Lewis, sir."

"So, you are Omicron," Michael said dryly, and handed over the rest of the folio. "That was my major concern, Sergeant." He gestured to David. "I'm bringing a recruit with me. He doesn't have ID yet, but his travel papers are in the folio."

The uniformed guard quickly and efficiently skimmed through the folio, and then passed it back.

"Apologies for the difficulty, sirs," he told the two men, and gestured for them to continue down the corridor deeper into the secured zone of the airport.

"Your job, sergeant," Michael replied, somewhat begrudgingly. "Carry on."

He led David past the guard and through a second door, into a windowed corridor looking down into a fully enclosed helipad with a jet-black helicopter sitting on it.

It was a weird hybrid of a vehicle, just like the one David had ridden in before, but he hadn't had a chance to look at that one as they'd hustled him aboard. It was a long and narrow vehicle, with an entrance just behind the cockpit, and another under the tail rotor where passengers could enter and exit. Where the side doors would be on a normal helicopter, a pair of short wings with almost-hidden intakes stretched out from the aircraft.

"That," the werewolf told his recruit, "is a Pendragon. They started as a prototype for a new Black Hawk-based jet-helicopter with limited supersonic capability. Then we took it apart, enchanted the bits and put it back together."

"It's a...magic helicopter?" David asked, disbelievingly. Somehow, monsters from myth and legend, along with vampires and Mages and a branch of the US government dealing with magic and the supernatural had managed to get hammered into his world view, but an enchanted helicopter *still* stretched his disbelief.

It was a feeling he was starting to get used to.

"Yes," Michael confirmed. "Get used to it. We mix magic and technology a lot for our work. Anything that isn't silver or used to fire silver bullets tends to be enchanted. The only reason silver escaped is because silver does to enchantments what nukes do to butter."

"So, I'm walking into Wonderland," the new agent said dryly.

———

A PRESUMABLY DIFFERENT storm was raging as the Pendragon finally drifted in for its landing at the ONSET HQ Campus. With the windows once again blacked out to prevent his learning the Campus's location the trip was...uncomfortable. After feeling the helicopter being thrown about like a toy for the last few hours, he could *hear* the pilot's sigh of relief even from where he was as the rotors were finally switched off.

Michael slid the door open and waved David out into the driving rain.

"Come on," he shouted over the wind. "The ground crew will deliver your things—you have an appointment with Warner."

"I do?" David shouted back.

"Yeah," the ONSET officer replied, stepping aside to let David exit the helicopter into the rain. "Actually, you're late for it, but I think she'll understand," Michael continued as the pair sprinted for the shelter of the nearest building. From there, they dodged from building to building until they reached one of the four tall buildings that anchored the Campus.

Entering the building, David found himself in a surprisingly adorned lobby. A stretch of blue carpet led to a security checkpoint flanked by marble pillars. Four marble pillars, spaced about two meters apart, lined each wall. The security checkpoint held the center of the far wall, and a close look revealed the armored weapon slits and the almost-unobtrusive machine gun barrels centered in the side walls above the dark leather couches.

The security guards in front of the checkpoint gave the pair about ten seconds to catch their breath before asking for ID and thumbprints.

"I don't have ID yet," David told them, glancing quickly over at Michael for reassurance.

"That's alright," the guard told him, and David relaxed. Somewhat. "Warner told us you were coming. We have your ID, but we have to check your thumbprint first."

The guard led them up to the checkpoint and presented the two men with a fabulously modern-looking set of biometric equipment. Hesitantly, David pressed his thumb against the scanner the guard indicated, and felt a line of warmth run over the panel. After a moment, the machine beeped, and the guard in the checkpoint gave a thumbs-up to the one standing with David and Michael.

"Confirms that you are David White, Agent-Trainee," the guard told him, and then passed him a black folio identical to Michael's. "Here are your ID cards for the Campus, sir. You'll be issued an agent's ID once you graduate. Good luck, sir!" He finished with a salute.

"The security guards are mundanes?" David asked once they'd cleared the checkpoint into a simply but comfortably decorated second lobby. Doors ran off to the left and right, and two elevators in front of them flanked a door labeled STAIRS.

"Yeah," Michael replied as he led David into the stairs and started up. Like the rest of the building they'd seen so far, the stairs were functional but not ugly. The same blue carpet covered the steps, and the railing was varnished dark blue steel.

"ONSET Security," the ONSET Commander continued his explanation. "OSPI also has security forces. ONSET has also trained and equipped about two battalions' worth of Marines for anti-supernatural combat—the Anti-Paranormal Companies. Between them and OSPI, there's also the better part of a short division or so of security personnel."

"A *division*?" David asked, incredulous.

"The Anti-Paranormals are the survivors of *two* divisions we deployed in Montana five years ago," the werewolf told him, a slight distance crossing his eyes. "And spread across the entire country, eight-thousand-odd men and women start looking like nowhere near enough," he finished grimly as they stopped at the top of a fourth flight of stairs. Neither man was breathing hard from the climb.

Michael led the way through a gray steel security door onto the building's fifth floor, where the men faced a second checkpoint. No marble pillars marked this room, but it also lacked machine guns. A heavy oak desk with another suite of biometric equipment took up the center of the room, and three men with slung assault rifles occupied it.

David presented his new ID folio to the men and gave his thumbprint to the machine. A few moments of processing later, and the guards passed them through.

They traveled down a short corridor marked with the same blue carpet but also brass nameplated doors to where a single door sat in the center of the end wall. A simple brass plate next to the door proclaimed: MAJ. TRACI WARNER. ONSET HQ BASE COMMANDANT.

"It's a standard induction interview," Michael told him. "Nothing to worry about. I'll be in the front lobby when you're done, to show you to your quarters."

David swallowed at the realization that the werewolf, whose presence had been a comfort so far in his tumble into Wonderland, wasn't coming into the office with him.

"All right," he replied, managing to keep his voice level. "See you shortly, sir."

It took the former police officer a moment to gather his courage and knock on the wooden door.

"Enter!"

———

THE OFFICE on the other side of the door was the first actual working space David had seen since his return to the HQ Campus. Filing cabinets lined the wall on his left, but the wall on his right was filled with an impressive collection of medals, citations and photos—what he'd heard called an "I love me" wall—above a set of low book-shelves.

Major Traci Warner sat at an undecorated desk in the middle of the room, flanked on the right of the desk by the United States flag and on the left by the circled diagonal lightning bolt of ONSET's unit flag. Behind the desk the wall held a painting of a large wolf, which seemed to glow with illumination from a hidden light source.

"Trainee White," she greeted him, and gestured to the single chair in front of her desk. "Have a seat."

David took the seat. "Thank you, ma'am," he said uncomfortably. For all the curiosity and determination that had led him here, the thought of what he'd agreed to do and just who these people were still scared him.

"This is just an induction interview," she told him, echoing Michael's words outside. "Normally, you'd have been given a decent tour of the Campus before this, but with the delay and the weather, we'll put that off until tomorrow I think."

"Thank you, ma'am," David said more wholeheartedly, relieved to have avoided a slog through the storm outside. Besides, he reflected, he'd seen most of the grounds already when he'd been convalescing there.

"By now, we have explained to you some of the nature of the super-natural world around us," Traci told David. "You're rare in our recruits, as you've seen ONSET personnel in action and have some idea of just what we do. There is a vast gap, however, between our day-to-day operations and the *mission* of the Omicron Offices. Do you know what that mission is, Trainee White?"

"No, sir," David admitted. He wondered what Warner meant, but as the conversation continued, he realized that he could *not* locate the source of the light on the painting behind Warner, and it was growing brighter—almost hurting his eyes and distracting him from his thoughts.

"That's not a surprise," she reassured him. "It's not always clear. The mission of this organization and our sister organization at OSPI is very simple: we are to protect the people of the United States of America, mundane *and* supernatural, from the horrors that slip through the Seal.

"The Office of Supernatural Policing and Investigation handles most of the day-to-day policing of the supernatural. We are the next line. When there's an outbreak of vampirism, it's an ONSET team that puts it down. When a crack opens and a dozen demons slip through, we deal with it. When an Empowered who's too strong or too dangerous for OSPI goes rogue, we're the ones sent to arrest him.

"We are the line between the innocent and the weak and those who abuse great strengths.

"Do you understand me?"

"Yes, ma'am," David replied. Hearing Warner put into words what he'd felt when he'd decided to join this organization, and hearing that desire—that *need*—to serve and protect labeled as ONSET's mission reassured him.

"Good," Warner told him. "Over the next four weeks, you will be trained in the various types of enemies we face, the capabilities of your fellows in ONSET and OSPI, and the weapons and magics at our disposal. We will also train you in combating supernaturals and will put you through intentional stress training to attempt to awaken your powers."

"What if I have no powers?" David asked. A part of him hoped that was true, while another part feared it. For all that he'd never shared his father's narrow-mindedness, the thought of turning into a "freak" bothered him. The light from the painting distracted him from his thoughts. It was growing extremely bright—indeed, it now looked as though Traci herself was glowing.

"You do," she said bluntly. She paused for a moment, looking at him oddly. "Are you all right?"

"I'm fine," he replied. "It's just the damned light on that painting."

Traci looked behind her and then back at him. "There's no light on the painting," she told him.

He looked at her, wondering if she was toying with him. "It's hurting my eyes, it's so bright," he told her harshly, and she looked at him for a long moment.

"White light? With some scattered blue and green speckles and some good chunks of red?" she asked.

David blinked against the light, trying to clear it out of his eyes, but then nodded. He hadn't seen the speckles before, but now she mentioned them, he could pick them out. "I thought you said there was no light," he demanded.

"There isn't," she said calmly. "That's the aura of the security spell woven into the painting. A security spell most *Mages* don't even notice."

"What?" David demanded. She couldn't be serious! Auras?

"You just answered your question about powers," Warner told David quietly. "You are demonstrating Second Sight—right now!"

———

DAVID DRIFTED out of Warner's office in a slight daze. Somehow, that moment of seeing the aura of the painting had woken something up, and *everything* seemed to have an aura now. The world was flipping out around him, and he had *no* idea what to expect now.

O'Brien glowed even brighter than Traci. The Commander was waiting in the lobby as promised, and he seemed to glow with an inner light he hadn't possessed before. A deep red, almost purple, light seemed to emanate from the werewolf, suffusing him with an eerie glow. A weave of blackness woven through the red spoke to David, somehow, and without knowing why, he felt a great sadness from the man.

"Are you okay, White?" O'Brien asked, and David realized he'd been staring dumbly at the other man for a good ten seconds.

"I don't know," David admitted. "I just...everything started glowing."

"Glowing?" the ONSET officer asked, then paused. "Second Sight."

David nodded. "That's what Warner said," he admitted. "It's...fucking weird."

"I lived through the sixties," O'Brien told him. "I know all about weird. Come on, I think we need to get you somewhere you can sit down."

It took only a few steps for the werewolf to grab David's shoulder and slowly support him back to the main security station at the entrance. The guard gave him an odd look, and Michael shook his head.

"He just turned on," he told the man. "Second Sight. One minute, nothing; next, he's seeing auras."

"I'll let front security know, too," the guard promised, waving them through.

The next few minutes were a blur of colored light to David, with new auras intruding on his vision all the time. Somehow, despite O'Brien's comments, it hadn't occurred to him just *how much* ONSET tended to enchant.

When every single piece of magic, as well as everything alive, glowed like crazy, it sank home, all right. Everything from the walls to the biometric scanners to the uniforms the guards wore glowed in a psychedelic rainbow of light and special effects. He vaguely remembered giving ID and thumbprints to get out of the building and giving them again to get into a second building.

"What's with him?" a gruff voice asked. David managed to focus enough to realize that the strange lights had faded there. The glows were down to only a handful of distinct sources, though a slight haze in the background suggested...something. He didn't know what yet.

"Second Sight hit him in the middle of his induction interview," O'Brien replied. "Can you give me a hand with him, Koburn?"

David shook his head. "I'm good," he slurred. "Less magic here," he finished, a little less slurred as he slowly cleared his head.

He was in a small sitting room with O'Brien supporting him and another man just standing from the couch. A few small paintings of animals—none of them glowing, thankfully—marked the brown walls, and the same blue carpet as the offices covered the floor. The black furniture—two couches and a trio of chairs—fit smoothly.

Most importantly right now, nothing except the two men was glowing. Michael continued to pulse purple, but the other man showed a soft but powerful pale blue that almost hid his roughhewn features.

"Right," the man, who David began to realize couldn't be more than five feet tall, replied. "We keep this area low-grade—mainly so we

can train folks with the Second Sight here without them going nuts."
He extended a hand. "I'm Commander Ryan Koburn. I'm the training
Commander for ONSET, so you'd better get better quick." He grinned
evilly. "I like my trainees whole before I break them."

"Thank you, sir," David said levelly, not entirely sure it was the
appropriate response, and Koburn laughed.

"He okay with you, Koburn?" O'Brien asked. "My team is
supposed to be drifting back in from leave today; I should go check up
on them if White is good."

"I'll take care of him," the short blond man replied. "You
know that."

"All right," O'Brien replied, lowering David onto one of the
couches. "Now, I'm your sponsor with ONSET, son," he told David,
"so if you have any major questions, the Commander can put you in
touch with me if he's not willing or able to answer them. You get
me, White?"

"Yes, sir," David replied. With his head finally beginning to clear,
he suspected just how much of a commitment the Commander had
made to get David into ONSET. He wondered why the man had bothered, though the thought of dealing with this kind of craziness *without*
people who understood it was terrifying.

"Good," the Commander told him. "Now rest up—having a power
spring on you like that can be draining as hell, I'm told, and our
training isn't exactly a walk in the park. O'Brien, we'll talk
again soon."

With a jaunty quick salute, O'Brien slipped out the door, leaving
White with just Koburn, who grinned at him.

"This is the training center," the man told David. "Includes dormitories, a shooting range, twelve different kinds of simulators and a
lead-sealed room for magic training. Until you finish our little course,
this is your home."

David nodded understanding, keeping his eyes half-closed against
the glare of the man's aura.

"Now, I'm going to add Second Sight training to your schedule,"
Koburn continued. "But we schedule the first week for basic training
and assessment anyways. The dorms are through there," he added,

pointing to a door off from the sitting area. "Two of your fellow trainees are here already and three more will be joining us before we start tomorrow."

With a slim but inhumanly strong hand, Koburn easily hauled David to his feet. "Until tomorrow, however, you need to rest. Meditate if you know how," he instructed as he half-led, half-carried David into the dorm. "Otherwise, be ready in the morning. In the morning," he added with a half-joking grin, "I get to break you again."

[6]

THE TRAINING BEGAN AT SIX AM THE FOLLOWING MORNING, WHEN DAVID was rudely awoken from a dreamless sleep by a resounding alarm and a voice that took him a moment to recognize as Koburn's bellowing "Reveille, reveille, assemble in five minutes."

David made it out of bed, into the black military-style fatigues that had been hung on his door at some point in the night and out into the hallway to assemble with about fifteen seconds to spare. He was the second-to-last one out, followed by a diminutive teenager in black-rimmed glasses whose fatigues made it clear he was quite possibly anorexic.

Three other men, including the youth, and two women joined David in standing around the front room, waiting for Koburn. The instructor, in his black bodysuit and jacket, was exactly on time, entering moments after the boy.

Every single person in the room glowed with a shifting mix of colors to David's eyes, and it distracted him. He didn't know what they meant, and he didn't know how to turn this Second Sight off. It left him off-pace and uneasy.

"At ease, people," Koburn told them, though only one of the

trainees—a heavy black man who was missing half of his right ear—
was standing at attention.

"Before anything else, we are going to assess you," the trainer said
calmly as he looked over the trainees. David wondered just how they
were going to do that, when the six trainees were only half-awake—
well, with the exception of the black man, who David figured to be ex-
military from his bearing, and David himself, who'd been through
worse than this in police training years before.

"Follow me," Koburn ordered, and led the trainees through a door
at the end of the hallway. The door led to a simple set of spiral metal
stairs leading down one floor to a short hallway with various doors
leading off of it. The hallway was floored in bare concrete, making it
the first area David had seen in the complex without blue carpet.

Koburn stopped at a door halfway down the corridor and pointed
to it. The sign on the door read SIMULATION TRAINING THEATER.

David followed the other trainees through into a small room on the
other side. Concrete walls hosted a small number of lockers and
several low benches. A horizontal locker was open, revealing a number
of what appeared to be submachine guns.

Koburn removed one and showed it to the trainees. "This is a paintball carbine," he said calmly. "Each is loaded with a full carbon dioxide
cartridge and a magazine of one hundred paintballs. You may take one
spare cartridge and one spare magazine. Make sure the magazine
matches the color of paintballs in your gun."

The trainer gestured at the door on the far side of the room.
"Beyond that door is a training theater fully set up with a replica of a
railway station. An opposing force is set up in there with identical
weapons and reloads to you, but with red paint. You are a team; take
them out. Any hit is considered a kill."

The trainees hesitated, looking at each other, and then, one by one,
starting with the black ex-military man and ending with the under-
sized teenager, took a paintball gun and entered the training theater.

———

DAVID LASTED, by his own count, one minute. In reflection afterward, he was almost proud, at least in comparison to the rest of the trainees. The only trainee to last longer than him was the black man, and he *had* managed to hit one of the opposing force. Of course, the man he'd hit had shot him at the same time.

The black man, whose name he had learned was Leonard Casey, a former sergeant from the 101st Airborne, had survived for almost five minutes beyond any of them but had only managed to take down one member of the opposing force himself before he'd been lured into an ambush and covered with paint.

"Your opposing force," Koburn told them as the trainees lay around the benches in the entry room to the theater, "was ONSET Four, currently assigned to the Campus on inactive reserve. One of you is the former commander of a police special tactics team"—he gestured at David—"two more of you are from our sister office at OSPI"—he waved at the two women—"and one of you is military"—he gestured at Casey—"but you really didn't stand a chance."

"Part of that is because ONSET Four's men are fully trained supernaturals," the trainer continued. "For example, the Mage used a series of illusions to lure Casey into the ambush."

Casey grunted in response. David wondered how it felt to realize that skill and training had been trumped by a single spell.

"However, *all* of you are here because you have been identified as either supernatural or high-likelihood potentials," Koburn told them. "Supernatural abilities are not the only things that separate you from ONSET Four. They are trained as a team, working together to make the best use of their abilities.

"You *will* be as good," the trainer continued. "Or you will *not* be ONSET Agents."

———

FOR THE NEXT NINE HOURS, Koburn drilled the entire group of trainees on small-unit tactics, marksmanship with a wide variety of weapons, and the general material that any SWAT or high-threat-response officer in the country would need to know. There was information on supernatural threats and responses that other high-threat-response personnel wouldn't need to know, but it was still mostly a normal course.

After nine hours, Koburn let them take a break—they'd eaten lunch during a lecture component—to "let the lesson sink in." He then announced that two people had special classes as soon as they finished dinner: David White and Eric Shanks.

Dinner was a slow meal, the trainees physically and mentally exhausted. David learned that Eric Shanks was the young teenager. Shanks was the youngest person in the room at nineteen, and David was the oldest at thirty-one. Casey, the ex-Airborne, was the next oldest at twenty-eight.

The rest of the trainees were in their early twenties. Both of the women confirmed Koburn's identification of them as being ex-OSPI personnel. One, a tall leggy blonde named Leila Stone, was already a trained Mage—an Inspector who had requested a transfer to ONSET. The other, a tiny redhead named Bella Samuels, had been a security officer for ONSET before springing a positive on a test for supernatural abilities and being offered a choice of Inspector training or ONSET.

The last of the trainees kept to himself, a light-skinned Asian man with long hair who watched the rest of the group in silence with shadowed eyes. When asked for his name, he gave it as Hiro Tsimote gruffly. He ignored further questions, and left once he'd finished his meal.

———

DAVID'S special class turned out to be in controlling his Sight. As he was still drained, despite the hearty meal, the class with Koburn proved extraordinarily difficult and brutal. By the end of two hours, David had learned to at least mute the auras so they were not as distracting, and believed he'd achieved a beginning understanding of what the colors meant.

At this point, David had been in one class or another for almost fourteen hours, and Koburn sent him away with a curt "Get some sleep; you'll need it."

He met Eric on the way back to the dormitory in the training bunker, and the youth looked shaken. Neither man felt like talking, and they made their way back in silence.

Only one of the trainees was still up. Tsimote was reading a small black-bound book as they entered. He looked up, and a tiny gesture suggested for David to come join him. David bid Shanks good night and joined the Asian man.

He was shocked as Tsimote reached out and touched him on the neck. A moment later, David realized the man had touched the scars from the vampire bite.

"You too," the Asian said in a hoarse voice. It wasn't a question, and Tsimote brushed aside his long hair to reveal a similar set of scars on his own neck. "They got my family," he said grimly, "and almost got me before I summoned flame and burnt them all away. I still nearly died."

"They'd killed an officer under my command," David replied softly. "I followed them into a warehouse. An ONSET team saved me, barely."

"I don't intend to fail this," Tsimote said calmly. "The others don't understand. They have no idea what's out there."

David considered this a foolish statement at best. Samuels and Stone had *worked* "out there". Casey had, from some of his comments, joined up after helping an ONSET team track down a supernatural killer in Iraq. And David had seen Shanks's eyes. There was something about the boy that suggested the boy knew as much about the dangers as any of them.

Unwilling to make an argument of it, he simply nodded slowly. "I don't think any of us intend to fail," he said finally, getting up to go sleep.

Tsimote watched him go in silence.

———

At six AM the next morning, the same blaring klaxon went off, and David slowly dragged himself to his feet to Koburn bellowing "Reveille!" again.

Exhaustion from the previous day conflicted with expecting it this time to have David out with the others exactly at the five-minute mark. Koburn was standing in the front of the room, tapping his foot impatiently.

"Follow me," he ordered once they'd all shambled into some semblance of order. Again, Casey was the most functional of them all, though David took a small amount of pride in being *almost* as awake and ready to go as the ex-soldier.

Koburn led the six trainees into a small lecture room that wouldn't have looked out of place in the police training academy David had gone through—and returned to twice, once for advanced training in investigation and tactics, and a second to teach some of the early classes. A projector sat in the middle of the room amidst twelve simple wooden desks. The ONSET trainer gestured for them all to sit and then propped himself against the table with the projector.

"Some of you," he said quietly, "have never seen real supernatural trouble and are wondering why the United States even has a secret branch of government, let alone supernatural strike teams.

"The rest of you"—his gesture took in David, Tsimote, Casey and Shanks—"have seen some of the horrors that are out there and understand why ONSET exists. Even *you*, however, are wondering why ONSET Campus is one of the most fortified locations on Earth. Why we have a small army of conventional troops, why we have *so much* firepower and technology at the command of what is, at the end, nothing more than a SWAT team.

"This lecture is on why," he said grimly, and hit the button on the projector. A frozen image of a mountainside with a PLAY icon on it appeared.

"This video clip is from late oh seven," he told them. "It is camera footage from the Commander's Leopard tank of Delta Company, Armored Battalion Thirteen of the Swiss Panzerbrigade Eleven. They were carrying out training exercises in the Alps when, well…watch."

The teacher hit a button, and the video clip started.

———

FOR A MOMENT, all the gun camera showed was frozen mountainside, then the camera rotated as the Commander reviewed the sixteen tanks crunching their way over the frozen field. The video was completely silent, so it was a complete shock when the tank on the end of the even line suddenly erupted into the air.

The sixty-plus-ton vehicle flipped completely end over end, slamming turret-first into the ground almost a hundred meters from its launch point with a visible crumpling.

Standing under where the tank had been driving was a monstrosity out of nightmare. Six or more meters tall, the creature looked like a moss-covered stone figure of a man—one someone had carved by rough description. Its rough mouth was open in a silent scream as it charged at the next tank in line.

There was no way the tank driver could have reacted, and the creature ripped the mighty armored vehicle in half with one yank of its immense arms. The professionalism of the Swiss army was demonstrated, however, in that the first shots hit the monster as it was attacking the second vehicle.

The camera was bouncing and wavering insanely as the tank started backpedaling, the formation rotating as the vehicles tried to open the distance and fire on the creature. The first few rounds did nothing, exploding on the troll's stone skin and stripping off moss.

The second salvo of rounds, however, showed that the Swiss had learned the first salvo's lessons. Bright red lines flashed across the camera's view as armor-piercing rounds drove into the creature's skin and detonated, lighting up the night as dozens of machine guns chattered to life as well.

The monster felt the armor-piercing rounds, raising its head in a bellow, silent on the film, which shook the trees around it. Whatever it felt wasn't enough to kill it, however, and it charged the line of tanks with a speed that left the camera only recording a blur.

David had to shake his head to clear dizziness as the camera spun to catch the stone creature slamming into two of the tanks simultaneously with the force of a train engine. Its broad arms crashed clean through the front armor but got stuck. For a moment, it stood still, a fist buried in each tank.

As it stood shaking its head in confusion, a second salvo of armor-piercing rounds slammed into it. This time, the Commander's tank was close enough to clearly see the rounds punching through the stone of the creature's flesh. Some kind of black ooze dripped from the wounds, and the creature spun around to face the other tanks. One of its hands tore free from one of the tanks it had struck.

The other brought the sixty-ton tank around with it, only breaking free in time to send it hurtling directly at the camera.

———

THE FILM STOPPED THERE and faded to a still shot of the same field. The smoldering wreckage of seven of the company's sixteen tanks littered it, and the photographer had caught six of the remaining tanks, in a carefully aligned circle, training their main guns on the broken stone pieces of the creature.

"That," Koburn said quietly, "was a greater troll. So far as we can tell, in eras of lower magical activity, they go to sleep like dragons. They wake up more readily than dragons, however, and *nine* have awoken in the European mountains in the last decade. It is only a matter of time until one wakes up in the Rockies, and they are, as you saw, incredibly hard to kill.

"Worse," he continued grimly, "is their shared attribute with the type of Empowered we also call a troll. Both must eat human flesh to survive—nothing else provides nutrition. Evidence suggests that a greater troll requires a *lot* of human flesh—we have not always been so lucky as to have a tank company literally drive over the troll.

"That said, at least we know what trolls are," he continued, and hit another button.

An image of a desolate town appeared on the screen at the front of the room. Desert was visible beyond the adobe houses and shacks, and sand blew through the street. The blowing sand caught forever in mid-gust explained why the bodies piled haphazardly through the streets were half-buried. The occasional half-buried AK-47 showed that they had not been defenseless. Several of the houses had holes in the walls; one had been completely demolished.

Just in the field of view of the first camera there were dozens, possibly hundreds, of bodies. The picture switched to another angle, looking into the town along a partially cleared highway littered with the wreckage of the town's dozen or so vehicles, and more piled bodies.

A third picture showed what had been the town's school. The teacher had clearly ordered the children to hide and then held the door shut with his own body. He'd been torn in two, the gore of his death still visible in a room protected from the elements by its walls, and splattered across the remnants of the students he'd tried to protect.

David swallowed hard as a fourth picture of the main market of the town came up. A handful of armed men had tried to make a stand behind a crude barricade thrown together from the remnants of the stalls. The picture showed half a dozen carrion birds picking at the piles of corpses.

They were the only living things in all of the pictures.

"The name of this town is classified," Koburn said quietly, as a fifth picture of the town—from the air, the bodies no longer visible with distance but the damage to the buildings still clear—appeared. "It's in southern Afghanistan, near the Pakistan border. The Taliban blame us for this. We...don't know what actually did it."

"What do you mean, we don't *know*?" Leila Stone, her voice choked, asked from behind David.

"This was discovered by a roving Army medical team just over a year ago," Koburn explained. "An OSPI team with an ONSET squad in support was sent in to investigate. Most of the people were killed by a creature with claws, and we *think* it was all the same creature.

"The OSPI team was led by a Mage Inspector, who tried to investigate with Second Sight." The instructor paused, his gaze locked on David, who returned his regard steadily. "The Inspector has been undergoing intensive psychiatric care on this Campus since. Our current best hope is that if we magically block out the memories, she will recover in another year. Such an operation is...delicate.

"We believe," he finished quietly, "that there were about two thousand people in the town. None of them escaped."

———

KOBURN FIDDLED with the projector again and a new image appeared on the screen. The burned wreckage of four armored personnel carriers framed a line of sandbags and a stunning vista looking out over snowy mountains.

The snow in the front of the scene was stained red. Dozens of bodies were scattered across the sandbags; the hastily dug machine gun pits were slaughterhouses. It was hard to tell with how badly the bodies were torn up, but it looked like they were wearing US Army winter camouflage.

"On October fourth, two thousand and four, a research team for the Office of Supernatural Policing and Security identified the presence of a major dimensional rift in the Rocky Mountains in Montana," Koburn said quietly. "Overhead imagery of the rift was quickly acquired."

The image of the slaughtered soldiers faded into a sterile overhead shot of a similar snowy mountain landscape. In the center of the image was a black-and-purple inkstain-like splotch. Around it were a number of small figures, difficult to make out.

The image zoomed in, centering on one of the figures. There was nothing to judge its size by, but it was roughly humanoid-shaped, naked with skin blacker than the darkest human. Massive curled horns emerged from the creature's temples, wrapping around to almost rest on the obviously male figure's shoulders.

"We estimated that the rift was allowing several dozen demons through every hour—three to four hundred a day," Koburn continued. "At the time, neither ONSET nor the Anti-Paranormals existed. The Brigadier commanding OSPI's High-Threat-Response teams requested and was denied the authorization to deploy small-scale nuclear weaponry—the threat was deemed insufficient. Instead, the Committee of Thirteen borrowed eight combat brigades—two divisions' worth of troops—from the Army, the Marines and the Montana and Washington National Guard.

"This," he said quietly, switching back to the original picture, "is what happened when the first two brigades thought they could handle the estimated twelve hundred demons that had come through when they arrived. Their assault turned into a retreat within two hours, and then into a desperate attempt to hold the line against the demons' counter-offensive."

A new image appeared on the screen. This one had been taken in action. Four tanks and a dozen APCs were charging across a clear snowy field. Lines of tracer fire and the muzzle flashes of the rifles of the infantry advancing with the tanks had been caught in the frozen tableau. So had the dozens of demons facing them, including one identical to the one Koburn had originally zoomed in on. Now with the tanks for scale, it was clear that the demon was easily twice as tall as a human. This one had an APC in its hands, held off the ground in the process of being thrown at one of the tanks.

"The remaining brigades arrived in time to prevent the line breaking, but the two units in the initial contact suffered in excess of ninety percent casualties," the instructor continued.

"The grind up the valley to get a team of OSPI Mages to the rift took three days," he told them. "We took more casualties in the four days of the Montana Incursion than in any other four-day period since the Vietnam War. Eight brigades and three OSPI High- Threat-Response Teams—out of four in existence at the time—assaulted that valley. Thirty-two thousand men and women."

Koburn paused, surveying his students as a slow slideshow of further images of combat and violence between demons of all sizes and colors on one side and the US Army on the other played behind him.

"Twelve thousand two hundred and fifty-six survived. Of those, eight thousand five hundred and thirty were permanently maimed. Of the surviving three thousand seven hundred and twenty-six, seven hundred and eighty-two suffered psychological traumas sufficient to result in discharge.

"The remaining twenty-nine hundred and forty-four soldiers formed the core of what is now the Anti-Paranormal Companies," Koburn finished. "They are a conventional military force trained and equipped to fight the supernatural."

The slideshow stopped on a picture of an under-construction mountainside base. Without the skyscrapers and walls, it took a moment to recognize the ONSET Campus.

"An inquiry by the Committee of Thirteen concluded that a lack of resources, information and authority hampered the fight against the Incursion. They also concluded that the rift suggested that we should expect more and more dangerous supernatural activity in the future.

"This inquiry was completed in June two thousand and five. The Office of the National Supernatural Enforcement Teams was established in February of two thousand and six," Koburn finished.

"It is our job to make sure that we *never again* see twenty thousand dead on our own soil."

HOURS OF LESSONS BLURRED TOGETHER OVER THE FOLLOWING DAYS. Lessons piled on lessons, in marksmanship, in supernatural politics, in the organization of the supernatural branch of the US Government.

David learned that a special committee of Congress, formally the Special Committee for Supernatural Affairs and informally the Committee of Thirteen, wielded the full power of Congress in supernatural affairs. He learned that the Familias were the body of the vampire politic in the United States, a group of nine vampire families of Italian and Russian descent that ran a huge portion of organized crime in the US.

The identifying marks of a hundred types of supernatural were drilled into their brains. The *many* different kinds of powers a supernatural could show. They learned the weapons and attacks all supernaturals were vulnerable to, like silver, and the more specific, like vampire's nonfatal but still debilitating allergy to full-spectrum light.

Hours upon hours were spent in gyms, honing reflexes and testing out new supernatural powers. Secured lead chambers were used to train the Mages, and David watched Tsimote wield fire like he was conducting a symphony.

Koburn had gone over multiple forms of martial arts with all of the trainees, enhancing existing training and focusing it into new forms. Mostly, he taught them a modified form of Krav Maga, as opposed to the Tae Kwan Do David had learned in his police training. Casey proved to be a master of Krav Maga, but this was insufficient.

Around the end of the second week, the burly black man came to quietly say goodbye to David. While Leonard Casey had proven some of his supernatural abilities, they boiled down to him being a glorified human bloodhound. He could follow anyone, anywhere, but Koburn had suggested—and Casey had eventually agreed—that it was a talent more useful to OSPI than to ONSET.

So, their number shrank by one, and David focused on his training with all his might.

He learned how to use his Second Sight fully and discovered that his enhanced perception extended to his other senses as well. The lights and auras of his Sight were no longer terrifying and strange. Now they were another tool in the arsenal Koburn had helped equip him with.

The lessons blurred hours to days, and days to weeks, and the next thing he knew, he was being roughly awoken early in the morning once more, and hustled down a set of stairs on the lower floor of the bunker—stairs he hadn't realized existed.

———

THE GRIZZLED INSTRUCTOR hadn't been kidding about breaking them, David reflected as the door slid shut behind him. He took the moment to reflect as he tucked into a dark corner, eyeing the rest of the shadowed tunnel—some kind of training complex *under* the basement to the bunker he'd been studying in for the last four weeks.

No one had come down with him, and he hoped that it meant that the others were getting their own final test, as they'd told him this was for him.

One last test, Koburn had told him. This was it, this shadowy underground complex, clear as day to his new senses. They hadn't given him a mission or anything. Simply woke him up at four in the morning, hustled him into the tight-fitting black bodysuit ONSET used as a uniform, and dropped him into the complex.

Now he stood underneath a vaulted concrete ceiling high enough for an elephant, and looked back at the metal door that had just clanged shut behind him. The tunnel stretched out to both sides of him, and he squared his shoulders.

It was too late to change his mind now. He'd thrown his lot in with ONSET, to serve and protect humanity from those who would abuse the powers that came from beyond the Seal. After four weeks of training, he was only barely beginning to feel he was ready, but he also understood just how understrength ONSET was compared to the threats it faced. The five men and women left in his class would increase the national agency's active supernatural strength by almost five percent.

ONSET needed David White, and that meant that whatever this exercise was, he'd deal with it. Well.

"So, what do we think of our little ex-lieutenant?" Warner asked Koburn, watching David on the monitor in the training center's surveillance hub. A massive multi-CPU server sat under each of the three desks splitting the room up, and the walls were covered in monitors. Right now, an entire wall of those monitors was showing the shadowy tunnel they'd dumped David White in.

The craggy trainer shrugged. "I've seen the video clip," he said quietly. "He hasn't shown *anything* like that in training or testing."

"But?" the Major invited.

"He *is* one of the strongest non-Mage perceivers we've tested yet," he told her. "We also put him on the resistance machine for bench pressing. He's no Michael," he continued with a nod at the werewolf Commander sitting quietly next to the guard who was normally responsible for the room, "but he was still benching a good six, seven hundred kilos with ease. Strength Empowered for sure."

"He isn't what we thought he was," Warner told them both.

"But he is still a viable agent," O'Brien interjected. "Perceivers are *damned* useful, and so is the ability to bench-press a Smart car. Not to mention that most of our recruits lack any qualification *other* than their supernatural abilities, and White was a senior police officer—and head of a tactical team, however part-time—without them."

"Plus," Koburn said softly, "it's more accurate to say he isn't what we think he is...*yet*. We *know* he can be what we see in that video. It's merely a question of what it will take to wake him up. I don't think artificial training is going to do it."

"If anything we can do will, it'll be his first meeting with Charles," O'Brien muttered.

———

THE SOUND of the almost-slithering footsteps was like an earthquake in David's enhanced hearing, and his hand slid down to the Silver-Mod M1911 automatic that Chief Hanson had given him. Koburn had pronounced the weapon "old but still perfectly usable for our purposes" on seeing it, and they'd never even asked him to turn in the silver bullets the Chief had given him with it. He'd only barely had time to grab the weapon before being hustled into these tunnels, but he'd been keeping it loaded. Not so much paranoia as...caution. For all his own commitment to the agency, thinking what his *father* would have thought about ONSET still left him uncomfortable.

The footsteps grew closer, and David drew the weapon, thumbing the safety off as he skimmed the massive shadowy tunnels for the source of the sound. He doubted there was a real threat there in the Campus's basements—but it was still better to be prepared.

The approaching sounds slowed and finally came to a halt, replaced by a sniffing noise. There was a *clink*, some kind of motion, and the sniffing sound repeated.

Wondering just what the hell was coming, David knelt, raising the pistol in a two-handed grip, aiming toward the direction of the sound. His heart began to beat faster and he could feel and smell the sweat on his palms.

He breathed evenly, calming his heart, and focused on the sounds —which had stopped.

For a long moment, there was silence, and then the slithering footsteps started up again—very slowly.

Taking a deep breath, David tucked one leg under him and rolled forward, around the corner toward the sound. He grunted with the impact, and then he came up, the gun training on the...dragon?

A massive lizard-like creature reared back, and his newly trained senses took in details with a suddenly detached mind. The dragon was a scaled and spiked hexapod, with massive legs bunched underneath it and tiny arms tucked under the wings that now spread wide. Part of him realized the wings were to balance the long, sinuous neck that dove toward him. Fire flashed through his veins, and ever so calmly, David raised the pistol again, even as his enhanced senses allowed him to estimate where the neck would be when he fired.

Even as he watched the physical dragon, he also saw the blurred outline of its future moments, as its jaws swung toward him and snapped shut—well clear of his head.

Halfway through raising the pistol, David stopped. A second later, the dragon's teeth snapped together, a good foot away from David, and the creature chuckled. The sound was surprisingly humanlike, coming from a creature twice David's height and five times that in length, but echoed in the tunnel as the massive twenty-foot wingspan slowly folded in.

"Yer supposed to be terribly a-feared of me and firing wildly," the dragon observed, a thick Irish brogue rolling out from behind its half-foot-long fangs and long, trailing whiskers to make the whole situation seem surreal. "But then, Ai tole them nae perceiver was going to be fooled by li'l ole me."

"Nice trick," David said, forcing his heartbeat down. "You're a dragon," he continued bluntly.

"That Ai am," the dragon agreed. "The name's Charles," he continued to brogue, "and it is my pleasurable task to inform ye that ye just passed your final test, barring the good Major's approval, o' course." The massive creature shrugged. "Till we hear from the good lady, will you join me for a cuppa tea in my lair?"

"Oh," said David faintly. "Of course."

"THAT WAS INTERESTING," Warner said quietly.

"Not really unexpected," Koburn reminded her. "He's a perceiver, and some of them see a half-second or so into the future. He knew that Charles wasn't going to actually bite him."

O'Brien was leaning in, looking intently at the closest screen. "You have this recorded?" he asked absently.

"Of course," Koburn told him.

"Rewind it," O'Brien ordered. "Show me when he reacted."

Koburn hit some keys on the computer, and the video skipped backward on the screen nearest Michael to the requested point. It ran for a few seconds and then O'Brien raised his hand.

"Show me that again, slowly."

Koburn slowed down the playback, and the three watched as David's gun rocketed up toward the dragon.

"I slowed it down more than that," Koburn muttered, checking the computer.

"Yes, you did," O'Brien replied. "But *he* was speeding up, until he realized there wasn't a threat." The werewolf turned to Warner. "Ma'am, knowing that Charles isn't a threat is enough to pass him, but with that extra snippet...I am perfectly willing to sponsor Candidate White as a full Agent."

"*If* he manages to empower and learn to control himself," Warner said slowly, "he will be an incredible asset. Until then, however, he only barely qualifies as ONSET-level abilities."

"I'll take him on ONSET Nine" O'Brien told her. "Keep him under my wing, so to speak."

Warner looked at the screen for a long moment and finally nodded.

"Very well," she said firmly. "He's yours."

DAVID FOLLOWED Charles through the tunnel. Sooner than he expected, they reached a large open metal door, leading into a spacious, well-lit room. A quick glance around the room showed that, while myth may have had dragons sleeping on beds of gold, Charles slept on a twenty-foot-long hybrid of a couch and a giant dog bed.

Facing the couch was a dragon-sized keyboard, linked to several large touch screens and a whole set of monitors, displays and other controls. Several massive power bars and Ethernet cables led back into the walls behind the displays, marking this as possibly the largest computing setup—in several senses—David had ever seen.

What looked like a giant deep freeze ran along one wall, and a third was covered with bookshelves. A kitchenette, clearly sized to be used by a dragon, was tucked into one corner, and a small table and human-sized chairs occupied another.

The floor was carpeted in a ridiculously deep version of ONSET's ubiquitous blue plush carpeting, and an odd assortment of paintings and decorations marked the walls. A dragon-sized door that wouldn't have looked out of place on a bank vault was half-hidden behind the couch,

"Quite the setup," David observed. "Surprisingly comfortable, I'll admit."

"It's all Ai have," the dragon said quietly. "Ai made a deal with yer gov'mint a lang time ago. Ai didn't show myself to the woirld, and they took care o' me." The dragon drifted over to his kitchen, where he began to delicately use the smaller arms—still as wide around as David's legs—tucked under his wings to make a pot of tea.

"They've kept their end," he brogued softly, the long whiskers twitching as he spoke, "so Ai keep mine. There are days when Ai miss the sky under me wings." The dragon shrugged his massive shoulders. "The world ain't ready to see a dragon o'er their pretty skies yet."

The dragon brought the pot of tea over to the table and poured David a cup of tea, those thick, smaller arms surprisingly delicate and controlled at the scale of the pot and teacup. The porcelain was, almost unsurprisingly, an exquisitely decorated blue-and-green set that was likely worth more than David's truck back home.

David sat and sipped the tea slowly as he gathered his thoughts. Once again, Omicron had managed to present him with something he hadn't been prepared for. Every time he thought he'd learned about everything and was ready to face *anything*, he was proven wrong.

He was getting used to the feeling of being completely shocked, but the sheer sense of wonder he felt at the size and grandeur of the immense—and intelligent—being sharing tea with him was new.

"They didn't mention anything about dragons to me in training," he told Charles.

"That's because there ain't dragons," Charles replied. "There's me, and Ai'm all that's awoken up this time 'round."

"And Charles here is one of ONSET's best-kept secrets," Warner's voice interjected into the conversation. David looked up to find her and O'Brien stepping in through a door half-hidden among the bookshelves.

Charles, as he'd said earlier, had been expecting them, and their arrival found him laying three more teacups on the table alongside his own bucket-sized one.

"MI-Nought is the only one, even among our allies, who knows Charles is here," Warner continued.

"And the idea of an Irish dragon gives them the heebie-jeebies," O'Brien observed as he took a cup of tea. "Thank you, Charles. For the help with the test, and the tea," he finished.

"They're fools," Charles said bluntly, with a growl that sent his spikes and whiskers to shivering. "Ai've no love for Patrick's Irish. They're the ones who kilt the Hibernia I loved."

"You're the dragon of the Saint Patrick myth?" David replied, shocked. Of all the things he'd expected to meet in service with ONSET, the dragon who'd fought St. Patrick so long ago was not one of them. Of course, Patrick was supposed to have *killed* that dragon...

Charles's growl shook the entire chamber. "*Saint,*" the dragon spat. "Book-burner and murderer, that one was, nae better than the worst o' the so-called 'barbarians.'"

Smoke trickled from the dragon's nostrils as he inhaled, and then slowly exhaled deeply as his whiskers and spines slowly stopped shaking. "But wa're not here to be talking on me ancient grudges," he said, his gravelly brogue calmer. "Major," he finished, gesturing to Warner.

"Thank you Charles," Warner said quietly. "For your help with the test, and, as always, for your eternal patience with the world that is."

Charles inclined his head to her, settling down on his couch without further words.

Warner turned to David. "Agent-Trainee White," she said formally, "over the last four weeks, you've demonstrated sufficient supernatural abilities that we believe you can keep up with one of our teams on an active-duty basis. While we would always prefer more training to less," she continued quietly, "we are so short on people, we really don't have a choice but to put you—and the other remaining trainees, if you were curious—onto active duty." She offered her hand across Charles's table.

"Welcome to ONSET, David," she told him less formally.

David shook her hand and then O'Brien's. The werewolf grinned at him.

"You've been assigned initially to my team," he told David. "Since that was to be the case, I had a talk with my team over the last week. My pair of Mages spent some time downstairs and made up this."

David's new Commander extended a sheathed knife across the table. "Formally, this is an ONSET-Issue Combat Knife, comma, Aetherically Modified, comma, Mod Six," he continued. "Informally, we call them mageblades," he finished as David took the knife and drew it from the sheath.

He handled the enchanted weapon with care, letting its internal glow and sparks of spells light its delicate lines and deadly edge. It was barely twelve inches long, including the grip, and no decoration or runes marred the blade. For all that, he could tell that there was more magic in this small blade than most people attributed to Excalibur.

"They are highly effective at killing demons, werewolves, vampires, elephants and small tanks," the werewolf told him dryly, "and pretty good at going through walls. The blade *will* cut anything you try to cut with it. Be very careful with it, and use it well. Welcome to my team."

David slowly and carefully sheathed the knife on his belt, and turned to face Charles as the dragon extended a claw for him to shake.

"Welcome to a small but important world, me young friend," he said simply.

———

THE HACKER HADN'T MANAGED to track down *anything* about that cop for weeks, but she wasn't exactly known for giving up. She'd posted on a few boards, conspiracy theorists and suchlike, seeing what would come up.

A blinking icon told her she had a reply on one of them. Five clicks later, and it was on her screen.

INTERESTING THEORY, Majestic, but really! We all know that the Grays control the government, and what use would they have for a supernatural hunting team? A magic department of the US government?! Hah!

I've got plenty of info on the Gray control of the USG, if you want to know the *real* truth.

CharDrake777.

THE HACKER KNOWN as Majestic leaned back in her chair, running her fingers through her hair as she regarded the post.

There had to be an answer; she knew that. There always was.

She just had to find the right place and the right tool with which to look.

[8]

DAVID FOLLOWED O'BRIEN INTO THE COMMON ROOM OF THE RESIDENCE—one of thirty-odd identical small buildings tucked into the southwest corner of the Campus—where ONSET Nine made its home with trepidation. While he'd seen O'Brien enough to make him mostly comfortable with the werewolf, the Commander's team was the people who'd saved his life a month before. Now they were also the people he'd be working with for the foreseeable future.

These were people he wanted to impress, but David figured it would take more than the two large suitcases he was carrying to do that. He'd surprised himself when he'd picked the cases up, as he knew from packing them how heavy they were. Every day, another little thing drove home to him the fact that he was just that little bit more than human now.

As time went by and more of those little things occurred, the dull ache of knowing his father would have disapproved slowly faded. His concern about just *what* he was becoming, however, was still with him as he entered his new home.

The common room was far nicer than he'd been expecting. Instead of the plainly decorated military austerity he'd encountered in the rest of the base, this was almost homelike.

"One common area and eight apartments per building, plus a kitchen and armory," Michael told him as David stopped and looked around the common room. "Most of ONSET's agents live in the provided apartments, so we make them comfortable. And we certainly get paid well enough to do so."

The common room was large but still oddly cozy, with a huge TV screen—currently turned off—along one wall. Three large plush green couches filled the sitting area, with hardwood chairs around several smaller tables off to the side. While the carpet on the ground was the exact same shade of blue as the rest of the facility, it seemed to be softer underfoot here. The room was occupied by the members of ONSET Strike Team Nine.

"Ladies and gentlemen," Michael said loudly, "I'd like to present the newest member of our prestigious team, Agent David White."

The nearest member of the team, a weedy young man with thin glasses, looked up at David from the laptop he was typing on and grinned.

"You're a lot prettier conscious and lacking vampire bites," the man told him.

"David," Michael interjected, "meet our Mage and wannabe hacker, Morgen Dilsner." The werewolf paused for a moment, considering. "Or is that 'hacker and wannabe Mage'? I can never remember."

"Would you prefer I fail to delete the camera tracks or to shield your furry face from fireballs next time?" Morgen replied sweetly.

"It's 'Mage, hacker and wannabe *smartass*'," another member of the team observed. This was a sturdily built older woman at the other table along the walls. Gray-shot brown hair failed to detract from her impression of ironbound competence, reinforced by the disassembled pieces of what appeared to be a machine gun on the table in front of her.

David smiled slightly at the woman, recognizing the bantering of a team that worked together often and well. If he was very lucky, he knew, he might be included in that bantering in a month or two. If he really screwed up, he never would be. He gave the older-looking woman a firm nod as Michael turned to her.

"David, be known to Alexandra Bourque," O'Brien introduced the woman with a gentle wave of the hand. "Formerly of the Marine Corps Special Operations Command, now ONSET Nine's heavy-weapons specialist. Don't get on her bad side; she's Empowered and likes to carry guns the Army normally attaches to tanks."

Moving on, O'Brien gestured to a smaller man, somehow even skinner than Dilsner. The man looked like a stiff breeze would blow him away, and there was a vague look around his eyes, which coupled with his long, ear-covering hair and delicate features to give him a very effeminate look.

"This is Malcolm Akono, our pilot and infiltration specialist," Michael introduced him, and the small man inclined his head in greeting. "And it's not you," Michael added, smiling at his subordinate, "he doesn't talk much to *anybody.*"

Akono gave his superior a look and turned back to David. "Welcome to the team," he said softly, even his voice somewhat dreamy.

Something about the man, beyond his far-away voice, vague look, or androgynous features, bothered David. It wasn't that Akono didn't feel trustworthy, just...very different.

"And here we have the member of the team voted least likely to get a credit card under their real name," Michael said, turning to the last member of the team in the room and taking a deep breath. "May I introduce Ixiltanequestelanaerith?"

"My credit card says Nathan, actually," the figure said in an unnaturally deep voice, and David took a long look at him. On first glance, he thought the man was black, with some sort of forehead tattoo. After a moment, however, he realized that the "black" was actually a deep burgundy, and the "tattoo" was in reality twelve small horns in two rows across the top of his forehead.

David began to take half a step backward, the memory of Koburn's lecture on the Montana Incursion still fresh in his mind, but stopped himself. While the *thing* sitting in the room with him was very definitely not human, it was also very definitely not an enemy.

"But you, Agent White," the demon continued, apparently unaware of David's internal conflict, "can call me Ix, like the rest of the team. Especially seeing as how, even with much practice, our esteemed Commander cannot pronounce my name *correctly.*"

"Thank you," David said faintly, still half-staring at the first real demon he'd ever seen.

When they'd taught him about demons, they'd told him that most of the ones that had come through were relatively minor. Some more powerful ones snuck through occasionally, such as the shock troops that had met US tanks on even footing in the Incursion, but they tended not to last long before the various supernatural defense forces around the world took them out.

They were, however, still the physical forms of beings the world hadn't seen in any real quantity in thousands of years. Beings that had spent those thousands of years locked up in the dimensional equivalent of a cupboard under the stairs.

David had been told that some of them liked the world the way it was, as opposed to the way their masters wanted it to be, and had joined the human defenders of Earth. He still hadn't expected to actually *meet* one.

"Where's Kate?" Michael asked the other members of the team, causing David to move his eyes away from Ix, who, if he'd noticed the stare, had genteelly ignored it.

"She has a date tonight," Bourque replied snapping together two bits of the dismantled weapon on the table in front of her. "She's upstairs prettying up."

"We're leaving in the morning," the team Commander observed.

"I'll be back by then," a new voice replied, from the stairs leading up to the second floor of apartments. David turned to the stairs to see the speaker step into the common room.

For every ounce of femininity that Bourque lacked, this girl probably had three. She was tall and slim, with a long blond braid that fell most of the way to her waist. Carefully done makeup enhanced her bright green eyes, and a small silver pendant of an encircled five-pointed star hung delicately in the cleavage exposed by her tight silver tank top. A short black skirt and long black boots completed a "date ensemble" that was as almost as much a weapon as Bourque's machine gun.

"David, this is Kate Mason," Michael introduced her. "She's our second Mage and resident little sister."

Kate breezed down into the room, smiling at David brightly before turning to Michael. The smile hit the cop, who was well aware he probably had at least five years on the Mage, somewhere under his ribs and made his heart jump.

"It's only an hour's drive into town," she told him, "and we're not leaving until the morning. I promise I'll be back by oh six hundred hours at the latest," she finished with an impish grin.

"No sleeping in the chopper," Michael told her calmly. "No hangovers. And *be careful.*"

"Yes, sir," she replied crisply, all impishness gone for a second. Only a second, however, before it returned in full force. "I'll see you all in the morning," she told the rest of the team, the bright smile returning in a flash.

A chorus of farewells came from the team, and she turned to look at David again.

"It's good to see you conscious and well," she told him, serious again. "Goddess's blessings on you—I look forward to working with you!"

With that, she breezed out of the room, leaving it seemingly darker in her absence. David found his gaze lingering on the door she'd left through, and he doubted he was the only one in the group.

"Also our tame whirlwind," Michael said finally in the sudden quiet. "I keep forgetting that part."

———

FROM THE COMMON ROOM, Michael led David up the stairs to the second floor of apartments. A single short hallway at the top of the stairs, painted a darker blue than the omnipresent shade of blue, boasted two doors on either side, each marked with a small nameplate, and a door at the far end that presumably led to the stairs up to the third floor.

The one on the right at the far end of the hall was blank, but Michael led David to the one on the left-hand side. The small name plate read DAVID WHITE.

To David's Sight, the plate glowed slightly, revealing a slight magical aura.

"The nameplate is an alarm, among other things," Michael told him, confirming his thought. "Not much of a security measure, but if they make it into the dormitories in this place, we have bigger issues than breaking and entering."

Michael opened the door and gestured for David to precede him. "Welcome to your new home away from home."

Wordlessly, David entered the apartment. The first thing he realized was the sheer size of the place: his brain hadn't quite done the math between the outside of the building and the fact that it was only split into four apartments per floor. The single-floor apartment was easily the size of a normal bungalow, and the open arrangement of the major rooms left almost the whole place visible.

He stood in a medium-sized living room, and he could see a kitchen and dinette assembly, equipped with cheap white and black appliances, to his right. A smaller room off to the side seemed to be an office cubbyhole, and a door leading off next to the office was presumably the bedroom.

Despite the size of the apartment, however, it was only sparsely furnished, with a single couch and coffee table in the living room, a table and chairs in the dinette area, and a small desk and chair tucked into the smaller office room. All of the furniture was cheap military standard issue.

"Sorry about the Spartan setup," Michael told him. "We generally leave the apartments for people to decorate themselves—we just provide help bringing the stuff in from Colorado Springs."

"So, that's where we are, huh?" David asked. It was the first time *anyone* had mentioned the Campus's location to him. He'd guessed the base was in the Rockies, and probably farther south, but to know where he was was comforting.

"Yup," his new Commander told him. "We're about eighty minutes' drive out of Colorado Springs—that's why I was concerned about Kate going on a date tonight. She has a ways to go."

"Didn't we fly in through Salt Lake?" the new agent asked. That seemed like a long detour up the Rockies to come here.

"Security measure," O'Brien replied. "Throws off people who may end up not getting the clearance to know where the Campus is. Speaking of which, here."

The werewolf extended a brown envelope. "You know that ID folio we gave you?" he asked. "These go in there. They're your full ONSET Agent identification and your Omicron-Delta clearance cards."

David took the envelope and put it very carefully, along with the ID folio, on the counter in the kitchen. Minor as the brown envelope and its contents might seem, they were the final confirmation that he'd made it there. He knew that there was some disappointment that he hadn't manifested greater abilities than he had shown, but it seemed like the ones he did have were enough.

They were enough for ONSET to want him, and perhaps even enough to make a difference. He wasn't here for power, or for the "fun" of being part of the most classified agency in the USA. He wasn't here because he *wanted* to be a supernatural. He was here to serve and protect.

"So, ONSET will help if I decide to move my stuff down from Charlesville?" David asked, his thoughts returning to the more mundane.

"Help?" O'Brien shook his head. "You'd have trouble getting yourself involved in the process. They'll probably just run the nearest OSPI security detail down and load up your things lock, stock and barrel. On the other hand, if you decide to keep the house, it's not like you can't afford new furniture."

David blinked. "You know, that brings up a thought," he said plaintively, realizing there was something he'd never asked. In all of his questions about ONSET, all of his lessons, all of his determination to succeed at becoming an ONSET Agent, one question had never even crossed his mind. "I don't think at any point it's been mentioned what I'm getting paid."

Michael looked at him, laughed, and quoted a number. The younger agent choked.

"That's *five times* what I was making in Charlesville," he protested. He'd expected some more money, but it hadn't been a factor. He hadn't cared—and he certainly hadn't expected a six-figure salary!

"In Charlesville, you were a small-town police officer," O'Brien told him gently. "A senior officer, true, but there are thousands like you in the country. *Here*, you are a supernatural trained in law enforcement, equipped and deployed as a member of a high-threat-response team operating on a national level. Did you really expect *not* to get paid more? Even a lot more?"

David shook his head slowly. It made sense. It was still a shock to the system.

"For now, you have a bed, a computer and a kitchen," Michael told him. "I suggest you get unpacked and start making a list of things to either grab from Charlesville or from the Springs when we get back. We are leaving in the morning, so get some rest."

"Where are we going?" David asked.

"Northern Louisiana," O'Brien told him. "We're relieving ONSET Thirteen as they go on their week off. I know some things about the possible situations down there, but I'll update everyone in the morning."

———

UNPACKING TOOK David longer than he would have expected in other circumstances. He'd really just thrown everything into the cases for the quick move, which made removing and untangling everything a complex task.

It was also a completely new storage setup, which he figured he wouldn't bother getting used to. Almost as soon as he'd finished unpacking, he loaded up a file on the desk terminal and started a list of things to add to the apartment.

Starting with food. The portions of ONSET training outside the training bunker had been David's first experience with the military's Meals, Ready to Eat, and he was sure it would not be his last. Nonetheless, he wanted more food in his fridge than the six MREs currently in there. In his newly acquired opinion, *nobody* should be forced to eat MREs unless there was no choice.

Tonight, however, he *had* no choice unless he wanted to try to find the cafeteria he knew had to be around there somewhere, so he picked one of the trays and prepared it.

As he ate, he continued to enter data at the computer. The apartment really was bare-bones, and if he was getting paid what Michael said he was, he could afford to upgrade.

Eventually, after slogging through several online sites with varying English and Swedish names for furniture, he checked his personal email for the first time since arriving on Campus.

Having answered a couple of personal emails from his old coworkers in as nondescript a way as he could, he went to bed.

———

MAJESTIC WAS ACTUALLY "WORKING" when the trigger she'd connected to David White's email account blinked up at her. Cursing, she ignored it. Personal curiosity had to wait—hacking corporate databases took all her attention and a lot of time.

Some hours later, her original task complete and someone's proprietary data on the way to someone else, she turned back to the alert. It was cold, but that didn't mean it was useless.

A little bit of digging brought up the IP address of the computer that had connected to the email server. A routing address, she recognized, not a personal computer.

She warmed up a few of her more interesting programs and went digging into that router address.

Sixteen point four seconds later, according to the log file, her entire computer crashed as her access attempt downloaded a nuke program to her highly secured computer.

9

THE MORNING SAW THE MEMBERS OF ONSET STRIKE TEAM NINE gathered in the common room on the ground floor of their residence, with Michael standing in front of his subordinates.

There were no briefing tools, no blackboard or computer screens. The massive TV screen along the wall was turned off. It was just four men, two women and a demon sitting around on couches.

"We're moving to ONSET's North Louisiana base," Michael reminded them all, "replacing ONSET Thirteen as they stand down to inactive reserve."

ONSET Teams, David now knew, were always on one of three statuses: active, meaning in the field at a secondary base; active reserve, meaning on the Campus; or inactive reserve, which meant completely off-duty and often entirely off-Campus.

"While on site, we will be primarily responsible for Louisiana and the surrounding states and sharing secondary responsibility for the southeastern quarter of the mainland United States," Michael told them.

"Remember that after the Texas Incursion, we're still short three teams," Michael went on grimly, "which means we're the primary response team for a seventh of the States, not an eighth."

The Texas Incursion was a smaller version of the Montana Incursion Koburn had used for the "why we exist" lecture that had occurred five months before David had even learned ONSET existed.

Incursions were still astonishingly rare, but when they happened, ONSET went to war. Fourteen ONSET teams—roughly a hundred supernaturals—and a battalion of the Anti-Paranormal Companies had gone up against a relatively minor incursion. Three teams had been wiped out and the remainder left under-strength, but the Incursion had been eliminated.

"Do we have any details on what's going on in our area of responsibility?" Kate, in uniform and fully professional now, David noted, asked.

"We do," Michael confirmed. "OSPI is performing research on a dimensional hole in southern Florida. They also have several investigations underway into supernatural crime in the area, including what we suspect may be an attempt by a group of fangs to move in on New Orleans organized crime." The Commander paused and surveyed his men. "Any of these investigations may require deployment of some or all of us to back up OSPI personnel, and dimensional research *always* requires a close eye kept on it.

"Things tend to come through those holes," he said grimly, "and after three-thousand-odd years in the dimensional equivalent of a broom closet, very little of what comes through is friendly."

Dimensional holes, David reflected, were one of the things he'd learned about that scared him. Not all other planes of existence were locked behind the Seal, but the links between the other planes weren't as defended as the link between Earth and the "broom closet" Solomon had shoved Earth's supernaturals into.

Ix grunted. "Not least because after three thousand years, the Masters Beyond have made mincemeat of anything that was friendly to humans. They can't stop the magical essence of mankind coming back," the demon said grimly, "but they could annihilate the vast majority of the beings that would have fought with you."

David grimaced. He was trying very hard to *forget* the little he'd been told about the Masters Beyond, the rulers of the demons. None of it was pleasant, and it all sounded rather Lovecraftian sometimes.

"Be that as it may," Michael told them all, "our purpose is, as always, primarily to support OSPI's operations and keep an eye out for major demonic or vampire activity. When needed, we will perform this Office's mandate and neutralize any supernatural threats to the United States. Clear?"

A chorus of "Clear, sir," accompanied by laughs and rude gestures, was his reply.

THE ARMORY SLASH change room that occupied the rear half of ONSET Nine's residence's main floor was spacious enough for all seven members of the team to gear up simultaneously.

David realized quite quickly that all six of the other members of the team were keeping an eye on him, to make sure he didn't do something wrong. The realization bothered him for a moment, but not for long. It was as much concern for his well-being as concern he'd slow the team down.

The first part of the gear the team was wearing was the ubiquitous black bodysuit he'd seen repeatedly on ONSET personnel. When David had first been told to put one on in training, he'd commented that they looked extremely, well, dorky. Koburn's response had been simple: the trainer had hung up a spare suit, picked up an assault rifle loaded with armor-piercing silver rounds, and emptied thirty bullets into the bodysuit.

He'd then put the rifle down, pointed at the smeared but unpenetrated suit, and asked if David still objected. Having seen the effectiveness of what was basically an enchanted full-body suit of Kevlar with ceramic inserts, David decided to suck up the dorky look of the outfit.

Among its advantages, it was actually relatively easy to put on. While David was slower than the rest of the team, it still only took him a minute or so until he closed the zipper up his side.

Very careful to ignore Kate Mason's gracefully outlined athletic curves, the newest agent picked up the shoulder holster with the Silver-Mod M1911 pistol and his spare magazines.

It said a lot about the reliability of OSPI's original Silver-Mod design that ONSET hadn't bothered to upgrade David's firearm. While the sidearms the rest of the team were belting on were a newer, more advanced weapon, the actual per-round effectiveness was supposedly about the same. Of course, the sleek Omicron Silver caseless auto-loaders, with their extra gas vents and propellant-encased bullets, held a good fifty percent more rounds—but that was unlikely to matter in most circumstances.

To balance the Silver-Mod 1911, David had hung the harness and scabbard for the mageblade knife on the other side of his body. Given the strict design constraints necessary to hold a weapon that would cut literally anything, the harnesses and scabbards the rest of the team wore were identical. A hard base locked around the guard of the blade, holding the blade suspended in a scabbard that was a minimum of a tenth of an inch away from the edge at any point. The base could be released quickly, though drawing the weapon was always an exercise in care. The rest of the harness was black Kevlar webbing, like the harnesses for the guns, designed to be slung on either side of the body.

Over the two weapon harnesses went a third Kevlar harness, clipping on to both, carrying and protecting the fragile components of the armor's core computing systems. It took only a moment for David to connect that harness to the fiber optic mesh linking the various sensors hiding in the bodysuit.

Finally, with the battle harness complete, David slung on the heavy uniform jacket with its circled diagonal lightning bolt insignia. As soon as he was done putting the jacket on, Michael, who'd been fully prepared for a while, passed him the M4-Omicron carbine ONSET used as a combat rifle.

The stock slotted against his upper arm and his hand gripped the barrel, just forward of the magazine that descended down a handful of inches in front of the grip and trigger. The barrel was larger than he remembered on the Army M4s he'd seen, but that was because the ONSET weapon had been redesigned for a heavy 7.62mm silver round instead of the original bullets.

Glancing around the room, David realized that the small team was carrying a scary amount of firepower, and that was before considering the fact that Morgen and Kate could probably destroy battleships with their minds. Akono and Ix shared the M4-Omicron with him and O'Brien, but Bourque had a light machine gun cradled in her arms, and the two Mages lacked any conventional weaponry beyond mageblades and Omicron Silvers.

"Seems a lot of gear to load on for a transport flight," David observed. It seemed a lot of gear for *anything* to the police officer he'd been. Koburn had pounded home why it was necessary, but it still scared him to be loading up military weapons and body armor for what remained basically a police position.

"It is," Michael responded. "Two reasons, however. First, all of this adds up to a lot of cubage in storage containers. Space on a Pendragon is limited, so we carry it aboard. Secondly," he continued grimly, "sometimes we get called in midflight. Like when we showed up in Charlesville. We need to be ready to kick ass and take names no matter what."

"Hoorah," Bourque interjected. "We can't predict when shit is going to go down. Get used to the gear," she instructed firmly, "as we don't take much of it *off* when on active duty."

"Wonderful," David observed calmly, considering the consequences of six men and women wearing the same armor for seven days. Ix probably didn't sweat, at least. "That's going to be a pleasant smell."

"We shower and sleep in rotations," Michael told him. "You can be out of harness doing those two things. Nothing else."

"Well, in that case," David said firmly, slinging the M4 over his shoulder, "let's get this show on the road, shall we?"

———

THE FLIGHT down to Louisiana was the first time David had ridden in a Pendragon helicopter without having the windows blacked out. The rest of the team freely allowed him a window seat, which allowed him to look out over the ONSET HQ Campus for the first time ever.

It was impressive. Settled into a small Colorado valley, the twenty-foot concrete walls surrounding the facility probably ran two thirds of a mile on a side. Four small skyscrapers marked the core of the Campus, but other buildings sprawled across almost a square mile of beyond-top-secret base.

On top of that, David knew that he'd only scratched the surface of the subterranean facilities under the Campus. Somewhere under there was one hell of a gun modification and manufacturing plant. ONSET modified heavy weapons but manufactured its own ammunition, rifles and sidearms.

Somehow, seeing the base from the air as opposed to being amongst the buildings drove home just how huge the Campus was. ONSET fielded twenty-one strike teams with a list strength of eight but an average *actual* strength of six, a total of over a hundred and thirty supernaturals, which now included David White. The security personnel, AP Companies, and general support structure for ONSET itself were easily fifteen or twenty times that number.

The helicopter continued to rise over the facility, until the whole Campus became a tiny postage stamp behind them. Once they reached cruising altitude, the chopper's stubby wings swung out and locked into place.

Moments later, the floor of the helicopter shook as the jets turned on, and the Campus shrank even more rapidly behind them as the stealth aircraft shot southeast at just under Mach One.

―――――

FROM THE MOMENT the rotors folded in and the jet engines came on to when the pilot turned the jets off and turned north above the old Louisiana town of Alexandria was a tad over an hour and a half. The chopper slowly dropped lower, heading toward the farmland northeast of the town.

The approach to the ground lasted a good five minutes, during which David started to wonder if ONSET put *all* their bases in mountains. Finally, however, the chopper dropped into a normal-looking farm field.

It was normal-looking from the air, anyway. No sooner had the chopper hit the ground before the nearby three-story red barn disgorged a flatbed truck and an armed escort.

ONSET Nine disembarked from the chopper, and the pilot turned the rotors back on for a momentary hop onto the flatbed.

The leader of the three armed men watching over the truck, a tall blond man whose mannerisms matched his plaid shirt and jean overalls, waved the ONSET team forward, and revealed himself to be wearing the same ONSET black bodysuit as they all wore underneath his "Farmer John" duds.

"I'm Lieutenant Alex Preston," he introduced himself. "I run the facilities at this base and command the team of security personnel." He gestured them into the large barn, which, while it looked like something out of a child's storybook, turned out to be fitted out as a modern military hangar on the inside.

Two more Pendragons held pride of place in the center of the hangar, but one wall held half a dozen cars of various makes and colors, only two of them with government plates. Other than the vehicles and the fueling equipment, the barn was completely Spartan. Concrete floors, fuel tanks and steel lockers were the only decoration. Not even a loose strand of grass marred the barn's military cleanliness.

Michael clearly knew where he was going as he walked confidently alongside Lieutenant Preston. The rest of the team followed the two men back into the barn and around behind the pumps.

Tucked into a corner, hidden from view of the front entrance behind a large fuel tank, was set of steel elevator doors with a biometric reader suite standing next to it and a pair of guards armed with bullpup shotguns.

"This leads down into the main facility," Preston told them, then gestured to the biometric and card readers attached to the elevator. "If you ladies and gentlemen can swipe yourself in, please? ONSET Thirteen left about ten minutes ago, but things are already cleaned up downstairs. As soon as you're all checked in on our system, I can brief O'Brien on our current situations."

One by one, ONSET Nine's members swiped themselves into the facilities' computers with their ID cards. Once Kate, the last person to enter her ID, had been beeped and cleared by the computers, Preston grinned at them all.

"That's the last immediate security procedure," he confirmed, and gestured at the now-open elevator. "Welcome to ONSET Louisiana Command."

10

LOUISIANA COMMAND'S AMENITIES, DAVID QUICKLY REALIZED, WERE relatively low. The facility was functionally an underground bunker. For the security personnel permanently assigned to the base, it wasn't as bad, since they actually lived off-site in homes of their own.

For the ONSET team, required to stay in the bunker 24/7, it was a different story. Eight small rooms, one common area with a TV and a single bookshelf made up the entire living space of the facility. A communications room, command center, and armory made up the rest of the tiny base. Unlike the Campus, not a scrap of blue carpet—or carpet of any kind—was to be seen covering the concrete.

By the Wednesday, the third day in the base, the team settled into a routine of pushing off boredom as long as possible. The rest of ONSET Nine had clearly expected something like this, as their luggage had disgorged a wide variety of time-occupiers, from Dilsner's PlayStation Vita to Bourque's cross-stitch.

David had settled for reading through the bookshelf. Most of it was trashy novels, but there were a solid two shelves of what he'd mentally begun referring to as "Secret Histories"—books on the events of the last hundred or so years nobody knew about.

He was reading through a book on the history of America's

Vampire Familias, a brutal mix between blood relations and criminal syndicates that had become very good at hiding their true nature behind intermediaries. According to the book, between the various supernatural groups and organizations and the Omicron Offices themselves, the average lifespan of a vampire after turning was less than three weeks. If that vampire was turned by or recruited by the Familias, however, they dropped into an intricate network of deception and concealment that nearly guaranteed their survival.

The thought that there were entire organizations of bloodsucking monsters like the punks who'd attacked Charlesville made David's blood run cold. That these organizations were deep-rooted organized crime syndicates, devoted to causing more harm than their unearthly appetites would have caused anyway, made him very glad he'd joined ONSET.

But, according to the book, the Familias were *old*, pre-dating not only ONSET but quite probably OSPI's early-twentieth-century origin. They were Omicron's most persistent enemy and, according to the book, weren't likely to go away anytime soon.

"All right, people," Michael's voice suddenly boomed across the ready room. David *felt* the rest of the group tense up as he dropped his book and looked up. For a moment, everyone in the room blurred a bit as his own tension activated his Sight, which started showing him the next few seconds' worth of motion.

Then he controlled his senses and picked the book up and put it away. With a wry thought, he wished his tension were as easy to control as his abilities.

"It looks like we have a situation, people," Michael told them. "An OSPI Inspector reported this morning that he was about to make an arrest in a case we've been watching for a while. That was eight hours ago, and we have not heard from him since.

"As of now," the werewolf continued, eyeing his people, "OSPI has advised us that he is presumed missing, and we are going in. This should *not* be a hell-for-leather run, and I want a team on site here. Ix, Bourque, Morgen," he barked, and those three worthies looked up.

"You three will remain here," Michael instructed. "Keep an eye on that damned dimensional research project and the rest of our little babies. Mason, Akono, White," he continued, turning to David and the others. "You're with me."

David rose to his feet, replacing the gloves he'd removed to read and grabbing the jacket to cover his combat harness. He was surprised that Michael had chosen him—he was, despite his age and experience compared to half the team, the team's newest member. He was also surprised, however, at how that simply made him more determined to prove Michael right to bring him.

"I'll brief you in the air," Michael told them. "Let's go."

―――――

As the four agents walked rapidly from the elevator to the Pendragon that had been moved out into the field, David brought the computer systems in his bodysuit fully online for the first time since training. With the black display glasses over his face, the computer projected a heads-up display across his field of vision, including data gleaned from the suit's sensors.

The ex-cop stopped outside the helicopter to plug the lead hanging from the end of his right sleeve into the base of the modified M4. As soon as he plugged the lead in, a small image popped up in his display, showing the view from the camera mounted on the top of the assault rifle. Matching the crosshairs on the camera, a second set of crosshairs appeared in his main field of view, with a circle marking the error of probability where the bullet would strike, given current conditions and his grip on the weapon.

The trained-in preparations soothed his uneasy mind and kept him from worrying about the fate of the OSPI Inspector reported overdue and missing.

Akono and Mason followed Michael into the chopper before David could catch up. By the time David had taken his seat, Akono had entered the cockpit and taken over the controls.

"Where am I headed?" the pilot asked.

"You have a waypoint in the computer," Michael told him. "It's a small Catholic church in northern Alexandria. Take us there."

As the helicopter lifted off, two small pictures popped up in David's HUD.

"The picture on the left," Michael told them all, "is OSPI Inspector Damien Riesling. He's been investigating a specific case of a serial killer for about two months, ever since we were called in when one of the killings the FBI was investigating turned out weird.

"He was pursuing a killer that seemed to keep popping up all over the country," Michael continued, "and the only link between the victims was that they were all gay men and none had blood drawn in the killing. All the deaths were strangulation, suffocation or blunt-force trauma.

"Riesling got a break about two weeks ago, when two more deaths showed up. Both were Catholic priests," the Commander told them, "and they'd only recently confessed that they were gay lovers—in fact, we found out about that confession after the fact. Only a small number of people had known about the confession, even though it seemed to be shaping up to have them drummed out of the priesthood.

"Riesling investigated the men who knew about the priests' confession—about forty of them—and matched them against his other killings. The man in the right-hand picture was confirmed as being in the area of over seventy percent of them," Michael said grimly. "His name is Rufus Carderone. At seven o'clock this morning, OSPI issued a warrant for his arrest on nine counts of murder, under the Supernatural Restraint and Enforcement Act. We have not heard from Damien since he informed OSPI he was headed to arrest Carderone. That was now nine hours ago."

"What do we know about this Carderone?" Kate asked.

"He is a fully ordained Catholic priest," Michael told them. "Which is going to raise a shitstorm all in itself, but we have more immediate concerns. Our evidence suggests that he is either a Mage or Empowered. We *know* he either is supernaturally strong or uses strength-enhancing magic, and there is evidence to suggest he is capable of at least short-range teleportation."

"How do we handle it?" David asked slowly, wondering what the answer would be. The thought of going up against a Catholic priest—

the faith of his birth, his *father's* faith—who wielded supernatural powers bothered him, but he was going to do his job.

"Malcolm secures the rear entrance," Michael said calmly. "Kate, you secure the front and call in local law enforcement. You know the drill; we're federal agents."

"Yes, sir," both replied.

"David," Michael continued, "you're with me on the entrance. We call for him to surrender, and do not engage unless attacked. Understand me, David? You do *not* shoot unless I order you or it is in immediate self-defense."

"Understood, sir," David confirmed with a sense of relief. He wasn't sure he was the best man to accompany Michael, but he was glad that the assumption wasn't that they were going in shooting.

"Folks, we're coming in on the church now," Akono reported. "Let's be glad it's Wednesday afternoon—Carderone should be the only one home."

Kate didn't seem to notice Akono's comment, as she'd lowered her helmet over her head. Presumably, that was for its sound-deadening qualities, as it looked like she'd used the communication system to make a call to the local police, and the magically noise cancelling on a Pendragon didn't work *inside* the helicopter.

"We'll go down by rope, and Akono will swing around in the air," Michael instructed David, pulling the rope winch out. "You first," the werewolf said, with a wicked grin.

11

THE FACT THAT IT WAS RAINING DIDN'T REALLY HELP DAVID AS HE HIT THE ground in the empty street outside the small church. Warm and soft as the drops were—so different from the cold driving rain of Maine—they failed to relax him. For the first time in his life, he was going somewhere with the knowledge that having to fight, quite possibly having to kill, was more likely than not.

The rain fell in large drops, a regular patter of them hitting against the ground around David as he thumped to the ground, his more-than-human muscles absorbing the impact with an ease that still unnerved him.

He glanced up and down the street, noting the quiet white-fenced houses, their driveways uniformly empty of vehicles. The early afternoon saw this suburb deserted, except for the two ONSET agents that stood in the rain, the helicopter whirring near-silently overhead.

"Kate's connected with the local police," Michael told him as the Pendragon swung away, circling around to the back of the small church. The building looked new but was built in an old style, designed to match the original missionary churches in this region. Brown stucco and white stone held up the triangle roof and its dark wooden steeple.

"They're on their way, but they'll stay out of the church unless we call them in," David's Commander continued. "They've been told it's a Federal matter and an FBI agent has gone missing."

"What about Riesling?" David asked as he took the safety off on his rifle.

"If we can find him, we do," Michael replied. "If we can't," he continued grimly, "Carderone has something else to answer for. Let's go."

The two agents crossed the small churchyard to the door and stopped, flanking it. Ever so calmly, Michael unslung the assault rifle he was carrying and gestured for David to go first.

Swallowing, David checked that he'd turned the safety off on his own rifle and, holding the rifle in his right hand, opened the door with his left. The heavy door swung open into a small lobby completely devoid of life.

Burgundy carpet stretched across the lobby, matching the long curtains that hung beside the doors on either side of the room, half-concealed behind baroque pillars. A set of heavy wooden doors, richly decorated with carvings of the crucifixion, stood at the far end of the room. The room was meticulously maintained and neatly furnished. Each wall had two wooden pews along them, behind the pillars and divided by the doors in the middle.

The two ONSET agents stalked forward onto that dark red carpet, gun barrels tracking over the doors on each side of the room, and the double door on the far side.

"Which way?" David asked quietly, breathing in the smell of incense and oiled wood, a familiar scent from his childhood.

"Forward, into the main sanctuary," Michael replied, and gestured for David to lead the way again.

David pushed the inner door open and entered into the main hall of the church. The same burgundy carpet and dark wood paneling continued into the larger room. A small stone basin stood next to the entry door, and heavy wooden pews lined the floor up to the raised pulpit at the end of the hall.

A balcony ran around the hall at the level of a second floor, supported by the same baroque pillars as had decorated the front room. From the ground, David couldn't tell if it held more seats or just decoration, as any view of it was blocked by heavy curtains slung from the roof.

The raised pulpit at the far end was fenced in by a dark wood railing framing a solid podium and half-concealing the door at the back of the pulpit. The pews started three feet away from the dais, and curtains hung down from the balcony to frame its occupant.

Like the pews on the floor, however, the pulpit was empty.

Michael moved up behind David, and an eerie growl reverberated from the werewolf that set the hairs on David's neck a-tingle.

"This isn't working," the ONSET Commander muttered, and then raised his voice.

"Father Carderone," he shouted. "Are you here?"

David, his Second Sight now fully active, saw the blur of potential at the door at the back of the pulpit before it opened and a figure walked out. Dressed in the full robes of a Catholic priest, the tall, fair-haired man was presumably Father Carderone.

"Who are you?" the man demanded, his eyes taking in the two ONSET agent's body armor and rifles. "What is the meaning of this violation of the house of God?"

"Father Carderone," Michael said calmly, "we are federal agents investigating the disappearance of an FBI Inspector by the name of Damien Riesling. He had advised us that he intended to interview you with regards to a case but then disappeared. Do you know what happened to him?"

"Riesling?" Carderone said slowly, walking out onto the floor of the church as the two armed men walked toward him. "Yes, I remember," he continued after a moment, stopping a good twenty feet from the agents, who stopped in turn.

"He defiled my church with his presence and made heinous accusations," the priest said, his calm voice contrary to the venom of his words. "Men like him, who do not admit their sins, are why our world is in the sad shape it is."

David watched the man's aura boil with emotion—rage, disgust, contempt—that gave as much lie to his calm tone as his words. The sight of those colors drove home just what this man—this *priest* of his father's faith—truly was. The sheer sickening contempt that inspired in him shocked David, and his hands shifted slightly on the rifle.

"What do you mean?" Michael said carefully.

"The man was a sodomite," Carderone said flatly. "The world may tolerate such, but I know the commands of God and I will not have them in my church. I evicted him from this holy ground, and I care not where he went!"

"I see," Michael said calmly, *his* aura belying his voice and words as well. Slowly and deliberately, the werewolf began to move forward. "Unfortunately, the 'commands of God' are generally not considered acceptable reasons for murder," the agent said softly.

"I have committed no murders," Carderone snapped, fear flickering through his aura, vanishing under rage. "I have shed no blood."

David remembered the comment that the major link between the killings that had led the FBI to conclude it was one killer was that all of them had been performed in a manner to minimize or remove the chance of spilling blood. With that realization, his hands tightened on the stock of his rifle.

Carderone believed every word he said, but to David, the blood of the man's victims shone upon his aura. Fear and rage outlined the deaths this man had wrought, and his excuses and lies were transparent as glass before David's Sight.

"Father Rufus Carderone," Michael said formally as he stalked toward the priest, "you are under arrest on the charges of first-degree murder, to be remanded to the custody of the Special Supernatural Courts as per the authority of the Supernatural Restraint and Enforcement Act. You have the right to remain silent. You have the right to an attorney. Due to the circumstances of these charges, one will be provided for you by the court. Do you understand these rights?"

"*You* are the one who does not understand," Carderone spat, and leapt forward. Two assault rifle barrels tracked him, but he grabbed the barrel of Michael's gun and yanked.

David had personal experience now with how strong Michael was, even in human form—the werewolf was even more inhumanly strong than David himself. Despite the werewolf's immense strength, the priest pulled the gun to the side, pivoting the werewolf around to hold him between himself and David's rifle.

For a long moment, the room held frozen in that tableau, and then, strained beyond any conceivable breaking point by the inhuman forces exerted on it, the barrel of the M4 snapped clear off.

Michael dropped the gun and grabbed for Carderone. The two locked arms, and then the priest threw the werewolf aside, slamming his burly form into the pews. With Michael clear, David had a clear shot.

To his own surprise, he didn't hesitate. Training and anger at the priest's hypocrisy clicked into place, and the circle of his targeting system dropped onto "Father" Carderone's chest with chilling speed.

The crash of the assault rifle firing echoed through the church, but even as David fired, he knew the priest would be gone. As the bullets flashed out, the priest faded out of his sight. For a moment, David had no idea where the man was, and then one of the massive wooden pews slammed into his back, crushing the ONSET Agent to the floor.

Michael barely danced out of the way of the crushing furniture, snarling at the priest David now saw standing behind him.

"You do not understand," the man repeated in a bellow, his calm demeanor now lost to the crazed eyes of a madman under his shock of blond hair. "I have been chosen and blessed by God to carry out His holy work! If He opposed this, would I be all that I am?"

David answered by throwing the pew back at the priest in a surge of strength. He managed to scramble to his feet as the priest vanished again, but this time David saw him reappear on the pulpit.

Turning to cover Michel, David sent another burst of bullets toward the pulpit. Again, the priest disappeared before the weapon fired, this time reappearing on the edge of the second-floor balcony.

Moments after reappearing, Carderone ripped one of the heavy curtain rods out of the pillar holding it and flung it at David, the metal spinning across the room with lethal speed. Seeing the motion begin moments before the priest appeared at the gap, David dove sideways, and the steel rod smashed two of the pews to kindling.

This time, David saw the priest in two places for a moment, the blur of motion heralding his arrival at the pulpit again. Michael saw the man appearing and rushed for the raised dais, changing forms into the immense black wolf as he did.

At the sight of Michael's transformation, Carderone began to froth. "Demon!" he screamed. "Accursed warrior of Hell, feel the wrath of *God*."

Carderone leapt over the pulpit, a heavy cudgel in his hand. He met Michael in midair, and the *crunch* of the cudgel hitting the werewolf echoed through the room. The massive black form flew sideways and slammed into the wall.

Michael slid down the wall, and for a moment, David truly feared his Commander was down, and that he had to face this madman alone. Only a moment passed, however, before Michael leapt to his feet and charged Carderone again, but the priest disappeared once more he could reach him.

Again, the priest stood on the balcony, and this time, he threw the cudgel at Michael, the impact sending the werewolf reeling back to the ground again. As Michael crumbled, David opened fire, spraying the second floor with silver bullets. His shots had no effect as the priest disappeared before they hit.

He reappeared at the far back of the church, standing directly in front of the massive cross that hung there.

"I have been anointed by God," he screamed at the two agents as he ripped the immense monstrosity of wood and iron from the wall. "You have neither the power nor the right to stop me!"

Michael met the priest's words with his own wordless scream. The echoing battle cry of an enraged werewolf echoed through the church, and David winced in pain as his Commander began to charge.

Even as Michael charged, Carderone lunged forward, the ten-foot cross almost light in his hands. With a sickening crunch, it tore through the werewolf, punching through Michael's furred body in a spray of blood.

The priest dropped the immense cross with a cold smile that faded as the werewolf rose again, tearing the cross from his body as the wounds healed before David's eyes.

With a snarl, Carderone ripped something from where the cross had stood and disappeared. David was watching, however, and saw his blurred form appear beside the blur of Michael's path, his Sight showing where the priest would appear.

David twisted his rifle around and emptied the last half-dozen rounds in the clip at the empty air where he *knew* Carderone would be.

The priest materialized with one of the bullets *in* his body, and two more slammed into his upper torso as the first ripped its way out. Blood sprayed across the church pews, and David came to a halt, the heavy pistol at full extension and his eyes on his enemy as the heavy silver candlestick in the priest's hands fell to the floor.

For an eternity, David White met Rufus Carderone's eyes and knew he'd killed the man.

Then the enraged and bloodied werewolf ripped the priest's head off.

12

By the time the Alexandria Police showed up, O'Brien had returned to human form and any sign of his injury had vanished. He ordered Kate, who'd responded to the gunfire in time to watch Carderone's head hit the floor, to have the cops secure a perimeter while the ONSET personnel swept the church. Kate had joined David and Michael at the front of the church's hall. Her presence helped calm David somewhat, as much because he didn't want to appear completely shattered in front of her as for anything she did.

"We're looking for three things," the werewolf calmly informed Kate and a still-shaken David after he had the two Agents with him. "Firstly, Damien Riesling, or at least some evidence as to *what* happened to him. Secondly, any supernatural objects. While Carderone appears to have been Empowered, not a Mage, that doesn't necessarily rule out enchanted toys, and we can't leave those to the local police. Finally," he concluded, "any evidence as to who else this sick fuck killed. Understood?"

David nodded somewhat sickly. A very large part of him just wanted to go outside and throw up. Whatever he *wanted*, however, David had been trained as a police investigator. He knew they needed evidence and as much information as they could find.

With that thought in mind, he headed toward the door at the back of the pulpit, where his memories of his childhood church told him the priest's rooms would be. To his surprise, Kate walked with him.

"Are you all right?" the Mage asked quietly. "It looks like it got ugly in here."

The hall of the church was a disaster zone of bullet holes and shattered furniture. Carderone's corpse now occupied a black body bag, but a massive bloodstain marked the spot he'd died.

David skirted that bloodstain and shook his head silently. He appreciated Kate's concern, but now wasn't the time. The shock of the violence, Michael's injury and terrifyingly rapid recovery, and the memory of Carderone's face were too fresh. He needed time and to see with own eyes the proof of the priest's crimes.

"He'd have killed you both," she reminded him. "You had no choice."

"I've been in exactly two firefights in my life," David told her, his voice weak even in his own ears as he voiced his disquiet. "First those vampires back home and now here. For some strange reason," he said bitterly, "I haven't got used to killing people yet."

"Want some advice on that?" the Mage asked, her voice still soft, as the pair stopped at the back of the nave of the church.

"What?" David asked, wondering just what the younger woman would say.

"Don't," Kate told him flatly. "Killing people is the ugliest part of our job, and if we didn't hate it, we'd be as bad the people we fight."

With that, the young woman turned toward the right door, leaving David to go left. Somehow, the thought that he wasn't the only one bothered made him feel a lot better as he entered the private areas of the church.

———

THERE WAS something inherently creepy about picking through the things of a man you'd just killed. The door behind the pulpit had led into a undecorated wooden antechamber, with several closets that proved to contain Carderone's priestly vestments.

A door at the back led into an office area, with an open door on the left leading to a bedroom and one on the right to a small kitchen. All of the furnishings were old oak, and sumptuous burgundy hangings marked the walls and matched the plush couch in the office. A surprisingly ordinary-looking black leather office chair stood pushed back from a massive oak desk, and paintings of the saints lined the upper walls.

The back rooms of the church were a small but comfortable home for a man who'd chosen to do truly horrible things. Somehow, their plush furnishings and small luxuries made David sick.

A part of his mind insisted that horrible men should live in horrific surroundings, not in neat little apartments in the backs of churches. With a shudder, he looked around and focused on the task at hand.

He swept his half of the back rooms with Second Sight once and then went back with his police training, checking for documents and evidence. While his Sight gave him some clues, he still trusted the training he'd used for years more than it.

No tingles of magic stood out to his Sight, nor did anything stand out as suspicious to his police training, but he eventually found himself staring at the priest's heavy wooden desk. It was a true monstrosity of solid, heavy oak, probably antique and brought into this church from the older building it had replaced. A filing cabinet made up one leg and eight drawers made up the other.

Several of the desk drawers stood open—Carderone must have been working at this desk when they'd arrived—and David quickly rifled through the papers, finding nothing out of the ordinary for a church this size.

For some reason, he still stood, looking at the desk. His training suggested that the kind of man the priest had been would have kept *some* sort of trophy list or record of his deeds. This desk was the center of so much of the priest's other holy work; it made a sort of twisted sense that he'd have organized his killings through it as well.

David focused harder, now bringing his Sight fully to bear on the desk, matching magic and intuition with training and experience. Traces of glittering past emotion swept through the air, tracing their transparent lines over the sad reality of the ownerless desk. The lines of the priest's life swept across that desk, marking which drawers were important and which ones weren't.

.   And one set of lines marked a spot, centered on the front of the desk's thick wooden top, where there *was* no drawer. These lines were red, with rage, and white, with satisfaction. Slowly, ever so slowly, David's fingers followed those lines, running along the bottom edge of the desktop. Where the lines converged, his fingers hit a latch, and a hidden drawer dropped out of the desk's top, sliding forward on smoothly greased hinges.

The cop checked that he was wearing the skintight black gloves of his suit and then removed the drawer's contents. One advantage of his suit was the knowledge that everything he saw was recorded, so photos were unnecessary.

The drawer had contained a red leather photo album, wrapped around with the transparent lines of emotion. The red leather was unmarked anywhere except on the very front, where a black metal stylized sun had been riveted to the leather. To David's Sight, the black sun glowed with a deep light, seeming blacker than should have been possible. He flinched from the sight of the symbol but then flipped the album open.

It was a forty-eight-photo album and held twenty-one pictures. Each was accompanied by a neatly written name, date and location.

The last photo showed a man with a massive purple bruise along the side of a face still in death. The neatly written details beneath, the ink still slightly wet under the plastic cover, were Damien Riesling's name and today's date.

For a long moment, David just stared at the album, feeling sick inside. He *knew* some murderers kept trophies, but none of his previous investigations in Charlesville had brought up anything like this. Swallowing, he activated his radio.

"Folks, I think Riesling's dead," he said grimly. "I just found Carderone's trophy album."

"He's definitely dead," Kate responded, her voice twisting with emotion. "I just found his body."

"Fuck" was Michael's only comment.

———

TWO HOURS LATER, a detachment from OSPI had arrived to take charge of the two bodies and the evidence. By then, Michael and Akono had carefully bagged Riesling's body and moved him into the still-taped-off lobby to lie alongside his killer.

David leaned against the front exit, studiously ignoring the black body bags and fighting with the sense of satisfaction that was starting to leak through his discomfort about the fight. Kate sat on one of the benches, watching the OSPI officers as Michael handed them the photo album with careful gloved hands.

"You found this?" Inspector Braun, the OSPI man in charge said incredulously as the rail-thin man slowly looked through the photo album.

"In a hidden compartment in his desk," David replied, touched by a sense of satisfaction that had nothing to do with the fight.

"We knew about twelve of these, son," the man said quietly. "The other eight are either still in their local PDs or were never even identified as homicides. Second Sight shouldn't have led you to this," Braun complained.

"I was the lead investigator in a small town," David told him. "Since I only had two other detectives reporting to me in the entire town, we cross-trained for everything from crime scene forensics to homicides and criminal psychology. No degrees," he finished dryly, "just lots of courses."

He focused intentionally on his pride in completing those courses, and his satisfaction at finding the evidence they needed. These were safe things to focus on. The sick feeling of Carderone's death—and the even more disturbing touch of satisfaction he was now feeling about it —where much less safe.

"This will help us close up a lot of dry ends," the Inspector told him, watching his own forensics team sweep into the church. "And rumor has it you're the man who took down Carderone, too?"

"That he is," Michael rumbled, stepping up behind the Inspector. "He saved my head from a run-in with a silver candlestick in the process, too. He's ONSET and not leaving," he added, with a mock glare at the Inspector. "Stop having ideas."

Braun chuckled softly. "Much as we'd like another investigator on the team," he told Michael and David, "sometimes it helps to have those same skills in the people who deal with the *very* sharp ends." He paused, looking at the front of the album again, this time at the black metal sun on it. "Do you know anything about this symbol?"

Both ONSET agents shook their heads, but David also looked at the sun again for a long moment.

"It looks wrong," he said softly. He couldn't find a better word to describe the effects of the Sight on the symbol. "To Second Sight, that is," he clarified. "But beyond that, no idea."

"Damn," Braun replied, then nodded to the two ONSET men. "If there's anything to it, we'll figure it out. In any case, your part of this is done," he told them. "We'll finish the forensics and the cleanup. Riesling will have a memorial service in a few days down in New Orleans, if you can attend."

"We'll see," Michael told him. "We should be just finishing up our tour of duty at Louisiana Command at that point, so we should be able to stop by."

"We'd appreciate it, Commander," the Inspector told him. "Revenge isn't our business, but justice is, and sometimes it helps to see the men who brought justice to those who hurt our own."

———

THE REMAINDER of ONSET Nine's stay in Louisiana command passed without incident. David finished the two shelves of histories, diving into the records of the Vampire Familias, the nationwide group called the Elfin, and a half-dozen other major and minor supernatural groups scattered across the country.

Mostly, he did it to fill in the details of the very broad-strokes history Koburn had given him in training. Partially, he did it to help the memory of Carderone's eyes fade. And lastly, he did it because Kate proved very knowledgeable about the secret histories and was willing to answer questions.

He was thankful for her help and also for her company. She was witty and intelligent and had understood that he needed to focus on anything other than Carderone. David was glad Kate had been around, and he found his awareness of her attractiveness fading as she proved to be a very good friend.

Time passed, as it did, and the last day, as they prepared to leave, Michael drew David aside.

"I just got a confirmation from OSPI," the Commander told him. "Riesling's memorial service is tomorrow morning. I've arranged for you and me to detour on our trip back to the Campus for active reserve to stop by. Unless you'd rather just go back to base," he added.

"No," David replied after a moment's thought. While his bullets had avenged Riesling's murder, they couldn't bring the man back. They owed the man something. "I think we owe him that much."

"Good," Michael said. "The rest of the team catches a Pendragon in a few hours, but we need to leave pretty soon if we're getting to New Orleans by nightfall. Go collect your things and change into civvies."

David nodded and headed back to the tiny quarters he'd had there. A quick shower and change later, he joined Michael in the front entrance. A concealed web harness hung under his denim jacket to hold his gun and mageblade, and he slung an overnight bag over his shoulder as he nodded to the werewolf.

"I'm good to go."

———

THE IDEA of a several-hour-long road trip in a government car with Michael left David somewhat nervous, but he'd agreed to the trip and settled into the car quietly. They hit the highway, headed south in silence. David wasn't up to asking questions, and Michael apparently didn't feel like talking.

The old blue Lincoln had been on the road for about twenty minutes before either of the pair of Agents said anything.

"So, I saw you read through that shelf of textbooks," Michael commented into the stretching silence.

"I didn't know to bring anything to do," David admitted, barely avoiding a sigh of relief that his boss had found something "safe" to talk about, "so it was what I could do that was productive."

"Fair enough," the Commander replied. "It helps a little bit, as I need to give you a bit of a rundown. We are going to an OSPI funeral. OSPI tends to get attached to specific areas and will get quite well known with the supernaturals in a region. Even with only one in twenty thousand of the general population being supernatural, that's still a lot in somewhere the size of New Orleans.

"This means that the local supernatural communities will be at Riesling's funeral," Michael explained, "so you need to know who you're dealing with."

"Who am I dealing with?" David asked, intentionally repeating the question back. The textbooks had made clear that the New Orleans voodoo community did have members with real magic, and some of the ones without magic made deals with real spirits. He wondered who *else* would be at the memorial.

"Firstly, you'll be dealing with OSPI people," Michael told him. "They're basically cops, so you should be okay. A good mix of mundanes and supernaturals, OSPI tends to run about twelve mundanes to a supernatural.

"Secondly, there are the local voodoo *prêtre*," the werewolf continued. "They're mostly Mages, with a few Empowered thrown in. Scary dudes, but generally on our side—hugely community-focused gentlemen."

"Do their communities know about them?" David asked. It wasn't something the book had been very clear on.

"There are a *lot* of *prêtre*," Michael replied. "Their communities think they're all magical, and certainly they can all practice low magic. Full Mages among groups like that are probably one in several hundred—which is still a lot more than the general population."

"So, our cops and the voodoo boys," David observed, ticking them off on his fingers. "And be extremely polite to the *prêtre*."

"Being extremely polite to everybody there is not a bad idea," Michael told him. "The third group will be Elfin, and Elfin are scary."

"Elves or Elfin?" David asked. His reading suggested there was a difference, but he wasn't fully clear on it. The Elfin were a nationwide organization that very definitely straddled the gray line of supernatural legalities. Elves were apparently a type of supernatural, and, despite the name, there didn't seem to be much connection between the two.

"Elfin," Michael confirmed. "Elves can be spooky and dreamy—Akono's one, if you missed it—but are mainly defined by the ability to create glamors—a kind of illusions. *Elfin* are members of the Elfin organization with all its semi-criminal aspects. Watch for the leaf brooches," he finished. "And be extra nice to them. They play by unspoken rules we've agreed to, and we don't want to unnecessarily piss any of them off."

"Unspoken rules?"

"They try to keep anything they think we *might* object to under wraps," Michael replied. "But they shut down anything we *do* object to without hassle. The legality in so many supernatural affairs is so gray that Omicron quite often can't arrest them when we think they're crossing lines, so the 'unspoken rules' save us a lot of problems."

"So, it's a criminal syndicate with a good PR department?" David asked. His sense of police justice growled at the thought of criminals getting away due to lawyers and legalities. That had never been a part of his job he'd liked.

"Not always, but sometimes," Michael replied. "And don't forget the Tolkien obsession among their founders. When dealing with Elfin, never forget the Tolkien obsession."

———

MAJESTIC WAS FINDING herself with a new appreciation for the worldview of conspiracy theorists, she realized. Skimming through news sites, looking for information on other topics, every so often she hit something that looked like it *could* be related to the whole mess with David White.

So far as she could tell, the police officer had just upped and disappeared shortly after he'd come back, and only a handful of blips on his personal email—all through that impossibly secured proxy server—suggested that the man still *existed*.

But that video from the warehouse still bugged her. It was just wrong. It suggested stuff she didn't think could possibly be real, but she'd *watched* it as it was recorded. She couldn't disbelieve it, which meant it had to be real.

So, now she watched for news that resembled it. There was a mess down in Louisiana. A Catholic priest had been killed by an FBI tactical team investigating the murder of a Federal agent.

One of the local journalists had managed to sneak past the security cordon and grab a picture of the inside of the church before being caught and hustled out. Unable to get it published due to the crackdown on information about the case, they'd dumped it online and Majestic had seen it.

The wreckage made of the inside of the church rang bells with her. It looked like the leftovers of the warehouse at the end of her video clip.

Other news had rung similar bells. Similar stories, where normal-appearing incidents had subtle but major security crackdowns around them, were all over the place now that she was looking for them.

She was sure that the answers were behind that godawful security program on that black server, but even *her* skill had so far failed to get through it.

13

IT WAS LATE EVENING BY THE TIME THE GOVERNMENT CAR AND THE PAIR OF ONSET agents made it to the Sheraton Hotel deep in New Orleans. Shifting out of the still-busy traffic on the road next to the streetcar line and into the drop-off zone, Michael pulled the car to stop.

"You go in and get the keys for our rooms," the senior agent told David. "I'll take the car around and meet you in the lobby."

"All right," David agreed, and grabbing his overnight bag from the backseat, got out of the car. The drive had failed to live up to his fearful expectation of awkwardness, but it had still been hours locked into a medium-sized car. The Empowered policeman was a big man, and he *hurt*.

The blue government car rolled away and around a corner as David stepped through the pillared entrance onto the plush carpet of the lobby.

The lobby was mostly empty except for a handful of people on the purple chairs in the sitting area near the Starbucks on the left-hand side, and a pair of clerks behind the long polished wooden reception desk along the right-hand side of the room. Potted palm trees split the reception desk in two, and separated the sitting area from the coffee bar and the restaurant beyond. The carpet was soft under David's feet and the lighting from the overhead half-dome lights comforting as David approached the desk.

"Checking in on two reservations," David said to the clerk. "Under O'Brien and White; should have been called in this morning." O'Brien had told him just before arriving that the Campus would have made the reservations for them. David was hardly used to other people arranging things for him, but he had to admit that ONSET was efficient.

"Yes, sir," the clerk confirmed. "All set up when your man called in this morning. We have two king rooms on the seventh floor. I'll need you to sign the paperwork for the account billing."

David nodded and took the papers from the young man. He skimmed down the sheets and was amused to notice that "FBI Division O" was paying for his room. Everything seemed in order, and he signed the bottom of the form.

"If you can sign this form as well, please, sir?" the clerk continued, passing him a second form with PUROLATOR stamped across the top. "We have packages waiting for you and Mr. O'Brien in your rooms."

David felt a twinge of paranoia but signed for the papers anyway as Michael came up behind him and accepted his own set of papers from the clerk.

"Thank you for staying at the Sheraton New Orleans, gentlemen," the clerk said passing them the room card-keys across the desk. "You have rooms 721 and 723, on the seventh floor. The elevators are at the back of the lobby." The youth pointed. "Have a good night."

With a quiet thank-you to the clerk, David and Michael crossed the lobby to the elevators. They waited a moment for an elevator, and then stepped in. As the wood-paneled doors closed and the pair leaned against the mirrored walls, David turned to Michael.

"They said we have packages waiting in our room," he said softly.

"I know," Michael replied, and David relaxed a bit. "I had dress clothes sent down from the Campus for us."

"I didn't have any dress clothes on Campus," David objected. For that matter, other than a dress police uniform in a closet in his house in Charlesville, he didn't have much in the way of formal clothes anywhere.

"They had your measurements," Michael said with a shrug. "Regard it as an early birthday present."

"Thank you, sir," the younger agent replied as he realized what his boss was saying. Even though his thirty-second birthday was almost nine months away, he kept silent and accepted the gift.

————

PARTING ways with Michael at the entrance to the hotel room, David stepped into the plush brown and beige room. Closing the door behind him, he padded across to the window, dropping his overnight bag onto the leather chair as he opened the blinds, looking out at the glimpse of river.

Turning back from the window to look around the room, he noted the single door leading to an oversized bathroom, the comfortable leather chair and the massive king sized bed. He had not been expecting this kind of comfort on a government budget.

Looking more closely at the dark bedclothes, David spotted the suit bag with the Purolator sticker on the bed. He regarded the bag warily for a long moment, wondering just what sort of suit his superior was likely to have purchased. Finally, he opened the bag and looked inside.

The suit the bag contained was black and conservatively cut. No pinstripes, dust or even misplaced creases marred the smooth fabric as he glanced over it. A white shirt, silk by the feel, was hung inside the jacket, and a dark silver tie was slung around the hangar.

A crinkle of plastic alerted him to more, and he opened the buttons on the shirt to reveal a package with the block letters of Omicron equipment labels. Apparently, the Campus had decided to include a "Vest, Ballistic Mesh, Aetherically Enhanced, Version Three" with the suit. Wrapped around the vest package were the black leather straps of concealed holsters for David's mageblade and gun.

David regarded the set of clothes for a long moment and then moved it over to the hangers in the closet. Whether or not it fit, he would find out in the morning, but he sincerely doubted there would be any problems with that.

It had been a long drive, and the ONSET agent was tired. With the suit cleared off the bed, he barely managed to remove his jacket and the holster under it before collapsing onto the large, far too comfortable bed.

———

THE IMAGE in the room's elegantly framed full-length mirror the next morning was a perfect match for generations of stereotypes of FBI officers. Most of those officers, however, wouldn't have been wearing enchanted body armor under the suit and balancing the shoulder holster that couldn't *quite* conceal an M1911 with a hidden magic knife.

Even so, the image was one that David barely recognized. His still-tousled hair was the only thing that anyone who knew him in Charlesville would have recognized, and he grinned at the officer in the mirror as he considered his hunting club's reaction to seeing him like this.

The smile faded as he realized that he would probably never be able to go hunting with them again. It would be too easy to slip, to do something that would reveal him to be more than human while hunting, and he didn't trust any of the men in the club enough to expect them to keep it quiet. Or to not panic, for that matter.

With a small sigh, David reached for a comb and the small bottle of hair gel sitting on the faux marble counter around the sink next to the full-length mirror.

A few minutes later had David's hair taking the neat form of the FBI stereotype as well. He quickly adjusted the suit jacket to make sure there were no visible bulges for the two weapons.

A part of him said goodbye to his tousled hair, knowing that here and now, neatening it up meant more than just looking pretty. Today, it was an acceptance that he'd changed forever—and that there was no going back.

He'd barely finished his preparations when there was a knock at the door of the suite. "Yes?" he answered. The only person who should have been knocking on his door was his Commander.

"Inspector Braun is on his way over," Michael told him through the door, and David nodded confirmation of his thought. "Are you ready?"

David looked at the door for a long moment before answering by opening it and stepping into the hall. Michael, wearing a very similar black suit, looked the junior agent up and down and then nodded.

"Presentable," he said firmly, although there was no way he knew what had gone on in David's mind as the junior Agent dressed. "Let's go check out."

———

INSPECTOR BRAUN and their blue car awaited them at the front entrance. David slid into the back seat as Michael joined the Inspector in the front seat. David barely got his seat belt on before the Inspector floored the gas and the car shot out into traffic. David grabbed hold of the handle on the door and held his breath for a moment.

Despite the initial shock, Braun proved to be a good driver, whipping the car through intersections and lane changes with a practiced hand to deliver them to the chapel fifteen minutes early. A temporary barrier blocked entrance into the parking lot, and crisply dressed men checked IDs before allowing the car in.

Behind the barrier, David saw an old, *old* church. The entrance had clearly once held a gate, but it had been removed at one point for modern tarmac. The rest of the church grounds were surrounded by a short stone wall topped by a cast-iron fence.

The church itself was a four-story wonder of gothic architecture. Buttressed and "guarded" by gargoyles, it could have been taken from the cover of half a dozen different gothic romance books.

"O'Brien," Braun said to the werewolf as they slowed to a halt in the parking lot, amongst a dozen other black government cars. "Watch your step. Rumor has it Riley is in town. Apparently, he knew Riesling back when they were both OSPI trainees."

"Riley won't be a problem," Michael replied firmly. "His issues with Omicron are decades dead."

David wondered who Riley was, and why his presence was a danger. One look at the sudden sharp edges on Michael's aura suggested that knowing was a good idea but also that Michael wouldn't be happy to answer.

"Some of his people aren't so sure," the Inspector warned. "Let's go."

The trio of Omicron men got out of the car, and David looked around at the church. The slowly growing crowd in the grass front yard of the church looked like it had been cut from a black-and-white movie, with every single member of it dressed in conservative suits. Very few colors other than pitch black and white seemed to be visible.

Glancing away from the crowd, David took a moment to step over next to Michael. "Who's Riley?"

"You'll find out," Michael said grimly, his eyes on something behind David.

David turned and noticed that three young men had detached themselves from the crowd and were heading toward the black OSPI car. Without thinking, he flashed to Sight and saw that all three's auras flashed with anger and arrogance, and were marked with the blue tinge he'd learned to recognize as Mages.

"Get behind me," Michael ordered, and David obeyed, his inhuman senses noting that one *physical* detail distinguished these three young men from most of the suited men and woman around the chapel. All three of them had a large lapel pin, almost a brooch, in the form of a silver leaf.

"Michael O'Brien," the leader, tall and slim with a long black braid stretching halfway down his back, said coldly. "We claim challenge under the code of the Hand."

"This is not the place," Michael told them, his voice equally cold. "This is a funeral, not a dueling ground."

"No outsider should have been taught *any* form of the Flame," the suited youth with the braid told Michael, and then moved.

Even David's Sight didn't give him enough time to warn Michael, but Michael clearly didn't need it. Even as the youth moved, muttering words of magic to accelerate his attack, Michael shifted to meet him.

There was a blur of motion, fast enough that even David almost missed the blows, and the Elfin youth was on the floor, spitting blood. Not knowing what the hell was going on; David stepped forward, reaching for his knife. Michael waved him back, however, and David retreated, accepting his Commander's wordless orders.

"Mordor take you, werewolf," the Elfin snarled, springing back to his feet.

He'd barely made it up before Michael's fist slammed into his chest, sending him stumbling back toward his friends, who had not interfered.

His friends, in fact, had barely moved, and David watched in surprise as the young attacker suddenly stopped in mid-motion, completely frozen. A fourth man, dressed identically to the first three Elfin men, had joined the gathering. He was older than the youths, though David judged him only five or so years older than his own thirty-one, with short-cropped black hair and piercing blue eyes. Unlike the younger Elfin, he openly wore a weapon—a yard-long sword, the hilt carved with some kind of hieroglyphs, strapped to his left hip.

"You should control your pups better, Riley," Michael said quietly. Given the attacker's impossibly frozen posture, he was not someone David wanted to be on the wrong side of.

"He will be punished," Riley said calmly, and his eyes held the frozen youths. "Ryan, Jason. Take Rico back to the car and wait for me. I will be along when the funeral is over."

At no point did the man raise his voice, but as he finished, he released Rico and the youth collapsed to the ground. Without the slightest murmur of dissent, the other two youths obeyed immediately, picking their fallen comrade up and half-supported, half-carried him away.

"Agent David White," Michael said, gesturing David forward, "be known to the Elfin Lord Jamie Riley, former OSPI Inspector."

The two titles explained a lot to David as he stepped forward to extend his hand. Not many Mages left Omicron, and those who left to pursue other careers were often ostracized. *This* man didn't seem to care about that tradition, but then, he was an Elfin Lord. That elite group was known for both their magical strength and their secular power over the Elfin Conclave.

"Agent White," Riley greeted him, shaking his hand and giving

David a slight nod of the head. "I regret that your first meeting with my people was in such circumstances. Funerals are somber enough without the interference of young fools."

"Fools are fools, regardless of the place," Michael interjected. "Come on. We all have a reason to be here, and Riley's idiots are not it."

Lord Riley acknowledged Michael's comment with a sharp nod but gestured for the three Omicron men to wait. "I had other reasons beyond restraining my 'pups' determination to defend the secrets of the Flame of Andúril to meet you, Commander O'Brien," he said quietly, and offered a manila envelope to the werewolf.

"What is this?" Michael asked, taking the envelope.

"We have had our own investigations into the affairs that...terminated at Father Carderone," Riley said simply, gesturing for the Agents to precede him into the church. "The memory stick in that envelope contains the sum of our investigations," he concluded. "I hope it proves of some assistance."

———

THE SIDE CHAPEL of the church was crowded almost to its full capacity. A smaller room than the main sanctuary, the chapel was still two thirds of the size of Carderone's church in Alexandria. Arched ceilings hung above them, and niches well above the height of a man held statues of the saints.

The two ONSET agents took seats at the back of the chapel, allowing the OSPI officers who'd known Riesling better to file into the front. A small cluster of men and a single woman that David now recognized as Elfin took up the back right-hand side of the chapel, gathered around Lord Riley, and the group of neatly clad men and women with hollow eyes David guessed to be the houngans filled the remaining space.

David sat in silence, watching the Catholic priest, who looked uncomfortably similar to the man who'd killed Riesling, take his place at the front of the room and clear his throat for silence.

"Ladies and gentlemen," the priest greeted them. "We are here to remember an officer and a brother. We are here to remember a brave man who died in the line of his duty, to serve and protect the innocents around him.

"We are here to remember Inspector Second Class Damien Riesling."

[14]

"WELCOME BACK TO HQ, AGENT WHITE, COMMANDER O'BRIEN," THE gate guard at the Campus greeted David and Michael after scanning their IDs. The east gate of the ONSET Headquarters was one of three gaps into the concrete wall, and several ominous metal hatches studded the wall nearby, suggesting that attempting to force entry was a bad idea.

Having confirmed their IDs, the guard entered a code into a keypad, and the steel bar that served as a barrier slid back into the wall, where massive steel gates stood ready to cut the Campus off from the outside world.

The government car that the two had picked up at the Colorado Springs airport slid through the gap in the concrete wall, and the bar smoothly slid back into place behind them, locking out the world that knew nothing of the Campus's existence.

"Do we really need this kind of security?" David asked as Michael maneuvered the car into the car pool. To his eyes, it almost looked ridiculous. No one had built a fortress like this since the Second World War, to his knowledge.

"We haven't yet," Michael admitted. "But we lost a local base—like the one in Louisiana—last year in Texas. We were using it for coordina-

tion between the forces we'd sent against the incursion, and a group of
demons took it out in a surprise attack. A good third of our casualties
in that campaign were due to losing command and control at a critical
moment."

"I thought all of our facilities were completely secret," David said.
So far as he could tell, everything Omicron was buried under about ten
different layers of secrecy and deception. It wasn't something he was
comfortable with, and he still wasn't sure he fully agreed with it, but
he did understand it.

"They are," his Commander confirmed. "Unless you're a supernatural. Then you generally know where OSPI operates from, and you
can work out where the nearest ONSET base is with a little bit of
watching and triangulating. So we secure, our facilities against the
worst." He shrugged. "I helped write the defense specifications for the
Campus. We had four worst-case scenarios: an attack by conventional
modern forces, infiltration, supernatural assault with the resources of a
full Familias, or a dragon. The Campus was designed to resist all four.
"

"At once?" David suggested as they got out of the car and collected
their bags from the trunk. The defenses around the base were insane.
Michael had helped design them? He knew that the werewolf was
older than he looked and had been with Omicron a long time, but
every so often, he got a hint that suggested that his Commander was a
lot more than just another team leader.

Michael barked a laugh and shook his head. "No, though we probably could. The defenses against a dragon attack are quite distinct from
the security to stop an infiltration or the heavy weapons to stop a
ground assault."

"How do you stop a dragon?" David finally asked as the pair left
the underground car pool, heading for ONSET Nine's dormitory. From
what he'd seen of Charles, he wasn't sure how it would be possible.
The dragon was fast and maneuverable on the ground, and formidably
armored. In the air, where it had evolved to fight...the thought
was scary.

"We retrofitted W80 warheads from decommissioned cruise
missiles onto Patriot interceptor missiles," Michael replied, his voice

suddenly quiet. "And if you don't know what that means, you don't *want* to."

For a long moment David, who could guess what a W80 warhead was, sat in silence, as he began to realize just how powerful the organization he worked for was. Scary as the thought of fighting a dragon in the air had been a moment before, the thought that ONSET could requisition nuclear warheads for its own defense was...much worse.

———

THE PAIR of officers returned to ONSET Nine's dormitory in subdued spirits. In the main room of the dormitory, they came upon Ix and Bourque playing a game of chess. Both wore the unmarked black bodysuit that formed the core of the ONSET uniform and combat gear, but without the rest of the harness that was slung over it for combat.

"You should go change into your blacks," Michael told David as they headed toward the stairs and their respective rooms. "We don't live in battle harness while on inactive, but the bodysuit is our best armor so we keep it on. You can throw clothes over it if you head off campus," the team Commander added.

"I can leave the base while we're on active reserve?" David queried.

Michael nodded. "We keep a tight training schedule this week, but outside of that, your time is your own. You can't go further than the Springs, and you'll have to be in body armor and carry a pager with a GPS beacon with you, but you only have to be here for your scheduled training. That won't be until morning," the Commander observed. "It's pretty late."

David returned the nod, and the two men split ways toward their own quarters. The cop slowly shed the civilian clothes he'd worn for the trip back from the funeral, and carefully pulled on the smooth black fabric of his bodysuit.

That done, he tossed the civvies in his laundry hamper and then carefully hung up the expensive suit Michael had got him. A quick check of the clothes he had with him revealed that only about half of them would fit over the bodysuit, so he settled for throwing a hooded sweater over the bodysuit as he glanced around the apartment.

It was quiet and empty, spacious as it was, and he was about to start a game of solitaire on the computer for a lack of anything better to do when he heard a knock on his door.

"Who is it?" he asked, wondering who would be knocking on his door at—he checked the clock—almost eight thirty in the evening.

"It's Kate," the team's younger Mage replied. "Can I come in?"

David gave his apartment a quick glance-over, but he really hadn't lived in it for long enough to create any sort of mess. He was glad to hear Kate's voice but also curious as to why she was knocking on his door.

"Come in," he told her.

The young woman opened the door and stepped in. She wore the same black bodysuit as he did, with an unzipped blue fleece sweater open over it, showing the circled silver star hanging on her frankly outlined chest.

He gestured Kate to the couch and pulled the chair over from the office into the living room. Setting it next to the couch, he sat down and looked over at the Mage.

"Good to see you, Kate," he said honestly. "What's up?"

"I wanted to check up on you," she told him with a soft smile. "The first mission can be pretty rough."

David smiled back at her. He appreciated the concern. He was sure most of the rest of the team shared it, but Kate was certainly the least threatening and most comforting of the group.

"Thank you," he said softly. "It's hard," he admitted. *Hard* was an understatement. Even though he'd mostly accepted that he'd done what had to be done, and even allowed himself a small sense of satis-faction at the realization that Carderone's killings were stopped, it still didn't take away the horror of seeing the priest's eyes when he closed his.

"I was raised Catholic," he continued. "Being in that church brought back a lot of memories. None of them really bad, but they're all going to be associated with Carderone now, whether I like it or not."

"Don't let one man's evil destroy your faith," Kate told him earnestly, her fingers touching the star hanging from her neck. "We have to have faith in something to do our jobs."

"I have faith in myself and in the law," David told her quietly. It had been a long time since he'd believed in the faith of his childhood. The oath he'd sworn as an officer defined what faith he had. It was a faith in men, not in unseen divinity.

"Remember to have faith in us as well," Kate murmured, her gaze holding his for a long moment. Something in her eyes made him uncomfortable, even as her presence reassured him, and he looked away.

"Killing is a part of our job," he said quietly. He'd known that from the beginning. ONSET was, after all, basically a group of tactical assault teams—a supernatural SWAT for the entire nation. Somehow, that knowledge had never really sunk in until he'd had to do it.

"Not always," Kate objected. "And not directly. Our *job* is to protect people. Killing is an ugly corollary to that sometimes, but what happens when people abuse supernatural powers *is* ugly."

David nodded slowly. He remembered his father's condemnation of anyone who was unusual, but also of anyone who abused power. According to the old man, power led to abuse by its very nature, and David had seen Carderone's trophy book. That man had taken a great gift—one much like the one David was finding within himself—and turned it to evil. Over twenty innocent men had died because of it.

"The Spider-Man coda," he said with a smile as a new thought occurred to him. "With great power comes great responsibility."

"Someone has to play police in a world with folks who have powers others don't," Kate told him. "We chose that role. For all our own reasons," she added, looking at him.

David shrugged. "Some of us are fighting for something," he agreed, putting into words the thoughts he had about the team, "and some are fighting against something. We're all here to protect others."

"That's why you're here, is it?" Kate asked, her voice a little more intent now to David's ears.

"To serve and protect," he quoted. "A policeman's oath and one I took very seriously."

Kate drew nearer to him, and her soft citrus scent hit David's nostrils. Unthinkingly, David pulled slightly away, and Kate stopped.

"When do we start training?" he asked, hoping to turn the conversation to less personal grounds.

"Eight in the morning," Kate replied, moving slightly down the couch, her expression unreadable to David.

"We should probably get some rest," he thought aloud. "I get the impression we'll need it."

"You're right," Kate admitted. "We tend to go for about ten hours." She stood up. "I'm glad you're okay, David," she told him. "If you need anyone to talk to, about anything, I'm just down the hall, okay?"

"Okay," David agreed as he walked her to his door. "Thank you."

———

DAVID WAS SURPRISED upon entering the training gym under one of the Campus's smaller buildings the next morning to see a black-banded hawk flying straight at him. He was even more surprised, however, when the hawk vanished into thin air moments before its claws stuck his face.

"Sorry, David," Akono murmured from where the other Agent stood near the door, half a dozen similar birds flying in circles around his head.

"How?" David asked. The gym was a good four floors below ground level, and there was no way the birds should have been down there.

"The birds aren't real," Kate told him from farther away, and David looked away from Akono's flock to take in the rest of the "gym".

Four stories below ground and two stories high, the room seemed almost Spartan at first glance. Minimal physical equipment was visible, and Kate and Morgen were simply standing in an empty space looking at each other now.

The floor was carefully polished hardwood, but the walls were stark concrete, thrown into harsh contrast by the powerful lights above.

A second glance around the room revealed several doors leading off into other rooms—the closest to David marked CAUTION: FIRING RANGE—and chunks of the apparently concrete wall looked like they were on rails, designed to slide aside to reveal storage space. One of those sections had been pulled open to reveal mats, protective gear and practice weaponry for martial arts.

Ix and Bourque stood upon the large mat they'd spread out next to that panel, and the distraction of David entering had apparently allowed the Empowered to take the demon off-guard, slamming him into the mats with a resounding crash.

"Welcome to Training Hall K," another voice said from David's other side, and he turned to find Michael leaning against the wall, observing his men. "Get comfortable," the werewolf Commander advised. "You'll be spending pretty much all of your time here while we're on active reserve."

With that, the Commander gave David a rough nod and removed himself from the wall to join Ix and Bourque on the training mat. Looking around the room, David figured there were worse places to spend his time. Those sliding walls probably hid just about any training tool he could imagine.

"Not real?" David finally asked as Kate and Morgen joined Akono and gestured him over to them. As he approached, the flock of birds flickered out, one by one, before David's astonished eyes.

"Glamors," the elf said in his soft voice. "Beings of the Dream, made flesh by will."

David blinked, confused by Akono's mostly nonsensical words, and Morgen laughed.

"*Never* ask an elf to explain glamors," the Mage told David dryly. "It's like asking a fish to explain water. They can do it all right, but nobody else is going to understand them."

"A glamor is something more than an illusion but less than real," Kate explained. "The Dreaming, so far as we can tell, is an alternate plane of existence or something along those lines. The elves live half in our world, half in the Dreaming. With a focus of will, they can bring something into the real world made of the essence of the Dreaming."

"The birds are real, then?" David asked, thankful for the Mage's somewhat more clear explanation. "Just from somewhere else?"

"No," Malcolm said softly. "They are *made* of the Dreaming; they are not *from* the Dreaming. They do not breathe; they are only an image. Only what I Dream them to be."

"Anything he can imagine, he can create," Kate told David softly. "Complicated machinery he has to imagine in full detail, which doesn't work very well, but mental archetypes are easy to create."

To demonstrate Kate's point, Akono smiled, and suddenly the elf was five feet off the floor, clad in full shining plate mail upon the back of a pure white stallion. David scrambled back from the sudden massive threat, but then the elf had shrunk back, standing where he'd begun.

"The Knight I can call easily," he explained dreamily. "Machines were alien to man when the Dreaming last came, and are alien to it still."

"Which doesn't stop him being a wizard with machines, too," O'Brien interrupted the conversation. "But the lesson can wait. You were rusty at the church," the Commander told David. "You're better unarmed than that. Or"—the werewolf grinned wickedly—"you *will* be."

FORTY-SOME MINUTES LATER, David groaned his way back up from his latest plunge to the mat and was truly grateful for the enhanced strength and prescience his strange new nature gave him.

Without them, he knew that Michael would have truly ripped him apart. As it was, the ability to see Michael coming had allowed him to land a handful of blows, but he'd still been thoroughly humbled. He'd still done better than he should have. *Much* better, in fact, so far as he could tell.

"I don't know that much Krav Maga," he said softly, as Michael gestured for him to take a rest. He'd found himself using the forms of the Israeli martial art far more than the Tae Kwon Do he'd trained in before ONSET. His main exposure to the style, however, had been his far-too-short training cycle under Koburn. The thought of what that meant was somewhat disturbing,

"Yes, you do, obviously," Michael told him dryly. "Koburn taught you."

"In three weeks?" the younger Agent queried. "That's impossible."

"After all you've seen, you doubt that we have a teacher who can plug the muscle memory for the core of a martial art into you in a week?" the Commander replied. "Koburn is a Sage—an Empowered teacher. He really did teach you that much."

David nodded slowly, internalizing the idea and realizing how much *else* Koburn had taught him that really shouldn't have been doable in the handful of weeks they'd had. The thought that the "Sage" had basically been implanting knowledge directly into his head was uncomfortable, but he was also somewhat grateful. Otherwise, his training would have taken months locked in that concrete bunker instead of weeks.

"Again?" Michael asked, and David shook his head. The thought of going up against Michael's terrifyingly superior strength and speed without some kind of break was too much.

"Give me a minute to catch my breath, at the very least," he responded, to Michael's laugh. The werewolf gestured to one of the doors leading off from the central gymnasium area.

"We should shift over to range training, anyway," the Commander told him. "We all have to get in our allotment of wasted bullets."

David nodded and followed his superior into the firing range. Blank concrete walls lined the long room. Ten separate stalls and target setups divided the range between them, and David took one of the stalls.

He drew the M1911 that Chief Hanson had given him, and settled into the comfortable rhythm of range training, sending one round after another down the long concrete range at the targets.

ONSET's training range had the trickiest targets he'd ever seen. They had targets appear and disappear at random intervals, in random places, and the only warning was a *plink* sound as the target appeared. The shooter then had to find the target in the admittedly limited range and shoot it in less than four seconds.

David didn't miss any of them.

"How is Agent White working out, Commander?" Warner asked Michael, and the werewolf paused to consider.

The pair was currently in a set of plush black leather chairs in Warner's office that the Major made a point of hiding when interviewing new Agents. Michael had changed from his training clothes into his normal blacks, but his combat harness remained slung over the uniform body armor.

"He saved my life in Alexandria," he finally pointed out. "I think that may bias my opinion."

"I don't know if I'd count that as a bias in this case so much as part of the assessment," the Major pointed out. "Is he fitting in with your team?"

"So far?" Michael considered. "It's only been a week, but I would say yes. He survived a week in an active duty bunker without driving them insane or vice versa. I've kept an eye on him, and his prescience is a good bit sharper than we thought it was. I think meeting up with Charles did wake a few things up, as he's faster than he was in training too—not as fast as on the tape, but almost as fast as me."

"He's also doing his best to learn as much as he can about us," the Commander continued. "He's devouring every one of the texts on the history of the Offices and magic in the world that we have. I don't even think he *likes* reading."

"That's a good thing," Warner observed, drumming her fingers on the armchairs leather in thought. "If and when he finally powers up to what we saw in that video, he'll be at least a Class 2—possibly even a full Class 1 Supernatural like you."

Michael shifted uncomfortably. Class 1 Supernaturals were rare. Full-blooded werewolves only reached the status after about twenty years of growth into their powers. Mages like Traci could spend years studying and never earn that rating without a prodigious natural talent. Traci herself only barely classified as the lowest end of the category.

Omicron classified supernaturals in a rating system from one to ten, with one being "Maxim guns of magic" and ten being "I can glow slightly in the dark." While OSPI would recruit any supernatural they found, ONSET generally regarded anyone less than Class 4 as simply too weak to carry the load of a strike team.

Right now, David's extraordinary perception and prescience, along with his strength and speed boosted him into roughly the middle of Class 4. The even greater speed, strength and awareness he'd shown in the warehouse video clips, however, would put him solidly into Class 2 and quite possibly to Class 1.

"I think he will do us proud," Michael finally said. "Whether he never shows those strengths again or fully Empowers later, he is determined to do his best, and that will carry him a long way."

"Good," Warner repeated. "If he does fully Empower later, you realize he'll be fast-tracked to command?"

Michael nodded. Since teams had to coordinate around the actions and powers of their strongest members, ONSET followed a policy of putting those strongest members in command. Every Commander was at least a Class 2, and most were Class 1s. A team led by a Selkie would need to operate very differently than a team led by a Mage or a werewolf. The concept went against the grain for many of their ex-military people, but it *worked*.

"He has more experience than half of the team leads we already have. Of course I do," he confirmed aloud.

"Does he?" Warner asked softly.

15

AFTER TWO DAYS OF LIVING IN HIS APARTMENT IN ONSET NINE'S
dormitory, David slowly reached the end of his ability to live with just
a desk, a bed and a kitchen. Knocking on Michael's office door, he
entered the small room tucked into the back of ONSET Nine's building
without waiting for an answer.

"Afternoon, David," the werewolf Commander said calmly from
behind the metal desk. The desk was typical of the room. A row of
unadorned black metal filing cabinets lined the back wall, and the desk
was made of the same material. Metal cabinets hung from the roof of
the room over the desk, providing Michael with space to store things
around his computer.

"So, how do I get furniture in this place?" David asked. His voice
was calm, he thought, but he was more than a little stretched. It was
hard to use what privacy he got when there was literally *nothing* in his
apartment. "Somehow," he continued, "I don't think I can get IKEA to
deliver."

The thought of the Swedish furniture giant delivering to the top
secret base, past the concrete walls and heavy weapons, amused
David. The inability to have anything delivered to a top secret base,
however, was the major issue with his getting furniture.

"Have you decided whether or not to bring furniture from your place in Charlesville?" O'Brien asked.

"No," David admitted. The thought hadn't actually crossed his mind. Six weeks had passed since he'd last been home in Charlesville, and his furniture there hadn't occurred to him.

His Commander leaned forward on his desk, layering his fingers together on top of the pile of paperwork on the black steel as he regarded David. David returned Michael's regard as flatly as he could. The thought of his home had brought back a stabbing feeling of homesickness.

"David, you've so far proven yourself beyond our expectations," O'Brien told him. "That comes at a price—among other things, higher expectations—but it's still impressive." The ONSET officer paused for a moment, and then pulled up a memo and regarded it.

"Something's going to come up shortly that will require a chunk of your time and effort," he said quietly. "We're going to need you fully in your own head, not distracted by lack of furniture and homesickness. Understand?"

David nodded slowly. He understood what Michael was saying, although he wasn't sure where it was leading—or what the "something" that was going to come up was.

"I'm going to cut your training short this once," the werewolf continued. He raised a finger from where his hands rested on the desk. "I expect you to make up for it twice over when you get back, and you'll still only have a week's leave," Michael said gruffly, "but I think you've earned an early break. Go home. Check which furniture you want to move and which you want to leave. I'll give you the number of a liaison officer with OSPI near to you, and you can let him know what you need. Sound fair?"

The junior Agent looked at his superior in surprise. He'd been fully prepared for the week of training he was supposed to receive before going on leave, but the thought of leaving sooner still sounded *very* good.

"More than fair," David finally admitted.

"Then get your ass the hell out of my office," Michael ordered. "I'll have a car run you down to the Springs airport later today. Go!"

THE CAB DROPPED David off at his front door and collected the cash the Agent had been given in advance to pay for the trip. He then squealed away, leaving the new ONSET man standing on his own doorstep, looking up at his house.

The house was his, with only a small mortgage. He'd learned the hard way to watch his debt when his family home had been seized after his parents' death to pay their mortgage. A year's salary with ONSET would allow him to pay off the mortgage in full, with more than enough left over for any living expenses he was likely to incur.

For a long few minutes, David simply stood on the threshold of his home and looked at the white-painted two-story home. It seemed so mundane and calm to his eyes now. Even his Sight revealed little about the home. Few emotions had attached themselves to this building over the years. Any emotions that had attached themselves to the wood and brick of the old house, time and multiple occupants had wiped away.

It certainly did not look like the home of a man with magic flowing in his veins. Its normalness struck David as a warning. If his home looked so normal, who knew what hid under the mundane trees and houses around him?

If he'd been so wrong about the nature of the world, how wrong might he be about the nature of people?

It was with a sigh and a shake of the head that David finally entered his house.

DAVID SPENT an hour cataloging the furniture in his house, deciding what he wanted to take with him—his bedroom suite, most of his kitchen utensils, his better living room set—and what he was going to leave—a second set of couches and the suite from his spare room.

After an hour, he dropped the pad of paper he'd been keeping track of everything onto the large bleached white oak desk he'd inherited from his father—take with him—and grabbed a beer from his fridge.

The beers were the only thing left in the fridge after he'd purged it before leaving.

He glanced at the clock and realized it was later than he'd thought. While he hadn't had a chance to reach out to Hanson, most of the unmarried off-duty cops would have gathered at Whistler's, the local cop bar by now. Given that he had a full week before he had to return to the Campus, David saw no reason that cataloging the furniture couldn't be finished tomorrow.

As he went to dress, he was surprised to realize that he didn't want to leave the mageblade behind. Even here, where he felt perfectly safe, he figured it was better safe than sorry.

With that thought in mind, he slung the knife's concealed holster over his plaid shirt and slung his old leather jacket on. He gave his image in the mirror a lopsided grin. The federal agent of last week was gone, and the plaid-shirted country boy he was used to looked back at him.

The lopsided grin faded as he realized that the image in the mirror wasn't familiar to him anymore.

———

WHISTLER'S WAS A LOW BUILDING, tucked in behind Charlesville's scenic downtown region. The tavern was older than any of the new buildings in the downtown and almost as old as the originals. Built of solid stone, it loomed out of the darkness like a dank behemoth, modern gas-lamp-imitation streetlights casting it into gloomy shadow.

The line of cars shadowed by the building looked almost out of place, but there was a space for David to jockey his truck into a parking spot between an extended cab truck and a red car, both of which he knew belonged other cops.

He turned the truck off and stepped out into the shadowed parking lot. There was no visible security in the parking lot, but everyone in town knew this was the police bar. No one would ever try to steal from these cars.

His gaze ran along the line of cars, ticking off names on his mental list as he recognized cars. Most of the usual bunch, the same bunch that made up the hunting club, was here tonight.

With a grin, David stepped up to the double doors into the windowless building and slung them open, entering the brightly lit interior with almost a mental sigh of relief. It was familiar, and it was comforting to be home.

"David!" a voice shouted. "As I live and breathe, David White is back among the living!"

David turned slowly, looking around the room. The stone walls were covered in paintings and photos of old police officers, back to sheriffs who'd served the town in the eighteenth century. One wall was devoted to relics and photos from the Civil War, and the men who'd gone to fight in the South.

Half a dozen booths in worn black pleather lined the far wall, but most of the customers were at heavy circular tables, their surfaces carved from the trunk of one great oak tree. A similar tree had been carved down to make the bar from behind which Lester Whistler, multiple great grandson of the Bill Whistler who'd founded the bar after being crippled in the line of duty as a sheriff in pre-Revolution America, had hailed David. Like the picture of his ancestor on the wall behind him, the younger man at the bar was sandy-haired and tall. Unlike the picture behind him, he was only just beginning to have a mustache long enough to wax into the family's trademark curls.

"Evening, Lester," David responded. "I figured I'd stop by since I was in town packing up."

"You're leavin' us forever, then?" the bartender asked.

"Haven't decided yet," David admitted. "I have a place to live near my new work, but I may end up keeping the house here, too."

"Well, come on," Lester said as the crowd began to leave their tables and gather toward David. "Say hi to folks!"

The former cop found himself deluged with one old comrade after another, and his arm almost wrenched out of its socket with hand-shakes. Eventually, the crowd died away, leaving him at the bar with Lester.

"Where's Buckley?" David finally asked. John Buckley had been

David's mentor on joining the force, and he hadn't noticed the tall Irishman around the bar at all.

"He had a later shift tonight," Lester, who always seemed to know everyone's schedule on the force, replied. "He should be joining us shortly. He should be here, actually," the bartender observed, his waxed mustache flexing as he turned to look up at the clock above his ancestor's painting.

David followed the bartender's gaze, but his eyes caught something under the clock. Filling the foot or so–high gap between Bill Whistler and the clock above him was a large stylized sun—carved from obsidian.

Before he could control himself, his Sight flashed on, and he found his eyes locked on the strange black sun, drawn to its impossible aura of sheer darkness. Whatever that sun represented, it couldn't possibly be *here*. Not in *Charlesville*.

A voice behind him broke the trance. "Hey, David!" Buckley shouted across the bar as the doors thumped closed behind him. "Good to see you, man."

David turned to greet his old mentor, but his Sight continued to flare as he looked into his friend's eyes. He finished turning, but his conscious motor control was gone as he looked into John Buckley's eyes. Black and purple auras flared around the man like lightning on a stormy night, and David White knew, with the certainty only magic could allow, that his oldest friend and comrade was evil to the bone.

16

DAVID MANAGED TO CONTROL HIMSELF AND NOT BLURT OUT ANYTHING OR go for the blade concealed under his jacket. Nonetheless, he knew he couldn't stay there. Even as he forced himself to trade pleasantries with his old friends, his Sight refused to go away.

He could tell now how much uncertainty lay beneath most of their greetings. They hadn't seen him in almost two months, and that was more than enough time for someone to slide out of a tight-knight group like a small-town police department.

Worst was the handful among the group touched with the black aura of that strange sun. Buckley was the worst, pulsing with it, but there were others. Most of them were men David had regarded as close friends until moments before. Until this strange revelation caused him to question everything he knew.

No one could have stayed in that room, with those thoughts in their head, for long. David made an excuse of his long flight and need to pack tomorrow and left the bar. He hoped that none of his old comrades realized he'd fled it.

His mind in turmoil, the ex-cop got into his truck and drove. Nothing in all his training had prepared him for this—for the revelations his abilities would give him about his home and his friends.

Part of him disbelieved what he'd seen. He *knew* those men; he knew they couldn't be what he'd seen. But the rest of him knew that his Sight could be misinterpreted but it never lied. Little things he'd seen before, little hints suggesting an inner circle to the department's social groupings and his own hunting club, struck home now.

The police officer he'd been refused to condemn these men—who *were* police officers—without any proof. The supernatural seer he had become *knew* that something was wrong in Charlesville.

He understood, now, why ONSET agents tended to live on the Campus. Not many had his abilities, but most had learned to read signs they didn't before. Even if it was only paranoia, it would be too easy for a supernatural to read the worst into the most mundane things.

David knew he wasn't being paranoid in this case. If that black sun meant *anything*, he had to warn the Chief. If a cancer was growing in Chief Hanson's own department, then the man in charge of protecting Charlesville from both the mundane and the supernatural had to know.

With some resolution finally in his thoughts, he turned the truck from its random circling of the small town toward the Chief's house.

———

IT WAS LATE when David arrived at the Hansons' house, and he hesitated for a long moment without ringing the doorbell. Here, in this pine-scented driveway far from the streetlights and shadows of Whistler's, his fears seemed almost silly.

He sighed. He may have misinterpreted what he had Seen, but he *knew* that icon on the wall. He didn't know what it was, but if the same symbol that was on a serial killer's trophy book was on the wall of a cop bar, something was very wrong.

David rang the doorbell.

There was a long silence after he did, and he began to think that the Chief was very asleep and he should come back in the morning. Maybe sunlight would burn away these fears.

Then the door swung open, and David found himself staring down the business end of an exact duplicate of the gun he'd left in his house. Moonlight glinted off the polished steel of Darryl Hanson's heavy silver-loaded automatic for a long moment before the police chief lowered the weapon.

"David!" he barked cheerily as he stood silhouetted in the bright light from the house behind him. "What are you doing here? It's bloody late," the chief, clad in a light blue bathrobe, observed.

"I know," David said softly, his fears seeming silly in the bright light of the house. He knew, however, that they weren't, and continued. "I needed to talk to you. You may have a problem."

The Chief's cheer diminished, to be replaced with an edged professionalism at odds with his bathrobe-clad appearance.

"Come in," he ordered, his voice suddenly as soft as David's. "Marge and I were just going to bed. I'll make coffee."

It turned out as they entered the house, however, that the thought was unnecessary. Marge, the silver-haired Mage clad in a light purple robe that matched her husband's, was already laying cups and a pot of coffee on the heavy wooden table in the living room. She gestured the two men to the massively comfortable chairs with a smile.

"And here I thought I'd put the pot on by accident of habit," she told David. "I should know better. I was never a seer or perceiver, but that doesn't mean I don't See on occasion."

"Tell me about this problem," Darryl ordered once David had taken a sip of the excellent coffee.

David took a deep breath and another sip of coffee, and then laid the cup down and explained what had happened at Whistler's, and what he'd seen on the wall and in Buckley's aura. He spoke quietly, as betraying the men he'd once trusted was hard. No matter what he suspected, they likely still thought of him as their friend.

"I never did like him," Marge said into the quiet after David had finished. Darryl had returned to his feet and was now stalking back and forth like an irritated bear.

"I did," the police chief rumbled. "Originally," he added. "I liked the fact that he'd take the new officers under his wing. Then I realized he was collecting them all into his hunting club, and started to get nervous." He glanced at David, and then glanced away and David knew he had been one of the "new officers" Buckley had collected until he'd been promoted past the Irishman.

"Police officers should have only one loyalty: the people they serve," Darryl continued. "His hunting club and little clique of followers risk that, but they've never done anything untoward—they still haven't," he reminded David sharply.

"You can't act on suspicion," David said, his voice still quiet. "No matter what I've Seen, that's all you have."

"Oh, I know," Darryl said grimly. "I know. But it whets a suspicion I already had. Suspicion of one's officers is a bad thing for a Police Chief to have, as it suggests his officers are failing in their charge," he continued, his voice suddenly soft and sad.

"But if they are failing"—the voice was suddenly sharp as ice —"then the Chief who *isn't* suspicious has failed *his* charge."

There was nothing David could say to that. For a long, long time, no one said anything.

"It's late," David said finally. "I should go back to my house. I have to finish packing up."

Darryl grunted. "I guess this is the end of you living in Charlesville?"

David paused. He hadn't even thought of that decision, but he realized now that the Chief was right. Charlesville had had a certain ideal to it to him until now. It had been a safe place, an ordinary place. Now he knew that the darker side of his job would stretch even here.

Being here would only bring back memories of good times, and memories of his father, and both of those would be only too painful. He now knew the good times had been at least partially false, and his father had been at least partially right.

"Yeah," he said softly, looking at his former chief regretfully. "I guess it is."

MAJESTIC HAD ACTUALLY MISSED David's return to the house, as she had almost forgotten the bug she'd planted in his house. When she found the link again, it was to a half-expected sight: men packing up the house of the ex-police officer.

She wondered for a moment if she could get a bug planted on the furniture, but brushed away the thought after a second of consideration. Even if one of her contacts was close enough to sneak in before everything left, it was unlikely all of it was going to White's new home, wherever that was. She also doubted anything would get into that home without being screened extraordinarily tightly.

Majestic *needed*, with all the drive of an addict whose fix was being denied, to know what was happening behind the reports she was tracking, and that black server she couldn't crack.

For all that need, for all that desire and curiosity, all the hacker could do was sit and watch the feed from the tiny electronic camera as her last clues about this mystery vanished into the back of a moving truck.

––––––

CLOSING up a house was easier than David had feared and harder than he'd hoped. The local OSPI representative and his men handled the physical aspects of the move, but that was only one part of it. The apartment on campus could hold less than half of his furniture, and it fell to David to decide which half would go.

Once he'd separated out the bedroom and office furniture that he'd inherited from his parents, he knew there wasn't much left he could bring. He marked one almost brand-new couch as a 'go,' and then told the OSPI men to donate the rest—none of it was worth transporting any distance, really.

Chief Hanson was a lifesaver, even more than the dozen or so burly soldiers who'd shown up to handle the move while treating David with an unexpected degree of respect. The police chief had volunteered to co-ordinate with the real estate agent who would handle the sale of David's small house.

Once everything was closed up, David found himself standing once more at the base of his lawn, looking at the house he'd striven so hard to purchase and keep after he'd lost his parent's home.

"It's hard to leave," Hanson said behind him, the chief's massive hand descending on David's own large shoulder. "I was born in a small mining town in North Virginia," the chief said softly. "It was a shit hole I couldn't wait to get away from, but the day I left I cried."

A black government car pulled up behind David and its driver, another one of OSPI's ubiquitous uniformed men, waved to David.

"You need to go," Hanson told David, who nodded.

He knew he couldn't stay. His Sight told him too many secrets for him to comfortably live among normal people. He wasn't one of them anymore, and sooner or later he'd slip up and drive that home.

He sighed. He'd scrimped and saved since his parents died to buy this home. He'd worked hard to make himself a home and a place in Charlesville, and that single night in a warehouse had woken up something in him. That something had stripped his home away.

David touched the mageblade under his jacket and turned to face his Chief. "Goodbye," he told the older man, his voice choked.

"It's not goodbye," the older mundane told the supernatural gently. "It's only till we meet again."

17

By the time David and his furniture made it back to the Campus, ONSET Nine had disappeared on their one-week break. He and the men helping him move found the dormitory common room completely empty on their arrival.

"It's the second floor, left room on the end," David told them. He hefted a chair with an ease no mundane could have matched, and headed upstairs. The chair's bulk provided more issue than its weight, as he hefted it one-handed to open the door.

As the door opened under his grip, he felt the chair begin to slip and half-panicked. Before he could turn to grab it, however, someone else's hands were there. The chair stable and the door open, David regained his grip on the furniture and looked over the leather-clad arm at Ix.

"Thank you," he told the demon honestly. He was still uncomfortable with Ix, but it made sense that the demon—who would have issues concealing himself as human—would remain on the base.

"Need a hand?" Ix asked. There was a sharp, gravelly edge to the creature's voice, marking the speaker as something not quite human.

"Sure," David answered, relaxing somewhat at the offer. Whatever his teammate's actual *species*, he certainly seemed to be a decent *person*. "The truck is out front. A squad of OSPI troops is unloading it."

The red-skinned almost-man nodded. "I'll go help them," he said briskly, and disappeared behind the black body of the chair.

WITH TWO SUPERNATURALS and a dozen competent young men working at it, it only took twenty minutes for David's furniture to leave the truck and make its way into the second-floor apartment.

With that finally done, David opened one of the boxes and pulled out a case of beer. He gestured to the OSPI men.

"Not sure if you're technically allowed," he admitted, "but here, have one anyway."

The Sergeant in charge of the squad laughed. "We're technically not," he advised the ONSET Agent, "but I believe it's traditional post-move."

Ix joined David and the OSPI men in the beer, and David was surprised at the men's ease drinking with two known supernaturals. A few months before, the thought would have scared the bejeesus out of him.

When the case of beer was gone, the Sergeant rose to his feet and gestured his men up.

"Come on, boys," he barked. "We've taken advantage of Agent White's gratitude, but we do have to get the truck back soon. Let's get a move on."

He barely raised his voice, but his men were on their feet and gathering the empty bottles together into one place without a moment's hesitation.

"It's been a pleasure, sirs," the man said to David. "I hope to see you about some more. I could use another free beer," he added with a wicked grin as he and his men trooped out, leaving the two supernaturals looking at the mess of boxes and furniture filling the living room of David's apartment.

IT TOOK David most of the next two days to truly unpack everything. He saw Ix every so often, and the demon made a point of accompanying him the first time he hit up one of the communal cafeterias for food.

As he lined up to partake of the government-paid-for "fine cuisine", David spotted Leila Stone collecting a tray of food and waved to her. She returned the wave, and the Mage made her way across the mostly empty room to David and Ix.

"David!" she greeted him. "How're you doing? Rumor around here has it that you fucking wandered into a bloody shitstorm on your first damned deployment."

David blinked at the stream of profanities interwoven with the question, and for a moment wondered how the Mage had ever remained an Inspector. With a smile for the woman, he realized it was probably why OSPI hadn't been sad to see her move to a less-public face of Omicron.

"It was unpleasant," he admitted as he began to shovel food on to his tray with half an eye on the blonde next to him. "We ended up having to fight—and kill—a murderer hunting gay men."

"I heard he was a goddamned priest," she replied.

"He was," David said shortly.

"There's no excuse for that shit," Stone said tightly. "I've been bloody stuck on the damned Campus since I finished training," she told David as they took a table together and he began to eat. "They assigned me to ONSET Twenty-One, but the fucking unit only exists on shithouse paper. It's me and two Empowered—we don't have even have a goddamn team Commander. We're just playing glorified fucking garrison around this bloody place."

The conversation drifted into normal life on the Campus, which Stone had spent more time in than David, and the active duties of ONSET, which David had spent more time in. Ix interjected on both sides of the conversation, revealing little about himself but proving a fount of information on ONSET.

While Stone swore worse than most cops David had ever met, she also had a perspective on ONSET that David didn't, and he appreciated the point of view. Dinner passed in conversation before David finally returned to his unpacking.

———

IT WAS noon the next day, the second to last before ONSET Nine went back on duty, before a knock on David's door heralded the return of another of Nine's members. He'd just finished setting up the leather couch that was the only new piece of furniture he'd brought, so he took the opportunity to collapse onto it as he shouted, "Come in!"

"I see you're all moved in," Kate observed as she stepped into his apartment. The blonde was dressed for the cooling Colorado autumn in black jeans and a light red zip sweater, unzipped low enough to show just a hint of cleavage.

"I brought most of my things up from Charlesville," David admitted. "I decided to sell my house there." For a moment, he considered telling Kate about *why* he was selling the house, but it seemed unnecessary. "How was your week off?"

"Quiet," Kate replied as she took a seat next to David on the couch. "Went to visit a friend of mine in Seattle. He owns a boat, so we spent most of the week on the water."

"Drink?" David offered. "I actually have more than water now," he added with a grin.

"Coffee, if you have it?" the blonde answered.

David threw on the pot in his coffee maker, and turned back to look at Kate. The younger woman had shed her sweater in the relative warmth of the apartment, revealing a clingy low-cut T-shirt underneath it. He had to admit to himself that his teammate was a very attractive young woman.

"How was your trip home?" Kate asked as David returned with the coffee. She took a cup and gently blew on it as he considered his answer.

"Different," he said quietly. "Everything seems the same, but there are so many things that bother me now that I never would have seen before."

That was about as much as David really wanted to say to anyone right now about the mess back home. He'd reported it when he'd returned and he'd left his suspicions and concerns with Chief Hanson who, as well as being capable of dealing with them, was also the appropriate authority to do so.

"For us, there is some truth to the claim that you can't go home," Kate told him. "I haven't been back to California in years. It's easier to see old friends in new places, where it's less jarring."

David nodded slowly. He saw her point, even if a part of him considered not returning to California a somewhat harsher task than not returning to Maine. That he'd found the darker side of his friends in the safe haven of his old hometown had made the betrayal worse.

He took a sip of his coffee to hide his discomfort, as he didn't want to talk about that to Kate just yet.

"How long did it take you to adjust?" he finally asked. He realized as he did that that he had no idea how long Mason had been with ONSET. He knew she was in her early twenties, so it couldn't have been too long.

"There are days I'm not sure I have!" she replied with a laugh. "It's hard to remember, sometimes, that the people I see outside of Omicron, even the other Wiccans, don't believe in magic in the sense I wield it. Oh, I could give them such heart attacks," she finished wickedly.

"Wiccans?" David asked slowly. The term wasn't something he was familiar with, though it did ring a bell somewhere.

"My coreligionists," Kate told him, touching the silver five-pointed star where it hung in her cleavage. "Think of it as tree-hugging turned into a religion," she advised with another wicked grin.

Religion wasn't something David knew—or cared to know—much about, so he let a semi-companionable silence descend over the room as he halfheartedly cast about for a subject change.

"Have you hit up the training room since you got back?" Kate finally asked into the silence.

"I've been too busy moving in," David admitted. "I probably should, though."

He'd promised Michael that he'd make up his missed training, he realized. With the move and the distraction of the events in Charlesville, he'd completely forgotten to take the time to do so.

"Well, if you'll let me go change into more appropriate clothing, I'll join you for a sparring match," Kate offered.

"Sounds good to me," David responded. While Krav Maga seemed to have been installed into his brain wholesale, he was sure that didn't mean he didn't have to practice and exercise to keep it there.

———

TRAINING HALL K was empty when David and Kate reached it in the early afternoon. They were the only members of ONSET Nine looking to train, it seemed, and the other team they shared the hall with was on active duty in Montana.

Kate showed David the set of controls hidden in a concealed panel by the door that opened the sliding concrete doors built into the underground walls.

"You go change," David told her after they'd opened the door to the floor mats. "I can grab the mats."

"Show-off," the Mage teased him as she entered the closet they'd opened. A number of padded karate gis were hung along one wall, and she grabbed one as David hauled the heavy mats out of the room easily.

Instead of ducking into a side room to change, however, she put the white robe over her shoulders and began to remove her T-shirt underneath it. She was mostly concealed from David by the gi, but he firmly focused his attention on the mat as she changed.

Kate's laugh let him know when she was done changing, and he turned back to her with his cheeks flushing. Much as he enjoyed the young woman's friendship, David remained aware of her physical attractiveness. Most of the time, it was a peripheral awareness, but every so often, she seemed to rub it in his face.

With a wry grin at his own thoughts, he gestured the gi-clad Mage to the mat and took one of the sets of padded robes and pants into a side room to change. He emerged in a few moments to the sight of Kate stretching her muscles.

He paused for a moment to watch. David recognized the smooth flow of her movements as that of someone long-practiced with the motions, and wondered how much of that was Koburn or another trainer's supernatural ability at work, how much was the years of training it suggested, and how much was just the woman's natural talent and flexibility.

After the moment of watching, he joined her on the mat and fell into his own stretch routine. For several minutes, only the grunts of stretching and the smack of bare feet on the mat sounded in the training hall.

Finally, David finished stretching and turned to look at Kate. By now, the Mage was done with her own stretches and was waiting for him.

"Ready?" she asked. "Don't hold back," she continued when he nodded. "I *hate* it when people hold back."

The pair assumed positions and, before David could even take a breath, Kate moved. She stepped forward into him and her fist snapped out, heading for his face. His forearm blocked it, knocking the blow aside as he stepped back for more space.

The Mage stepped forward aggressively, and for a moment, David gave more ground, blocking each of her strikes with precision. He slowly released his Sight, allowing himself to predict her blows and block them all.

Finally into the rhythm, he suddenly moved from defense to offense. He knew she was going to overextend, and grabbed her arm as she did so. A shift of his weight, and the Mage was stumbling across the mat as his open hand slammed into her back, shoving her away faster.

Kate turned and gave him a flash of a grin before driving back at him. This time, David moved into her blows, blocking and returning with strikes of his own. It didn't take him long to realize he was vastly stronger than she was, and in the back of his mind, he started to worry.

He began to pull his blows, ever so slightly, so as not to strike with full force when he hit. The slight pull meant that Kate blocked more and more of his blows, but that was fine with him. With his longer reach and greater strength, he was now in control of the match and they both knew it.

Then he pulled a blow a bit *too* much, and Kate's eyes flashed.

"I *said*," she panted, "*don't hold back*." The Mage spat three words that David didn't understand, and then *moved*.

A blur that might have been a fist slammed into David's right shoulder, sending him stumbling back. A second blur, definitely a fist to his Empowered eyes but *glowing* to his Sight, slammed into his left thigh, taking the leg out from under him. As he began to fall, her first fist blurred back again and impacted on his chest.

With a burst of light, David was lifted off his feet and thrown clear across the room, slamming into the pile of mats in the storage closet with a loud crash.

———

For a long moment, David simply lay in the mats, catching his breath from how thoroughly and suddenly he'd been defeated. He slowly rose from them, rubbing his aching chest, to the sound of applause.

He glanced over at the noise to realize that, at some point, Michael O'Brien had entered the room to watch the sparring match. He was the one now applauding.

"She means it when she says not to hold back," the werewolf told David, inclining his head to Kate. Like David, the Mage was still catching her breath. "That's called Aureus Pugnus—the Golden Fist. The full name is much longer and more dramatic, but it was created by Hermetic magicians, so what can you expect?" he asked with a small smile.

"It's a combination of martial arts and magic," O'Brien continued, as Kate gestured that she was still catching her breath. "The Elfin have a similar form, called the Flame of Andúril—you'll remember Riley's idiots complaining about it—and I believe the vampire houses use a style called Spell Fang. Kate is usually generous enough *not* to use Aureus on the rest of us."

"It's a good thing to have in reserve," the Mage added, having finally caught her breath. "I do know others who can sustain the form for longer. It really takes it out of me," she finished ruefully.

"It's an unpleasant surprise," David told her as he reached the mat. "But I *like* unpleasant surprises for our enemies," he reminded her with a smile, just in case she'd taken his words the wrong way.

Michael nodded, and then sighed. "Speaking of unpleasant surprises," he said softly, "Kate, can I get you to give David and me some privacy?" he asked.

The young Mage raised an eyebrow but nodded. She grabbed her neatly stacked pile of clothing by the mats and disappeared off into one of the changing rooms. David found himself wondering just what the hell was going on, and turned to Michael.

"What's up?" he asked as Kate disappeared through the door out of the hall. He was still sweaty and clad in the gi, but he suspected that Michael didn't much care.

"It's about Carderone," Michael said grimly, his voice low enough to almost be a growl. "The Catholic Church has decided they want 'independent verification of our story,'" he continued in a half-singsong. "They're sending their own investigator, a Monsignor Cameron Rodriguez."

"It makes sense," David admitted. "We did kill one of their priests, after all."

"Oh, it makes sense," Michael agreed, his voice still a growl. "But any senior Ordo Longinus official could have done it. The Church's supernaturals are just as present in America as anywhere else."

David had heard vague references to the Ordo Longinus since joining ONSET. It was the supernatural branch of the Catholic Church. If you were a supernatural and a priest, you were part of the Ordo. In some parts of the world, Ordo priests were the only line of defense against the supernatural.

Logically, there would be senior Ordo priests in America, so who were they sending? Before David could ask, however, Michael answered.

"Rodriguez is coming from the Vatican itself," he told David, and his voice was soft now, not a growl. "He's a Papal Investigator, promoted *from* the Ordo Longinus but no longer a member of it. That makes him one of the Hounds of God, the Pope and Cardinals' personal enforcers and investigators into the supernatural."

"Damn," David replied, his own voice soft. He'd caught one vague reference to the Hounds of God, and it had just been a mention of the term in reference to the Church.

"He wants to interview you specifically," Michael told him, and David caught his breath. "This means he knows my reputation and hopes to get more out of you than me."

"What should I tell him?" David asked after he managed to breathe again.

"The truth," his Commander replied. "We did exactly what we should have done, so there's no point in lying. You're going to miss our next active deployment," he continued, "as we won't let him into the Campus. You'll have to meet Rodriguez at OSPI Headquarters in New York."

David's mind reeled. He'd been just about ready to go out on another active duty cycle with his team, and now he was being completely yanked out for an *interview*?

"It sucks, David," Michael told him. "But we don't have a choice. Even if he wanted to talk to me, you're more easily spared. The extra time to train won't hurt you, though the rest of us will miss your Sight."

The younger Agent nodded slowly. "When do I leave?"

"In the morning," O'Brien instructed. "Pack to be there for a week; I don't know how long they'll keep you."

"Understood," David replied. With a glance to make sure his boss had nothing more to say, he headed for the change rooms.

"David," Michael said after a moment, just before the junior man left the room.

"Yes sir?" David asked.

"Watch your step with Rodriguez," the old werewolf ordered. "The Hounds have another, even less pleasant nickname.

"To those who've come up against them, they're the Inquisitors."

18

DAVID WAS SLOWLY BECOMING MORE FAMILIAR WITH THE TRANSITION WHEN he traveled back into the "mundane" world from the ONSET Campus. Remembering that, to the rest of the world, nothing had really changed was hard sometimes.

His longest exposure to it, however, was the several-hour wait for his flight at the Colorado Springs airport. An ONSET car had whisked him down to the airport and dropped him off, with only a small carry-on bag.

As a Federal Agent, David *could* travel on public flights armed, but the thought seemed mildly silly to him when he was moving from secured building to secured building. So, for the first time in weeks, he'd shed the concealed holsters under his crisp new black suit—not the highly expensive one Michael had bought him, but a cheaper one he'd picked up while waiting for ONSET Nine to return from their leave.

Unarmed or not, his government ID whisked him through security with an astonishing speed, and he found himself one of the first passengers on the plane to New York.

The flight was only supposed to be three hours long, so David settled down into the chair and pulled the provided blindfold over his eyes. He wasn't sure what a Papal Investigator's idea of an interview would be like, but he suspected he'd need all the sleep he could get before it.

———

OSPI HEADQUARTERS WAS TUCKED AWAY in a quieter street of Manhattan's skyscraper core. Rising thirty stories above the streets, it was an unassuming block of concrete and brick from the sixties that almost vanished into the crowd of similar buildings all around New York.

David was delivered to the front doors of the skyscraper by a suited young man who had quietly ignored his attempts at conversation. Upon reaching their destination, the young OSPI man had pulled up along the curb and popped the automatic locks.

"This is it," he said simply. David gave the quiet youth a curt nod, a little annoyed at the man's complete lack of companionability, and stepped into Manhattan's streets.

Even in this quieter street, cars zipped past and crowds surged back and forth. The sheer noise and pressure of the New York crowd hammered against David's calm. Even with his Sight all but turned off, the blur of auras and motion pressed on him.

He still took a moment, standing like a rock in the midst of those rushing crowds, to look at the building before him. Only the stark carving of the Office's initials into the stonework above the door gave any clue at first that he was in the right place, but his continued regard revealed more.

The building might have looked superficially identical to those around it, but it still differed in half a dozen small ways. The other buildings around it were divided only by cramped alleys, where the OSPI building had a small park—lacking in any trees tall enough to block fields of fire—on one side, and a double-wide and suspiciously clean truck access alley on the other. His Empowered gaze noticed that the glass in the upper floor windows was thicker and denser than in the surrounding buildings, and there were no windows on the lower level. The four sets of heavy oaken double doors were the only break in the gray concrete on the ground floor.

Those doors opened readily enough as David finally entered the building, revealing a second set of doors six feet away. These doors were also heavy oak, each of them bearing an American flag carved into their surface. Unlike the outside doors, the interior doors were marked to his Sight as enchanted with security spells, and more mundane training spotted the recessed slots above them that would allow solid steel doors to seal the entrance in a lockdown.

He barely allowed his assessment of the doors to slow him as he crossed the entryway and stepped through into the public lobby of the Headquarters of the United States Office of Supernatural Policing and Investigation.

THE LOBBY WAS ONLY SLIGHTLY LESS plain than the gap between the doors. It was a medium-sized room, wider along the entry wall than it was deep. A large curved desk occupied pride of place on the far wall, its heavy wood forming a psychological barrier between the receptionist behind it and anyone forced to occupy the uncomfortable black plastic benches that lined the concrete walls around a repressively cold and empty concrete floor.

Right now, those benches were empty, and the only occupants of the room other than David and the secretary were an American flag in each corner. A handful of outright ugly landscape paintings dotted the walls. The receptionist didn't even seem to have noticed his arrival.

David approached the desk, vaguely intimidated by the stark austerity of the surroundings. He knew OSPI had to keep a low profile, but this Spartan, ugly lobby would have looked at home in a free clinic in the slums.

As he crossed the room, he began to realize its true purpose, however. The desk was heavily enchanted and would likely protect its occupant from almost any attack. The roof was too low—even lower than it had been in the gap between the doors—and almost certainly contained some nasty surprises for an unaware attacker. One of the ugly paintings had turned somewhat on its hanging, revealing a hatch David recognized from the Campus's defenses as being a weapon slit.

The room was designed to function as a killing ground if anyone assaulted the skyscraper, and as David stepped up to the receptionist's desk, he Saw the woman behind it for the first time and knew she was no secretary but a highly trained Mage who could add her own power to the strength of the defenses.

"Can I help you?" she asked coldly.

"David White," he identified himself, looking at her carefully and allowing the FBI-style suit he was wearing to do much of the talking. "I believe I should have an appointment?"

The woman touched something in front of her—an LCD touch-screen concealed by the desk so as not to break the image of the poor and Spartan lobby, David realized—and then looked back up with a smile that softened her face incredibly.

"Good afternoon, Agent White," she greeted him, her eyes meeting his for the first time and dancing with a spark of humor. "Welcome to OSPI HQ. We apologize for the lobby, but we're renovating."

"How long have you been renovating?" David asked, with a glance around at the very permanent looking benches.

"About forty years," she responded with a grin, and offered him her hand across the desk. "Inspector Deanna McDonald, Agent. You are expected." She touched the screen again and the door on her right popped slightly out with a click, and then swung open as its motors caught it.

"Director Morrison is waiting for you in the main lobby," McDonald told David. "If he doesn't ambush you, ask the receptionists in there to point him out." She glanced down and then lowered her voice. "According to my memo, you are *not* to meet Father Rodriguez without speaking to Director Morrison."

"Understood," David confirmed, wondering who this Director Morrison was and what he wanted. Nobody had said anything to him about a briefing before the interview, though he realized now that it made sense.

"Go on through," the Inspector instructed, and David obeyed, stepping through the automatically opened door into a second, much larger room—OSPI's *real* lobby.

———

THE SECOND LOBBY was a far more ornate affair that the concealed abattoir David had just passed through. Bare concrete gave way to a familiar plush blue carpet, which, unlike the ever-present flooring at ONSET Campus, was decorated with evenly spaced gold sunbursts.

The sunburst motif was repeated on the marble columns that decorated the walls at two-yard intervals around the room. A single gold sunburst marked with a stylized Omicron was engraved onto each white marble column at eye level.

The furniture in the room was all a uniform navy blue. A cluster of four couches stood to David's right around a large hotel-style fireplace, and three more stood in the far corner beyond the elevator doors to his left.

Another large solid-oak desk blocked the access to the second set of elevator doors in the far right corner of the room, and its elegant style contrasted sharply with the recognizable biometric suite set up around the single door leading to the elevator area.

The couches held a scattered handful of men and women in business suits, and a quartet of uniformed receptionists slash guards stood behind the desk. None of the four were openly armed, and David's Sight confirmed all were mundane, but he doubted they were defenseless.

"Agent White!" a voice greeted him, and David turned toward the couches on his left to see that a man had left them and was walking toward David with his hand extended.

David took the man's hand firmly. "Director Morrison?" he queried.

"Indeed," the director replied. He was a tall man, head and shoulders taller than David, and whip thin with it. His face was only lightly marked by age, but his hair was pure white and his three-piece charcoal suit was the ultimate in conservatism.

"Walk with me, Agent," the Director instructed, and headed toward the biometric scanners allowing access to the rest of the building.

"Director," David acquiesced, and followed the older man.

"I imagine you're wondering why you were ambushed here," Morrison said calmly as he and David both presented ID and thumbs for the scanners.

"Just a little bit," David admitted, eyeing the Director carefully. He wasn't even entirely sure what agency the Director was with. The man carried himself with authority and calm, but the security guards weren't deferential enough for him to have been the Director of OSPI. Besides, Mark Anderson held that position. David knew that name.

"I'm with the ISA Office," Morrison explained as he gestured David to the elevator.

David blanked. For all of his study of America's Omicron Branch, he didn't remember that office.

"International Supernatural Affairs," Morrison elaborated after a moment of silence. "My office is relatively small, and we never impact ONSETs operations much, so I'm not surprised you don't know about us," he continued.

"We interact with the other supernatural government agencies around the world, and other groups in the know—like the Vatican," Morrison said quietly as the elevator door closed behind them.

"This is the first time a Papal Investigator has set foot on US soil in fourteen years," the old man told David, running his fingers through his white hair. "Now, I'm sure Michael told you to tell him the truth, the whole truth and nothing but the truth, right?"

"Right," David confirmed, eyeing the man. He wasn't sure he liked where this conversation was going.

"Now, Michael is entirely correct in his assessment that we have nothing to fear in this case," Morrison told David. "However, that does not mean we have nothing to *hide*," he softly. "So, tell him the truth. Just don't tell him *everything*."

"What am I not allowed to tell him?" David asked carefully. He had the feeling he was stepping into a minefield, and he wasn't trained for diplomatic minesweeping.

"No details about your team," Morrison said flatly. "He knows O'Brien is your team Commander, but do *not* mention anything about any other member of your team. Mention nothing about your training, or the Campus, or the Louisiana base. Even the location you took off from is irrelevant and classified."

"So..." David considered, and trailed off as the elevator came to a halt. Morrison laid one delicate finger on the CLOSE DOORS button before the doors could open, and raised an expressive old eyebrow at him. "Tell him what happened in the church," David summarized quietly and somewhat uncomfortably. "Tell him what we found there and about Carderone. Nothing else about ONSET?"

"Exactly," the Director said in a satisfied voice. "Tell him the truth about what's relevant—and don't give him *anything* that isn't relevant. It's more important than you might think," he added.

The old man released the button and the elevator door slid open. "Monsignor Rodriguez is in room 1612," he instructed. "That's to your right and down at the end of the corridor. Go!" he barked.

David left the elevator and allowed its doors to close on Director Morrison before he let loose a sigh of relief. He had never liked even office politics, and this was *way* over his head.

A quick glance down the blue-carpeted corridor spotted the number 1612 on a gold number plate on one of the brown wooden doors lining the wood-paneled hallway.

Time to go face the Hound of God.

———

THE ROOM on the other side of the door was plainly decorated. There were no shelves or wall ornaments to conceal the two cameras mounted up by the ceiling, but carved wooden pillars marked each corner. A long wooden conference table and a dozen black leather chairs were the only furniture.

A single man occupied the room, and he rose to his feet as David entered. He wore a black cassock, closed with a row of dark mahogany buttons running from the high collar at his neck most of the way to where the robe's hem brushed the ground.

"Agent White, I presume?" he greeted David in a heavy Italian accent while proffering his hand.

"I am," David confirmed as he took the man's hand. "You are

Monsignor Rodriguez?"

The priest nodded calmly as they shook, and David was taken aback by how small the man appeared. He was a good inch shorter than David's own five four and lacked the breadth that made people assume the agent was taller. The man's fair hair and laugh-lined face gave an impression of cheerful humor, but his eyes told a very different story.

Rodriguez's eyes were a blue so cold, David almost shivered as he crossed gazes with the man, and even the low level of Sight David had active revealed an aura that had been perfectly regimented and controlled. David was used to auras revealing much about a man, but this priest's aura revealed *nothing*.

Despite his small stature, the priest terrified David. He tried very hard not to let that show as he held Rodriguez's gaze.

"Please, Agent White, take a seat," the priest said softly. "This is not an interrogation, simply an interview."

David nodded and took the proffered chair. Rodriguez remained standing, walking slowly and silently around the table to look at David over it. For a moment, the silence in the room was eerie, and David's Empowered senses tingled.

He drew on his Second Sight to study the priest, and turned his gaze on the other man. He blinked in astonishment as he realized the source of the tingle in his senses: the priest was turning the full power of a Sight as strong as his own on him.

For an eternal moment, the two men looked deep into each other's souls. Rodriguez's control only concealed so much and revealed in its existence almost as much as it concealed. The priest's aura showed a firm determination, as well as an honesty and honor that could be bent but never broken; and a stubbornness to rival David's own.

Finally, Rodriguez blinked and released his Sight. Quietly, without comment, David released his, and the two men's gazes met with normal eyes.

"You are an exceptional man, David White," the Monsignor said finally. "I find your Omicron branch tends to underestimate strong perceivers. Mother Church *requires* abilities such as mine and yours to be a Papal Investigator.

"Knowing your abilities makes this easier," he continued. "I can be more confident that there was no error in judgment when the man who judged can see souls."

"I appreciate the confidence," David said carefully, surprised at the open expression of it by this extraordinarily powerful man.

"Now, understand that I have reviewed your OSPI's evidence file and the reports that were filed on this incident—with what I presume was adequate censoring, given the liberal use of black marker," Rodriguez said dryly. "What I want from you is what you remember of the event itself—what you saw and heard before Carderone attacked, how the fight progressed, and how he died."

David paused for a moment, marshaling his recollections of that church into a coherent framework, and then began to retell the events. He gave as much detail as he could remember, and more as Rodriguez used careful questions to bring up things he hadn't considered.

The Investigator never sat during the entire ten minutes that David spoke. Still, he barely moved, standing on the other side of the table like a black-clad statue. Finally, when David had finished speaking, Rodriguez relaxed slightly and sat in the chair opposite David.

"Thank you, Agent White," he said softly. "Reports only tell me so much—and it's far easier to lie on paper than in person to someone like us. I can guarantee"—a flash of harshness crept into his voice now —"that the Church will accept your actions as justified and necessary. Carderone was a monster, and the Church should have dealt with him ourselves. It was *our* failure, not yours, that led to the entirely unnecessary death of your Inspector Riesling."

David managed not to openly sigh in relief, but he knew that it was a waste of effort. While Rodriguez's control of his aura prevented easy betrayal of his emotions, David had no such control.

His statement finished, Rodriguez shuffled through the papers on the conference table and removed a familiar red-leather photo album, marked with its black metal sun.

"You found this, I understand?" he asked.

"Yes," David confirmed. His gaze was now riveted to the sun, which he'd seen duplicated in his hometown bar. What did it mean?

"Do you know what the sun means?" the priest asked, echoing David's thoughts.

"No," David admitted. "I've seen it elsewhere," he said slowly, "but I have no idea what it means."

"It's a symbol of the Antichrist, among other things," Rodriguez said softly. "Whatever its meanings, it shouldn't have been in a Catholic church. I suspect its presence may help reveal why the Ordo Longinus missed Carderone. You said you saw it somewhere else?"

David hesitated. He wasn't sure he wanted this man, this small unassuming man who utterly terrified him, digging into Charlesville. On the other hand, he was pretty sure the Monsignor had no real authority outside the Catholic Church. This might not stop him, but...

"I saw a similar decoration in a bar in my hometown," he finally admitted. "It...stank of evil almost as badly as the one on that book."

"That makes no sense," Rodriguez replied in a mutter that David wasn't entirely sure he was meant to hear. For a few long moments, the two men sat in silence, both of their eyes drawn toward and repelled from the evil emanating from the black sun to their Sight.

"But that is my problem now," the Monsignor finally sighed, looking up at David. His voice was soft, but his eyes were ice-cold again and David really did shiver this time. "The Ordo *should* have found Carderone. They failed. You did your job in stopping him. Now it's my turn to find out why you had to," he finished grimly.

The Catholic Priest rose to his feet and offered his hand. "Thank you, Agent White. I now have my own investigation to launch, but I doubt I will need ONSET's help in the future."

"Thank you, Monsignor," David replied shaking the proffered hand. "But if the Order is corrupted, will you be safe?" Even though the man scared him, he could tell that Rodriguez was an ally—a powerful one—for Omicron in keeping the peace.

"I am the voice and hand of the Pope, the Vicar of God on Earth," the Monsignor said softly. "No Catholic will lay a hand upon me. Besides," he finished, his voice still equally soft and cold, but something different in his aura, "no one expects the Papal Inquisition."

David was still blinking at the unexpected joke as the Inquisitor calmly walked out of the room.

19

DAVID REMAINED IN THE CONFERENCE ROOM FOR SEVERAL MINUTES AFTER Rodriguez left. The interview had taken less than half an hour, but it had left him shaken. For all that the priest seemed to be on the same side as ONSET, he'd still been unnerving to deal with.

No one had given David any instructions for when the interview was over, so he eventually decided to head down to reception and check to see if they had any instructions for him.

He'd barely made it out of the door before a familiar voice shouted down the corridor, "Hey, David!"

David stopped and turned to find the hulking form of Leonard Casey barreling down on him. With a grunt of laughter, the black ex-Airborne punched him lightly in the arm. A smaller woman in an identical uniform followed him at a distance.

"Figured it was you when they told me to catch an 'Agent White' before he left the building," Casey rumbled at David. "ONSET ain't big enough for there to be two of you. Pam," he said, gesturing the woman forward, "this is David White. David, this is my fire team partner, Pam Uphoff."

David gave the slightly built woman a nod of recognition. "You were told to catch me?" he asked.

"Yeah," the larger man confirmed. "A couple of our grand poobahs want to debrief you. I got tagged by my unit Commander as being free."

"Unit Commander?" David queried, as he gestured for Casey to lead the way. "I thought you'd been headed for an Inspectorship."

"So did I," the OSPI man admitted as he and Pam guided David away from the elevators and toward a set of stairs. "I think they barely finished getting the fax of my profile from ONSET before I got co-opted into a special program, though."

"What program?" the ONSET man asked, curious. So far as it had been explained to him, OSPI had Inspectors and Security teams, and the Security teams were mundanes like ONSET's Anti-Paranormal Companies.

"We're part of the Stutters," Pam answered him as the trio climbed up the stairs. "That's SSTTR, or Special Supernatural Tactics, Technology, and Recon. Also known as the dirty tricks command."

"I thought most of that fell under ONSET's jurisdiction," David asked carefully as Casey led him out of the stairwell into another blue-carpeted and beige walled corridor.

"ONSET is combat teams," Casey told him. "Stutter is designed to disable and capture enemies we don't need to bring the heavy hammer down on—or need alive."

It sounded to David like a recipe for an inter-force rivalry, but he didn't have a chance to say anything as the SSTTR man swung open a door leading into another conference room, similar to the one he'd just left. This one, however, contained half a dozen men, including an intrigued-looking Director Morrison.

THE DEBRIEFING WAS MERCIFULLY SHORT, and David found himself rapidly hustled back to yet *another* black government car. He wondered if the arrival and departure of so many blatant government vehicles from this supposedly commercial high-rise stood out to those surrounding it.

By the time they got him to the airport and handed him his plane ticket back to Colorado Springs, he'd been in New York for less than eight hours. The whole affair seemed rushed to him, like he wasn't welcome in OSPI headquarters, and he wondered to what extent that was true.

Before ONSET had been an independent office, it had been the OSPI High Threat Response teams. He knew Michael, who'd been involved in those teams, seemed to think it had been a move for the better, as did most of the ONSET people he knew who'd talked about it.

He was left wondering as he boarded his plane, however, how the organization that massive chunk of funding and influence had been ripped away from had felt about it.

————

DAVID RETURNED to the Campus to an empty dormitory. ONSET Nine had left without him, a helicopter whisking them away to another week-long assignment that he'd been removed from. No one had expected his New York trip to take a single day.

Six days was a long time to burn without training, so he called Koburn up and talked his way into special unarmed training sessions with the Sage. While he was faster and stronger than the trainer, the trainer continually pulled out tricks David hadn't seen before.

Between training and setting up his new home, his week vanished surprisingly quickly. He grabbed time to have lunch with Leila Stone again, but only once, as she was busy with her team finally going on a deployment at the end of the week.

When ONSET Nine finally returned late Sunday evening, they found him in the dormitory common room, cleaning the disassembled parts of the M1911 that Chief Hanson had given him.

"Look who's had the lazy week," Michael said loudly as he tromped through the common room, followed by the rest of the team.

David looked up from the parts of the gun and returned his Commander's grin. "Rumor has it that you guys weren't doing much more over in California," he replied.

"Probably less," Bourque grouched as she slouched past David and collapsed into a chair, slinging her locked and unloaded machine gun onto the ground beside her.

"Secure that," Michael half-barked. "Come on, people, let's get the gear off, *then* we can harass the local layabout. Did you at least clean up around here?" he added to David, who shook his head laughingly as the team trooped past him into the armory behind the common room.

―――――

THE TEAM slowly drifted back into the common room, freshly showered and with body armor and weapons stored in their lockers. They collapsed into chairs and glanced at the television, which Morgen had turned on with the new *Star Wars* movie playing at low volume.

Kate, the last of the team to come back downstairs, had just settled on the chair across from David when the door to the outside of the dormitory swung open.

"TEN-HUT," a masculine voice bellowed, and the members of ONSET Nine leapt to their feet and snapped to attention as two men in full ONSET combat gear stepped into the room. A moment later, Major Warner followed them.

David looked at her uncomfortably. He could guess why ONSET's second-in-command would show up in the common room of a reserve team. He suspected their time off was about to be cut short for real work.

"Ladies, gentlemen," she addressed them calmly. "At ease."

The team rapidly drifted together into the middle of the room as she regarded them. For all his discomfort, David was with them. He might not think he was fully ready, even with the last three weeks of training, but he knew he'd proven himself. If there was a job to do, he was going to be right there with the rest of his team.

"Our friends over at ISA have forwarded a request to us," she told them. "The Royal Canadian Mounted Paranormal Police have a situation in Montreal that they would very much like to have a strike team for. Unfortunately, Canada's Joint Task Force Hercules has one team currently tied up assisting operations in the Middle East, and the other is apparently somewhere in the Arctic Circle, dealing with a minor Incursion."

It made sense, David reflected, that other countries had organizations like OSPI and ONSET. He couldn't help feeling, however, that "Joint Task Force Hercules" was a much better name than 'the Office for the National Supernatural Enforcement Teams.'

"Therefore, the RCMPP has requested to borrow an ONSET team to support this operation. You've been designated," she finished. "We've coordinated in the past with both JTF-H and the RCMPP to everybody's satisfaction, and I expect this time to be the same."

"What's the mission?" Michael asked calmly. David, like the rest of the team he was sure, was listening carefully to the answer.

"The RCMPP has located a complex they have confirmed to belong to a major Vampire Familias," she told her subordinate. "While we have yet to confirm which Family, we *have* linked it to some of the intelligence provided by the Elfin. Carderone was funneling money from his parish's charitable donations to a shell company that owns part of the complex.

"Even without that information, however, the Canadians don't want that boil on the universe to exist for one day longer than it has to."

"When do we leave?" Akono asked, the elf's dreamy tones somehow much scarier than normal.

20

"What's Canada like?" David asked Michael as ONSET Nine busied themselves in their armory, pulling on their full gear. He hadn't lived far away from the northern country, but he'd never made it up there and didn't trust rumor for an accurate opinion.

The werewolf Commander paused for a moment, sliding his assault rifle back into his locker and gesturing for his subordinates to do the same. "No rifles," he ordered. "We're trying to be at least somewhat covert." He pulled a submachine gun, the curved grip and magazine shape of a Heckler & Koch MP5, out of a locker and slung that instead.

He checked that the rest of the team was doing the same, and then turned his gaze back to David. "Canada?" he responded, appraisingly. "Good coffee. Decent hockey. Lots of ice. That really sums up ninety percent of what you need to know. Oh, and the Quebecois, the folks around where we're going, speak French."

"French?" Ix asked, the demon pulling a black knitted cap down to the augmented reality goggles to cover his giveaway horns. David wasn't sure it would help if anyone got a close enough look to see the inhuman red tinge to the demon's black skin, but from a distance, it would work.

"Older language from over in Europe," Michael answered. "Second language of the Canadians."

"None of us speak it," Bourque objected, pausing in her process of attaching various small and medium weapons about the combat suit. David agreed with her that not speaking the language in the area would be a pretty major problem, and wondered how Michael was planning to get around it.

"All the RCMPPs do," Michael told her. "As well as English. We'll be fine."

David settled the low-profile AR goggles over his face and checked the safety on his M1911 before holstering the pistol opposite his mage-blade and slinging his own MP5 over his shoulder. If Michael was expecting them to be able to rely on the Canadians for translation, then they'd be working pretty closely with them. He wondered why the Canadians needed an ONSET team if there would be enough of them for that.

"What sort of resistance do we expect?" he asked, putting the question into words as he brought his suit computers online for a systems test.

"Not sure yet," Michael admitted. "We'll be rendezvousing with a Sergeant-Major Bordeaux from the Mounties on the ground at the Pierre Elliott Trudeau Airport. He will be in charge of the operation and will brief us en route."

"That leaves only one question," Morgen said, the Mage sliding his own Silver auto-loader into its holster with an audible thunk. "When do we leave?"

Michael glanced around the room at the team and met David's eyes for a moment. David gave a slight nod, and the werewolf Commander grinned.

"Now."

———

IT WAS the first time David had ever been loaded into a Pendragon making full speed. The trip to Louisiana had been done at the helicopters' normal subsonic cruising speed, and the trip to Carderone's church hadn't been far enough to need it.

This time, ONSET Nine was in a hurry, and Malcolm Akono knew it. As soon as the door shut behind the last team member, the helicopter was already moving, and the elf ordered the team to strap in.

A slight touch of sweat filled the air as the helicopter body-slammed its way into the sky, but David was simply thankful that no one had thrown up. The initial lurch upward had almost brought his breakfast back up.

Seconds after leaving the ground, a sonic boom crackled through the mountains around the ONSET HQ Campus as the Pendragon went to full speed. The helicopter had been designed to outrun any civilian aircraft in existence *before* Omicron's Mage-technicians had taken it apart and enchanted the pieces.

At full speed, the chopper had to avoid populated areas like the plague, as even magic couldn't conceal the sonic boom of an aircraft screaming along above the speed of sound. For those inside, the super-sonic ride was uncomfortable at best, as even the slightest turn threw the passengers against their safety belts. With all the precautions and the circuitous route, it took the helicopter ninety-six minutes to cross the continent from the Rocky Mountains in Colorado to Montreal in Quebec.

———

"WELCOME TO MONTREAL, LADIES AND GENTLEMEN," the RCMPP officer standing on the helipad greeted them as the American team drifted out of the Pendragon into the river-fresh air of Montreal. He was dressed in an ordinary-looking business suit, short and dark-haired with an Asian angle and coloring to his face and eyes. "I am Sergeant-Major Jean Bordeaux, commanding officer of the Quebec detachment of the RCMPP. You made incredible time," he finished, looking at the sleek black jet-copter behind them.

"Our government and our Office both highly value the cooperation between our countries," Michael told the Sergeant-Major. "We were ordered into the field as soon as your request reached the Campus."

"We appreciate the speediness of your response, Commander," the RCMPP office replied. "Normally, I'd have Joint Task Force support, but they're currently tied up in the Middle East and the Yukon."

"I understand completely, Sergeant-Major," Michael replied. "We have three teams in the Middle East ourselves, coordinating with the Europeans and the Israelis."

This was the first David had heard about ONSET operations in the Middle East beyond the story of Casey's recruitment, but it made sense. America was tied up in providing enough security support against IS that it made sense they'd be helping with supernatural security, too.

The RCMPP officer nodded, and gestured for the team to come with him.

"We have transportation to the operations center ready," he told them. "This is a secure pad, but we should still get you out of sight."

David, looking around at the conspicuously black-clad and armed strike team, agreed completely with the officer. He and the rest of the team willingly followed Bordeaux to the unmarked white van sitting near the edge of the pad.

The driver waved out the window at them. "Bienvenue à Montréal," he greeted them warmly.

"Ils sont américains, Pierre," Bordeaux responded in the same language, "ils ne parlent pas français."

"Sorry," the driver immediately said to the American agents. "Welcome to Montreal, Officers."

"Thank you," Michael responded, with a quick glance at Bordeaux. "The back's unlocked?" he asked.

"Jump right on in," Pierre replied. "It'll be nice to show these *sang* they can't fuck with people like they do."

"That's what we're here for," Michael told the driver before following his people into the back of the van, where long benches waited for them.

———

THE OPERATIONS CENTER turned out to be an unmarked eighteen-wheeler truck tucked away, with several other unmarked vans, into an alley next to a Chinese restaurant and behind a large hardware store emblazoned CANADIAN TIRE. Behind the cover of the vans blocking the alley entrance, men in blue coveralls and black body armor quietly loaded and checked shotguns and submachine guns.

Bordeaux led the American team into the trailer, which turned out to be a fully functional mobile command center, with the front end hosting a flatscreen display that covered the entire wall. Right now, the display showed a satellite photo of an ordinary-looking warehouse. Blinking red lights and circles on the photo were the only marks to distinguish the image from any other warehouse anywhere.

David was impressed. ONSET had better setups—hell, Charles's "personal computer" was probably vastly more capable—but those were immobile, not fitted into the back of an eighteen-wheeler.

"This is our tactical display," the RCMPP officer said unnecessarily. "Our surveillance technicians"—he gestured at the half-dozen men in gray and blue sitting at computers in the surprisingly spacious trailer —"are combining data from surveillance satellite footage and our onsite observers to give us the best image possible of what is going on at the warehouse."

"We have current satellite footage?" Michael asked.

"Over the course of the next six hours, we've been granted special access to a total of seventeen spy satellites—mostly American and French, but two are ours and one is British—to keep continuous surveillance on the warehouse," Bordeaux replied. "We shouldn't need it for that long."

Spy satellites? David was again surprised by the reach of the supernatural organizations of the world. Turning away from the screen, he looked out the window at the back of the truck at the early evening sky. "It's almost dark," he observed to the two Commanders. Everything he'd read suggested that vampires were almost as vulnerable to sunlight as myth and fiction made them out to be. "Shouldn't we wait till morning to raid vampires?"

"Oui," the Canadian replied, "normally, we would. However, in this case, your prompt arrival has given an opportunity we didn't expect.

"We have acquired intelligence since our original request for help that a VIV—Very Important Vamp—from the family running this place arrived there last night and is leaving tonight."

"That…is a very good reason to go now," Michael said softly, and David found himself in full agreement. His encounter with vampires had left him very willing to blow holes in plans of theirs. "I'm glad we came so quickly."

"So am I," Bordeaux admitted. "Most of my people are glorified ERT—Emergency Response Teams. I have sixty men, but only five are Empowered, and I'm the only Mage."

And *that*, David realized, was why they'd wanted an ONSET team. As the assessment of his own survival chances of going into the Charlesville warehouse had made quite clear after the fact, mundanes didn't stand much chance against vampires.

"What sort of resistance are we looking at?" Bourque asked, interjecting herself into the conversation firmly.

"Each of these red circles is a confirmed guard on the outside of the building," Bordeaux told them, turning back to the tactical display. Nine red circles marked the outside and roof of the building. "The blinking lights are where we've *seen* guards that aren't our definites, but we're not sure where they are now. All of the outside guards are uninfected," he finished. "They're all armed. Only one of our observers got a really good look at the weapon. He confirmed a small suppressed SMG."

"How many men and vamps inside the building?" Michael queried.

Before Bordeaux could answer, one of the techs hit a button, and the tactical display changed color, showing a number of blotches of green over the warehouse of varying intensities. David looked at the screen, which looked distinctly like an IR image.

"One of the American satellites we grabbed footage from had thermal scanners," the tech told them all. "The bright blotches are either normal guys or possibly Empowered lackeys," he explained. "This group"—he gestured at a cluster of bright blotches—"is in an area the plans of the building show as a large storage closet and they aren't moving around as much as the rest—probably prisoners.

"These, however," the tech continued, and five darker blotches of green were suddenly surrounded by blinking blue circles, "have body temperatures much lower than anybody else. Probably at about the twenty-two Celsius mark," he finished. David took a moment to convert the temperature in his head, and then nodded his understanding.

"Vampires," Michael said coldly.

"Five of them," Bordeaux confirmed. "Nothing has left the building since this picture was taken that could have concealed a vampire, and only two normals have left. Based off the thermals and our observations, there are forty-four ordinary men and women in there, nine of whom appear to be prisoners, and five vamps."

"Doable," Michael replied, looking at the map again. "Can you integrate this with our combat information system?"

"Your Charles just emailed the interface software to us," the tech told him. "You'll have the area map, the satellite photos, and our analysis sent to you real-time."

David liked the sound of that kind of connectedness, though he had to wonder if the tech would be as enthused with the software if he knew that Charles was a twenty-foot-long, fire-breathing dragon.

"Thank you," the werewolf told them. "How long till sundown?"

Bordeaux checked the sky and then his watch.

"About ninety minutes."

"Then what's the plan?" Michael asked the Canadians. "We've got ourselves a Very Important Vampire to properly welcome to your fine city."

"Our observers are also our snipers," Bordeaux told the Americans bluntly. "As soon as we're there, they will take out the exterior guards, clearing us our way in. There are two major and three minor entrances." The Sergeant-Major highlighted the doors on the map.

"The loading dock is our best point of ingress, and I want to put two of my squads—twenty men—and most of your team there," Bordeaux continued. "The main entrance, here"—he highlighted two sets of double doors—"is covered by four snipers, and I'll put my heavy weapons squad there. Two silver-loaded machine guns and an

AG-shrapnel grenade launcher should discourage any attempt to escape through there.

"These two entrances here and here are closest to where the vamps are located, and are probably their first lines of escape," the Canadian continued, highlighting the doors. "I'm putting my best teams at them. I will be accompanying my Alpha squad, and I'd like you, Commander, to accompany Bravo."

"Certainly," Michael agreed.

David looked over the map, committing it—and the plan—to memory. It all sounded good to him.

"The last entrance is here, at the very back of the warehouse," Bordeaux told them, dropping a last highlight onto the screen, and David looked at it carefully. "There is a guard on it, but it's far away from most of the folks inside the building. We've only got one sniper covering it, however, and the team covering it is my only supernatural-less team. I'd like one of your people to provide them with support, just in case."

Michael looked back at the team, and David met his Commander's eyes squarely as they fell on him. At the back, out of the way and lowest risk sounded like the perfect place to put your greenest team member, and David knew it. He didn't particularly *like* it, but he did know it.

"Agent White," the werewolf barked.

"Sir!" David responded crisply.

"You'll accompany..." Michael paused and looked at Bordeaux. "... which team, Sergeant-Major?"

"My Epsilon squad," Bordeaux told them.

"The Mounties' Epsilon squad," Michael finished. "You'll keep them safe, and they'll keep you safe, clear?"

"As crystal, sir," David replied. On the one hand, he was disappointed in the fact that he was being removed from the main fight as a possible liability. On the other hand...only the greatest strength of willpower kept his hand from touching the scars on his neck. He remembered vampire bites. Unprofessional as it was, he both hated and feared vampires. The entire "species," such as it was.

"Agent Mason," Michael continued, turning to Kate. "You'll take command of the rest of Strike Nine and accompany the main strike force. I will accompany Bravo squad."

"Understood," the Mage replied crisply.

"Then let's go join the people we're riding with," the werewolf Commander finished briskly. "We've got a lot of work to do, and only till sundown to do it!"

21

DAVID WAS POINTED AT EPSILON SQUAD'S VAN, AND MADE HIS WAY ACROSS the astonishingly clean alley to join them.

"I'm Agent David White, with ONSET," he introduced himself. "I'm being assigned as your support."

"Nice to see you, Agent White," the team leader greeted him. "I'm Sergeant Angela Devereux."

In the heavy body armor the entire team wore, it was difficult to tell who other than the team leader was male or female, but Devereux had her helmet off, and the tight-wrapped braid of blond hair around her head hinted at sweeping waves of hair that would have left no doubt as to her gender. She smiled at David, and he found himself smiling back unhesitatingly.

"Now you're here," she continued, "we should get a move on. We have the furthest to go." The blonde leader settled her helmet with its Plexiglas visor on her head and turned to her team. "Let's get going, people! We have some *sang* to uninfect—the hard way!"

The Mountie team was on their feet immediately, doing final checks on their weapons as they efficiently trooped into the back of the unmarked powder-blue van. David found their obvious competence reassuring. He finished his own checks and joined the team in the van.

As soon as they were all settled in and the van started into motion, Devereux leaned over to touch her helmet to David's so he could hear her over the sound of the van. She didn't quite have her head on his shoulder, but the nearness sent an unexpected thrill through him, for which he scolded himself. He'd only just met this woman and was about to go into a fight. He didn't have time to be distracted.

"Now, there's something you need to understand before we get there," she said softly.

"Yes, ma'am?" he asked, trying to subtly inform her that he did not intend to challenge her authority.

She laughed; a soft sound that seemed out of place in the well-armored fighter beside him. "Not a question of authority," she told him. "Michael wouldn't have assigned you to us if he thought you would cause problems."

"You know Michael?" David asked, surprised. He presumed the werewolf had been to Canada before, but it seemed odd that anyone they were working with would have specifically heard of him.

"I was his Canadian liaison when the Brigadier commanded the Provisional Force in Montana," the Mountie replied. "Yeah, I know him. But that's not my point."

Michael had *commanded* the Omicron force in Montana? As David thought back on what he'd learned about the Montana Incursion, he realized that there'd only ever been references to "the Brigadier," and the leader's name had never been mentioned. Another one of the secrets ONSET seemed to love, and another question mark about David's Commander. Michael wasn't a Brigadier anymore. When had he stopped being one—and why?

"What is it, then?" he asked, putting aside the question about Michael's history.

"You have a full Omicron combat information suite," Devereux said. It wasn't a question. "You have full coms and minute-to-minute tactical updates. My men don't."

"I...see," David replied. Now that he thought about it, it made sense. The fully upgraded combat information suite built into Omicron's combat body armor was expensive, and even Omicron's Anti-Paranormal troopers didn't get the full deal.

"Now, I have a suit *based* on your Omicron gear and do have that coms and update capacity, but I'm the only one of the team other than you who does," she told him. "If you see something I miss, or see *anything* you think my team needs to know, do not hesitate to tell them. Understood?"

"Yes, ma'am," David confirmed. He hesitated for a moment, but something about this woman reassured him, so he continued. "I'm also mildly prescient," he told her softly. "If I have enough warning of something, I will pass it on."

"So, if you say something weird, we do it before asking why?" she asked, the slight smile audible in her voice though he couldn't see it.

"That sums it up, yeah," he agreed, somewhat self-consciously. He didn't *like* people relying on his prescience, but it was too much of an edge to ignore.

Before either of them could say more, the van reached the last of the waypoints on his HUD and drifted to a stop.

"All right, people," Devereux said over the squad radio channel. "We walk from here."

———

THE TEAM DISEMBARKED from the van efficiently and spread out to cover the access points toward the warehouse. The Mounties kept full three hundred and sixty–degree surveillance as they moved toward the target, carefully keeping out of sight of a small restaurant on the corner they'd dismounted at.

They were perhaps a minute from the van when David spotted something that made the connection to Carderone even clearer— blocking half of the alley they were moving into was an eighteen-wheeler truck with a familiar black sun on the side. The ONSET Agent's Sight didn't show anything supernatural around *this* sun, part of the logo of a company called "Stellar Noir Shipping".

As the Mounties' team cleared the truck, a voice broke onto their channel.

"Epsilon-Lead, this is Eagle Five," the observer/sniper reported. "A second guard is now covering the entrance. I can't take both before one sounds the alarm."

"Understood, Eagle Five," Devereux said calmly over the radio and David was impressed with her cool. "We'll take them close-range. Epsilon-Eight, Epsilon-Nine."

That was all she said, but two of her men stopped and slung their MP5s over their shoulders, drawing heavy pistols and attaching ugly-looking silencers. Even knowing what was coming, the thought of the unexpected silent death that would have to claim the outside guards bothered David. He guessed he was still just too much a cop to be comfortable with shooting somebody without ordering them to surrender first.

The team moved silently along the back alley toward the warehouse. Eventually, David's exceptional hearing caught the sound of voices ahead of them, and he raised his hand.

"Two men, about one hundred fifty meters that way," he said softly, pointing toward where his enhanced senses had heard the speakers.

"We'll advance thirty and I'll try and get them on a directional mike," Devereux ordered, removing that piece of equipment from her belt.

The team moved more slowly, drawing closer into range, until David could clearly see the guards standing in front of the old warehouse. Here, in this centuries-old city and industrial park, he almost felt hemmed in by the ancient brick and mortar, and the target complex looked no different from a hundred other century-old warehouses. David touched the team leader, pointing at the men against the brick wall, and Devereux raised the mike.

"*Putains vampires*," a voice said harshly in David's ears. "*Quelque grand Don est ici du sud, et ils sont et ils capotent.*"

"*Ils sont patrons*," a second voice replied resignedly.

David glanced over at Devereux. "What are they saying?" he whispered over the radio, feeling somewhat helpless. He didn't like relying on other people, though at least the Mountie officer was more reliable than most.

"They're bitching about a Don from down south putting the

vampires in an uproar," she replied quietly. "These men are probably Mafia when the *sang* haven't called them in."

"They *know* who they work for?" David asked, stunned. The thought of anyone knowingly working for vampires horrified him. Suddenly, he didn't feel quite so bad about the thought of snipers.

"At this level?" she replied. "Yes. Eight, Nine," she continued, switching channels. "Infiltrate and disable."

A pair of clicks on the radio was her only answer, but the two men holding the silenced pistols slipped away along the alley. David watched them go, his SMG unlocked and his Empowered senses stretching for the slightest sign that the guards knew what was coming. Even here, he could smell the river through the industrial smells and sounds. The river and someone's salty, garlicky cooking. He focused his senses, keeping them on the guards and pushing away unnecessary input.

"Epsilon Team, report," a call came over the radio, recognizably Bordeaux's voice.

"This is Epsilon-Lead," Devereux reported. "An additional guard joined our first one. I have men moving in to disable."

"Understood," the Sergeant-Major replied. "We'll hold the snipers until your guards are down."

Devereux clicked her radio but kept her gaze firmly set down the alley, to where the two guards stood outside the door. Their men were nearly invisible in their dark clothes.

It was, David reflected, scarily quiet. Even he could barely identify where the infiltrators were, and it was blatantly obvious that neither guard knew they were in danger before the two Mounties opened fire.

One guard had enough time to curse *"Tabernac!"* before a second shot ended any response; the other took the single round through the throat and dropped in silence. To David's enhanced nose, the scent of blood filled the alley with an overpowering stench. The men's sudden deaths bothered him, but he was surprised to find himself completely lacking in sympathy for men who knowingly served vampires.

"Targets down," one of the two cops reported over the radio, and Devereux passed it on.

Moments later, a series of reports came over the command net that the snipers had taken the rest of the guards.

"Everyone, cover your entrances," Bordeaux ordered over the radio. "The main team will enter in fifteen seconds."

David checked the MP5 he was carrying and moved into a position pointed out by Devereux, joining the rest of the team in covering the entrance. He felt more than saw the team leader take up a position to his left, her weapon trained on the door as well.

"Epsilon-Lead," Devereux reported. "We're good to go."

Moments after the last secondary team reported their readiness, an explosion tore through the night as the main team's shaped charges blew in the main entrance.

Gunfire followed, and Epsilon team's members quietly unlocked their weapons and aimed at the closed door in the old brick wall.

"We have entry," a voice said over the radio. "Alpha team is moving to secure the prisoners."

David hoped that Alpha team made it in time. Given that the vampires had to regard their prisoners as a renewable food source, there was a distinct possibility that someone would just shoot them all to stop them being rescued.

Swearing and gunfire over the radio interrupted his thought. Then a cry of "They're coming out!" echoed over the radio, and the machine guns covering the front entrance opened up with a loud sound like tearing cloth.

"*Tabernac*," someone shouted, and the radio crackled with the volume. "That *sang* is in body armor; the bullets aren't slowing him."

David winced, and his fingers tightened on his gun. He had his own area of responsibility—the front guard team was Michael's.

As if to finish his thought, the roar of a transforming werewolf echoed over the radio. There was a sharp curse from the machine-gunners, and silence from that team for a moment. Finally, "Front entrance secure" sounded over the radio in a voice that sounded slightly sick.

"This is Alpha Team," another voice reported. "Prisoners are secured. We have one vampire down. Mason is damned fast with those fire bolts."

Relief flooded David, both for the prisoners and for the news that Mason was okay. He didn't know her well yet, but he'd already come to think of her as a dear friend, very much the "team's little sister," as Michael had described her at David's first meeting.

"Bravo Team, reporting the main offices secure," David heard Bourque's voice. "Bravo lead is down, with two others, none dead. One vampire confirmed shish-kebabed. Looks like we got the files intact."

"There are two more vampires," Bordeaux snapped over the radio. "Find them, people!"

David reached out with his senses, trying to find any hint through his Sight or other enhanced senses as to where the vampires were. Around him, Epsilon team shifted slightly, the Mounties tightening their grip on their guns and moving slightly in toward the door. Suddenly, David's Sight flashed a warning, and he knew they were too far in toward the door.

Even as he opened his mouth, it was already too late. As soon as one of the cops came close enough to reach the door, it suddenly exploded outward in a hail of shrapnel and ball bearings as the claymores someone had attached to the other side detonated.

Three of the Mounties went down in the explosion, and two men came charging out on its heels. David fired quickly as they charged out, his three-round burst catching one in the upper chest and throwing him back into the building. He knew that he would see the man's face again in his dreams, but the death flashed by so fast he barely had time to realize he'd shot someone.

David hit the ground as the other man sprayed the alleyway with fully automatic fire until his gun clicked on empty and he charged Devereux. The Mountie leader calmly shot him in the face as he did, but over half her team was down now, moaning and wounded.

The ONSET Agent's prescience flashed another warning, and he sprang back to his feet and faced the door in time to watch a figure *blur* out of it. Silver bullets from the remaining team members splashed off body armor much like the Mounties' own, and there was a sickening thud as the blur reached the two closest Mounties.

Both went down in a heap, and David caught a glimpse of a

youngish man in black body armor over an expensive suit. Fangs protruded from the man's mouth, and for an eternal instant, David was back in another warehouse, in another country.

Then fear flashed to rage, and he and Devereux both opened fire as the vampire sprang toward them. Bullets pinged off the body armor, leaving smears of silver behind as the vampire reached the team leader.

Devereux blocked his first strike with her MP5, but the force of it drove both of her arms back with a sickening crack as her forearms shattered. Fear flashed through David again as the woman crumpled backward with broken arms. Not fear for himself—fear for *her*.

Before the vampire could strike again, David channeled his fear to draw on the future and fire one carefully aimed burst. Three silver bullets punched into the back of the vampire's exposed neck, shattering the creature's spine and sending him plummeting forward to the ground.

David's heart was beating fast, so fast, yet his breath seemed to come so slowly. He watched Devereux stumble backward, barely holding in a scream as she dropped her gun from her shattered arms, his heart leaping as he began to run toward her. Then his prescience triggered again as he realized he was the last cop still standing—and there was someone *else* in the alley.

He spun and interposed his MP5 between himself and a descending knife. With a blur, the SMG split in two under the enchanted blade—but it stopped the knife strike. David's enhanced strength took the strike with ease, and he dodged backward.

Something woke inside him as he dropped the halves of the submachine gun and yanked his pistol out, firing as he drew. A single silver round punched through the other man's leg before the same flashing silver knife turned the Chief's gift into so much scrap metal.

The knife came at David again, and this time he went for the wrist holding it. The waking feeling *exploded* inside him, and he *knew* where the wrist would be, and his hand struck with lightning swiftness as the attacker seemed to move in slow motion.

He caught the vampire's wrist and spun. The man, unarmored and dressed only in a gray suit, shifted with David, adjusting to the grip with literally inhuman speed and striking back. David caught the man's other hand without thinking. For a moment, both of them stressed their arms to the utmost pushing against each other, and then the vampire let go.

The knife went spinning in one direction as the vampire went another and David a third. Both men hit the walls of the alley and were on their feet in moments. Fire burned through David's muscles, searing away pain, searing away fear.

"Who are you?" the man snarled.

"Agent David White," David snapped back. "Who the hell are you?"

"*I?*" the vampire laughed. "I am Marcus Dresden, and I was putting men like you in their graves five centuries before you were *born*. Mantled or not, you are fucked. Run," he suggested with a cold smile.

David didn't. The fire continued to burn through him, and the vampire seemed slow and no stronger than himself. He could win. He *knew* he could win. The thought terrified him.

"If I have no fucking clue what I can do," he told the vampire quietly as the flame continued to surge inside him, "how the hell can you?"

Marcus charged, and David's mageblade flashed out of its sheath like a spark of fire. He knew where the vampire would be and at what moment, and he struck perfectly. *Nobody* should have blocked it. With the fire burning through him, he knew that even *Michael* would have been struck.

Marcus blocked. The vampire's hand struck out impossibly fast and struck David's wrist with enough force to shatter concrete. Only David's enhanced strength allowed him to survive the blow intact and still hold on to the knife, but the block distracted Marcus, and David's snap-kick response caught the vampire by surprise. Even surprised, the ancient vampire dodged out of the way.

David struck with his free hand, a bladed strike driving at the nerve cluster at the old vampire's right shoulder. With a snarl, the vampire blocked David's attack and kicked low.

The Agent jumped over the kick, landing just out of reach of the monster, and the two supernaturals paused, facing each other.

"Fuck you," the vampire spat, and attacked.

No one David had ever fought, not the vampires in the warehouse, not the priest Carderone, not even his practice matches against Michael, had moved that fast. Every strike happened at the speed of thought.

For a moment, David matched it. He rode the Sight and the burning fire within him, and parried every blow, dodged every kick. For an eternal moment, an ancient vampire attacked him with everything it had. And he stopped it.

Then he blocked a moment too slow, and Marcus Dresden slammed his fist into David's chest. Ribs *cracked* and the younger man flew backward, crashing into the alley wall with a shock of exhaled air.

Pain flared through him and breathing stabbed his side as the vampire stalked toward him. He barely managed to get to his feet, and he knew in that moment that if the vampire touched him again, he would die.

All of his speed left him, the fire draining away in a spasm of pain and fear, and Marcus Dresden smiled.

"I lived before your *country*, and will survive past its end," the vampire told David. "You should have run."

The strike, when it came, was impossibly fast. No human could have dodged it.

David knew where it would strike and slid sideways. His free hand snaked out and caught Marcus's wrist. For a moment of shock, Marcus lurched forward, drawn by his own inertia. The vampire hit the alley wall exactly where David had been a moment before, and the mageblade in David's other hand slashed down in one stroke.

There were two thuds as Marcus's remains hit the alley's dirty concrete.

———

MOMENTS after the vampire was down, David was on his knees as the adrenaline left him and he gasped for breath, for oxygen, for the cool air of the river city. He slowly raised himself up despite the pain in his chest and met Devereux's eyes. They were the eyes of a competent fighter who had seen the supernatural for years.

And those eyes stared at him in awe, shock, and fear. He knew how she felt. He felt it himself. Fear and shock at his own speed. He had no idea what had just happened, but he'd won. His body felt burnt and his chest hurt, yet he knew that he would be fine. What *was* he? What kind of monster could *do* that?

"You need to call in," Devereux told him. "I can't. We need a medic."

Pain as well as shock marred her voice and shattered David's shocked reverie. He hit his radio immediately.

"This is Agent White," he said softly, expecting his voice to somehow show the fire that had just burned through his flesh, "Epsilon team got hit—hit hard. We need medical help *now*." He paused. "Confirmed two vampires down," he finished finally.

He then grabbed the med kit one of the team had been carrying and pushed past his own pain to perform first aid on the worst of the wounded. Epsilon team was hit *bad*, and David could not—*would* not let them die. He threw every ounce of strength he had left into trying to save them. Trying to save *all* of them.

He'd bound up the worst of the wounds and was trying to immobilize the fractured neck of one of the men the first vampire had taken out when a heavy hand suddenly settled on his shoulder.

"The medics are here," Michael said gently. "Let them do their jobs."

David slowly backed away as the white uniformed paramedic took over, setting the poor man's neck in a professional immobilization collar. Michael's hand remained on his shoulder, and David was impossibly grateful for its reassuring weight and strength.

"Do you know who that man was?" Michael asked, gesturing at the decapitated corpse nearby.

"He called himself Marcus Dresden," David replied. The pain was gone, and only fear burned through him now. Fear of himself. Fear of what he'd just done.

"The Father Dresden himself," Michael affirmed in a soft tone. "I've lost two entire teams to that bastard. He'd disable our best two or three men with darts loaded with aqueous silver and then annihilate the rest. Usually leaving the one or two most senior men alive. He *founded* the Familias in America, David."

"What?!" David exclaimed, startled. He knew the vampire had been strong, had been fast—faster and as strong as David himself. He hadn't known that the vampire had been *that* strong.

"You just took down a five hundred and eighty-something-year-old vampire who was Infected during the end of the Hundred Years' War in the fifteenth century," Michael told him gently. "A man who defeated *me* twice."

David looked back at the body of the vampire, then looked around at the wounded from Epsilon squad. Hearing from Michael's mouth just what the vampire he'd killed had been drove away his guilt at killing the thing, but not the other guilt. Not the guilt of still standing when others were not. Of having failed to find that fire sooner—of having failed to save them.

"Not fast enough," he said softly.

"We're downloading the video from Devereux's and your tactical helmets," Michael told him softly. "But I doubt it will suggest anything I can't see from the aftermath. There was nothing you could have done to keep Epsilon any safer than you did, and you stopped one of the most wanted fiends in the world from escaping.

"Well done, Agent White. Well done indeed."

[22]

DAVID PAUSED OUTSIDE THE HOSPITAL DOOR THE NEXT MORNING, uncertain of himself. The hallway of the military hospital at the Canadian Forces Base Montreal gave him no relief from his own mind. The walls were white, and with this entire wing of the hospital cordoned off to hold the casualties from the warehouse raid, there were few people in sight.

Barely twenty hours had passed since the raid had concluded, and everyone involved, including the American team, had been restricted to this base hospital. David hadn't seen Michael since they'd arrived in these stark hallways and he had joined the rest of the team in collapsing into dreamless sleep.

Nine of the RCMPP officers hadn't been lucky enough to make it to sleep. They'd either died in the fight or died after arrival. He knew that elsewhere in the building, grim-faced doctors still fought for the lives of some of the strike team's wounded. Of the sixty Mounties that had assaulted the warehouse, twenty-one Canadian officers had been standing at the end, fewer than half unwounded.

Since then, he'd walked these corridors in silence, staying carefully out of the way of the Canadian Forces doctors and nurses who were attending to the RCMPP officers. None of ONSET Nine's members were injured, but the Canadians seemed to be intent on keeping everyone involved in the incident under complete lockdown.

He'd checked in on the members of Epsilon team to learn that though some were still critical, most were stable, except for one who the nurse had gently informed him had been dead on arrival—his chest ripped apart by the Familias's claymores.

David made a point of learning the name of the dead man: Jean Charquest. Somehow, he'd needed to know the name of the man who'd died because he'd failed to warn them fast enough. He *had known* the door was about to blow. He hadn't spoken fast enough.

Checking on Epsilon's team members had been easy, as none of them had been conscious and it had simply been a matter of asking the nurses. A minute ago, however, one of the nurses had found him and told him that Sergeant Devereux was awake.

"I thought you'd want to know," the young uniformed man had told David before whisking off to deal with another patient.

David had wanted to know, he realized after the nurse had told him. He'd wanted to know about Devereux more than any other member of her team. That thought had surprised him and made him uncomfortable. As surely as he'd saved her life, he knew she'd saved his by stopping the first vampire getting to him. Whatever had followed, at the moment that they'd killed that vampire, he hadn't been ready to fight it hand to hand.

And now he stood outside the white hospital door with its plastic mounted tray containing manila folders and its tiny, closed window. Part of him wanted to run away, to never see Devereux or any of her men again, to forget entirely.

He knew that was cowardice, however, and faced the door squarely for a long moment, while facing a surprising thought inside his own mind just as squarely: he did not *want* to leave without seeing her.

David knocked. "Come in" was the immediate response, and with a deep breath, he opened the door and stepped into the hospital room.

The small room was no less stark than the rest of the military base, with sterile white walls surrounding a functional set of basic medical equipment. A full suite of medical monitors and IV leads were attached to the wall on the far side of the bed. The nearer side was occupied by a sink and a counter running along the wall. The entire room was gently lit by the afternoon sunlight streaming in through a window with pale yellow curtains, an unusual spot of color in the sterile military hospital.

"Hello, Agent White," the room's occupant greeted him, and David turned his attention to the central feature of the room: a large reclining bed currently raised just enough for Devereux to see around the room.

"Good afternoon, Sergeant Devereux," he replied. The formality sounded stiff and trite in his ears. They'd fought alongside each other and saved each other's lives, but he really knew nothing about the woman in the bed.

She smiled up at him from the bed, half covered by a blanket and covered the rest of the way only by a flimsy hospital gown. Her blond hair, now undone from its tight braid, sprawled around her on the covers, framing her face like the sun. Both of her forearms were visible on the bed, encased in beige plaster casts. He suddenly felt guilty, to see her so vulnerable when he was the cause of her injury.

"Please," she said finally, breaking the silence, "call me Angela. It seems silly to call each other by our ranks when we're alone."

David's heart jumped, and the adult part of him told it to stop acting like a teenager. He had no idea where the spark fueling this *idiocy* had come from, but this brave woman deserved better than to be gawked at.

"Then you should call me David," he replied, and was almost surprised at how little of that lurch of his heart showed in his voice.

"Have a seat," Angela told him, her fingers—and only her fingers—gesturing to a chair by the bed. Wordlessly, David obeyed, pulling it up next to the top of the bed. "You weren't hurt?"

David shook his head. "No"—he coughed to clear his throat, and then continued—"none of the ONSET people were badly hurt."

Now that he thought about it, that lack of injury seemed odd. Michael, he knew, had charged a vampire-led breakout attempt that had almost made it out in the face of machine guns before he intervened. He knew Kate had acquired some minor injuries dealing with another vampire, and the rest of the team had been supporting, not in front, but Michael should surely have picked up something.

For that matter, he'd thought he'd cracked a rib or something when Dresden had hit him, but the nurse who'd examined him said all he had was minor bruising.

"You were lucky," Angela replied, and David winced.

"I'm sorry," he said quickly. "I should have been faster—I knew the door was going to blow."

"Prescience, right," the blonde in the bed replied, and shook her head fiercely. "Prescience be fucked," she continued. "You had what, half a second? A second? Even if you'd managed to say something, we couldn't have got back from the door in time. And you're the only reason any of Epsilon survived. I think we got off lightly."

David paused, unable to respond, and Angela continued.

"We only had one man dead, and that's because you stood over our wounded and fought harder than I thought any man possibly could, even an Empowered," she told him, and her eyes flashed in a way that made David uncomfortable. "You saved my men's lives—*my* life. I won't forget that."

Overwhelmed by the fierceness of her response, David raised a hand to slow her tirade. She truly believed he'd saved them. While a part of his mind continued to scream "my fault, my fault," the rest of him was familiar with the concept of survivor's guilt. Angela's determination that he was not at fault might not have salved everything, but it certainly made it easier.

"Thank you," he said finally. "It was...hard, being the last one standing."

"The rest of us lived because you were," she replied, and her voice was firm. "Conversation done, over."

"Just like that, huh?" he asked.

"Exactly like that," Angela replied, and her smile made David's heart ache. "When are you folks heading out?"

"I'm not sure," David admitted. He suspected that Michael's absence was because the werewolf Commander was trying to free his men, but he didn't know for sure. "Your government seems to be trying to bury us all."

"The Ministry of the Paranormal doesn't like to admit that it exists to *itself*," Angela told him wryly. "They won't hold on to you guys too long, but they're going to spin this mess to the press as hard as possible."

David nodded, but there really didn't seem to be anything to say to that, and as he remained silent, he felt a touch on his hand and looked down. Angela had shifted her hand over onto his, and her fingers touched his softly.

"You have any family, David?" she asked.

"Not really," he admitted. "Two cousins by an aunt who moved away from Charlesville—it was a great scandal when she left, and I don't know them well. My parents died in a car crash the year after I became a police officer."

He didn't like to think about his family. He had an email address for his aunt, and he'd kept in touch with her every so often since his parents' funeral, but they weren't close. He had been close to his parents—they'd funded his education and supported his application to the police force. It was only after they'd died that he'd found out they'd done it by mortgaging the family home to the max—a home he'd lost to the debt collectors when a fledgling policeman couldn't cover the bill.

A lot of his father's sins had been forgiven when David had discovered the sacrifices his parents had made to get him through college. He was still glad that Max White couldn't see what his son had become.

"I'm sorry," Angela told him, and something in her voice told him that his thoughts had shown on his face. He realized he was seeing her aura unintentionally, and colors swirled through it he hadn't seen before. Grief and sadness he recognized, but he wasn't sure about the others.

"What about you?" he asked, to break the train of thought as he shook away his Sight. "Any family?"

Angela laughed, and the darkness that had settled on David as he thought of his parents faded at the sound.

"I'm half-Quebecois, half-Italian," she responded. "I'm related to half of Montreal, and they insist on keeping in touch. They all think I push papers around for the RCMP in Toronto," Angela added softly, and the thought of the secrecy they both kept around their real work shadowed the room again.

"How do you keep it all secret?" David asked. It was a question he hadn't yet dared to ask of his ONSET team members, but here, in this small hospital room with this attractive blonde woman, it was easier to ask.

"A lot more easily than the Ministry thinks," she told him. "The secret about keeping the supernatural secret is that it's easier the less you try—no one believes it. They don't *want* to believe it. Those who know, know, and those who don't know, don't want to."

David thought about it for a long moment. Would he have believed someone if they'd told him about ONSET or the Royal Canadian Mounted Paranormal Police before he'd encountered vampires? Or would he have dismissed it as a joke or a prank?

He knew the answer, now he thought about it, and for the first time in a while, the long running deception behind the supernatural agencies of the world made sense. The supernatural wasn't secret because shadowy government organizations like his employers kept it that way —those organizations worked in secret because no one would believe they existed.

"I never thought about it that way," he admitted to the woman with her hand on his, and she smiled at him. With a jolt, he realized that asking about family was also a good way to discover if someone was married.

With a gentle movement of her unoccupied fingers, Angela raised the bed to a roughly sitting position, carefully adjusting her arms as he did. She was now a lot closer to David, and she leaned toward him without words.

The kiss was completely unexpected, but at the same time, he knew it was coming. It lingered for a long moment, soft and uninterruptible. When they broke, he found himself looking deep into Angela's eyes and knew that he wasn't the only one whose heart had found a spark of companionship and—yes—attraction under the threat of vampires.

"Normally, I'd be even more appreciative of you saving my life," she said softly, "but given that I can't even undress right now, and we're in the middle of a military base, I think that's off the agenda for the moment."

"I may accept a rain check," David heard himself say without any intervening center of intelligence between the origin of the words and his mouth. Angela's smile suggested it wasn't as much of a faux pas as he'd thought.

"Good," she told him, and kissed him again. When they came up for air, her hand gestured at the sink and counter next to the bed. "There's a pen and paper there," she instructed. "Write this down." She gave him a phone number, and he obeyed her instructions.

"Call me, eh? You great Yankee goof," Angela told him with a bright smile.

"I just may, Miss Canuck," David responded, her smile dragging one out of his suddenly lightened heart. "I think I just may at that."

———

MAJESTIC THOUGHT she'd managed to refine her paranoias by this point. After weeks, she'd managed to break down a set of criteria against which she measured news reports, to see if they were worth looking into.

She knew she was a very logical person, not prone to exaggerations or flights of fancy, so the number of reports left under her criteria scared her. A dozen reports in the two months since the fight in the warehouse. *Hundreds* when she started running her criteria back in time.

It was almost as if a massive undercover operation was going on to control and contain something…weird. She kept coming back to her theory about the supernatural. If it was real—if those punks in the warehouse had really been vampires, and that cop…a hero out of a Greek myth or something—then it made the pieces fit together.

But if she was right, who would believe her? A massive effort must have been made to keep this undercover, and trying to break that cover could be dangerous. The hacker had brushed way too close to a couple of conspiracies in the past, and only her ironclad levels of anonymity had saved her from being a specific target. Majestic knew she was on dangerous ground.

But there was something about that cop. She'd dug into his record. Parents killed in car crash. Unmarried. No close family. Nonetheless, well known in his community. One of the good ones, the cops people went to for help instinctively when they had problems.

But Majestic had years of experience reading between the lines. White was a good one, yes, but ironbound in his ethics, too. There were hints in the mentions of him that he was too stiff for a small town, where a minor crime by a popular person could be hushed up.

He didn't seem the type to buy into this sort of conspiracy, yet given how thoroughly the man seemed to have disappeared, that was almost certainly what had happened.

Even as her thoughts went to the police officer whose timing had dragged Majestic's curiosity into this mess, another report pinged her filters: an incident in Montreal. Local police claimed a successful drug bust, but the media had dug up reports of dozens of wounded and a massive gun battle. Security was tight on information—far tighter than it should have been. Like it was in so many of these cases.

Majestic looked away from the articles her feed was bringing up, and glanced at another window on her screen. This one showed a graphical representation of data flowing in and out of the black server she'd last seen White ping his email from, and that she'd repeatedly failed to hack. The computer she'd used for the attempts had eventually had its hard drive so fragged by multiple nuke programs, she'd had to scrap it for parts.

Her gaze drifted back to the window with the profile of David White on it. It might be time to fall back on a more...old-fashioned method of hacking.

[23]

M<small>ICHAEL</small> O'B<small>RIEN</small> <small>STRODE THROUGH THE SMALL</small> W<small>ASHINGTON</small> DC secondary airport in a foul mood. The sight and sound and smell of the bustling crowd around him barely registered on his consciousness as he made his way toward the terminal housing the private and chartered planes.

A government Learjet waited for him there, ready to whisk him back up to Montreal, where the writ he'd just been given by the Committee of Thirteen *should* be enough to break his people free of the Canadian's Ministry of the Paranormal.

He'd thought, when he'd originally headed back to the States, that a simple request from Director Morrison of the International Supernatural Affairs office should have been enough to break his people free. To give the aging Director credit, Michael knew the man had spent an entire day on the phone to one person or another, trying his damnedest. In the end, all the man had been able to do was get Michael an introduction to Senator Lyle Quatrell, senior Senator of the Committee of Thirteen.

Thankfully, the Committee had a *lot* more influence to bring to bear than the ISA Director, and from the sounds of it, the Ministry of the Paranormal was going to see reason. Finally, Michael had been back in the US for three days, and his people had been locked in a Canadian Forces Base for all that time.

With a sigh, Michael slipped through a door away from the bustling crowd of the public terminal. The quiet of the private terminals corridors hit him like a wave of cool air, and he finally allowed himself to take in his surroundings.

Where the public terminal was the usual utilitarian tiles and drywall, the private terminal was *much* nicer. A red carpet, still thick despite the many feet that must have trod over it, covered the floor, and dark brown wallpaper blended into wood paneling on the walls.

Not that the security was any less tight, Michael reflected as he was waved to a security scanner that was identical to the one in the public terminal. The werewolf wasn't carrying any weapons—he didn't expect to need them and was quite capable of defending himself without them—so it was a very quick check.

"Your plane is waiting at gate three," the calm guard in a brown-and-red uniform informed Michael after glancing over his travel papers. "From my understanding, there are a handful of other passengers, but they are already in the building."

The ONSET Commander nodded his thanks and set off down the plushly carpeted corridors. From what Senator Quatrell had said, they were holding a diplomatic flight for him, so he wasn't surprised to be the last one there.

"Brigadier O'Brien," a voice said quietly beside him.

Michael quickly concealed his shock and turned to face the speaker. His denial of that identity faded on his lips as he recognized the black cassock and the neck pin of the silver spear.

"I no longer hold that rank," he said finally, before taking a stab at the identity of his ambusher, "Monsignor Rodriguez."

"Indeed?" the Papal Investigator replied calmly with a slight bow. "I thought you were merely retired from command of the Anti-Paranormals. I can see how commanding an ONSET Strike team might qualify as a…quiet retirement from being in command of all supernatural high threat response in America."

Michael quickly glanced up and down the corridor, but the two supernaturals were alone. "Even here, it is unwise to speak of these things," he said softly. "What do you want?"

"Like your Agent White," Rodriguez said quietly, "my senses are Empowered. We are quite alone. If you will spare me a few minutes of your time, however, I have arranged a more private location."

Michael glanced at his watch and realized the plane had already been held over an hour for him. He looked at the slight figure of the Pope's man and wondered just what was worth this amount of effort.

"All right," he agreed.

Rodriguez waved for Michael to follow him and swept off down the corridor, Michael trailing him bemusedly. Barely ten steps down the corridor, however, the priest paused and brushed aside a curtain to reveal an alcove tucked into the wall. Another man in a simple black cassock with the silver spear of the Ordo Longinus stood in the alcove.

At the sight of Rodriguez, the guard opened the door hidden in the alcove and gestured them through. The door closed behind them with a click, and Michael and Rodriguez were alone again.

The room concealed behind the curtain was a small conference room, perhaps large enough for a meeting of ten men. Its decorations were identical to the outside, and the wooden table matched the paneling exactly.

"The management here maintains a few small private meeting rooms like this one for travelers who don't have time to detour for their meeting," Rodriguez explained to Michael. "I arranged for one to be free for us while my taxi to this airport was being 'unavoidably delayed.'"

"Delayed, huh?" Michael asked dryly. "What's going on here Monsignor?"

"Understand one thing, first, Commander O'Brien," the priest replied, using the correct title now and not the one Michael had given up years ago. "I am not here. We did not meet. I am under strict orders from the Cardinals not to discuss my investigation here. Do you understand?"

Bemused again by the cloak-and-dagger, Michael nodded as he took a seat. "I understand. Say your piece...or don't, as the case may be," the werewolf finished with a small smile.

The priest did not return the smile; he turned away from Michael and crossed his hands behind his back. For a moment, he remained silent, and then he turned back to the ONSET man, who felt himself being measured by the other man's Sight.

"As I'm sure you were briefed after my interview with David White," Rodriguez told him finally, "I left OSPI HQ determined to investigate how Carderone went undiscovered amongst the Church. I now know why."

Michael sat wordlessly and gestured for the priest to continue after the silence stretched on for a moment.

"Bluntly, Commander, we failed our flock—and you," the Papal Investigator said quietly. "It was the Order's job to catch Carderone before he went mad. We failed. Not because the Order didn't find him but because members of it covered up his actions from the rest of the Order. They even, I discovered, attempted to cover it up from the police."

The ONSET Commander now sat up much straighter, his attention focused on the Catholic Priest. This was news. This was *bad* news.

"My investigations revealed that the Ordo Longinus in America was rotten to the core," Rodriguez continued. "Many of the priests had fallen in with a group calling itself Black Sun, as did Carderone and others outside the Order.

"This group encouraged them to believe themselves as chosen by God, placed above mortal men to punish their transgressions. This," the black-clad man said softly, "is exactly the arrogance the Ordo Longinus exists to try and prevent.

"The rot had spread far and high," he explained quickly, "and we in Rome missed it. No longer!"

"How bad?" Michael asked.

Rodriguez shook himself. "I ordered one hundred and twenty-two priests, mostly Ordo Longinus but including fifteen non-Order supernatural priests, interned for return to Rome." He checked his watch. "Their plane left fifteen minutes ago. Among them," he said grimly, "was Prelate Ambrose. He betrayed the Church, the Order, and God Himself. He will be punished."

"From the sounds of it," Michael said carefully, "the Cardinals seem to regard this as an internal Catholic affair. Why tell me?" He was stunned at Rodriguez's numbers, for all his apparent calm. There were barely three hundred priests in the Ordo Longinus in America. The Pope's Inquisitor had just arrested a third of them.

Rodriguez reached inside his cassock and withdrew a metallic gray object, about three inches across by five inches long. Michael recognized it as a portable hard drive just before the priest slid it across the table to them.

"This 'Black Sun' came *to* the Catholic Church in America, not *from* it," Rodriguez explained slowly as Michael took the hard drive. "Prelate Ambrose clearly was dealing with its true leaders, however, but his files of those dealings were locked under a high-power encryption key on his computer. Copies of those files are already on their way to Rome, but I suspect the American government has even better cryptologists than the Vatican.

"Any information stored on those disks is likely a greater threat to the US than to Rome, which means I cannot in good conscience leave Omicron in the dark," the priest told him finally. "I must do as God guides me, and this is what I feel must be done. Take the hard drive. Find the answers you must find."

"Thank you," Michael told the other man sincerely as he pocketed the drive. "For your honesty and your help."

"It is my duty, not merely my job," Rodriguez replied. "Now, we both have planes to catch. We may meet again, but only time and the Lord will reveal that."

With that, Rodriguez swept out of the room, the door swinging shut with a thud behind him. Michael considered the portable hard drive for a long moment, and then pulled his cell phone out.

"This is Commander Michael O'Brien," he said into the phone calmly as it connected him to the OSPI station in Washington. "I need an Omicron-Charlie clearance courier to deliver a package to ONSET HQ." He looked at his watch, considered how delayed his flight already was, and added, "Soon."

DAVID AND THE OTHER MEMBERS OF ONSET NINE HAD SETTLED IN FOR A long wait by the fourth day they'd been ensconced on the Canadian Forces Base. Evening found them playing cards on the flimsy wooden table in the common area of the wing of rooms they'd been given. They'd drawn the uncomfortable plastic chairs around the table and settled it in the fading light from the single window.

David glanced at his hole card as he regarded the others. He had a six up and a six in the hole. "Hit me," he told Ix, then groaned as the demon dealt him a king. He flipped the hole card over, showing the others he'd busted.

Kate, sitting to David's left, gestured for Ix to pass her a card. She took an eight to go with her four and then held. She'd been somewhat more aloof than usual to David over the last few days, but he chalked it up to stress and strain.

Akono took an Ace to go with his open five. "Hit me again," he said dreamily, then flipped his hole card—an eight—when he received a jack. The elf had been bothered the least by the four days locked up in a hospital wing, but David had realized that elves really didn't live entirely in the normal world.

Neither, apparently, did the Canadian Ministry of the Paranormal.

While the individual nurses and guards around them had treated the ONSET team with respect, their orders were also ironbound—the ONSET team was *not* leaving. David honestly didn't know how Michael had managed to leave, as by the second day, they'd been restricted to this wing of rooms.

He hadn't had a chance to see Angela again, even when news had come to them that the remaining wounded were being shifted to a Ministry hospital near Toronto. She'd sent David farewells through a friendly nurse, but returning them through the same young man was all he could do.

"I'll stand," Dilsner answered when Ix turned to him. The techno-Mage had spent most of the four days they'd been locked in hiding behind a laptop, ignoring the rest of the team.

Bourque had passed on the game and sat in the corner, knitting a cardigan. He'd seen it before, but it still struck him as an incongruous hobby for the harsh and burly heavy weapons specialist.

"And dealer takes one," Ix said aloud in his growling voice. He tossed another king down next to his three, then quietly flipped his hole card to show a queen and his bust. Even after four days locked in a small number of rooms, David knew almost nothing about the demon. He was an enigma, even beyond being a being that was once an enemy.

"Can I get into the game?" a quiet voice said from behind David, and the distracted team members looked up to find Michael standing in the doorway. David realized the Commander looked tired, but followed the rest of the team in standing up and clamoring for news, the blackjack game forgotten.

"Quiet down, people," Michael said firmly, and the team slowly quieted. The werewolf walked into the room and took a chair, gesturing for the others to do the same. "First question first: we have been cleared to leave. The Ministry received a specific request from the Committee of Thirteen, and Mr. Wellington has conceded the point. We'll be leaving whenever you're ready."

Michael looked utterly exhausted. David was shocked that it had taken an appeal all the way up to the Committee to free them, but it did at least explain the werewolf Commander's state.

"Questions you *haven't* asked," the Commander continued, "one: the Mounties have officially thanked us and ONSET for our assistance. Their assessment reports and my own are already at the Campus, as are glowing endorsements on all of your files. You did well, people— very well." Michael paused to allow them to settle down, and then went on. "Two: our inactive reserve time has ended, so you are all officially on your one-week-cycle leave as soon as we leave this hospital.

"Pack your things," he ordered. As the team began to move away, he gestured at David. "David? Can I have a word?"

David felt a twinge of concern but stepped over to his Commander. "Yes, sir?"

"Come with me," Michael ordered, and led the way off of the hallway and down a floor, into a military gymnasium attached to the hospital. The wooden floor had been cleared of any equipment, and RCMPP officers guarded the doors.

"We didn't have time when this mess first wrapped to a conclusion to discuss your fight with Dresden," the werewolf told David as he continued to lead the way into the center of the gym floor with its painted lines.

"It was still sinking in then, sir," David admitted. "I'm still not sure what to make of it."

"I am," Michael said quietly. "You fully powered up—to the level of ability we knew you to possess from the beginning. Have you been able to repeat any of it since?"

David thought for a long moment as the pair stood there, alone in the empty gym. He remembered the sensation of running at that "full power" now, the feeling of fire running through his veins, but...

"I haven't tried," he admitted, "but I haven't felt like that since then."

"We need to test it, David," Michael told him. "Do you remember what it felt like?" At David's nod, he continued. "Focus on that thought. Try and draw that feeling into you, and then try to hit me."

Given the empty and guarded state of the gym, Michael's apparent idea of testing wasn't really a surprise to David, and he nodded silently. He stepped away from Michael and focused inward.

He focused on that memory of heat and flame, and tried to bring it forth. He closed his eyes, drawing on the meditations he'd been taught to control his Sight and tried to bring the fire up from inside him.

Then he felt...something. A spark flared inside him, and he moved at Michael. Before he was even halfway there, he knew the spark had failed, and Michael's block seemed blurringly fast.

The next thing David knew, he was on the floor where his Commander's block had thrown him.

"Apparently not," he said breathlessly as he slowly clambered back to his feet. Even given his past experience with Michael, that strike had been a humiliating failure. "I had something but nowhere near enough."

"These things take time and practice," Michael told him. "At least you know what to try for now. You have somewhere to begin."

"What if I can never gain conscious control?" David asked. He now had to admit he *had* the strength they attributed to him, which terrified him, but it wouldn't help him much if he couldn't control it.

"You will," his Commander said firmly. "Now we *know* you can do it, it's just a question of practice. You said you had something just now —more time and you'll have more."

David nodded, conceding the point. It also seemed like he triggered under stress, he realized. Most likely, anytime he *needed* his powers, he'd have them. Not that that wasn't terrifying enough all on its own.

"What now?" he asked.

"Don't go back to Campus," Michael told him. "Go on holiday... somewhere. Hell, *anywhere*. Denver's nice and near the Campus for when you have to head back. You need a break, son."

The younger man looked away from his Commander but nodded. "Denver, huh?" he said, considering.

A break sounded *very* good.

[25]

ON HITTING THE GROUND IN DENVER, THE SUITED AND NEATLY DRESSED crowds in Denver International Airport drove home to the rumpled and worn David that he'd been wearing the same clothes since changing out of his combat gear four days before.

His taxi delivered him to a chain hotel with faux marble pillars holding up a stone roof over the drop-off area. He paid the man and walked into the small lobby. Dark red carpet ran over the floor, and dark beige walls made the tall potted plant stand out plainly.

He booked a room for the next several nights and headed past the desk to the main-floor rooms. To his right, a sign noted that hotel guests received a discount at the nearby nightclub and bar just across the street. David swallowed immediate temptation and continued to his room.

He glanced around the room, noting the large white bed, the dark wooden desk in the corner, the television, and the tiny—invisible to those without Empowered senses—security camera in the far corner of the roof. The only really unusual feature of the room, which he'd paid extra for, was the Jacuzzi tub in one corner.

Ignoring the camera, David entered the white-tiled bathroom and stripped off for a much-needed shower. The hotel provided the normal assortment of tiny bottles, which was more than enough for his needs.

Later, when finally feeling clean, he opened the duffel bag that was all the personal gear he'd brought with him to Montreal. His combat gear had gone back via Pendragon, leaving him with the sparse selection of clothes in the bag. He had one spare shirt, already worn once but mostly clean, and the suit he had worn to fly there.

David looked at the sparse pile of clothing dissatisfiedly and decided to go shopping.

————

SEVERAL HOURS LATER, David returned to his hotel room with several bags full of clothes, and wearing a new coat that the saleswoman had assured him looked "amazing" on him.

It was a shoulder-to-ankle duster of heavy navy blue wool. Six small but heavy silver buttons closed the front of the duster, and he was surprised at the freedom of movement he had while wearing the full-length coat.

Under it, he wore a brand-new pair of black jeans and a dark scarlet sweater, proof against the late autumn mountain chill. He looked, he realized with a wry grin as he looked in the mirror, like the stubbled and long-coated heroes of bad action movies.

A newly purchased razor, however, made short work of the stubble. He'd discovered while shopping that he'd not only been paid by ONSET since starting work, the bank had already processed the payment for his old house. The number of digits on his bank balance was surprising to the small-town cop that still lurked somewhere deep inside him.

Cleanly shaven, showered and wearing new clothes, David finally felt fully human for the first time in a couple of days. His watch and the dark sky outside told him it was evening, almost nine o'clock.

He left the hotel into the fading remnants of a Colorado sunset. Rather than catching a taxi anywhere, he walked over to the grassy verge between the hotel and the road. The smells of cooking wafted on the air as he looked over at the strip mall of restaurants on the opposite side of the road. Cars and pedestrians passed both ways, the noise traveling far through the streetlight-broken darkness.

Turning away from the restaurants, his path took him north to the club his hotel had given him a discount ticket for. After the week he'd had, David wanted a drink.

———

MAJESTIC HAD LEFT A TRACKER PROGRAM, hooked in to several hotel and airline databases, watching for David White's name. He was her only link to the secret she was nibbling around the edge of, and her curiosity was driving her crazy.

She'd been out for the day, and when she returned home in the evening, her computer was flashing multiple hits on that program. One glance at the locations, and her heart leapt into her throat. Denver.

Here. She knew the hotel he was booked at. She'd used to *work* there. Now she could find a way to reach White. Majestic was a *superb* hacker and had learned a thousand tricks of the trade. By now, she'd coded up a program that she was almost certain could get her through that security node's ungodly defenses—but only from the other side.

With that thought, she began to start loading the ISP of the hotel in question. She'd cracked it before, so she was sure she could be into their systems by midnight at the latest.

She needed her program loaded into the conspiracy's own computers, and David White was the only person she knew with access to them.

———

DAVID WALKED up to the entrance of the medium-sized club to find the doors wide open with no line. It was only nine o'clock, and the bar was probably only barely open. A shining neon sign proclaimed that the Black Iron Club was open.

The bouncer at the front door eyed David up and down, obviously noting both his age and his muscular frame. David gave the man a raised eyebrow, and he then grunted, "Five bucks admission."

David gave the man the money and entered the club. It was less well lit than he was used to, and most of the lights seemed to be black lights. White-painted Celtic knotwork covered all of the walls at about head height. A scattering of dancers, all younger than him but still older than the late teens he'd expected, held down the lowered dance pit as David skirted it to get to the bar.

He took a seat at the bar and ordered a shot of whiskey. With the lack of customers, he got it almost immediately and shot it back. His second was ordered on the rocks, and he turned to watch the rest of the club as he drank it.

Over the course of the next two hours, the club slowly filled up. A good portion of the crowd appeared heavily into black and silver. The reminder of the vampires from Charlesville resulted in two more quick shots, in addition to a regular metronome of a whiskey on the rocks every fifteen minutes.

David knew the bartender was watching him, as he'd had a *lot* to drink, and didn't care. His hotel was five minutes' walk away, and the whiskey was good. He could afford to drink.

"Can you still stand after that?" a soft feminine voice asked after he'd taken the two quick shots.

David looked up at the speaker to find a tall dark-skinned woman looking at him. She was both taller and slimmer than him, with soft brown eyes gazing down at where he sat on the stool. Her black hair, only slightly darker than her skin, was braided around her head like a crown, silver hairpins holding it up. His eyes continued to track down, to her high breasts, mostly exposed by an elegant silver-ribbed red-and-black corset over a floor-length flowing black skirt.

Wordlessly and calmly, he rose smoothly to his feet and pulled the stool next to him out from the bar. With his Sight activating without a thought, he sensed her amusement and willingness as he gently took her by her bare arm and guided her to the stool. Her skirt flared out as she sat, revealing stiletto-heeled boots that continued higher up her legs than he could see.

He then retook his seat and smiled at the...lady. She was definitely *not* a girl, with the slight lines on her face suggesting her to be nearly his own age. While her clothes were in the same vein as the clothes worn by the younger women in the bar, hers took the ideal to a much higher degree of sophistication.

"May I buy you a drink?" he asked after finishing his current whiskey.

"That you may," she conceded with a wink. "My name is Jasmine, by the way," she offered.

"David," he replied, his brain somewhat fuzzy. "What would you like?" he asked. A part of his brain suggested that he probably *shouldn't* be buying a girl a drink in a bar, but the rest replied that he'd made no commitment to Angela other than to phone her.

"That whiskey looks fine," she replied, and he ordered two more whiskeys on the rocks.

They spoke of inconsequential things for a few minutes as they drank. His Sight meant that he *knew*, without a doubt, what she was after, but there was no reason to push the fact.

When the whiskeys were finally done, Jasmine rose to her feet and offered him her hand. "Shall we dance?"

Smoothly, belying the copious amounts of alcohol he'd consumed, David rose to his feet to join her. She took him out onto the dance floor as a slower song started and the crowd paired off. Jasmine closed into his arms and pressed her breasts against him. Parts of his brain shut off as blood rushed to a lower portion of his body, and her smirk suggested that she knew *exactly* what she'd just done to him.

They danced wordlessly, and David's hands slid down her back to rest naturally on the curves of her ass. She made no complaint, only expanding her smirk and pressing slightly harder against him.

When the song finally came to an end, Jasmine rested her head on his shoulder and flicked his ear with her tongue.

"You're in the hotel next door?" she questioned.

He nodded, not trusting himself to answer verbally.

"Let's go."

Angela never crossed his mind.

———

THEY MADE their way back to his hotel room hand in hand like giddy teenagers. The darker, soberer part of David's mind had no illusions about the likely duration of this encounter, but the protesting voice was buried under whiskey, and the rest of him didn't care.

When they entered his hotel room and he turned on the light, Jasmine gave a cry of delight at the sight of the Jacuzzi. She turned and leapt on David, pressing her chest against his and her lips against his as they kissed for the first time.

Her tongue quested across his lips for a moment, and he returned the favor as he closed and locked the door behind them. They parted finally, breathless, and eyed each other, momentarily shy.

"Can we use the Jacuzzi?" the woman asked, her lips slightly parted.

David glanced at the time, and then realized he didn't care if it was nearly midnight. He wanted this woman, and that meant anything was kosher.

"Sure," he replied. He crossed to the white tub, discarding the navy blue duster beside the door as he did, and turned on the water. He took several moments to ensure the temperature of the water entering the tub was just right, and then turned around to look back at Jasmine.

She had shed the corset and long skirt while his back was turned, and stood before him a goddess in knee-high boots. He drank in the sight of her for a long moment before crossing to her.

They kissed passionately, fervently as they undressed, until David pulled back and gestured for her to precede him into the Jacuzzi.

———

IT WAS JUST after midnight when Majestic finally broke into not merely the hotel's computers but also their security system. Cross-referencing the guest list with the security system, she loaded the camera to White's room.

For a long moment, the hacker simply sat there, watching what she'd found. In the scene shown, the police officer she was looking for was not alone. A black woman was also in the room, sharing a bubbling Jacuzzi for a purpose other than getting clean.

There was no sound over the camera, and Majestic was grateful for that. She suspected that the rooms next to White's were getting quite the earful.

Emotions warred in the hacker's mind Part of her sparked with lust at the sight of the couple's lovemaking, and another part with inexplicable anger at the woman in the hotel room.

She shook her head against the emotions and began to check for the information she needed. A smile crossed the hacker's face as she found the emergency alert feed to the room's computer. She could override that to turn the TV on and carry *her* signal.

More checks brought up the phone line, and pre-set up a program to make sure the hotel's phones carried no record of her call. With her having an unknown amount of time to have everything ready for the morning, Majestic threw herself thoroughly into her preparations and planning.

Anything, after all, to distract herself from the realization that, after months of obsessively pursuing this man for entirely intellectual reasons, it had been a *long* time since anyone bent *her* over anything like that.

[26]

MICHAEL WALKED INTO CHARLES'S LAIR TO THE UNEXPECTED SIGHT OF IT having been converted into a mass computing center. Half a dozen skinny young men and a trio of young women had set up tables and laptops scattered around the large and comfortable den under the Campus.

All of the laptops were connected to power bars and ran blue Ethernet cables over to the massive computing setup Charles used to surf the internet. The dragon and Morgen Dilsner were by the dragon's "desk", talking quietly.

"Michael!" Morgen shouted loudly as soon as he realized the Commander was in the room. "Come join us."

Michael crossed the den, noting as he passed the slight ozone smell and a chill in the air. The latter was explained when he noticed the plastic piping connecting the air-circulation vents with two massive air conditioning units set up in front of Charles's bookshelves, now covered in white sheets to protect them. Instead of cooling the laptops and, yes, the server towers he now saw had been tucked under the tables, they'd decided to try and freeze the room.

"Where *did* you get this drive?" Morgen asked, gesturing at the central section of Charles's setup, where Michael saw that the hard drive Rodriguez had given him was hooked up with some large cables.

"I can't say," the werewolf replied gruffly, a little intimidated by the sheer mass of computing power—machine and otherwise—in the room. "But it looks interesting."

"We broke intar the first layer of encryption six hours ago," Charles said softly—for him. The room rumbled with his voice, and Michael blinked at the incongruity of the perfectly pronounced technical term in the midst of the thick brogue.

"What did we find?" the Commander demanded, then paused as he fully translated Charles's statement. "First layer?"

"Whoever encrypted this thing was good," Morgen explained grimly as he walked over to a human-sized keyboard and mouse by Charles's setup. He brought up something on the screen, a single icon, and then double-clicked it.

Michael examined the resulting screen for a moment and shrugged. "Looks like Outlook to me," he confessed. He couldn't tell any difference between this and any other email program.

"That's what was under the first encryption layer," his hacker replied. "An email program and an archive of about nine years of emails. The major keywords showing up were references to the Catholic Church, a mother, a sister and a brother. Looked like a senior Catholic official's personal email."

Michael nodded slowly, unwilling to say more. He wasn't sure how much his people would be able to guess about the source of the disk from analyzing it, but he'd promised Rodriguez not to reveal it himself.

"The first encryption was very high-grade commercial software with some customization," Dilsner continued. "However, it was one most of us here"—he gestured at the small crowd of cryptographers still working away as the techno-Mage explained things to the boss —"had broken for practice. So, it only took us sixteen-odd hours to break once we'd pulled all this together."

"But all you found was his personal email?" Michael asked, disappointed.

"That's what 'tis supposed tae look like we found," Charles replied softly.

"The emails were from Prelate Ambrose," Morgen said quietly. "Which I'm sure you knew," he added before continuing. "In a casual look-up of the name, we found out three very interesting facts.

"One, Prelate Ambrose *has* no sister—never has. Two"—the Mage counted off the points on his fingers—"his mother has been dead for six years. Lastly, his brother's *name* is never mentioned in these emails. In fact, no one is mentioned by name."

"As soon a' we took tae looking, we find doubled-up messages," Charles continued for Morgen. "'Twere all a lie, a fake."

"So we looked at the 'email archive,'" Morgen finished. "The entire damned thing is a carefully generated cover for the encrypted data. What's underneath is an encryption we've never seen. However," he continued, raising a finger, "the email program has done us one bit of good—it *is* the decryption software. Once we find the key, we'll have the whole kit and caboodle."

"How long will that take?" Michael asked.

The hacker shrugged and gestured at the laptops and towers set up in the room. "We have an ungodly amount of computing power running through thousands of possible keys on hundreds of copies of the original data every second as we speak. Every minute or so, it'll pop up a possible, and we'll take a look, and maybe use it to refine our testing sequence. We'll keep getting closer until we get it."

"How long?" the werewolf, who was perfectly willing to admit his lack of real technical skill, repeated.

"We could strike lucky and have it today," Morgen said quietly. "But we could also have to run through every possible key permutation. It's a multi-terabyte key, Michael—*thousands* of characters. Each time we find even one bit, it cuts our time down by eight, but we could still be looking at weeks—possibly months. Anyone without our... advantages would be looking at *years*."

"Keep working," Michael ordered, and Dilsner gave him a dirty look.

———

DAVID WOKE UP ALONE, and for a moment, he didn't remember anything of the night before. Then the smell of sex and perfume hanging through the hotel room hit him, and he bolted upright as memory returned.

The other side of the bed was empty, without even a note. Only the scent and the slightly damp impression of Jasmine's form in the bed suggested it had not all been a dream.

The ONSET Agent sank his aching head into his hands. Apparently, he'd done a little too well at drinking to try and forget what had happened. He'd forgotten all about Angela, and now sparks of guilt drove against his conscience. While they'd made no commitments to each other, David White wasn't the kind of man to take that as a license to fool around.

Jasmine had obviously left not long after they'd finished having sex, and he doubted she'd slept at all, simply waited for him to fall asleep. It wasn't, he reflected, as if he'd had any illusions about the nature of the encounter, but it still seemed…rude.

With a grunt of pain, David turned to stand up. As he did, a crackling pop sounded as the TV turned on. Blinking against his hangover, David saw that the screen showed an oddly greenlit view of familiar-looking scene: a security checkpoint—metal detector, glass booth. The room shown was empty.

That didn't last. Even as David began to wonder what was going on, a stream of six figures, eerily silent in the film, moved onto the camera. They ignored the metal detector, which went off at their studded clothing as they passed through.

When the lead figure reached the door shown in the video and ripped it off without slowing, David realized what he was watching. The room was familiar because he'd been in it only a couple of months before. This was the warehouse in Charlesville where his life had turned upside down.

The video then changed, cut by an unknown editor, to the inside of the warehouse. Struts and racks of crates and pallets shone an eerie green in the light-gathering optics of the camera. So did the silver studs on the vampire punks who'd sneaked in there.

David watched his own figure—recognizably so, as the image

zoomed in on his face when he appeared—enter the camera's view. Bound in place, both by his hangover and by the impossibility of what he was watching, he watched the ensuing battle. He winced as he watched his arms being broken and then saw the men and women of ONSET Nine inexplicably descend through the presumably solid roof.

On the video, he saw Michael transform into a werewolf and Kate throw flames from her fingers. Things that everyone knew were impossible and even a cursory scan of the tape would likely show were not special effects.

The video ended, just as the black-clad figure David thought was Morgen left the room, presumably heading to attempt to prevent just this kind of tape from being left.

Before David could gather his thoughts at all, the hotel room phone rang. He stared at it, numb with the shock of watching his own brutal induction to the world of the supernatural as ONSET had seen it.

The phone rang twice more before he finally grabbed the presence of mind to take the receiver and answer it.

"Yes," he said flatly, wondering what would be on the other end.

"David White," a crisp mechanical voice said flatly. It wasn't a recording or a computer generation, he didn't think, but it definitely wasn't a human voice either.

"You saw our tape," the voice continued. "We also have original, unedited files from the warehouse. If you do not do as we ask, those files and this tape will be forwarded to the Associated Press, where they will cause questions to be asked that your new employers would almost certainly dislike."

"I...I don't know what you're talking about," David told the voice, desperately trying to lie.

"You do," the voice replied, still flat and mechanical. "You encountered vampires in that warehouse, which you demonstrated superhuman strength and speed in combating. Those who rescued you employed blatant magic and shapeshifting. These are not mundane happenings.

"After these happenings, you were recruited by the group that rescued you," the voice continued. "We want to know what this group is."

"You want me to answer twenty questions?" David asked, still trying to recover his mental balance. An hour ago, he'd believed no one outside the Omicron Branch knew any of the true details of the incident in Charlesville. Now that safe assumption was shattered.

"No," the voice answered. "We desire more information than you can readily supply us and from more reliable sources. There has been a package left for you with the hotel's front desk. It contains a USB drive. You will smuggle this drive into your new employers' headquarters and place it in any computer. It will run automatically. Once done, you will destroy the drive."

"And if I refuse?" David asked, considering the level of betrayal they were asking of him. He had *no* idea what was on that drive. He could be agreeing to upload a virus to destroy ONSET's computer system. This strange voice had a threat against Omicron, but it wasn't much of one against David himself.

"If the drive has not been run in one of your computers within fourteen days," the flat voice said harshly, "these files will be forwarded to a man at the Associated Press who will take them with the seriousness they deserve...and they will be sent from your email account. Your employers will believe *you* betrayed them."

David didn't answer the voice for a long time. He didn't know how ONSET would handle the betrayal of one of their own, but somehow, he didn't think it would be with a slap on the hand and a hundred-dollar fine. If these people *could* do something like that, they could very well destroy everything he'd done with ONSET—have him driven out of the one place he could fit in now.

But he also knew ONSET. He knew their resources in the affairs he'd dealt with, the skill and level of technology they brought to bear on issues. He doubted that anyone could deceive Omicron's investigators for long enough to damage him.

"Go to hell," he said thickly. "No one would believe the tapes, or your deception. You won't get the chance, either. Run," he instructed, "hide. But we are Omicron—and we *will find you*."

"I doubt that," the voice told him. "*We* are Majestic. You have fourteen days."

Then the line cut off with a click.

———

AFTER KILLING the phone line connection, Majestic spent a moment eyeing the naked form of the police officer on the video feed she was watching as she cursed. Who was *he* to threaten *her*? Even as she watched, however, he was grabbing a cellphone.

Suddenly afraid, she took one last glance at White, who was now dialing a number, and disconnected the video feed. She then set her mind to the task of erasing every trace of her presence in the system as quickly as possible.

With that done, she leaned back in her chair and considered. A friend, who had no idea what Majestic did for a living, had dropped off the USB drive at the front desk for her. She couldn't risk prying closely enough to see if he'd picked it up, but she doubted the agent would. Somehow, she'd thought he'd be more vulnerable to that threat.

Now she'd failed. Other options had to be considered, and Majestic was angrier than she'd ever been. She knew she couldn't be tracked— but these were the same people who had that impenetrable server. Fear touched her as much as anger.

This was White's doing. She was going to find a way to punish him for it. And there was *always* a way. Slowly controlling her emotions, Majestic brought up her file of research on White. The direct approach had failed, but that didn't mean there weren't other approaches.

———

DAVID SAT on the edge of the messy hotel bed for a long time, ignoring the tangle of sheets and blankets around and behind him. He'd never before had anyone attempt to blackmail him, and the attempt had shocked him to his core.

Reporting it to his superiors had been the right thing to do, and they'd told him to stay put while they tried to track down the source of the phone call and the video feed he'd received.

He hoped they could track it down. If that video reached the news... He shuddered. There were a lot of people out there like his father, and the video showed his face very clearly. He'd never be able to leave the Campus again without being seen as some kind of freak.

His cell phone rang, and he answered it quickly.

"White."

"Agent White, this is Inspector Hill with OSPI Internet Security," the voice on the other side said calmly. "Your report was forwarded to us and we just swept the hotel computers remotely. I have a team heading over to request physical access, but we couldn't find *anything*."

To his astonishment, David was sure he could hear a hint of doubt in the Inspector's voice. Without his Sight, however, David was no judge of people and couldn't quite tell.

"They covered their tracks?"

"It appears so," the Inspector confirmed. "As I said, I have a team en route. I'd suggest you clear out of there, however. We'll contact you if we need you."

David sat on the bed for a long moment, looking at the cell phone. He wasn't entirely sure the Inspector believed he wasn't crazy or making this up, but at least he'd reported it.

With a sigh, David called the airport to book a flight back to Colorado Springs. His holiday had just become much less entertaining.

———

ANGER HAD NEVER BEEN something to distract Majestic. It was something that drove her, made her focus. Now she dug through her research on David White, looking for the vulnerability that her intuition told her had to be there.

It didn't take her long to find. After all, she'd been tracking his emails all along. She knew that the only person he corresponded with even semi-regularly through his personal email was Darryl Hanson—his old police chief.

Finding Hanson's computer proved more difficult than she'd expected. Finally, she tracked down his ISP—a small company specializing in rural internet—and found his connection.

Her utilities and tricks got her through his firewall, too. It was harder than it should have been, a lot harder, but Majestic didn't consider herself the best for nothing. Once in, she took a moment to analyze the firewall. It shared features and coding with that black server that had crashed her. Not as powerful but an earlier form of the same code. She was on the right track.

Attaching a worm to an email was child's play for a hacker—literally. It was what stupid children who wanted to be hackers did. Attaching a worm to an email coming from a white-listed address so that the most powerful firewall she'd ever seen missed it and it ran without the user ever even knowing it existed...*that* was the kind of thing you needed a hacker like Majestic for.

Most notably, the worm wasn't on its own email. It would wait until Hansen sent an email of his own, and then piggyback itself on that email through these bastards' firewall.

Then, *then*, let David White think he'd beaten her just by being stubborn!

27

DAVID RETURNED TO AN EMPTY DORMITORY. MOST OF ONSET NINE WAS still away, busy with their vacation or other time away from the Campus. It was Thursday night, and the team wouldn't go back on active duty until Monday.

He thanked the driver for getting him home and carried his own bags upstairs. These days, his major limitation with carrying suitcases was the number of handles he could hold. His two newly purchased suitcases, with their newly purchased contents, were no problem.

The sight of his old brown couches in his apartment living room was a relief, something familiar in his life even as his brain fought an internal war. He had no hesitation that he'd done the right thing, but Hill's attitude worried him.

Picking through his suitcase, a crinkling of paper caught his attention, and he pulled out the slip with Angela's phone number. He pulled up a tall wooden barstool to the kitchen counter and dropped the slip of paper and stared at it.

Jasmine had been a mistake; he knew that. Alcohol and frustration and loneliness combined with an opportunity, and he'd taken it. Angela wouldn't approve. He doubted she'd hold it against him, but *he* did.

He'd liked the Canadian woman, he really had. He had *no* idea, however, what to do about that. The life he'd chosen wasn't going to let him get up to Canada often, and he doubted the RCMPP were much for letting their people to leave the country either.

It was something he'd have to think about, and he tucked the number into a drawer on his desk. Putting the thought aside with the paper, he booted his computer up. Before he'd left, Chief Hansen had promised him pictures of the annual Fireman's Fall Ball fireworks in Charlesville.

Opening his email found the Chief's email sitting there amidst a scattering of spam. A few moments later, he was downloading the pictures of the fireworks and wondering why it was taking so long.

———

THE WORM PINGED a server Majestic had rented in Russia for just this purpose thirteen hours after it had been placed on Chief Hansen's computer. With no idea of when the email would go through, she was busy doing something completely different when the little icon popped up in her screen, informing her it had made contact.

Apologizing to the other members of her guild, she dropped out of the raid and logged off the server. This was far more important than the game.

The blinking icon linked to a program screen that listed the details of the connection with the agent. It was coming from inside the firewall and had user access inside. It couldn't give her much of a channel past that black security node, but it was a channel.

Now she had access to the systems behind it. Now she had a chance.

With a smile of pleasure that the mere video game she'd been playing could never match, Majestic began to warm up programs. The first step was to give herself permanent access through that black-wall security. Then she'd move on to other things, like digging for the information this strange conspiracy wanted to conceal—and she therefore wanted to know.

28

SATURDAY MORNING SAW MICHAEL ARRIVING IN CHARLES'S LAIR WITH A carrying tray full of large, steaming-hot cups of coffee. It had become something of a daily ritual now, helping him keep up to date with their process. While the scent of the liquid tar Morgen and his fellow sysadmins and cryptographers preferred as coffee bothered Michael's oversensitive nose, he had to admit they deserved the coddling right now.

At seven thirty, the entirety of the ten-human and one-dragon team was assembled in the dragon's cavernous layer, but Michael realized they weren't running the same program as before. Now they were all...paging through text?

"Michael!" Morgen greeted him, scooping a cup of coffee as the werewolf put the tray down on Charles's table. "I was about to call you. We broke it."

"The encryption?!" Michael demanded, fully focusing on the techno-Mage. "When? How?"

"About"—Morgen checked his watch—"twenty-six minutes ago. And as for how, Dorian!"

At the Mage's bark, a pale-skinned youth with a shaved head and a tiny tattoo of a crucifix over each eyebrow joined them.

"Sir!" Dorian greeted Michael with a snappy salute, only slightly marred by the wince as the cup of coffee in his hand slopped onto his forehead.

"Tell him the key," Morgen instructed.

Dorian grabbed a book from the worktable behind Morgen and handed it to Michael. The book was small, with very fine pages and a thick cover, and Michael had opened it to the bookmark before realizing it was a Bible. He skimmed down the page, but the words were only somewhat familiar, and he looked up at the others questioningly.

"It's in Latin," the shaved and tattooed sys-admin told him. "Isaiah fourteen, verses twelve through twenty."

Michael blinked at the text in front of him, and then slowly closed the book. "Well done," he said slowly. "How did you recognize it?"

The tattooed man, who Michael realized was probably in his late thirties, shrugged. "I was in a seminary to be a Catholic Priest once," he admitted. "I kept up the study, even after they kicked me out for sleeping with a nun."

"Do you have the English version?" the Commander asked slowly, deciding to ignore the excessive explanation.

Morgen grabbed an open copy of the Bible from his own workstation with a nod and a grin and handed it to Michael. The Mage had been less respectful of the book than his ex-priest co-worker, and the relevant passage stood out in yellow highlighter.

12: How you are fallen from heaven,
O Day Star, son of Dawn!
How you are cut down to the ground,
you who laid the nations low!
13: You said in your heart,
'I will ascend to heaven;
I will raise my throne
above the stars of God;
I will sit on the mount of assembly
on the heights of Zaphon;
14: I will ascend to the tops of the clouds,
I will make myself like the Most High.'
15: But you are brought down to Sheol,
to the depths of the Pit.

16: Those who see you will stare at you,
and ponder over you:
'Is this the man who made the earth tremble,
who shook kingdoms,
17: who made the world like a desert
and overthrew its cities,
who would not let his prisoners go home?'
18: All the kings of the nations lie in glory,
each in his own tomb;
19: but you are cast out, away from your grave,
like loathsome carrion,
clothed with the dead, those pierced by the sword,
who go down to the stones of the Pit,
like a corpse trampled underfoot.
20: You will not be joined with them in burial,
because you have destroyed your land,
you have killed your people.

"The Day Star in question is sometimes translated as Lucifer, or Satan," Dorian explained as Michael finished reading the passage. "The verse is considered one of the sources of the story of his fall."

"It seems our Prelate had a bit of a high opinion of himself, even as he knew he was a traitor," Morgen said quietly.

"It also shows some sense of guilt, I would guess," Michael replied slowly. "Should help the church interrogate him."

"Nobody's interrogating him now," Morgen said.

"Yes, they are," Michael said grimly. "They shipped him back to Rome to face trial and interrogation."

"Didn't you hear?" Morgen asked. "The Spanish Guardia Civil's coastal department just announced it last night—Prelate Ambrose and a number of his staff and other priests were killed when their chartered plane went down in the middle of the Atlantic last week."

A chill ran through the werewolf. He *hadn't* heard that. Somehow, he doubted that it was mere accident that had crashed the plane carrying every single one of Monsignor Rodriguez's prisoners. A surprisingly large part of him was suddenly thankful that the Papal Investigator had missed that flight to meet with Michael.

"Both of ye," Charles suddenly rumbled. "Come take a look ae this."

Morgen and Michael crossed to the dragon, who was quickly assembled a montage of communications and documents across his huge screens.

"Ai think we found this just in time," the dragon said grimly as his claws gently used the mouse to highlight portions of text. "The Black Sun are planning something big—tomorrer. And if I read this right, it sounds like they're summoning a daemon. A big 'un."

Michael's gaze skimmed across the highlighted portions of the documents, detailing a date, a time, personnel, equipment, supplies and abilities to be present. ONSET knew more about what was necessary to summon a demon than many of the idiots who tried to do so. He *knew* what those supplies were used for—and the date was tomorrow!

"Where is it?" he demanded, but the dragon shook his head.

"Compile this and send it to Major Warner," Michael ordered sharply. "Let her know I'm on my way up. And find me *where* they're holding this damned ritual!"

———

WARNER WAS WAITING when Michael arrived, reading over the file the cryptography squad had sent upstairs, and gestured to one of the plush chairs she kept for official meetings. Michael took the chair and waited, eyeing the flags and painting behind the Major as she finished the document.

"This is bad," she said quietly after finishing it. "With the supplies and people they've gathered, we're looking at possibly the largest summoning ritual attempted in North America—and its being done by a group with protection as a bona fide religion."

"That hasn't stopped us before," Michael said flatly.

"No," she agreed. "And it won't this time, either. But we'll have to bounce this up to Colonel Ardent for approval. It may even end up with the Committee—possibly the President."

"Ma'am, we have less than thirty hours before it was *scheduled*,"

Michael reminded her. "We don't know where it is and we don't know if they'll have changed it, knowing that Ambrose was arrested."

"It may be that knowing about this is why Ambrose died," Warner told him softly. "They may have counted on everything being aboard that plane. *However* you got that hard drive, it possibly saved this information from being lost."

And saved Rodriguez from dying on that plane, Michael reflected.

"Thirty hours is barely enough time to put together a strike force as it is," he observed. "If we wait until we have the go-ahead, we could be scrambling at the last minute. And we may need authorization to violate civilian computers to *find* the damn ritual."

"Agreed," the Major answered. "Let Dilsner know he's cleared to do whatever it takes—I'll have a court order to him within the hour. I want *you* to get into contact with Major Anderson with the Anti-Paranormals and with OSPI. We don't have many ONSET teams free right now, so we'll need mundane personnel to make up the gap."

"How many teams can I pull?" Michael asked.

"We're stripped to the bone right now," Warner said slowly. "I need to keep a reserve here for other emergencies, and most of our active teams are getting dragged down by one brush fire or another. Your team is just back from their week off, correct?"

"They should all be in as of this morning," he confirmed.

"I don't think we can free up anything beyond ONSET Nine," she told him grimly. "On the other hand, it doesn't look like we should expect any major supernatural resistance, so one ONSET team, with Anti-Paranormals and maybe OSPI security teams supporting you, should be enough."

"I can't say I like it," Michael said, thinking. "But if it's what I've got, I can work with it. We need that go-ahead as soon as possible," he reminded her.

"Then we both have work to do," she replied. "You go do your job and I'll do mine."

———

MAJESTIC HAD SPENT the two days after David had opened the email setting up her access into her target systems very, very carefully. Once she'd done so, she slipped in and starting looking for data. She hit an internal security wall almost instantly—her worm was in a personal computer, after all. That didn't take long to circumvent, and she was soon in the main system.

The first thing she noticed was a complete paucity of system administrators. Normally, a secure system had dozens of them, many ex-hackers. She found none in this system right off the bat, and that made her go looking.

All of the system admin–level accounts were logged into one area of the network. While that area looked juicy, with some odd computing setups, she made a mental note to avoid it until the admins had separated out more. She had no desire to charge into the lion's den like that.

Not when there was *so* much else to look through! The internal security on the system was still pretty tight, but nothing compared to what she'd broken through to get there. Quickly, layer after layer of security opened before her as she dug into the files.

The documents she found lacked context. References to "Omicron", "OSPI", "ONSET", and other items went completely over her head. As she began to read through, Majestic began to build a mental image of the context as she slowly assembled enough information to build herself a fake user on the system.

Once she was done, anything she did would appear to originate from a terminal well inside the facility—and she now knew that she was accessing the computers of a covert facility called the "ONSET Headquarters Campus".

Using that datum as a search point, she found the Campus's electronic library, and a whole new world opened before her eyes. Everything she'd suspected and feared after finding those videos was true.

Vampires, werewolves, superhuman police officers, it all hung together in a framework the files in that library neatly provided—especially to someone to whom the classification levels were irrelevant.

It really was the biggest secret of the century, and now Majestic knew it. And because she knew it, she began to understand why it was secret. She might think this was amazing and cool, but even she found some of the information terrifying. The world wouldn't take knowing all this well at all.

Majestic knew, instinctively, that she was smarter than most of the human race. She also knew she could handle this knowledge better than that same most of the human race.

Now she had that knowledge. She shared the secret the government had tried so hard to hide, and she knew, beyond any doubt, that she would never tell another living soul what she'd found.

29

DAVID SPENT MOST OF HIS WEEK EITHER HOLED UP IN HIS APARTMENT OR exercising like crazy in the Campus's gyms. Leila Stone had invited him to join her and some other off-duty officers for dinner one night, but he'd pled paperwork and begged off.

Most of the team had returned on Friday night, and Kate had come by, knocking on his door to see if he was there. They'd had a short, quiet conversation, but he'd eased away from his concerns about Angela. Somehow, he didn't feel that Kate wanted to know.

He knew that there was always a time limit of sorts on how long you waited for someone to call, and that he was rapidly approaching it. However, he still wasn't comfortable with the thought. Even if things did work out, she was a long way away.

David passed the remainder of his time off in an almost teenage state of pre-relationship anxiety.

———

DAVID ENTERED the ground floor of the dormitory to find the common room occupied only by Akono and Bourque. Bourque had CNN playing on the TV, and Akono was sitting in a corner, creating and releasing various strange visions with his glamors.

He gave both of them a nod and settled on a second couch to watch the news with Bourque. Not much was happening in the world that morning, apparently, but it helped pass the time as other members of the team slowly drifted down.

Kate greeted David with a quiet "Hi, David, how was your trip to Denver?" as she settled onto the opposite side of the couch from him.

"All right," he answered carefully. "I got some shopping done, picked up some new suits so I can look the part of the Man in Black better."

Kate giggled. In her skirt and knit sweater, David couldn't think of anything less like the archetypal Man in Black than Kate Mason, but, like him, that's exactly what she was.

"You look so out of place in a suit," she teased him, relaxing slightly, and he rewarded her with a smile as she began to break down his bad mood.

Kate made it easy to forget his worry about Angela and join in the banter of the team as the others gathered around. Soon, only Morgen and Michael were missing, and the team knew they were waiting to hear from Michael what their week's assignment would be.

Morgen drifted in from outside around nine thirty in the morning, his hair unkempt, his shirt food-stained, generally looking like he'd been awake for days. Kate was the first to express that opinion.

"You look like shit," she said calmly.

"You try running on caffeine and magic for a week without sleep," he retorted. "Someone wake me up when Michael gets here; let him know we found it if he hasn't checked his email by then."

He ignored further attempts to communicate as he carefully walked up the stairs to his apartment. The rest of the team eyed each other uncertainly. David found himself wondering if the hacker spending his "off" week running without sleep was normal. Everyone else looked just as confused as he did.

"Anyone have the feeling something strange is going on?" David finally asked.

"Yes," Akono said simply. "The only item usually capable of

keeping Morgen awake for a week at a time is a new video game, and he plays those *in* his apartment."

Silence slowly enveloped the common room's occupants. Only the TV newscaster, now reduced to a low volume, made any noise as the team slipped unconsciously into waiting mode.

After about half an hour, the group slowly dispersed to take up activities. No one left the common room, and all of the activities were inconsequential. Bourque knitted. Kate pulled out a pink handheld game console. Ix pulled a book out of thin air that a moment's inspection revealed to be a "bodice-ripper" romance novel. Akono went back to practicing his glamors.

David grabbed the TV remote and began channel-surfing. Nothing that was on could hold his mind, and he continued to flip from channel to channel, hoping something would pop up.

Finally, just before noon, the door to the common room swung open and Michael walked in. The werewolf Commander looked grim, and all activity in the room stopped. As David turned the TV off, dead silence descended on the room as every member of ONSET Strike Team Nine turned their gaze on their commanding officer.

"Where's Morgen?" Michael asked.

"He said to tell you 'we found it', then went upstairs to sleep," Ix volunteered, his romance novel having disappeared back into thin air. "Something about running on magic and caffeine for a week," the red-skinned demon added.

"Fair enough," the werewolf grunted. "Someone want to grab him? He's the one this is revolving on? As he said, he helped find it."

Kate nodded and went upstairs to collect her fellow Mage. When they returned, she leaned against the wall by the stairs, and Morgen, rubbing sleep from his eyes, claimed one of the wooden backed chairs in the room.

Michael looked around at all of them and then barked, "Now sit up and pay attention!"

It was, David reflected, an unusually unnecessary order. Every member of the team still had their full focus on Michael O'Brien.

Sure he had their attention, the Commander crossed to the flatscreen TV and booted up the computer tucked away behind it. He slotted a USB flash drive into it, and a few moments later, a black iron star, creepily familiar to David, popped up on the screen.

"Some of you saw this symbol after we took down that Catholic priest, Carderone," Michael told his people.

David had seen it later, too. Back home in Charlesville, a thought that still gave him the shivers. Both places he'd seen it, it had radiated pure evil.

"Now, the Elfin were also investigating Carderone, and they found this symbol was specifically associated with a group called the Church of the Black Sun," the Commander continued. "This is odd, as we found it on the personal belongings of a Catholic priest.

"The Catholic Church also found this odd, and it was one of the items they looked at when they investigated how Carderone managed to carry out his murders without being caught by the Church's internal authorities," he explained. "Their investigation was thorough—*very* thorough. My information is that they arrested a significant portion of the Ordo Longinus in North America."

David blinked at Michael in surprise. He knew that Rodriguez had been investigating the Church here, but he hadn't learned of the results of that investigation.

"Through various avenues, we acquired significant quantities of information from that investigation," Michael told them. "Sifting through that information, we came up with evidence suggesting that a massive demon-summoning ritual was being planned. However, despite the scale of the threat, we had no idea *where* until Dilsner ran a crosscheck. Why don't you explain it?" he asked, gesturing to the hacker.

Morgen looked tired but also thoroughly excited.

"While we were digging through the files on this ritual, we ran across a reference to Stellar Noir Shipping being the company making the delivery," he told them all. "This reminded me of some of the Elfin's investigation into Carderone—the funneling of funds that we followed to Montreal.

"The company that technically owned that warehouse was Stellar Noir Shipping," he explained. "I ran through a number of their ship-ment logs and managed to match up some of their outgoing shipment manifests with the manifests we had for the ritual. Thanks to the Familias Dresden, we now know that the Church of the Black Sun plans to summon their demon…here."

With Morgen's last word, Michael switched the image from the iron sun to an overhead image of what appeared to be a lodge of some kind. Snow on the ground around the lodge—in mid-autumn—suggested it to be northerly and high in the mountains.

"This is a hunting lodge, owned by a senior member of the Church of the Black Sun, in northern Washington State," the werewolf explained slowly, "about a hundred miles south of the Canadian border, and further from anything that can actually count as civilization. There is one road leading to it.

"According to the information we have, both the data on the Church and the files extracted in Montreal, the Black Sun has concentrated a massive stockpile of summoning supplies, multiple high and low Mages, and an unknown number of weapons at this lodge.

"They plan to summon into this world a demon called Ekhmez," Michael said finally. "We know almost nothing about him, but they believe his power will be unstoppable if they succeed." He paused and looked at the demon among their own ranks. "Ix, do you know him?"

The human-looking creature considered for a moment, running his long fingers along the ridge of horns across his forehead. "No," he finally admitted. "That doesn't mean much," he continued. "There are many demons beyond the Seal, and they're not exactly a bunch for remembering names—or even using the same names, often enough."

Michael nodded and turned back to the screen.

"We have to assume that their ritual is going ahead as planned," he told his people. "We are coordinating with OSPI on this mission, as ONSET currently only has this team and a company of Apes available."

"We're it?" Kate asked. "Isn't that a little underpowered?"

"Unless the ritual is completed, we don't expect heavy supernatural resistance," Michael replied. "We also have a full company of Anti-Paranormals—a hundred and sixty men, including their heavy weapons teams—and it looks like we'll have four platoon equivalents of OSPI's security people, as well as the SSTTR team. That's over three hundred mundanes equipped to deal with the supernatural, and the Stutters' forty supernaturals.

"We're the spear point," he told his people, "but we're not doing all the work." He gestured to the map and clicked the mouse, and four flashing blue circles appeared on the screen, one of them on the road, the other three in the hills around the lodge.

"AP Company Six will be splitting their heavy weapons platoon into four components, each of which will be attached to an OSPI platoon and positioned at one of these locations. Their job," Michael said grimly, "is to make sure no one gets away."

"The Apes will be joining us on the ground. They will insert at the same points as the OSPI platoons by heavy-lift chopper at H-hour minus two and attempt to quietly encircle the lodge.

"At H-hour, we will launch a Pendragon-borne assault onto the lodge's roof as AP Six seizes the exits. Our task," the werewolf explained, "is to penetrate the ritual space and disrupt the ritual—if necessary, by killing all of the participants.

"We don't know where the ritual space is, and we do not currently have blueprints for the building," he admitted. "This is going to make our job harder."

That was an understatement in David's opinion. The lodge was three stories high and sprawled across an impressive area of ground for something built in so remote an area. Searching it room by room was going to suck.

"Do we have the sanction for that kind of force?" Bourque asked in response to the order to kill the ritual participants.

"That decision will be made as soon as the Committee of Thirteen gets together for an emergency meeting late this evening," Michael replied. "Until that session is over, we do not have a go on the mission. However, due to the necessity of the timeline, we will be rendezvousing with AP Six and the OSPI men in Washington within the hour. Pack your gear, people," he ordered. "We may get called back before we go in, but we are damned well going to be ready to go in!"

———

Dᴀᴠɪᴅ ᴡᴀs most of the way through loading up for the mission when he went to grab his M1911 and remembered that he didn't *have* it anymore. The old automatic had saved his life when Dresden had come at him, but it had ended up in two pieces and no one had been able to fix it.

"David," Michael barked, as he was looking at the empty spot in his locker that should have held his sidearm. "Come here."

The younger agent crossed to his Commander, carefully not noticing the languorous stretches Kate seemed to feel obligated to do where he could see them once she had the skintight combat suit on.

"Yes, sir?"

"Here, take this," his Commander ordered, handing him a black gunmetal case. "Meant to give it you before, but we haven't been on active duty since you lost your Colt."

David opened the case to reveal the futuristic lines of the Omicron Silver caseless sidearm. Michael then passed him four of the metal magazines that held the rounds and took the gun out, holding it carefully so David could see it all.

The gun consisted of a standard pistol grip, but the barrel had an angled shroud attached that cut down at thirty degrees and left just over an inch gap past the trigger. Two slits ran along the triangular barrel shroud, venting the gas to the side, and another curved over the top of the weapon.

"Magazine holds fourteen forty-five caliber caseless rounds and goes in the grip, like most other handguns," the werewolf grunted. "Watch your hands here and here," he said, pointing at the two vents on the side and the one on the top. "Gas vents mainly through the rear vent, canceling much of the recoil," he continued. "Still, the side vents get pretty hot. Do *not* touch the barrel shroud after burst fire."

David blinked. "Burst fire" wasn't a term he associated with a sidearm, but now he looked, the little switch on the side of the barrel had an extra position for ʙᴜʀsᴛ along with sᴀꜰᴇ and ʀᴇᴀᴅʏ. Burst fire from a .45 handgun wasn't something *he'd* want to try unless desperate, and would likely break an un-Empowered human's arm. He nodded his acceptance of the quick lesson and took the firearm from Michael.

Removing the old holster from his belt and replacing it was a matter of moments, and he slid the new magazines into the ammo pouch on the combat harness. The new sidearm now locked and loaded, he turned to look at Michael.

The werewolf Commander wasn't in harness like the rest of them, but he regarded them all calmly, with a bit of a twinkle in his eye, David thought.

"You'll be rendezvousing with AP Six and the OSPI personnel at an Omicron-owned covert facility in Montana—a leftover staging barracks from the Incursion," Michael told them. "I will meet you there by H-hour minus three at the absolute latest with the go or no-go from the Committee of Thirteen. Until I get there, Agent Mason is in command. Understood?"

David spared Kate a glance as he chorused "Yes, sir" with the rest of the team. The young Mage seemed only mildly perturbed at being placed in command of a team that was, to a man, woman and demon, older than her.

She caught his gaze and returned it levelly, without any of the small smiles she usually gave him. He quickly glanced away. Sometime while they were in Montreal, Kate had become somewhat colder with him. Still friendly—still friends, he was pretty sure—but still a little cool.

He wasn't sure what to make of that just yet.

30

THE PENDRAGON SET DOWN IN THE LAST FLEETING RAYS OF DAYLIGHT AS the sun descended behind a mountain to the west of them. The mostly dead grass around them rippled away from the draft as the rotors slowed to a halt and Akono turned the chopper's engines off.

ONSET Nine's members, faceless under black-fronted helmets, disembarked in the field. David shivered against the autumn chill as he and his fellows crossed to where a tall man in camouflage gear waved them over to him.

"Welcome to our base site for this little excursion," the gangling Asian man told them. "I'm Captain Narita, CO of Anti-Paranormal Company Six."

On closer inspection, David saw that Captain Narita looked cheery, but his face showed a story of wearing service. His left eye was clearly, to David's Empowered vision, made of glass, which fit with a long and ugly scar running from just in front of his left ear all the way over to his right cheekbone. A matching chunk was missing from his nose. The vast majority of the Anti-Paranormals, David suddenly remembered, were the remnants of the two divisions of Army and National Guard who'd been drafted to fight the Montana Incursion.

"Good to see you, Captain," Mason greeted him. While her face was invisible behind her faceplate, David could hear the smile in her voice.

"OSPI's heavy choppers will be arriving just after dawn," Narita reported as he led the way toward a number of prefab structures. "Their tactical platoons are with them. The Stutters came in by Pendragon about fifteen minutes ago."

David realized, taking a moment to look around, that several of the enchanted gunships occupied the snow-covered field. A chill breeze was beginning to sweep through the valley of the base site, and it was shifting enough of the camo fabric over the vehicles to allow someone with David's senses to count eight—nine, including Akono's—of the aircraft.

"The Pendragons will be playing air support tomorrow, with the exception of your delivery drop," the AP captain continued. "The Stutters will be going in with my ground element—can't say I'm not glad to have them! You ONSET boys and girls have your own job," he conceded, "but having Stutter's forty-odd supernaturals on the ground with us is a nice boost."

"Have you done any surveillance of the target site?" Bourque asked as the team followed the captain into a large central structure. Heated air hit them all like a brick wall, warm and muggy after the chill of the evening.

"We have four Predator drones running shifts, surveying the lodge," Narita responded. "One has been modified with thaumic detectors, and we've confirmed the presence of unusually large quantities of magic, including at least four true Mages."

"Those are our problem," Kate said grimly, gesturing for the team to sit down. The inside of the building was mainly set up as a cafeteria, with a command center taking up one corner of the room. The team and Captain Narita took over a table as they continued.

"Have you located the entrances?" David asked, wondering how the APs intended to insert three quarters of a company—a hundred and twenty men, give or take—into an admittedly large structure with standard doors, especially when ONSET Nine's Mages were going through the roof.

"We're not using them," the Captain replied with a grin. His scar twisted the cheerful expression, making it incredibly sinister. "My demo team is making up shaped charges as we speak. As I understand it, once we have the go-ahead, property damage is not on our list of concerns."

———

THE SUNSET THROUGH THE MOUNTAINS, David reflected later on, was beautiful. An eerie red glow now surrounded the peak the sun had sneaked behind on its final descent out of sight from the tiny valley they were using as a staging area for the mission.

Twilight had brought a further chill with it, and David was glad for the insulation in his combat armor. He'd found a suitably sized rock to watch the sunset from, to wait for the news in private.

Out here, only the wind and the occasional wolf howl disturbed him. Narita had sentries out, but the AP men were mostly at the southern end of the valley, where the company's trucks blocked a small dirt road that wove its way down toward Montana. No one was bothering him here, tucked away in a corner of the camp.

His rock stood at the edge of the cliff at the north end of the valley. Beneath him, a sheer face dropped over a thousand feet to a river valley below. He suspected too much time would have passed for him to call Angela when he got back to the Campus, and out here, he forced himself to face the reason why he hadn't called her.

He remembered her face after he'd killed Dresden. The mixed shock and horror. The *fear* at what he'd done—at what he was. That was what drove him away from his comrades tonight, he knew. The fear of what he had become.

They had all known for some time what they were and had adjusted to it. David wasn't used to it yet. He wasn't used to being supernatural, and he was afraid. Afraid of his own nature. Afraid of what his father would once have thought.

He didn't want to become a monster, and he was afraid that it would be all too easy. He'd already seen it—Carderone, given gifts beyond mortal men, turning them to an evil beyond mortal men as well. David White faced the night wind coming in over the lip of the cliff and faced his fear squarely. He was afraid of becoming like Carderone, twisted into evil by his own power. He couldn't deny it. He didn't know if he could *ever* overcome that fear, somehow prove to himself that he was not tempted. But at least today, he knew what he feared.

"To serve and protect," he whispered to the night air. His oath. His duty. If he failed at all other courses, if there was nothing else left to him, then there was that oath. That duty. *That* was his answer to his own fears. As long as he held to his oath, he *would not fail.*

David straightened from a slouch he hadn't even realized he'd sunk into and faced the biting wind. He remained afraid of what he would become. He would not deny that to himself now.

David White laughed. He understood his enemy now. Understanding didn't mean *victory*. It meant a fighting chance. David faced that bitterly cold wind and understood, for the first time, the battle he had to fight within himself to accept the choice he'd already made.

He *was* Empowered, and only by fully wielding the powers that he had discovered were his birthright could he truly serve and protect, as he'd sworn to do. As he must do, if he was to prove he was no monster.

David returned to the utilitarian barracks ONSET Nine was sleeping in to find Kate Mason, wrapped in a standard-issue blanket, sitting on a rock by the building, staring off across the calm alpine meadow.

He paused, behind her and out of her sight. Kate had been slightly more distant with him than usual since Montreal, though he wasn't sure why. From what he'd seen, she'd generally been quieter and more distant with everybody.

Whatever the reason, she was sitting out here in the cold, and David wondered just what was going on. He suspected it might be part of why she'd suddenly been placed in apparent second-in-command of the team.

"Penny for your thoughts," he said finally, approaching her from behind.

She started and turned to look at him. "I didn't hear you coming," she accused him.

"If I clomped around the way I used to, I'd give myself a headache," David observed. "Like I said, penny for your thoughts."

"Not sure I have change," the Mage replied. "Pull up a rock if you want, though."

David glanced around quickly, noting a major lack of appropriate rocks, before shrugging and settling on the ground. While the grass was cold, it was pretty dry.

"I hadn't realized you were out here," Kate told him as he sat.

"You weren't paying attention," David replied gently. "I left the barracks an hour ago."

"Damn," she said softly. "I wasn't at all, was I?" She looked away from David for a moment, staring across the meadow again. "It's been one hell of a week," she told him quietly. "Since Montreal."

"What happened?" David asked. The team hadn't talked much about Montreal while locked in that Canadian hospital, and when Kate had come back from her leave, she'd been closed off.

"The vampire I killed," she said softly. "He was a Mage too—a powerful one. I reached deeper than I ever had before to fight him. When it was done, I'd...changed."

"Changed?" David repeated. She looked the exact same to him, but the thought caused him to *look* at her, with his Sight. The instant he did, he knew what she meant. The pale blue color that wove through her aura marking her as a Mage was no longer pale. It now pulsed with a deep azure fire.

"What do you know about ranking among Mages?" Kate asked, and David blinked at the apparent non sequitur.

"Not much," he admitted.

"Ah," she said quietly. "Then this may take some explaining.

"We don't rank ourselves," she began. "It's not even really something we have control over. At a point in our lives, something happens. We become a Mage—a weak one, what the US College of Arcana calls a First Circle Initiate. Eventually, you meet a challenge and master it, growing more powerful and becoming a First Circle Master.

"It continues on this way for five Circles, Initiate and Master," she continued. "You can intentionally seek out a trial, but often life will bring you one."

"Like it's fated?" David asked.

"No..." Kate trailed off. "More like something recognizes what you've done and makes you stronger. Some...*awareness* at the core of the magic. We call it the Deep Magic."

"And this vampire Mage was one of your trials?" David asked, putting together the pieces.

"I accepted a while back that I was a Third Circle Initiate," Kate told him. "I'd tried to induce a trial with the College, which usually works if you're meant to be more powerful. It failed, which meant that an Initiate of Third was all I'd ever be.

"Then came Montreal, and the vampire, and suddenly I was a Third Circle Master—moving from mid-Class 3 supernatural on ONSET's classifications to borderline between Class 3 and Class 2."

"I...see," David said softly. And he did. That sort of change could easily be as shocking in its own way as, say, suddenly finding out you're a supernatural after thirteen years of adult life.

"When I reported to the College, they suggested I try to induce a trial again," she continued. "Sometimes, a spontaneously induced trial opens up new abilities."

Kate met David's gaze, and to his Sight, her eyes now glowed with azure flame.

"It worked, David," she told him. "Now I have to learn to master the magic of a Fourth Circle Initiate, and it scares me. And while I'm doing that, ONSET has decided I'm a Class 2 supernatural."

"Which means?"

"Which means I'm now a candidate to command an ONSET team," Kate told him. "Hence being left in command while Michael is gone. They're testing to see if I can cut it."

"Being in command overnight isn't a big deal," David reminded her. "You'd have to find some new and amazing way to screw up to create a problem overnight."

She laughed and gave him the same small smile he remembered.

"It's odd for you to be counseling me," she told him. "I forget that you're more experienced at the whole cop-and-leader shtick than most of us. I've been used to helping you adjust to our job."

"That's probably a good sign, you know," David said. "If you can convince *me* to accept being an ONSET agent, then I'm pretty sure you can convince ONSET agents to walk into hell. We're pretty easy to convince to do that," he added dryly.

———

THEY WERE all woken in the morning to the loud chatter of rotors as ten Chinook heavy helicopters descended into the formerly calm alpine meadow. David and the rest of ONSET Nine fell out into the field, dressed in full combat gear by the time the last rotor whirr faded away.

Captain Narita joined them as Michael swung out of one of the helicopters, accompanied by a man who looked in his mid-twenties with bleached-white hair.

"Ladies, gentlemen," Michael greeted them. "This is Captain Anderson, CO of OSPI's Special Supernatural Tactics Technology and Reconnaissance platoon."

"You know," Narita observed, eyeing the white-haired Captain, "some of us drove up here."

"Well now," Anderson drawled, "that's why we brought the choppers—so you don't have to drive to the target."

"Noisy, aren't they?" Akono murmured, the elf's dreamy tones managing their usual effect of being heard regardless of volume.

"I'm splitting my Mages up," Anderson replied in a slow, irritatingly calm accented drawl. "One per chopper should do it."

David wondered, as he eyed the apparently Texan SSTTR Captain, if the man's accent was real or put on—and if the man had any idea how annoying it was.

"Does that mean we're going in?" Narita asked—the scarred Asian pointedly asking Michael and not Anderson.

"We do indeed have a go," Michael confirmed. "Saddle your people up, Narita. You leave as soon as the Chinooks have refueled."

31

Magically silenced from the outside or not, a Pendragon's rotors still echoed through the helicopter gunship's passenger compartment. David and the other members of ONSET Nine sat in silence, only the short, sharp breathing of men and women about to go into combat cutting through the echo of rotors in the chopper's belly.

"T-minus three minutes," Akono said quietly over the team's radio. "Ape Six Actual has confirmed his people are on the ground. Entrances are covered and entry charges are placed."

No one said anything in response. No one needed to. Outside the window, mountains whipped past them. Inside, David checked the magazines on both his M4-Omicron and his Omicron Silver. Both were seated and full. Holstering the caseless pistol, he checked that the thong on his mageblade was on but loose enough to be quickly released.

"T-minus two minutes," Akono reported into the silence. "Slowing us down and beginning final approach. If you've any prayers left to say, now is the time."

David glanced around at his teammates. Blank faceplates looked back at him, and he knew that was all they could see of him. While he understood the necessary anonymity of ONSET combat gear, at a moment like this, he wished he could see his companion's faces—he could see their auras, but that wasn't the same.

"T-minus one minute," the pilot said quietly.

"Unstrap and hold on," Michael ordered, unbuckling himself and rising to his feet as he spoke.

David *felt* the tension in the small helicopter around him, the scent and Sight of nervous anticipation. They knew what was coming, and they were ready.

"Bringing us in now," Akono snapped. "One roof entrance—it's chained and padlocked, Commander!"

"This is a damned gunship!" the werewolf barked. "Blow it open. All units," he continued, presumably switching to a channel reaching everyone on the operation, "Go."

The sound of the Pendragon's automatic cannon opening fire was the opening note in the crescendo of explosions that followed.

———

DAVID HIT THE ROOF RUNNING, following Michael forward toward the shattered and smoldering hole that had been a locked and chained door a moment before. The heat from the fires still flickering around the staircase they bolted down was palpable even through his insulated suit.

Gunfire echoed up the spiral staircase and David reached the bottom to find the shattered body of a man, still holding the Uzi that had been his death sentence.

Michael was waiting just outside the door in a hallway that stretched away in both directions. Plush brown carpeting crushed beneath the ONSET team's feet, and expensive-looking textured beige wallpaper smoked around the bullet holes behind the werewolf.

"Split up," the Commander ordered. "Maintain radio contact, watch your tactical nets. Move!"

David went left with Ix at his side. As they moved, he kicked down the flimsy wooden doors on the left, and the red-skinned demon kicked down the ones on the right.

The rooms were empty. The hallway was filled with well-appointed bedrooms, but the only sign of life they'd seen was the one gunman at the stairwell down from the roof.

As if to put the lie to David's thought, the sound of gunfire began to echo up from the ground floor. The heavy bark of M4s conflicted with the sharper noise of Uzi submachine guns.

"This is Bravo-Three Actual," a breathless voice reported over the radio, identifying itself as the leader of AP Six's Bravo Platoon's Third Squad. "We have engaged armed opposition—SMGs and automatic rifles. We have them pinned down, but it's a mutual affair. Estimate fifteen to twenty hostiles."

David and Ix hit a staircase as gunfire continued to echo through the building. The two exchanged a look, and David gestured for Ix to continue along the corridor they were in. With a nod, the demon moved away, and David took the stairs down another floor.

Even the gunfire didn't conceal the sound of running footsteps to his enhanced senses, and he broke through the dark wood door at the bottom of this flight of staircases to face a trio of men charging forward, Uzis in hand.

As guns swung toward him with lethal intent, a moment of shock shook him. For a second, a spasm of fear at being in deadly danger held him, but then his training took over. His Sight warned him to step sideways as the three men fired, the Uzis firing uselessly down the corridor, and then told him where his own bullets were going.

Six shots later, he was stepping over the twitching bodies of the dying men. Part of him screamed in horror, but he ground the screams down as he headed down the hallway in the direction the armed men had come from.

Ten meters behind, a barely closed door was marked with the familiar black iron sun. Grinding his teeth against its *wrongness*, David shoved the door open and inhaled sharply. While the rest of the lodge had been well appointed, *this* was something more. The brown plush carpet gave way to a pure mahogany hardwood floor, and David was sure he could see a fur rug just down the corridor. Mahogany hardwood paneling rose halfway up the corridor walls, and the upper half was a continuous woodland mural.

As he moved along this new hallway, careful to be as quiet as possible on the hardwood floor, David realized that there was something plainly *wrong* about the mural on the wall. The angles and scales of the animals and trees were all subtly wrong. And the sun…every ten feet was another sun, and they were all black.

More running footsteps sounded, and David sank to one side of the hallway, trying to hide behind a solid mahogany table holding a black iron sculpture of what appeared to be an unnaturally skinny man with a sun for a head.

Two more men, these in body armor and carrying ugly-looking bullpup weapons with drum magazines, were hustling along the corridor. To David's Sight, both had auras slightly tinged with red, marking them as Empowered.

One of them spotted David behind his flimsy cover and fired the weapon as David dove out of the way. A three-round burst of heavy shot obliterated the statue and its stand as David mentally classified the ugly weapons as *assault shotgun—highly dangerous*.

He returned fire before the second gunman could shoot, his three-round burst shattering the man's skull. Nerves pulsed in death, and a dying finger twitched around the trigger of his weapon. The first man was blown across the hall into the wall as the heavy shotgun emptied a single shell into his upper torso.

Again, David ground down the sick feeling of having killed and his nausea at the remains scattered across the hall as he charged deeper into this more luxuriously appointed area of the lodge. He used his combat information suite to ping the location to his teammates. There was *something* here.

Then his hearing, stretched to its inhuman limits to hear anything under the continuing gunfire from the lower floors as more Ape squads clashed with defenders, heard something different.

First, it was only chanting, but as he headed toward the sound, he began to hear the crackling noise of several fires burning. Finally, he reached a large set of double doors that his Empowered senses told him was the source of the chanting.

Slowly, ever so slowly, David checked that he was still getting a feed from the camera on his M4 and slowly poked the barrel and its camera mount around the corner of the door, peering into the room.

It was apparently the inner sanctum of the Black Sun's temple. The room was set up like a chapel, with six split rows of chairs leading up to a raised stage. Stairs led up either side of the stage, flanking two massive braziers whose flames sparked up to the roof, resplendent in unnatural colors David could See were fueled by magic.

If there'd been anyone in the audience seats, they'd left to help defend the ritual. Five men, all dressed in blood-red robes out of a cheap fantasy horror, stood in a rough circle around a roughly hewn stone. The rest of the room was shrouded in deep red hangings and shining mahogany, and the stone stood out.

It, like the angles in the murals outside the room, was vaguely *wrong*, and David knew even without his Sight that the rock was the key to the ritual they were performing. The braziers, the unnatural flames, the stone altar and the robed Mages all fit together.

Here was the sanctum where the Black Sun would bring their demon into the world.

————

WITH A DEEP BREATH, David focused, trying to See as much as he could through the mundane filter of the gun-mounted camera. The ritual continued as he slowly picked out the lines of power connecting the robed men to the stone and each other, and the one robed man that was the focal point.

He gently, ever so gently, settled the crosshairs of his M4 on the man's head as he continued to chant. One shot, and it would all be over. Even if they could retrieve the ritual without its leader, it would cost the Mages enough time for the rest of ONSET Nine to get here.

David hesitated. His disgust at the deaths he'd caused getting here surged up in rebellion. He was a *police officer*, not a killer. Shooting without warning, gunning down an unarmed man without mercy; these were his *enemy's* tools. Taking the shot would take him one step closer to becoming like Carderone—absolutely certain of his right to carry out evil acts.

His finger rested on the trigger of his rifle, and he knew every moment risked both discovery and the completion of the ritual. Slowly,

David lowered the rifle a few degrees. He stared through the scope for an eternal moment, and then fired.

The single bullet flashed across the room and smashed into the ritual leader's knee. The silver round blasted out the front of his kneecap in a spray of blood that splashed over the stone altar as the Mage crumpled forward.

David focused through his rifle, hearing the sounds of confusion and anger in the room. Mages scattered away, raising shields of magic and throwing bolts of fire at nonexistent targets. Now he fired again, and again, more to suppress than to actually do any harm. He had to slow this ritual.

Only his prescience warned him of the man behind him—he never heard the footsteps over the commotion in the sanctum. His Sight warned him of pain, and he spun in place, yanking the assault rifle from the gap in the door he'd been aiming through.

A shaved bald man in a brown robe had stepped out of a hidden door along the corridor David had passed through. The black T-shape of an Uzi machine pistol was extended in his hands, pointing at David as the man pulled the trigger. This time, there was no way David could dodge.

David felt the bullets before they even hit him, ripping through his flesh in both the present and the future, but he held his focus long enough to drop the M4's video crosshair on the bald man's head and fire three rounds.

The Uzi's hammer clicked onto empty just as David's burst ripped the man's head apart. David stood frozen, knowing he'd been shot, knowing he was dying.

He fell. The bullets from the Uzi, he saw, had thrown the door behind him wide open, and he watched in horror as the crippled body of the man he'd shot first erupted into flame. The flame shot up from the altar, incinerating the Mage's flesh, and formed into the shape of a man.

David saw the demon they'd come to stop take form before his very eyes, and knew he didn't have the time left to warn his comrades.

And then shock took him into darkness.

32

MICHAEL CURSED TO HIMSELF AS THE VITAL SIGNS FOR DAVID WHITE ON his helmet display flatlined. The werewolf had been watching the junior agent's progress since he'd pinged an unusual find, but he'd also been trying to break Bravo Three clear of their deadlock with the cultist defenders.

"White is down," Ix said over the radio in clipped tones. "I'm moving to investigate and provide medical."

Medical assistance was likely to be unnecessary, Michael reflected grimly. According to his suit, he wasn't getting a transmission from David's health monitors. The younger man was almost certainly dead.

The momentary distraction almost proved fatal, as Michael took one step farther than he planned—past the end of the wall. He found himself staring at the backs of over a dozen brown-robed men and women with automatic weapons, several of them turning to him.

The werewolf jerked his assault rifle up and opened fire, emptying a thirty-round magazine of silver bullets across the hallway before diving across the hallway to take cover on the other side.

Gunfire echoed after him, followed by screams, and then silence. In the moment of calm, Michael realized he'd been shot. At least three bullets had gone through him, and two more were still inside him.

With a grunt, the werewolf *focused* and slowly forced the two remaining bullets out, thanking whatever deity happened to be listening that these idiots weren't using silver. Regeneration complete, he poked his reloaded assault rifle around the corner.

The brown-robed men and women were down. Most, by their scent and lack of motion, were dead. Bravo Three had followed up his surprise rear attack with an assault of their own, and their medic was giving rough and ready first aid to the handful of cultist survivors.

The squad leader, an older man whose features were entirely obscured by the large and ugly black glasses of his combat gear, crossed to Michael.

"Most of the resistance seems to be dying down," he reported. "We got the ping from your man. Do you need support at the target?"

"My man is down," Michael responded sharply, his HUD still showing the blinking icon of David's location. "I'll take whatever support I can get."

"Understood," the sergeant confirmed. "Kabongo, Culligan, stay with these idiots. Star, you're with us. We've got a super in need of first aid."

The medic left the hastily patched-up survivors to the pair of soldiers detailed to watch them and joined up with the rest of the squad as they formed up around Michael.

"Let's go," the werewolf ordered crisply.

———

As MICHAEL LED the way deeper into the mountain lodge, toward the blinking icon of the mark David had put on the map for a point of interest, his superhuman ears noted that the gunfire had all but stopped. From the slowly descending quiet in the cult's hidden head-quarters, the fight was almost over.

The cultists' numbers and equipment bothered Michael. They hadn't expected nearly so many men—and certainly not men this fanatical and equipped with military-grade weapons.

"ONSET Nine, this is Nine Actual," the werewolf said gruffly, activating his radio. "Check in, over."

"This is Nine Deuce," Kate's voice responded immediately. "I'm with Ape Six Actual, we have the main entrance secured and are coordinating with our covering teams. No one's made a break for it, over."

"This is Nine Four," Dilsner replied. "I've found their coms center. This is one hell of a network hub for the middle of bloody nowhere. I'm secure, over," the Mage added as an afterthought.

"This is Ape Six Charlie Actual for your Nine Six," a voice said over the radio. "We just finished sweeping the east wing—looks like it was their barracks. Your gal took some bad hits and is being medevaced with our wounded. Paramedics say she's probably going to make it."

"Thanks, Charlie Actual," Michael replied. He'd known about Bourque's injuries from her combat suit, but the paramedic's assessment of her survival chances was more useful than the suit's transmission of her pulse and blood pressure.

"Nine Three here," Akono reported as Michael cut his link to Ape-Six-Charlie squad. "Still over your head. Confirm on Nine Deuce—our boys in the hills are bored. Nobody even tried to run, over."

Michael growled, low in his throat, as he hit a set of stairs running, taking three at a time before forcing himself to slow so the AP soldiers could keep up. Only a supreme effort of will kept the transformation at bay. He was worried—and angry. There shouldn't have been this many cultists here, and they shouldn't have been heavily armed. Two of his team were down and he didn't even know what David had run into.

"Nine Five," Ix said in his clipped, inhuman, tones. "Closing on Nine Seven."

"I'm close," Michael responded. "Stabilize him and check for gear failure, got it? Over."

"Check," the demon replied. There was a moment's pause, and the demon didn't drop the line. "Actual," he continued in a strained voice. "I can't get closer. Watch your-grrgh!"

The demon's voice cut off as his vitals—already very different from the other members of the team—went crazy. His pulse dropped to single digits and body temperature plummeted.

"Shit," Michael cursed, his sense of foreboding crystallizing into a chill of fear. He turned to his contingent of Apes. "Hold here; some-thing's going *very* wrong. Dig in and wait for my signal."

They were on the second floor, less than ten meters from the spot David had marked, and maybe three times that from David himself. With a nod, the sergeant began to order his men to break down doors and find a barricade.

Without the detail to slow him down, Michael allowed the transfor-mation to take him. His ears caught gasps from the soldiers behind him as his skin *flowed,* the form of the massive wolf subsuming him and all of his gear.

He sniffed the air, relying on superhuman senses instead of the technology that had gone Elsewhere when he transformed. An odd scent caught his nose from the direction he was headed. It smelt like incense but cut with gunpowder—and burning blood.

The massive wolf launched into a run.

————

He hit the area where he figured David's marker would have been, and understood why the junior agent had left it. This richly and strangely decorated section of the lodge was almost certainly the temple area. David had found the sanctum.

The scent of blood drew Michael on, and the werewolf found the shattered corpses of the two guards David had gunned down. He sniffed at the bodies and the heavy assault shotguns.

Both were dead, and he was running short on time—*David,* if there was any chance for him at all, was running short on time. The werewolf left the bodies, cringing as his paws sank into the sticky pool of half-dried blood.

He could feel himself leaving a trail of bloody pawprints as he ran down the corridor, and it distracted him at a crucial moment. Michael rounded a corner at full speed and was almost too focused on his sticking to the floor to pay attention to the man standing there.

With no time to process any oddities, Michael leapt for the throat, long fangs bared to rip out the throat of the damned cultist getting between him and any chance of saving his junior agent.

The hand that caught the massive werewolf in midair and flung him against the wall was a complete surprise. Michael himself couldn't have done that to a werewolf of his age and power, and he assessed his new opponent carefully as he sprang back to his feet.

It was not a man. It *looked* like a man, wearing a burnt cultist's robe over a neat business suit, but it smelled all wrong. Even if Michael hadn't been a werewolf, the fact that the face was still regrowing itself out of a charred mess would have given the game away. Or the eyes, where green flame burned instead of eyeballs.

Undistracted, Michael felt the power of a greater demon and knew they'd failed. Only once before had the werewolf had stood in the presence of a being of this power—and this time, he was alone.

The werewolf charged forward anyway, changing into a hybrid form of man and wolf as he did—a creature of fang and claw and muscle, perfect for this kind of close-range brawl. His claws extended, slashing for the demon's stolen flesh.

Each strike was blocked easily, casually. As each clawed blow flashed out, a hand easily interposed itself, stopping the strike. Finally, the demon stepped back and lashed out at Michael in turn.

The werewolf dropped, dodging under the blow and stabbing forward with both hands. He felt his claws drive deep into the flesh of his enemy, and his gorge rose. This flesh was not living. He'd just driven his claws into a walking corpse sustained by the sheer power of the entity that had claimed it.

His claws stuck in the dead flesh, the demon's next blow sent him flying through the air. He bounced off the wall and around the corner. He landed next to the corpses of David's victims, multiple bones broken.

He *focused*, and even as the demon walked sedately around the corner, his bones clicked back into place with loud cracking noises and a scream of pain. His transformation undid itself as the demon came, and Michael faced the monster as a man.

An unimaginably strong man. With two assault shotguns right to hand.

As the demon threw a bolt of green flame at Michael, the werewolf rolled away, grabbing up a shotgun in each hand. Years of practice found the safeties and flicked them to automatic.

Another bolt of green flame burned a clean strip through the top of Michael's hair as he dropped to a crouch and lifted the guns, pulling the triggers as they bore on the demon and unleashing a hail of full-auto fire.

Even through the earplugs that had returned with his human form, the cacophony of two assault shotguns hurt. The shotguns slammed back against his hands with too much for even *his* endurance, and he felt even his left wrist shatter, the gun dropping from his grip before it emptied.

The second gun fell to the ground as it worked its way to vertical, having filled the corridor with a wall of lead. The smell of the pellets was enough for Michael to know they weren't silver, and that was bad news.

The smoke from the shotgun bursts faded, and the demon grinned at Michael. The side walls had been demolished, the murals obliterated by flame and lead. The robe that had hung over the demon was gone, its fabric disintegrating under the hail. But the claw wounds Michael had inflicted were gone, and the shotguns had done nothing to the demon itself, not even marring the suit.

For the first time, the demon spoke. "Nice try," it told Michael mockingly, the voice low and smooth as silk. Then it punched him in the chest. Michael flew backward, crashing through the twisted murals with a crash. He hit the floor of the room beyond and *bounced*, crashing into the outer wall of the building with enough force to punch through its solid wood—and take Michael into darkness.

———

THE BRIEF FLASH of unconsciousness faded, and Michael pulled himself out of the wreckage of a neatly trimmed hedge along the edge of the lodge's grounds. Hard leafless branches prodded into his back even as his regeneration fixed broken bones with painful *cracks*.

He waited a moment, focusing on healing his injuries, and looked back at the hunting lodge he'd just been punched out of. A massive hole marked the nearest wall around the second floor, bits of which were scattered around the bushes he'd landed on. As he watched, a suited figure walked up to the edge of the hole and calmly jumped out of the building.

"All helicopters and heavy weapons," he said into his radio, coughing to clear the taste of his own blood from his throat, "this is Nine Actual. Our primary mission is a failure," he said grimly, his voice clearer now as he pulled a laser target designator, somehow intact despite everything, from his harness. "I'm designating a target for a full fire mission. The demon is heading east, and I want him hit with everything we've got."

"Hold that thought," a drawling voice interjected onto the radio network. Michael froze at the sound of Anderson's words, the laser designator half-raised.

"This is Stutter Actual," Anderson continued. "Abort the direct-fire mission. Do not, I repeat, do *not* fire on the demon. I'm uploading a fire pattern to all helicopters and guns. My Bravo team is setting up a trap in the hills. We're going to herd him in."

Michael took a very deep breath, his body aching with the effort of regenerating so much damage, and switched to a direct channel with Anderson.

"Are you *mad*, Stutter?" he demanded.

"No," the SSTTR Commander said flatly. "My man Casey is already on the ground and laying out a path while keeping an eye on that thing. This was the backup plan, remember? Your mission was to stop the summoning, but you failed. This is *my* mission now, understand?"

Michael stood on the cold ground, watching the demon run to the east as artillery fire began to fall around it, trying to drive it in a specific direction. "He's not stupid, Captain. He'll realize what you're doing."

"His choices are to go where we want or walk into an AG-shrapnel shell," the Texan drawled harshly. "Either we take him alive or he dies. Think of what we'd lose if he dies, Commander," he implored. "He's a *high court* demon. He's a major player in the Masters Beyond's plans for invasion. We *have* to take him alive."

"He's too dangerous," Michael argued. "Last time we faced a high court demon, it took a *nuke* to put him down, Anderson! Unless you didn't tell me something, that's not an option here!"

"It's not your decision," Anderson said sharply. "It's not mine, either. The Director gave his orders. If the demon was summoned, we were to take him alive." The Texan's voice softened. "I agree with your point, Commander, but we need what he can tell us. And I have my orders."

With a click, Anderson cut the connection, and Michael inhaled sharply, catching the iron tang of blood. The scent brought back the thought of David, and he switched to another channel.

"Did anyone make it to Seven?!" he demanded.

"This is Nine Five," Ix reported, his voice showing no sign of his earlier problems. "I'm sorry for earlier," he continued. "The bastard is higher-court than I am—I can't fight him!"

Michael nodded, and then remembered the demon couldn't see him. "Understood, Five," he said quietly. That wasn't something he'd been aware of, but it explained why Ix had collapsed when a high court demon had approached. "Did you get to Seven?"

"Just reached his position," the demon confirmed. "Checking him over now." There was a pause, and Michael looked around him, making sure there were no more threats and that the cascade of explosions herding the demon was moving away.

"He'll live," Ix reported, and Michael quickly checked his data feed on David.

"I'm still showing him flatlined," the werewolf observed. "Is there damage to the gear?"

"His gear is totaled, but he's definitely going to make it," the demon said cheerily. "He's lost a lot of blood and is still in shock—but he's regenerating."

[33]

DAVID WOKE UP TO PAIN. IT WAS A DULL SENSATION IN HIS CHEST AND upper left leg, like there was cotton wrapped around injuries that should have hurt more. He twitched in pain and felt something sticky under his hand. The cop slowly opened his eyes and looked at his hand.

He was lying on a polished hardwood floor, and he wasn't entirely sure how he'd ended up on the ground. He remembered the mission—assaulting the mountain lodge to stop the ritual. What had happened?

Then it finally sank in what the sticky red substance his hand was in—that he was lying in—was. It was blood. A massive pool of blood spread out around him. His *own* blood.

David remembered. He remembered turning and shooting at the other man, and being shot in turn. With a lurch, he rose to a half-sitting position to look toward where the cultist had shot at him from. The man lay in a crumpled heap, blood spattering the wall around him.

The wounded man slowly looked around, still stiff. The doors to the ritual chamber had been torn down, and the once-elegant pews and hangings of the sanctum were a mess. Fire had claimed many of the hangings, and bullet holes had been torn through the sanctum. Bodies were scattered everywhere, and David was *sure* he hadn't shot them all. The carnage was far beyond his capabilities—many of the Mage-priests had been ripped to pieces.

His blood-soaked hand, unthinkingly checking out the body armor he was wearing, found a hole, and David looked down. His black combat bodysuit was shredded and soaked in blood. An ugly-looking hole in his upper left leg showed where one bullet had clearly gone through, but the chest of the suit was so mangled, there was no way to tell how many bullets had hit him.

Even as he began to panic, a hand settled down on his shoulder. David turned quickly to see the red-skinned and horned form of ONSET Nine's demon member, Ix's helmet missing for some reason.

"Take it easy," he rumbled. "So far as I can tell, blood loss knocked you unconscious for about twenty-two minutes. You should be dead."

"Dead?" David repeated, staring uncomprehendingly at the demon. Even with the state of his body armor, that seemed...a bit much to take in.

"You have already regenerated most of your injuries," the demon told him quietly. "That wound in your leg alone should have bled you out in the time you've been unconscious. I got here before it fully sealed up—your femoral artery had been nicked—not enough to kill you quickly, but more than enough to kill you in the end. Your armor probably saved your life—it looked like most of the rounds bounced off, so the ones that got through were, again, not enough to kill you quickly. And *not quickly* apparently wasn't quickly enough," Ix finished.

David's mind struggled with the idea, although part of him remembered the Uzi firing and knew that he'd been lucky just to receive the wounds Ix described—and should still have died from them. But...*regeneration?*

He tried to stand, but Ix's grip tightened, holding him down. "You're a lot more tired than you think," the demon agent told him. "Stay down for a moment. Here." With the last, Ix pulled a chocolate bar from a pocket hidden inside his bodysuit and handed it to David, who found that he was starving. "Eat."

"How's everyone else?" David asked, between bites.

"We're still doing a tally now, but Michael has ordered the team to

ONSET: TO SERVE AND PROTECT 281

converge here," the other agent said. "From what I've heard, Bourque got beaten up pretty bad and was airlifted out with the Apes' wounded."

"The demon?" the wounded agent asked, finishing the chocolate bar. He watched as Ix's inhuman face suddenly went even flatter.

"Summoned," another voice said from behind them. "Then kicked mine and Ix's asses and broke out of the building," Michael continued as the burly werewolf crouched down beside David.

"Why aren't we pursuing?" David demanded, scrabbling for his gun before Michael's hand sank down on his other shoulder.

"We've been stood down," the werewolf replied, his voice a low growl. "The Stutter platoon has tactical control. We failed to prevent the summoning, and the demon's *capture*, not destruction, is their mission in that case."

He paused for a moment, and then admitted, "While I disagree with the objective, they *are* more qualified to carry out that mission than we are."

David nodded, and silence descended on the bloody hallway. Kate and Morgen drifted in a few minutes later, but no one in the team said a word, just exchanging silent nods.

Eventually, they helped David to his feet, and ONSET Nine made their way down to the Black Sun cult's lodge's lobby to continue waiting. Their job was over. Now all they could do was wait to hear whether or not the SSTTR team succeeded.

———

THE LOBBY WAS LESS ORNATELY DECORATED than the sumptuous inner sanctum where David had almost died, but it had still been gorgeous before a running gunfight had torn through it. Now blood spattered the shag carpeting and bullet holes marred the oak paneling half-covered by torn deep blue curtains. A dozen padded brown armchairs were set up in small clusters of three, but one cluster had been all but obliterated by a grenade.

The heavy wooden double doors were closed, their carefully carved wood miraculously untouched by the violence that had occurred around them. Two AP soldiers stood by the windows next to the doors, peering out, while another pair manned a heavy machine gun set up pointing at the door.

"Expecting trouble?" David heard Michael murmur to the corporal in charge of the fire team.

"Not unless that demon gets past the Stutters," the soldier replied. "But we've got a lot of wounded in the building who are waiting for the second round of evacs, and it's better safe than sorry."

David ignored the rest of the conversation as Kate helped him to an undamaged armchair. *Everything* hurt, but especially his chest. But then, from what Ix had said and he remembered, he was healing from at least two gut shots, a theoretically *fatal* leg wound, and a punctured lung. Somehow. The pain was fading, too. Fading slowly, perhaps, but far faster than it should have.

"Are you all right?" Kate asked after he winced in pain.

"I should be dead," he observed quietly, half-reminding himself as he explained to her. He knew that intellectually, but it was hard to accept. Even with the oh-so-clear memory of bullets ripping through his flesh.

"Given that, I'm laughing," he told her, wincing as another surge of pain shot through his leg. A part of him wanted to think that the pain was being concentrated along with the healing, but he also knew better. If anything, even the pain was reduced as his body healed far too quickly from something it shouldn't have been able to repair.

"We should have evaced you," Dilsner told David, setting himself down in the chair beside David.

"The Apes had folks worse wounded," Michael told the Mage, joining the collection of agents. "And Bourque was pretty bad off too—they've all made it to the hospital, though. I just got the status update."

"And the demon?" David asked as Ix settled down on the floor with the rest of ONSET Nine.

"No news," Michael said shortly. David waited a moment, but the Commander gave no further commentary. The junior agent opened his mouth to ask what Michael *did* know, but another massive surge of pain lanced across his chest as he did, and he fell back into his chair with a gasp.

Closing his eyes against the pain, nasty even as it faded, he felt Kate's hand on his shoulder and appreciated the support. Neither Mage on ONSET Nine was a healer, but he knew he didn't need one. His injuries had healed; he was going to recover. All he really wanted was a painkiller.

"We screwed up pretty bad," David said quietly. "*I* screwed up pretty bad. I was the only one at the sanctum."

"Shit happens," Michael said bluntly. "None of us know enough about a ritual summoning to know what stage it was at. If it was at a point where *anything* you did triggered it, it was probably too late for us to stop it at all."

Silence held for another moment, and then Morgen spoke up.

"What happens if SSTTR fails to capture it?" the Mage asked softly.

"Then we find David another set of body armor and fulfill the mandate of our Office," Michael replied, equally softly. "We kill the bastard."

———

THE FIRST SIGN that anything changed was the guards at the windows perking up, checking their weapons and eyeing something approaching toward the door. One of them stepped over and swung one of the heavy doors open.

The familiarly large form of Leonard Casey stepped through the open door, his helmet off and his rifle slung. The SSTTR Empowered glanced at the machine gun sitting in the middle of the lobby and stepped carefully sideways, out of its line of fire.

He approached the ONSET team and saluted Michael crisply. "Captain Anderson sends his regards, Commander," he said briskly.

"At ease, Sergeant," Michael replied. David realized that his Commander had a point—hidden in the snow camouflage Casey was wearing were the chevrons of a Sergeant. Apparently, SSTTR still used Army ranks.

"What's the news?" the ONSET Commander continued, and David looked back up at the tracker's face.

"We got him," Casey said flatly. "Herded him into a pit trap and dropped a containment coffin on the bastard. The captain sent me to advise you as soon as we confirmed the seal. Doesn't matter how strong the bastard is when he's inside two inches of pure silver."

David pursed his lips in a silent whistle as he met the former ONSET aspirant's eyes and gave the man a nod. Casey looked back at him in surprise, taking in the bullet-ridden state of David's armor and clothing.

"You look like shit, White," he said harshly.

"I'm still breathing," David replied softly. "Congratulations."

He didn't need anyone to explain to him that this kind of coup for the SSTTR team was going to cause problems for ONSET down the road—interoffice rivalries worked that way. Casey was a friend, though, and the big grin on the man's face suggested he had been in at the catch. David couldn't begrudge him his accomplishment.

"Your people are playing with fire," Michael said grimly. "You have *no* idea what you're getting into."

The grin faded to a flat line, and Casey's gaze turned to Michael. "SSTTR is capable of taking care of ourselves," he said coldly. "Ekhmez's containment unit has been loaded onto a transport chopper and is on its way back to OSPI Headquarters. An OSPI cleanup team is on its way here to go through the computer records we recovered."

"There were a lot of those," Morgen said quietly, and part of the tension diffused. "We got in there before they could even touch the computers. Their servers, their workstations…it's encrypted, but it's all there. Every piece of information this cult collected."

Casey whistled, and he wasn't the only one surprised. In this day and age, information was a deadly weapon. Capturing the complete files of a hostile organization was almost as big a coup for ONSET as capturing Ekhmez was for SSTTR.

INFORMATION OVERLOAD. It was a major problem with hacking, especially when you were successful beyond your wildest dreams and had only been digging for curiosity's sake in the first place. Majestic had no goal in ONSET's system, no target pay data to steal for an employer.

Context was everything, and she was only slowly building that. She had decent access now, and she was pretty sure ONSET's IT security wasn't going to find her. Files, programs, wireless networks, all of it opened before her, and she had only the slightest inkling of how it all went together.

She needed a target. Needed a place to start her search and come back to—a data point around which she could build her context.

With a grin, Majestic looked at the directories in front of her and warmed up her search tools. She *had* a data point.

His name was David White.

[34]

"WALK WITH ME, DAVID," MICHAEL SAID QUIETLY, AND DAVID LOOKED UP at his Commander questioningly. The junior agent had only just returned to the main floor of ONSET Nine's barracks after changing into civilian clothes.

"What is it?" he asked. They'd returned to the Campus above Colorado Springs barely an hour before, the helicopters delivering the unwounded ONSET and AP men and women into a surreally twilit mountain scene.

"Just walk with me," the werewolf repeated, and gestured for David to head outside. The rest of ONSET Nine looked at them curiously, but no one said anything. They still had no news on Alexandra —no one on the team was even sure how badly she'd been wounded beyond "badly".

Wondering what was going on, David grabbed the blue canvas duster he'd picked up in Denver the week before. Michael was already wearing a black leather bomber jacket.

Michael led the way out into the campus grounds in the darkening twilight, and David breathed deeply of the fresh mountain air. ONSET Campus had the population of a small town, but there weren't many vehicles coming or going, which allowed the air to retain a clean mountain crispness.

Dead leaves crunched underfoot. The trees around them looked skeletal, with only a few leaves still hanging on. The air smelled odd to David's Maine-bred nose, with a scent he wasn't sure of but suspected meant snow.

This late in the year, he was surprised that somewhere as far up into the mountains as the Campus hadn't had snow yet. It was cold, though, and David shivered as it bit through the duster.

"I'm going to be writing my report on the Cult tonight," Michael said finally. "There were some things I needed to say to you before I do, though."

"To me?" David asked. He hesitated, wondering if he was in trouble for having failed to stop the summoning.

"You should have died, David," the werewolf said bluntly as he removed a pack of cigarettes from his jacket. The younger Agent looked at them askance. He hadn't known that Michael smoked. "Three rounds through the abdomen. Two through the left lung. Clipped femoral artery. You shouldn't have died instantly, but your life expectancy was less than the time it took you to wake up."

"You make it sound like it's a big deal," David observed. He suspected that Michael, for example, had survived worse in Montreal.

"Until yesterday, I would have said only two members of my team could have survived that injury," his Commander replied, continuing to lead them away from any of the buildings on the campus. "Myself, and Ix. Cigarette?" he offered

"No, thank you," David replied. "Those things can kill you," he added.

"Take the damn smoke, David," Michael snapped, and David slowly took the white cylinder from his boss. "That's what I wanted to talk to you about," he continued as he lit his own cigarette and inhaled. "It won't kill you." He lit David's cigarette.

David breathed in the smoke and found himself disagreeing strongly with the statement as his lungs tried to claw their way up his throat.

"A fully trained Class 2 regenerator could have survived your wounds," Michael continued once David had finished coughing. "You are not fully trained. Until yesterday, we didn't even know you *were* a regenerator."

Now that the realization had come up, David could think of a few times he'd healed faster than he should have. The first time on Campus, when he'd put it up to ONSET's medical and magic capabilities. The broken ribs from his fight with Dresden. He'd been regenerating all along, but until he'd been repeatedly shot, it hadn't been this obvious.

"It's that big a deal?" David asked, holding the cigarette away from him, even as his enhanced nose twitched at the acrid smell.

"Minor regeneration isn't," Michael said quietly. "It's relatively common among supernaturals, actually. But that's just faster healing. To survive what you survived, without training in focusing the healing energy... There is a high likelihood that you are a Class 1 regenerator, as able to regenerate as I am," he concluded.

"Our level of regeneration is generally the province of vampires, werewolves and a handful of Empowered. That's growing back limbs and recovering from near-fatal wounds almost instantly. That and not aging."

"Not...aging?" David repeated, suddenly beginning to realize why they were so far away from everyone.

"Minor regenerators will live a long time," the werewolf said quietly. "Akono, like most elves, is one. He has a life expectancy of around a hundred and eighty healthy years."

"And major regenerators?" the Empowered cop standing next to him asked.

"How old do you think I am?" Michael asked suddenly.

David eyed the other man. He knew Michael was older than him. He'd heard rumors of what the werewolf had got up to in the past, and knew him to be older than he looked, yet...he wouldn't put O'Brien over forty.

"Forty-odd?" he guessed finally.

"I was twenty-five when I volunteered for the very first tour of duty in Vietnam," Michael said grimly. "I was born a year to the day before the Pearl Harbor attack. I'm over seventy years old, David, and have spent more than forty of those years in the service of the American people, one way or another.

"I am a werewolf, a major regenerator," he continued. "I barely age, as the regeneration sees it as damage and fixes it. Mostly."

"Mostly?"

"We don't have a lot of evidence, but we think the major regenerators do age over time," Michael told him. "But it's so slowly, it may as well not be happening. I probably have another thousand years in me."

"Damn," David said softly, looking at his Commander in a new light. "You're telling me I can expect to live for over a thousand years?"

"Yes," his Commander told him bluntly. "You can die. Wounds inflicted by silver will kill you. Disease...maybe. *Enough* physical damage can do it—but we're talking instantly fatal injuries—complete destruction of the brain, being blown apart, that kind of thing."

"Decapitation?" David asked, thinking of a certain TV series, and Michael laughed.

"More likely than not," Michael agreed. "But the only reliable ways to kill men and women like us are silver and magic. Anything else and the odds are weighted in your favor."

"So, I'm..." The younger man trailed off.

"Close to immortal," Michael said bluntly. "There are maybe two thousand men and women in the world who share that status with us. Our bodies will tolerate no long-term damage—not cancer, not age, not even tar from cigarettes in your lungs. Smoke up," he ordered, "because goddammit, David, you'll outlive everyone here regardless."

———

DAVID FOLLOWED Michael blindly across the barren ground of the ONSET Campus in late fall, lost in his own thoughts as a chill wind swept over the wall and blew his duster in waves around him. His Commander said nothing to him and the pair smoked their cigarettes down to the filters.

The younger man *still* didn't like the taste, but he saw Michael's point. Just this once, today, as he faced a future that stretched for a very long time, he was willing to try it. It was starting to look like he should be willing to try anything.

The sky continued to darken above them, and the lights along the main paths began to flicker on in groups, their pools of light illuminating sections of the stark buildings and pathways. The trees had finished losing their leaves, and the grass was brown, waiting only for the first snows of winter to definitely claim the campus.

Like the summer and the trees, David knew he'd reached the end of a phase in his life. Whatever happened now, things had changed forever. How did you face the world when you knew you'd live to see most of it turn to dust? How did you *accept* that everything you saw would turn to dust while you lived on? What kind of monster *could* accept that?

"How do we deal?" he finally asked Michael as they stepped onto one of the lit pathways. "You tell me I'll outlive all of this"—he gestured around at the buildings—"but how am I supposed to accept that?"

"You're not," Michael replied softly, stopping and turning to look at David. "Don't worry about the future; don't plan based on the knowledge you'll live long past this place and these people. I think, for us more than for any other, it is essential that we live in the present. If we take the long view, it *will* kill us."

David stopped alongside the werewolf and looked at the brooding darkness of the Campus's buildings. Lit windows scattered across the upper floors of the structures marked where parts of the organization worked far past regular hours.

"The easiest way for a regenerator to die is suicide, isn't it?" he said quietly. Most enemies wouldn't know how to hurt a regenerator, let alone kill them. Most regenerators, though, would know how to hurt themselves. They would know that a silver bullet to the head would end any of them.

"Yes," Michael said flatly, then gestured along the lit pathway toward the slumbering bulk of the Campus's main administration building. "We should get moving. You have an appointment with Major Warner."

"I do?" David questioned, surprised.

"That's what I was sent to tell you," his superior told him. "I needed to talk to you first, though. We regenerators try and keep a lot of the details of what being one of us means to ourselves. Traci has different things to tell you than I did."

The younger man nodded, and looked at the admin building. He began to walk toward it, then stopped and turned back to Michael.

"What happens now?" he asked, softly.

"We live," the werewolf replied. "For as long as we live—not one day more or one day less. Go talk to the Major, David. Whatever the future holds, we have a job to do today."

DAVID PASSED through the security checkpoints in the Campus's Administration building with the blasé air of past experience. While he had not been up to Major Warner's office since that first meeting almost three months before, similar security measures took up every non-residential building on the Campus, as ubiquitous as the deep blue carpeting.

He reached Warner's office at the end of the short corridor with its brass nameplates and knocked once.

"Enter," she ordered immediately, and David stepped through the door. Unlike his last visit, the single chair on his side of her desk was a comfortable armchair, not a straight-backed wooden terror. The filing cabinets, the flags, the low bookshelves, they all looked the same.

This time around, David noted the aura of the painting behind the uniformed Mage as soon as he entered, and winced slightly at the memory of the first time he'd seen that bright white aura.

"Have a seat, Agent White," Major Warner instructed, gesturing him to the armchair. Sitting behind the desk, the redhead's small size was easily missed, and her calm green eyes seemed much more authoritative.

"Thank you, ma'am," David replied, sinking into the surprisingly comfortable leather chair and facing the day-to-day head of his organization. "May I ask what this is about?"

"I know that Michael gave you a long regenerator-to-regenerator talk before he sent you up here," she told him softly, "so I won't bore you with the details of what this change means. Given how quiet the regenerators in our ranks keep some of the details, you probably now know more about the long-term consequences than I do. You're here so we can discuss some more...short-term consequences."

"Like what, ma'am?" he asked, wondering what she meant.

"When you came to us, we tested you extensively for supernatural abilities," Warner reminded him. "We know about your potential, but we can only rely on the abilities you are in control of, and those are basically your prescience and your strength. You are an exceptional man but not necessarily in ways that lend themselves to ONSET's mission. Everyone here is exceptional, David," she reminded him as he started to object.

He was all too aware that he was hardly exceptional compared to anyone else on ONSET Nine. Even Bourque, the team's other Empowered, was stronger and probably a more capable fighter than he was. Without his sparks of major power, he'd have nothing.

"You were a Class 4 supernatural," she told him. "That meant you were borderline—an individual assessment case. You're hardly the only Class 4 in ONSET—Nine's Akono and Bourque are both Class 4s. You were judged sufficiently capable of combat that you were accepted."

David nodded, wondering where this was going. He suspected by now that it wasn't really Omicron's policy in general to tell people where they rated on that scale. The only person, he realized, who'd mentioned it was Kate—in the context of her promotion.

Surely, regeneration wouldn't raise him that high.

"After Montreal, we considered reassessing you, but Michael advised me you had no control over the ability," Warner continued. "We left you at 4, with a note on the file that you were capable of Class 1–grade feats under sufficient duress. Then somebody emptied an Uzi into you, and you lived."

David nodded silently. The thought still stung. It still brought back that memory of bullets tearing through his flesh, and the blackness after. The thought that he should have died without ever waking up was nerve-wracking.

"The analysts haven't crunched it yet," the Major told him, "but I'm reasonably confident you will have been upgraded to a Class 2 Supernatural. I'm sure by now you've realized most of our people really fall into the Class 3 and 4 categories."

Class 2. David knew, from talking to Kate, that she'd been offered a Commander's position just for reaching that Class in her training. But he wasn't training—just waking abilities he wasn't entirely sure he had control over.

"You also have police procedural experience most of our people lack," Warner continued, apparently taking his silence as an invitation to continue. "You were trained as a tactical team leader, though I understand the team was only deployed once under your command. You are also older than over sixty percent of our people, with more experience in general.

"We are prepared to offer you a slot at the next Commander Training Session. We only run it when we have enough candidates," she explained. "Marking you as a candidate does mean you are increased in seniority and effectively take on a second-in-command role."

"Kate already holds that role in ONSET Nine," David objected.

"Yes, she does," Warner confirmed. "And with her and Ix, who, being a *demon*, obviously cannot command a team, ONSET Nine already has two Class Twos to support its Class One. We're going to have to move you anyway, so we would like to move you to a team in need of a candidate for a second-in-command."

Without moving from his chair, David reeled across the room. They were offering him more authority—more trust. More *power*—and the power he already wielded terrified him. His father's old axiom of "power corrupts" rang through his head, and a part of him was convinced it would only put him on the slippery slope to what he feared.

Part of him *knew* he couldn't be trusted with that much power. He feared he'd fail them, and he opened his mouth to refuse. Before he spoke, he met Major Warner's eyes and Saw.

He'd looked at the Major before with his Sight, but not since he'd fully mastered the ability, and certainly not since the additional abilities woke up in Montreal and Montana.

He looked at her and saw her confidence. He saw the assured competence of the professional soldier and officer who served as the day-to-day Commander of ONSET. And woven through her competence he saw her day-to-day struggle against temptation. In her aura, he saw the same fear of corruption in her as he felt in himself. He knew she'd seen far more people abuse their powers than he had. She knew the consequences, and the temptation, intimately.

David White looked into his leader's soul in that moment and saw a mirror of everything that drove him. The same oath drove Major Warner as drove him.

If she could use that oath to sustain her faith in herself in the face of temptation, how could he do less? For all his strengths, a high-Circle Mage's temptations were far more immediate, more...insidious. Every day, Major Warner faced the temptation to make her life that little bit easier by abusing her power. Every day, she refused.

David's refusal died unborn on his tongue as he blinked and the moment passed.

Warner looked at him strangely, as if questioning what he'd Seen, and he shook his head.

"I accept your offer," he told her, as much an oath to himself as an acceptance to her. "I will serve and protect to the best of my ability. And I will trust *you* that this is the best use of my ability," he finished.

"Thank you," Warner said quietly.

The two stood in silence for a moment, and then Warner's phone rang, interrupting the power of the scene. Gesturing for David to hold on a moment, she answered the phone.

"Major Warner."

She waited a moment, and David watched the green eyes go completely flat and her lips press to a thin line.

"Thank you," she said quietly. "I will inform the team."

She turned to David. "I hate to make you the bearer of bad news, David," Major Traci Warner said softly to her agent, "but that was the hospital in Montana. Alexandra Bourque just died."

[35]

THE NEXT DAY PASSED IN NEAR-SILENCE IN ONSET NINE'S APARTMENT
building. Michael flew off to Montana the very next morning, and the
rest of the team gathered in the common room. No words passed
between any of them, but they all took comfort in each other's presence. David's promotion attracted some gentle prodding early on, but
even that faded into the general malaise of Bourque's death.

Morgen was missing for most of the first day but returned in the
early afternoon and threw himself into a chair in front of the dead television. David was playing a very quiet hand of blackjack with Kate
and Ix, the three feeling the emptiness of the room.

"What is it?" Kate asked, looking up from the game.

"I'm supposed to be doing analysis on the data I pulled from those
bastards' computers," the techno-Mage said flatly, "except that
someone at OSPI has pulled strings and yoinked the entire analysis
operation over to New York. The damned disks were pulled right off
of my chopper and couriered to OSPI before any of us even got a
chance to look at them."

"The last thing we need right now is an interoffice pissing match,"
David said quietly. "They *do* have a larger analysis department than
we do."

"Normally, this would not be grounds for concern," Ix growled. "However, given the seizure of a high court demon, it is likely a bad idea to have Ekhmez and those responsible for tracking down his cult in the same building." The demon looked around at the other ONSET agents as he dealt out a new hand, including a set of cards for Morgen.

After a moment, the hacker joined them, accepting the cards.

"It's a security risk," he said bluntly. "We don't know what the bastard is capable of." He glanced at his hole card and tapped his king. "Hit me."

"You think he might escape?" David asked, looking at his own hole card. He had an eight showing and a queen in the hole. "I'll stay."

"Possible," Kate replied, checking the card next to her own queen. "I'll stay," she told Ix, then continued. "There are other powers Ekhmez might have that could be more dangerous."

"It is notable that most of the high court demons can influence the minds of their inferiors," Ix said flatly as he dealt himself a three to go with his four showing. "Certainly, my encounter with Ekhmez was... uncomfortable. I had not yet encountered a higher court demon than myself on Earth, so the realization that I could not act against him is difficult to accept."

"You're saying he could take over OSPI?" David asked in horror, his fingers pressing hard against the card table.

"Unlikely," Ix said calmly. "Even among demons, who have issues resisting the powers of higher courts, it is usually only an influence. He would find it difficult to force his enemies to become his allies. Card, Morgen?"

"No, I'll stand," the Mage replied. "Also," he said, turning to David, "the OSPI pukes aren't useless. They'll know if he's doing something like that and counteract it. They've got some good Mages over in New York."

Ix dealt himself a five and then flipped over his nine to show he'd busted. "Show cards."

Kate flipped over her ace first, revealing a perfect twenty-one none of the others matched.

"You're all being paranoid," she reminded them. "OSPI really does have a bigger analysis department than us. That's why they grabbed the data. Let them do their job and give us a target. Then we can go kick the bastards' asses to hell."

A growl ran around the room. Alexandra's death had not fully sunk home yet, but they intended to make someone pay for it. Dearly.

———

MICHAEL MADE his way into Kalispell Regional Medical Center in a somber mood. The ONSET Commander had been out of the state for less than twenty-four hours before being called back.

The receptionist at the front desk had clearly been told to expect him.

"If you'll wait here, please," she asked, leading him to a plainly furnished side office. "Dr. Lincoln will be with you shortly."

The girl vanished with surprising alacrity, and Michael smiled to himself. Even though he was dressed in a conservative black suit, most people were *still* uncomfortable around him.

The werewolf looked around the office and noted its bare surfaces. A pair of filing cabinets against one wall, in institutional green. A simple metal desk, the sole furnishings on it a silent computer and a picture he couldn't see the front of. Not much to suggest that Dr. Lincoln spent much time here.

As if summoned by the thought, the doctor finally arrived. A surprisingly short man, Lincoln barely made it to Michael's shoulder. Skinny and dark-skinned, he surprised Michael. The werewolf had hardly expected a doctor in Montana to be black.

"Have a seat, Mr. O'Brien," Lincoln said softly, as Michael was still standing.

"Thank you," Michael replied, doing so. "My name is Michael, please, Dr. Lincoln."

The small man nodded nervously as he took his seat and faced the ONSET Commander across the desk.

"I don't presume to ask what happened," he said eventually. "Suffice to say we don't see a lot of government agents or gunshot wounds."

"You were the closest hospital," Michael replied. "Some of our people wouldn't have lived if we'd gone further."

While Bourque had *not* lived, Michael had been given a quick rundown on the status of the AP men who'd come to this same hospital. While they had all been moved on as soon as they had been stabilized, several had lived who hadn't been expected to make it that long. Captain Narita had specifically labeled Dr. Lincoln as the cause of that.

"Yes, that is true," Lincoln replied quickly. "Still, we were not expecting so many, so quickly. Those sorts of wounds are not our specialty."

"This is a quiet area," Michael agreed. "You and your people performed wonders."

The small man seemed to relax slightly. "But not miracles," he answered, his speech somewhat slower. "I am sorry."

"How bad was Alexandra?" Michael asked, after a moment of silence.

"Honestly, I am amazed she made it here," the doctor replied, his words very slow now. "She had a number of minor wounds, but the one that killed her was her stomach. She took a shotgun slug there, and it did not fully pass through. While it was present, she could not properly digest and would have starved," he said in a voice now distant and clinical, as though describing an article he'd read.

"When we attempted to remove it, she began bleeding profusely and died before we could stop the bleeding. We were not prepared for blood loss that drastic."

Lincoln fell silent; his gaze focused somewhere far away from Michael. The ONSET officer allowed the doctor his silence for a few long moments and then cleared his throat.

"Her body is ready for transport, as requested?" he asked.

"Yes," the small man confirmed. "We were not given a next-of-kin listing," he noted.

"They have been notified," Michael replied, wincing internally. He'd left that duty to Major Warner while he came here to collect her body. Alexandra had an ex-husband and two daughters. While her husband had had custody of the children for the last ten years and one of the daughters was now adult and married, she'd still been on good terms with them. She had effectively sacrificed her marriage on the altar of service in ONSET.

"The US Government is handling all funeral arrangements," he continued. "My understanding is that a significant disbursement is slated for Kalispell Regional in thanks for your assistance and discretion."

He stressed the last word carefully. While no one would be so crude as to *say* so, the major boost to the hospital's funding was nothing more or less than a giant bribe to keep their mouths shut about this whole mess.

Lincoln nodded without comment. "I'll take you to speak with our morgue director," he offered. "You can make the transportation arrangements directly with her."

"Thank you, Dr. Lincoln," Michael replied. "My colleagues made clear that you are the reason as many of our people survived as did. We cannot thank you enough."

Maybe it was Michael's imagination, but the little doctor seemed to stand a tiny bit taller and straighter as he led the way out of the office.

CURIOSITY ALWAYS HAD to give way to paying the bills, and it had been days since Majestic had last had a chance to trawl through ONSET's files and servers. Each time she went through, she found new layers of security she had to circumvent. The system was the most secure she had *ever* hacked her way into, and she made a habit of raiding the Pentagon yearly to make sure she was still up to the task of doing it without being found.

Searching by *David White* began to give context to large portions of the system. Over *here* was payroll and human resources, and the read/write protections on those files defeated even her. Not that she needed to change anything there; just looking at some of the salary figures made her blink. Salaries alone for the organization probably ran somewhere around a billion dollars.

Over here were equipment records, recording the issue of weapons, armor, rooms, ammunition, food, even furniture to David White. Skimming through the list of items issued to him and others was an experience in itself. What the hell was an "ONSET-Issue Combat Knife, comma, Aetherically Modified, comma, Mod Six?" What did the "Class Four Technological Aetheric Focus" note attached to the issue of a laptop to one of his teammates mean? Digging back through the library gave some of the answers, but the idea of a magical *computer* made Majestic laugh.

Until she remembered the choke point security. Yeah, it was technically possible to have a reactive firewall like that, but no program should have even detected her. A magical computer suddenly didn't sound so unlikely anymore.

The jackpot of the night was personnel files. David White's personnel file, to be specific. It gave his name, place of birth, parents, social security number—all things she already knew—and several ID numbers she hadn't been aware of.

Then it listed details of his supernatural powers. "Supernatural Strength" was listed as confirmed, with specific ratings she didn't understand. "Aura Perception" and "Precognition" were the same, numbers and descriptions she'd have to reference. Then...*Major Regeneration?!* That seemed...somewhat self-explanatory.

The last entry was more complex. "Agent has demonstrated extreme levels of supernaturally enhanced speed under significant stress. This ability has not been confirmed under controlled conditions, but data suggests at least A-rated Empowered Speed, and possibly as high as AA or AAA."

A summary line at the bottom of that list labeled David White as 'class two supernatural, potential class one rating on achievement of potential abilities.' Another line labeled him as a candidate for some 'Commander Training Session,' though no more details were given.

The document closed with an itemized list of what appeared to be reports. Not efficiency reports, Majestic presumed. After all, he'd only been with the organization a few months.

She clicked on one. It gave a date of a few weeks before and a location in Montreal. Further reading rang repeated bells in her head, until the hacker pulled up her list of red-flag new stories.

The "drug bust" in Montreal had been an ONSET raid on a

vampire holding. David White had been there—in the middle of it, according to this report. Each of these reports gave the true details of an incident that had been buried and hidden.

Setting her computer to download *all* the incident reports linked to David White, she looked back up at the numbers at the top of the document. She stared at them blankly for a moment and then realized what one of them was.

It was an identifier code for a communication network. With that code, she could pick out his radio from ONSET's network. Maybe talk to him.

Not, she realized, that he likely wanted to talk to *her*.

[36]

DAVID HAD ALMOST FORGOTTEN ABOUT HIS TRANSFER IN THE MIDST OF
ONSET Nine's grief for their fallen member. On the second morning,
however, he received an internal electronic memo requesting that he
confirm with Campus Facilities when his belongings were packed and
ready to move over to the dormitory for ONSET Team Thirteen.

While it made sense that he room with his new team, he wasn't
ready for the move yet. The thought of moving away from his
comrades as they dealt with one permanent loss was a lot to bear, and
his initial packing was lackadaisical at best.

He'd been at it for less than two hours before a knock on his door
interrupted him.

"Come in," he answered, grateful for any interruption from the
unpleasant task.

Kate and Ix walked in together and surveyed the room.

"Got your memo, I see," Kate said quietly. "Warner let me know
you'd be moving, and I grabbed Ix on my way here."

"What's up, guys?" he asked slowly, taking in the young woman's
words. He noticed that both the Mage and the demon were dressed in
comfortable sweats and T-shirts.

"I have moved between teams four times in my service with your people," Ix growled. "It is not an easy task. We are here to provide you a distraction while you pack."

Kate shot the demon a glance. "It was a tossup between whether it would be you or me moved, you know," she told David. "We're here to help you move."

"And provide a distraction," David repeated Ix's words, understanding the truth. "Thank you."

Kate flashed him a bright smile and then said two words David didn't understand. Sparks flickered out from her fingers and formed into a set of brown boxes. They looked like cardboard, but David didn't need his Sight to know they'd hold a lot more than it looked like.

"Then let's get to it," she said briskly.

———

WITH TWO HELPERS, the work of packing was both easier and faster. Kate made it vastly easier by repeatedly demonstrating a spell she referred to as her "packing cantrip." It grabbed all of a type of object— say, socks—from where they happened to be in a room and folded them neatly into a box.

David's clothes and books fell victim to the cantrip, leaving only the more awkward individual items for the three ONSET agents to pack into Kate's enchanted boxes themselves. Empowered strength or no, David *knew* the fully packed boxes were lighter than they ought to be.

By midafternoon, they were actually done with packing, and David called the Facilities office to have the strapping soldiers it employed come move his furniture into trucks and across Campus.

His new CO must have bribed Facilities to tell him when that call was made, because he beat the trucks there. The work of packing barely done, the three had only just joined the others in the common room. This meant David was still in sweaty work clothes when Commander McDermott arrived in ONSET Nine's common room.

This put him in stark contrast with Lorne McDermott, who was dressed in the ONSET black bodysuit uniform, with two ribbons on his chest—for, unless David misread them, the Navy Cross and the Distinguished Service Medal, two of the Navy's highest awards for valor. The Commander barely matched David's own unspectacular five-foot-four height, dark hair slicked back with some kind of oil. David met his new superior's eyes and barely kept from reacting visibly. The man's eyes were pure black, lacking iris or whites.

"Agent White," he greeted David, offering his hand. The Commander's motions were graceful, flowing and somehow dangerous.

"Commander," David replied, shaking the man's hand.

"I've heard good things about you, David," McDermott told him. "O'Brien gave me a phone call after the decision was made you'd be coming to my team. He told me I was lucky to get you."

"Did he say anything about Alexandra's funeral?" David asked.

"He told me that if I didn't let you get to it, he'd 'eat my blubbery butt,' I believe was how he put it," McDermott said serenely. "This Friday," he added, glancing around at the rest of the team. "I just found out before I came over here. Alexandra played wet nurse for my first command, back when ONSET first stole me from the SEALs."

"What about her family?" Kate asked.

"My understanding is that the funeral is taking place in Colorado Springs so her family can attend," the Commander replied. "You are all receiving special leave to attend, along with those of us who served with her for a while."

"Thank you for the notice, sir," Kate replied.

"You'd have heard soon anyway, so don't give me that, young lady," McDermott replied with a wink. Despite the deadly grace with which he moved, it was almost impossible *not* to like the man.

"Now, I need to introduce David to his new team," the Commander continued. "Don't worry, he's not going far," he promised, "but it is time to go. I'll wait outside for a minute," he concluded.

The Commander gave a slight bow and stepped out of the dormitory. David looked around at his now-former teammates helplessly. What did you say at a time like this? He'd worked with them for mere months, but he was going to miss them all.

Akono broke the ice first, the elf seeming to materialize out of nowhere to step forward and offer his slim hand to David. David took it and was surprised once more by the firmness of the elf's grip.

"It's been a pleasure, David. Don't go too far; we'll keep in touch," Akono told him, then without warning kissed him on the lips.

While David was still spluttering, Kate stepped in front of him and, with a swift "My turn," kissed him as well.

Morgen and Ix broke down into uproarious laughter, and much of the tension of the last few days drained away. The team had been hit with a double loss, of Bourque to a cultist's shotgun and of David to promotion, but they would survive.

The goodbyes after that were still painful but short.

———

MCDERMOTT HAD WAITED out the goodbyes, which took far more than a minute, and was standing outside by a boxy five-ton truck, talking to the three black-uniformed Facilities men. He turned when he saw David and stepped over to him.

"Looks like our moving team is ready to go grab your things," he told the junior agent.

David took a moment to thank the men for their help, which was met with grins.

"It makes a nice break from watching screens with crosshairs for threats that never come," one of them replied. The others nodded, and with a wave, they entered ONSET Nine's building.

The younger man watched them go and realized he'd never thought about just who manned the incredible defenses around this base. Between the security personnel he'd encountered and the men necessary to man defenses of that level, there were a *lot* of soldiers on this base. Somehow, he doubted they had the full apartment suites each that the ONSET Agents enjoyed.

That thought carried him, wordlessly, to McDermott's black government-issue Lincoln. He got in the passenger seat as his new Commander got behind the wheel.

"Just so you know," McDermott told him as the heavy car smoothly rolled away, "you're a replacement for one of our people—Jason Shi. He took a silver bullet to the head during a raid on a vampire safe house in New Jersey. That was a few weeks ago, but keep it in mind, son."

"Noted, sir," David acknowledged quietly. "Who else is on the team?"

"I'll wait until we're there to introduce them," McDermott told him. "We tend to get the more aquatic missions—we're unofficially ONSET's Coast Guard slash amphibian team. This is mainly because I'm a Selkie, and one of our people is a water elementalist. You're going to need scuba and aquatic training."

David considered for a moment, wondering just what a Selkie *was*, and then nodded at McDermott's last comment. Just because he probably wouldn't *die* from drowning didn't mean it wouldn't be excruciatingly unpleasant. Relying on his powers not to die as he walked underwater seemed like a moderately bad idea.

The drive wasn't a long one—while ONSET Thirteen's dormitory was on the opposite side of the Campus from ONSET Nine's, the entire Campus was less than a mile across. Driving around it never took long.

They parked beside the building, basically identical to the one they'd left a few minutes before except that it had rose bushes around the entrance, which Nine's building lacked.

"Those are Kelly's fault," McDermott noted as they walked up to the rose bushes. "She likes plants, and I'm too big of a softy to remind her of the concept of 'clear field of fire.'"

The concept of the Selkie ex-Seal as a "softy" was hard for David to swallow, but he suspected it might be more truth than it seemed at first as he followed the other man into his new home.

The main floor common room shared similarities with the room in Nine's dormitory. The same flatscreen television with the cupboard beneath it for computer access stood at one wall. The plush green couches and hardwood chairs were the same, as was the ever-present blue carpet. The chairs and tables were pushed together to form a circular meeting-slash-eating area in the corner next to the door, and potted plants occupied all four corners. The couches were formed into a U around the television screen, and a pool table was in the corner beside the stairs leading up and the door into the armory.

Two men and three women were scattered around the room in civilian dress. Whatever they had been doing when David and McDermott entered had been dropped, and the five rose to their feet with an instinctual simultaneity.

"Ladies and gentlemen," McDermott greeted them. "I'd like you to welcome David White, our new second-in-command."

A large tanned man, towering over both David and the Commander, was closest and offered his hand to David. His head was completely shaven, and his eyes locked on David's with a harsh, measuring gaze.

"This is Chris Johnston," the Commander introduced him to David, "more commonly known as Stone. He's our local Empowered, with the ability to make his skin granite."

"That sounds useful," David admitted as he took Stone's hand. Stone immediately exerted full force—Empowered force. Barely managing not to wince initially, David returned the big man's supernatural strength pound for pound and then squeezed a bit more. After a moment of silent struggle, Stone relented.

"It is," he responded, his voice oddly quiet and high-pitched for such a large man. For the first time, David noticed the ugly scar on the man's throat as Stone nodded firmly and stepped back, allowing one of the women to take his place.

"This is Kelly Walsh," the Commander introduced her. Walsh was a tall woman, nearly matching Stone's six-foot-plus frame, but far thinner with it. A bright golden braid looped around her head, and dark blue eyes glinted at him.

"Kelly is our resident green thumb," McDermott continued. "And you'll only think that's a minor power until the first time you see her tell a tree to beat someone up—and it does."

As he took Kelly's hand, David was grateful for his regeneration. A slight warmth in his hand healed the bruising from Stone before he shook her hand.

"You just have to know how to talk to them," she told him gruffly.

Her grip was firm but not the bone-breaker Stone had tried to exert. She shook hands swiftly and then joined Stone on the couch.

The third member of ONSET Thirteen was the first less-than-massive person David had seen since McDermott himself. She was a brunette of around five three, an inch or so shorter than David and somewhat stocky with it. She was dressed in a shade of deep blue that brought out the dazzling blue of her eyes.

"This is Mary Lynch," McDermott told David. "She's our water elementalist. Likes to go surfing without a board," he added with a grin.

"Boards are for those afraid of the water," Lynch told her Commander, her voice a delightful brook-like burble. She shook hands with David and stepped aside, waiting by the door, unlike Walsh and Stone.

The last woman on the team was another woman of average height, slimmer than Lynch and raven-haired instead of brunette. Her dark eyes matched her hair as she met David's eyes firmly. Lines drawn on her face and a few traces of silver in her hair suggested an age much older than the rest of the team's late twenties.

"This is Kate Hellet," their Commander told David. "She's our team's Mage and resident mother. She does a good job of keeping us all in line and on task."

"You all need it," Hellet said quietly. "I used to teach kindergarten," she told David. "It was good practice for dealing with this lot."

She shook his hand and joined Lynch by the side of the door as the last member of the team stepped forward with a minor grin. The shortest member of the team by a good four inches, the last man was heavily stocky with it and could probably have played a dwarf in a Tolkien film if he grew a beard.

"Lastly, this is James Pell," McDermott told David. "OSPI used to think he was a mundane Inspector, until the day he got into a half-wrecked car with no engine and caught a werewolf in it."

"How does *that* work?" David asked, incredulous.

"I didn't know the car wasn't working," Pell said simply. "Vehicles just do what I want them to. Even if they're broken. Or shouldn't be able to do it in the first place."

"Don't test him on the last one," Hellet replied. "Yes, he can make a car break-dance. It probably won't drive again afterwards, though."

"It did eventually," Pell argued.

"It took you longer to fix it than it did to get it to dance," she told him.

The teasing was interrupted by a knock on the door announcing that David's things had arrived.

[37]

DAVID DIDN'T REALLY HAVE TIME TO SETTLE IN WITH HIS NEW TEAM BEFORE he was back with his old one, on his way down to Colorado Springs in the back of Kate's car. He'd spent most of the three days rearranging his furniture to make subtly clear to his mind that he had changed locations. The apartments were laid out identically, so he *knew* an unchanged layout would have confused him.

The rest of the time had been spent in a water tank in one of the underground training facilities, having McDermott, ably aided by Koburn, David's original instructor, teaching him scuba and snorkel use. David was glad for Koburn's assistance. Without the Sage's ability to magically instill skill, he doubted he would have acquired even the very basic competency he had acquired.

Thoughts on his week and mental review of his underwater training helped keep him distracted on the long, silent trip down to the city. Akono and Ix occupied the back seat. Akono was silently working on a glamor to cover Ix's obviously inhuman face. People like David and Kate, with Second Sight, would be able to tell what was going on. They, however, weren't what he was hiding from. They were going to a funeral amongst normal people—people who didn't know about the supernatural.

They hit the city limit around when Akono pronounced the glamor complete, the first words anyone had spoken that morning. David twisted around to look at Ix, who was now an African-American man of a heavy build.

"Works," David said shortly. Like the others, he really didn't feel like talking much as they drove through the city to the funeral home. A motley mix of rental cars from Bourque's family, personal vehicles of ONSET personnel and black government cars filled the church parking lot.

The four agents exited the car and were met by Michael standing on the edge of the parking lot by the steps leading up into the blocky church building with its tall white cross.

"Morning," the werewolf greeted them. "Sorry for not making it back to Campus," he told them, "I've been tied up in Washington when we haven't been making arrangements for this."

"Washington?" David asked.

"OSPI has pulled an intelligence gold mine out of that database Morgen grabbed," Michael said quietly, eyeing the crowd moving into the church. Most of Alexandra's family and non-ONSET friends were giving the black-suited Omicron men and women a wide berth, and he continued. As he watched, Morgen exited a black government car with a number of other Campus sys-admins, and Michael waved him over.

"I can't say more here," he continued once Morgen had joined them on the steps of the church, "but I think we'll be avenging Alexandra soon enough."

Nodding to them all, Michael led the way into the church.

———

"MANY PEOPLE CAN BE RELIED upon to speak their beliefs loudly and without thought for consequences," Michael said quietly, the microphone carrying his voice to the assembled mourners.

"Not so many are willing to stand up for their beliefs. Fewer still are willing to fight for their beliefs. Alexandra Bourque was a member of that last group.

"She believed that the people of America deserved protecting from the darkest sides of mankind," Michael told them. "She believed it so strongly that she gave up an aspiring career as a marketing analyst—one that would have kept her and her family comfortable for the rest of their lives—to join the Marines.

"Alexandra believed so strongly that when she left the Marines, even married and with a child"—his gaze drifted to Alexandra's ex-husband and children in the very front row—"she joined the FBI when we recruited her." Here, before her family and the world, that lie would have to stand. No one except her co-workers needed to know who she'd *really* worked for.

"It wasn't an easy course for her, and we all know the sacrifices she made along the way," he continued. "Her marriage failed upon the strictures of duty." Mr. Bourque looked uncomfortable, but Michael hardly blamed the man. The parting had been due to her inability to spend enough time with the family, not an unwillingness of the family to support her.

"Mrs. Bourque knew what her duty in a high-threat-response team entailed," Michael continued grimly. "Friends around her paid the price of our freedom. She was forced, on several occasions, to kill to protect those she wanted to keep safe.

"But Alexandra Bourque kept the faith and the fires burning," he said loudly now, and the mike echoed his voice across the small chapel. "She died as she chose long ago—standing between her people and those who would do them harm."

Michael let the tears flow now. He let the family and his comrades see that moment of weakness. He'd seen too many friends fall in the line of duty, and knew that his long lifespan would bring many more such losses.

"Alexandra Bourque was a friend," he said, his voice soft again, mellowed by his tears. "She was a comrade I was proud to serve and fight alongside, and rewarded to command.

"But above all else, she was a cop. A protector. A guardian of our people, sworn to serve and protect.

"Do not forget her choice," he begged them. "She is no longer with us, and I mourn that, but I know that she is pleased, wherever she has gone. Alexandra *made a difference*. None of us can ask for more than that.

"Thank you," he said finally, softly. He turned to face the coffin—a closed coffin, just in case. Her wounds, and the injuries inflicted as they tried to save her, were coverable but still ugly. It was safer this way.

Firmly and slowly, Michael O'Brien gave Alexandra Bourque one last pristine salute.

———

WHILE ONSET PERSONNEL mostly ate in their apartments or their dorm common rooms, today many of them gathered in a mess hall. ONSET Nine had occupied an entire table, and ONSET Thirteen, David's new team, took over the next one.

Bourque had once served on Thirteen, though only McDermott and Pell had known her. The rest of the team had cycled through since then. Between casualties and transfers, ONSET units often changed up rapidly.

It was a silent, somber gathering. While no more complete teams were present, a scattering of agents and admin personnel who'd worked closely with Alexandra Bourque were gathered in the Spartan hall. The chairs were uncomfortable, the tables cheap and quickly empty of food, but they stayed regardless.

No one was sure what they were holding vigil for, least of all David, who sat with McDermott at the end of ONSET Thirteen's table. But they held the vigil nonetheless, and he, unlike the others, knew that they were actually waiting for something. No Sight would tell him what, though.

It was almost ten o'clock at night when the answer came. The door to the mess hall swung open and Major Warner stepped in. She was wearing a rumpled gray skirted suit and looked like she'd been traveling. In both hands she held a black briefcase, and two men in black civilian suits followed her through the door.

The gathered men and women eyed her carefully. Those who had noticed—like David—had been surprised that the Major had missed Alexandra's funeral.

"They told me you would all be here," she said quietly, and even without volume, her voice carried through the silent hall.

"I am sorry I missed Alexandra's funeral," she continued. "I wish with all my heart I could have been, but even that must give way before the wishes of the President of the United States."

The President? David wondered what was going on, and given the rustling around him, he didn't think he was alone.

"I, and Colonel Ardent, have spent most of the last two days closeted with either the Committee of Thirteen or the President," Warner told them in explanation of her absence. "We were reviewing with them the evidence we extracted from the Church of the Black Sun's lodge."

The sound that ran through the crowd of mourners was not questioning this time. It was *hungry*, and David felt that hunger in himself. The Church had killed one of their own—several, actually, but there was more distance from the two Anti-Paranormal men who'd died than there was with Alexandra.

"It was a gold mine, people," she told them quietly. "Financial records, membership lists, everything we needed to know exactly where they were, who they were and what they were doing.

"We took all of that and the footage of the demon-summoning to the President," she continued. "Colonel Ardent pressed for the Committee to declare them a demon cult, removing religious protections."

They can do that? David questioned in amazement. It was one hell of a violation of civil rights, but given the circumstances, he could understand that.

"The Committee felt that the situation was more dire than that, based off of OSPI's recommendations, and took it to the President himself."

Scuttlebutt that David had heard suggested that the President had major issues with Omicron's very existence and found the whole affair highly uncomfortable. He couldn't have been happy about being dragged into this.

"As of an hour ago, the President issued, and the Committee confirmed for Congress, Executive Order Omicron Ninety-One," Warner told them grimly, removing a sheet of paper from her briefcase.

"As per the terms of this Order, the so-called Church of the Black Sun is now classified as both a demon cult and a terrorist organization," she read from the paper. "As such, it is a threat to the national security of the United States and the President has ordered extraordinary measures.

"All religious protections awarded to the Church have been revoked," she continued to read, her voice formal. "All rights of religious freedom related to the Church have been revoked. All financial and physical assets of the Church are to be frozen and confiscated.

"All known members of the Church of the Black Sun are temporarily stripped of the following civil rights: the right to assembly, the right to free speech, the right against self-incrimination, the right to *habeas corpus* and the right to freedom of religion." Warner's reading of the list continued into dead silence, each suspended right hitting the silent air like a falling tombstone.

"Per this order, all known members of the Church of the Black Sun are to be detained immediately. Interrogations under truth magic will determine the innocent and the guilty.

"These orders of seizure and detainment will be carried out by the Office of the National Supernatural Enforcement Teams and the Office of Supernatural Policing and Investigation as soon as reasonably possible."

Warner lowered the paper and looked at all of them. David was frozen in shock, and he doubted he was the only one. They had *that* kind of authority? Morgen had filled them in on some of the information they'd learned about the Church. It was a nationwide organization, with over a hundred chapter houses and other properties. They'd just been ordered to arrest over *five thousand* people—and many of the rights those people assumed they possessed had just been stripped away.

Part of him insisted that this was wrong, but the rest accepted that this was *necessary*. These people had already summoned one demon. If they weren't stopped, who knew what they could unleash upon America? Upon the *world*?

"The order is signed by the President himself, and counter-signed by all three Justices of the Omicron Court," Warner said softly, as if she knew what David was thinking. He half-expected that she suspected—too many people in the room would be thinking the same thing. "It is fully legal, and we will carry out these orders as soon as possible.

"An operations plan is being prepared by OSPI, and this operation will almost certainly require the combined strength of our ONSET teams and OSPI's personnel," she continued. "You will all be briefed on your individual team roles in the morning. This will be the largest operation the Omicron branch of the US Government has undertaken since the Provisional Force took on the Montana Incursion.

"This threat to the safety of our people will not be tolerated. Get some rest, people," she ordered. "Tomorrow, you'll need it."

THE MORNING CAME WITH A RENEWED SENSE OF PURPOSE. DAVID DRESSED simply, knowing that he'd be changing into combat gear soon enough, and descended down to ONSET Thirteen's common room.

He wasn't the last one down, but Stone and Hellet were already there. Hellet was reading a ridiculously thick hardcover book at the circle of tables, and Stone was busy watching television on the couch. Both of them looked up as David entered. Hellet bookmarked her page and lowered her book, but Stone gave an oddly pitched grunt and turned back to the television.

The ex-teacher gestured for David to join her, and he did so gladly, taking the chance to look at the book. It was some sort of encyclopedia of western European mythology.

"Some light reading for the morning?" he asked as he pulled a chair out and joined her at the table.

"I like to research the myths from around the world," she replied, patting the book affectionately. "Every so often, I compare it to the supernatural creatures and people we have encountered and see how accurate the myth was."

"And?" he queried. He'd heard the rough rundown on a few of the myths—mainly werewolves and vampires—compared to reality, but he hadn't really looked too much at it himself.

"Some of them are very accurate," she replied. "Werewolves, for example. An untrained werewolf only shifts under the moon, silver hurts them, et cetera, et cetera. Others, like vampires, are dangerous to believe. Crosses and stakes don't bother vampires much, and believing that they will can get you killed."

David nodded, remembering his reading. Vampires were vulnerable to sunlight, but it was more painfully crippling than fatal. Silver was the best weapon against them, like against most supernaturals. Staking one through the heart *might* kill it, but it was no magic bullet.

"Then we have the grab bag the 'scientists' like to call Empowered, like yourself," she continued. "You, to all intents and purposes, are the walking vision of a Greek hero or a modern four-color superhero. Others in the category, like Pell or Stone over there, are harder to identify."

"What about Commander McDermott?" David asked. He figured that was a safe way to find out just what a Selkie really was. All he knew was that they were seal shapeshifters.

"Lorne is a Selkie," Hellet said aloud, thoughtfully. "They're an odd bunch, both in myth and reality. Myth talks about their sealskin, required for them to transform. Steal it away, and they're locked in human form.

"In practice, that's not as good an idea as you might think," she said dryly. "Some are relatively helpless in that form, but it depends on the kind of seal. Lorne is a leopard seal Selkie—think several hundred pounds of solid-muscle fury. Even in human form, he is a powerfully strong man, and, like most shapeshifters, he regenerates almost any injury."

David considered that, noting as Pell and Lynch came down the stairs. Pell joined David and Hellet with a nod to them both, while Lynch nodded in the pair's general direction and joined Stone on the couches before the TV.

"The sealskin part of the myth isn't true," Hellet continued, and then glanced over at Pell. "I'm giving David a lecture on comparative myth and reality on Selkies," she told him. "Feel free to be bored."

The dwarfish man grinned. "Nah, I'm always good to listen to someone talk about the boss," he told them.

"Like I said," she said in response, "the sealskin part of the myth isn't entirely true. The Commander doesn't keep an actual sealskin under his uniform or anything so dramatic. *However*, all Selkies apparently have some token required for them to complete the change."

"And absolutely none of us like having the fact, or the nature of said token, advertised," a dry voice interjected. David looked up to find McDermott standing at the entrance to the dormitory, only about five feet from where they were sitting.

The three at the tables scrambled to stand and salute; but the Commander waved them back down to their seats about halfway up.

"Of course," he continued in the same dry voice, "none of you *know* what my token is. So, I'm probably safe." And he winked. David relaxed slightly as the Selkie smiled at his team.

"Are we all here?" he asked, and David glanced around the room. As if conjured by the question, Walsh, the last member of the team, appeared at the top of the stairs.

"All right," McDermott continued. He crossed to the flatscreen set into the wall and opened the computer console. "Sorry, Stone, I'm taking over the screen," he told the Empowered.

"Go for it, sir," the hulking man said quietly, pushing his entire couch slightly back so the rest of the team could gather around.

The television screen faded, replaced by the lightning-crossed O and police badge of the Omicron Branch, and the subtitle CLASSIFIED: *TOP SECRET OMICRON-DELTA.*

McDermott entered a code into the keyboard, and the seal faded to background as a different title blazed onto the screen: OPERATION SUN NET.

"This is the operation plan we got out of OSPI's analysis department last night," the team Commander told his people. "I've looked at the numbers, and it's a scarily large number of our people.

"All in all, we are committing twenty ONSET Strike Teams and almost every OSPI Tactical Team. That's just over a hundred supernaturals with the ONSET teams and just under two thousand OSPI

Tactical Police. Call it twenty-one hundred sets of boots on the ground."

"That's a lot of people, boss," Lynch interjected. "What the hell do they think we need that for? And if we're throwing that many folks around, where's Stutter? Those boys aren't up to our level, but they're still a full platoon of supernaturals!"

The numbers, David realized looking at the map, left the entire Omicron branch drastically short of people to do anything *else*. With that much of ONSET and basically every tactical team OSPI had tied up, it left the country very vulnerable. And Lynch's point about SSTTR rang true as well. They were the ones who'd grabbed Ekhmez at the end, why weren't they involved in this?

"The Stutter team," their Commander told them, "was already tied up in an internal affair over at OSPI when we broke this information. As for the total numbers," McDermott said grimly, "that is a minimal strike force at each target location. We are looking at an average of two sites per state, including Alaska and Hawaii. That, for those of us who don't like math or lost count of the states, is over a *hundred* target sites. We know how vulnerable this makes us, people," he told them. "But we want to hit them all.

"We estimate between twenty and fifty targets on site at each location, and an average of fifteen to thirty targets we will have to sweep up individually afterwards.

"Last number I heard," he elaborated, "was that we have a list of over six thousand individual names that warrants have been issued for. We expect to grab between sixty and seventy percent of those people at the target sites."

"All respect to OSPI's analysts, but how do we expect that?" Pell asked. "These people could be anywhere."

"We don't have addresses for all of those names yet," McDermott admitted. "Once we do, those of anyone we miss in Sun Net will be passed to local police departments. *However*, we also have the worship schedule of the church. Tonight, at six PM in their local times, they will be opening services. The services and socials will run to around eleven.

"We will move in at six thirty Pacific Standard Time," he continued, bringing up a map of the continental United States with time zones marked and tiny red dots for target zones. "This means that even in the Eastern Time Zone, most of them will still be in the target zone."

David eyed the map. "What about Hawaii?" he asked.

"The Hawaii operation is somewhat more complex, but I'm assured it will still go down at our target time," McDermott told him. "All operations are intended to go down simultaneously to make sure no target gets prior warning." He checked his watch. "That is in just under thirteen hours from now."

"What's our role?" Stone asked.

"Good question," the Commander replied. "We can't really influence the result of any other operation but our own. This is our target."

The screen changed again, to an overhead view of a building set along a river. An attractive Victorian-style hotel stood on the shore of a meager river, with a boathouse attached to the hotel embracing a small natural inlet.

"This is the Solis Niger building," McDermott told them. "It was the Salinas River Hotel till about two years ago, when the Solis Niger Corporation bought it and closed it for their uses. Solis Niger—Latin for *Black Sun*, for those of you lacking a classical education—is a shell company for the Church of the Black Sun."

"So, it's a Black Sun site," Lynch said softly. "A church of sorts?"

"Exactly," the Selkie officer told them. "It's situated about ten miles inland, along the Salinas River, from Salinas. It's about two hours away from here by Pendragon.

"We've been given this target due to the availability of a water approach," he continued. "It's been assigned to an ONSET team, as we think they've been using this building as an armory and training center, and it's isolated enough and has enough living space that we think they may have supernaturals there. Possibly even some minor demons."

"Damn," Stone growled. "Sounds like fun."

"Or something like that," Walsh said grimly. "What's our approach?"

"We split into two elements," McDermott replied, bringing up a series of screens illustrating his words as he spoke. "Mary and I"—he nodded to the team's water elementalist—"will approach through the river and infiltrate through the boathouse. David"—he nodded to David—"will command our second element, which will consist of him, Stone, Kate and Kelly. You four will approach from our joint drop-off point to the north, through this copse of trees." He touched a small clustering of trees that David, a New England boy, wouldn't have honored with that description.

"Pell will provide air cover from the Pendragon and make sure anyone who tries to escape by vehicle comes right back to us," the Commander continued. "Remember, people, our orders are to take prisoners. We are sanctioned for whatever force is necessary, but we want these people *alive*. We don't go in shooting," he ordered bluntly, his gaze on Stone.

"Understood," the big man whispered.

"Is everyone clear?" McDermott asked, looking around. His gaze met David's, and the Agent returned it levelly. This would be David's first time in command of ONSET Agents, and the thought made him nervous.

Nonetheless, he fully intended to do his job.

"Then that's it," he said softly. "We will suit up at four this afternoon. Be ready."

[39]

THE TENSION IN ONSET THIRTEEN'S COMMON ROOM WAS THICK ENOUGH
to be cut with a knife. Operation Sun Net was the most complex operation any of them had been on, dwarfed only by the outright war Hellet
and Pell had fought in against the Incursion in Montana. Unlike the
Incursion, though, they were on their own. If they screwed up, it
would affect thousands of others, but none of those others could
help them.

David knew that his own presence didn't help with the tension. He
was an unknown factor, a new addition and untested in this team. To
him, *they* were the unknown factors, and he found himself wishing he
were back with ONSET Nine.

But that wasn't possible, so David, like the rest of ONSET Thirteen,
sat in silence in the common room. McDermott sat off from the rest of
the team in one corner, a communications headset on his head and a
guitar on his lap as he played through a series of soft ballads. Walsh
was sitting next to a row of potted plants, crooning softly to them and
making them dance along with the Commander's music.

Lynch and Hellet both had materialized books from somewhere
and had claimed chairs away from McDermott's music. Pell was
making a variety of small mechanical devices assemble, disassemble,

and reassemble themselves into various forms. After a while of watching, David realized that each of the forms was actually functioning. He was moving through a cycle of about twelve different devices, including a short-range radar dish and what might have been a harpoon gun.

Through McDermott's music and Walsh and Pell's playing with their powers, Stone simply sat against one wall, watching the room. David assured himself that it was only paranoia that insisted the massive man was watching him.

David wasn't aware of the time when Stone stood up and walked over to him.

"White," he said in that quiet, high-pitched voice that seemed so strange coming from such a large man. "Walk with me for a minute, will you?"

David nodded slowly. He stood and eyed the tanned Stone for a moment, then gestured for the other man to lead the way. He had a sneaking suspicion what was going on, and he also knew that if the other man wanted to play power games, they needed to be finished quickly.

The pair of men grabbed their coats against the late autumn mountain chill and walked out into the cold air. David carefully buttoned up his long blue duster, making sure he was free to move even as he kept an eye on the larger man.

Stone led them around behind the back of the dormitory, into the lee of the building against the wind. David noted calmly in the back of his head that there were also no windows and likely no cameras bearing on this quiet spot, shaded from wind and other outside influence.

"You didn't bring me out here to walk in circles," David told Stone dryly. "So, say your piece."

The bigger man tugged his heavy brown bomber jacket tighter and turned to face David, his tanned face red with the cold.

"That's how you want it, huh?" he whispered. "And here I was planning on sugar-coating things for you."

"In," David checked his watch, "about seven or eight hours, you and I are going to go get shot at together. We may as well get this out of the way now."

Stone said nothing for a moment, then blurted, "You don't know this team. You don't know us at all, what we can do, how we operate.

"I *do* know these people," he continued. "I've worked with them and been second-in-command of this team for a year. I won't let you get them killed because you don't know them."

"I wasn't planning on it," David told him, but Stone continued as if he hadn't heard him.

"So, this is the deal," the big man said flatly. "You can play figure-head as much as you want, but when we go into action tonight, you do what *I* say, or I frag you."

David looked at the bigger man in shock. He'd asked the other man to be up-front, but he hadn't expected him to be quite that blunt.

"This isn't the time for power games," he said slowly. "You're what, twenty-five, Stone? I'm thirty-one. I've spent the last twelve years in the police. I've organized; I've led. I've fought this Church of the Black Sun before. But it boils down to this: Omicron says I'm in command, and that means I need to be in command.

"So, you *will* follow my orders," he told Stone firmly. "And if you try and frag me, you will regret it until the end of fucking time. Do I make myself clear, son?"

In retrospect, David realized the patronizing *son* was a mistake, but he only realized that as Stone's fist came swinging for his face. He barely ducked under the strike, and his palm slapped hard against Stone's wrist to deflect a second fist.

He jumped backward, out of Stone's reach, and looked coldly at the younger man. For a moment, the two men stood there, staring at each other. David met Stone's eyes and knew that, unless he wanted to get "accidentally" killed on the mission, he was going to have to prove himself to the younger man. There were a lot of ways to do that, but there was only one fast way.

David reached up and undid the buttons on the heavy blue duster. He removed the coat and tossed it onto the snowbank next to the building, leaving him in his black ONSET armored bodysuit.

"Lose the jacket, Stone," he said grimly. "It'll get in the way."

Stone didn't hesitate, tossing his own heavy leather jacket onto

David's duster and raising his fists into a boxer's defensive position. The two men circled each other, assessing. Stone had almost a foot on David in height but only a couple of inches in arm length, and David was actually broader across the shoulders than the bigger man. Stone was light on his feet for such a big man, David noted, and quick with it.

Stone struck first, jabbing sharply at David's chest. David met the blow with his open hand, trying to pull the other man and throw him. He felt the flesh under his hand turn cold and hard, and the sheer weight and momentum of Stone's suddenly rock arm kept the other man going past him, throwing both of them off balance.

They separated and circled again. David waited until a patch of snow was behind Stone and then moved forward, striking at the other man's shoulder and midriff. Stone deflected the first strike, and the second slammed into his stomach.

It felt like hitting a brick wall, and David *felt* his fingers break as his left hand slammed into the stone-covered flesh of Johnston's midriff. The other man barely moved, and *his* rock-hard—literally—fist slammed into David's shoulder.

David stumbled back and shifted away from Stone as the telltale warmth ran through his fingers, which *snapped* back into place with a bolt of excruciating pain. He winced against the pain, and Stone struck, iron-hard fists shooting toward David's chest and stomach.

Even distracted by pain, the older man deflected the strikes. He didn't try and throw Stone this time, simply focusing on knocking the blows away. As Stone recovered, David struck back, sliding under Stone's extended fists to slam another blow against the big man's solar plexus.

This time, he was expecting to hit the stone wall of Stone's skin, and turned the blow into more of a shove, saving him from more broken fingers. The bigger man stumbled back but jabbed forward as he did.

David wasn't expecting the counterstroke, and it slammed into his ribs with a crunching noise. He flew backward and hit the ground with a thump, and *knew* he had broken ribs.

With a painfully deep breath, he focused the healing warmth he was starting to expect and gain some control over into his chest. Stabbing pain shot through him as his ribs popped back into place. Opening his eyes, he saw Stone coming toward him, and without thinking, lashed out.

His foot slammed up, barely missing Stone's groin to smash into his upper pelvic bone. Unlike the previous strikes, he hit flesh, not stone, and the bigger man stumbled backward. David got his legs underneath and sprang to his feet, his open hand moving in a powerful strike as he did.

He hit Stone in the chest with his open hand, feeling rock through the other man's armored bodysuit. Stone or not, the bigger man grunted as the blow lifted him off his feet and tossed him away to land on the snowbank the two jackets covered.

David paused, waiting for the other man to stand, but Stone merely rolled over to face him.

"I thought I'd broken your ribs," he said slowly, "I was *checking* on you."

"You did break my ribs," David told him. "I healed them."

The two men stared at each other for a moment, and then Stone began to laugh, rubbing his lower stomach where David had kicked him.

"That was nearly a very low blow," he told David. "Sir."

Taking the *sir* as the concession he was sure it was, David stepped over to the bigger man and hauled him to his feet.

"I wasn't thinking," he told Stone. "But if you cause trouble on this mission, I may kick that low intentionally."

Stone continued to grip his hand after standing, and David met his gaze evenly. The grip turned into a firm, non-breaking handshake.

"You fuck up, I'll still frag you," Stone told David, his strange high-pitched voice calm. "Till then, you're the boss. Boss."

"I can live with that condition."

———

Majestic kept an eye on the communications network she'd hacked into at ONSET now. She knew it was interfering with her normal work, but other than stealing a multinational conglomerate's third-quarter results before their publication, she hadn't had much to do that week.

She'd seeded enough warning tripwires into ONSET's system that she knew that their sys-admins were no longer distracted by whatever had kept them tied up when she originally penetrated the system. She had to be more careful now, and limited her access to their files.

That didn't mean she'd *stopped* reading through their files, and she'd been saving a lot of it to her computer. There were now enough files and incriminating information on Majestic's hard drive to blow an entire secret branch of the US government wide open.

However, she'd also dug up enough to know just how powerful this "Omicron Branch" was. The very top of it appeared to be a Senate Committee—one that wielded the full power of Congress in affairs of the supernatural.

She had enough to expose everything, but she'd read and seen too much. Even with all these files, going public would probably be a dramatic failure. People would think she was crazy. And she had no illusions about the government's willingness to silence one criminal hacker who knew too much.

Part of her wanted to kill the connections, delete her probes and tripwires, destroy the files on her computer and forget everything. Another part, to her great surprise, wondered what she could do to help them. To help, specifically, David White, to whom she'd done a great disservice.

So, when the chatter level on ONSET's network went up, she paid attention. Then she started digging into their files again, looking for the details of "Operation Sun Net".

40

No one commented on their absence or their snow-covered coats when David and Stone returned to the common room. David met the other man's gaze as they hung up their coats and gave him a firm nod. Stone returned it and joined Pell at the table where the pilot continued to shift his mechanical parts through their continuing series of forms.

David picked up a book, yet another of ONSET's many books detailing previous supernatural incidents and events in the world, and began to read. He had a layman's knowledge of world history, but he knew that these events weren't known to anyone outside the small, secret supernatural communities and agencies of the world—and were far more immediately relevant to him now than most history.

Shortly after the pair came back in, McDermott packed up his guitar and, in apparent response to some message on his headset, exited the building himself. The loss of his music left the room in an uncomfortable silence that reigned for a long time.

David focused on his book—a record of a number of incidents involving trolls in central Europe. The label was applied to a small subset of supernaturals that had to eat human flesh to fuel their powers. Some of these supernaturals were people who awoke to the powers and a hunger they couldn't sate. Some, however, seemed to just wake up out of the hills and come down to the valleys hunting.

It was a sufficiently complex study that it drew David's complete focus, and he lost track of time until he realized that McDermott had returned and was gesturing for everyone's attention.

"It's six o'clock, people," the Selkie said quietly once they were all looking at him. "So, five Pacific—T-minus one and a half hours. That makes it time for us to load up and get ready to move out. Our target's event will be underway in an hour, so let's get our part of the party ready."

It was as if some unspoken agreement had been concluded, and the team began to quietly talk to each other as they trooped into the armory behind the common room. Lockers lined the room and banged open as the team began to load up.

The combat load-out started with the black armored bodysuit, which David was already wearing. The first items he removed from the locker were a number of shaped plates, aetherically enhanced ceramic inserts to his bodysuit. They slipped into carefully designed pockets on the suit, covering various vital regions.

Next came the electronics harness. Two long CPU cases, as much enchanted armor as electronics, clipped to straps and a battery that tucked behind his lower back. More ceramic plates attached to the same straps, covering them and adding an inhuman curve to his torso. A second harness attached on to the base electronics net and slung over his left shoulder, holding a shoulder holster in place for the Omicron Silver pistol.

The holster in place, he checked the chamber—empty—and other mechanisms of the surprisingly simple high-tech firearm. Finally, he took a long block of shining silver bullets with their plastic explosive bases and slid it into the base of the pistol. A panel slid home over them with a soft sound. Checking that the safety was on, David slid the pistol into its holster and attached it to the tiny electronic lead connecting the weapon's electronic sight to his upgraded helmet systems. Four more magazines slid into armored pouches on the harness.

David now slung out the third part of his harness. This one held the unimaginably sharp blade of his mageblade, the enchanted knife that had served him so well. The knife pressed against the right side of his lower torso, and the fabric clipped onto the rest of the harness.

Now only the M4-Omicron remained of the kit, and David checked its chamber and mechanisms just as he'd done with the Silver. His inspection done, he slotted a magazine home and packed four more magazines away in more armored pouches.

Slinging the rifle, he turned to look around at the rest of the team. To his surprise, he realized he was not the last one done. Pell was helping Lynch and Walsh check their weapons. He was even more surprised to realize that Stone wasn't ready yet.

Seeing that David was, the big man gestured him over. "Can you give me a hand here, White?" he asked.

Surprised *again* at the younger man's apparent friendliness after their earlier altercation, David joined him. "What do you need?" he asked.

"Hold these," Stone asked and passed David two round drums. Each was over two inches thick and easily ten across. "Thanks."

His hands no longer occupied, the big man quickly attached a pair of pockets unlike anything David had ever seen to his combat harness. He retrieved the drums and slotted them in.

"What *are* those?" David finally asked.

"Custom-built hundred-round drums," Stone replied quietly, reaching into his locker and removing his main weapon—a meter-long stock of metal with an odd crystalline sleeve around the barrel. "Belt feed wasn't particularly useful for me—recoil doesn't bother me, so I don't need a tripod, and the belt kept hitting me and jamming. So, we modified the gun."

As he was speaking, the big man was checking the breach and mechanism of the big M60 machine gun and pulling out a third of the ridiculously huge ammo drums.

"This girl started life as a short-barreled M60E4," he told David. "We stripped out some of the recoil gadgets and added in what downstairs calls 'aetherically enhanced' cooling equipment." He tapped the crystalline sleeve on the end of the weapon to show what he meant. "Then they modified it for drum loading. Hold her for me?" he asked.

Bemusedly, David took the only barely man-portable weapon from the big Empowered and held it as Stone inspected the docking sleeve for his drum. With a high-pitched mutter of "clear," Stone snapped the drum onto the weapon. Holding on to the weapon for a moment, David hefted it. With his strength, he could hold the weapon in the same stance as a rifle, and the drum hung to the right and out, away from the shooter.

Empowered strength or not, David knew he couldn't *fire* the thing. Alexandra had used Empowered strength to carry heavy weapons like this and their ammo, but she'd used a bipod or tripod like anyone else to use the guns. Strength only went so far with recoil. Stone, however, could turn the shoulder and arm firing the weapon to rock...which meant recoil really *wouldn't* bother him.

David handed the huge weapon back to its owner with a new spark of respect for the big man. He knew that was the point, but it still made an impression.

Stone took the weapon with practiced ease and swung it into the same ready position as the others carried their much smaller M4s.

"Your girl, huh?" David asked as he looked at the Rambo-esque profile of his new squad mate.

"Yup," Stone agreed. "I call her Becky."

"Becky, by the way," Pell's voice interjected as the other man, a squat dwarf compared to Stone or even David, joined them, "is the name of his ex-wife. I met her," he added. "The gun is aptly named."

A chuckle ran around the room, and then all their eyes snapped to Commander McDermott standing in the center of the room. His uniform was all covered in an odd, almost wet-looking material, and all the pockets and holsters were sealed. Unlike the rest, he did not hold an M4 or a "Becky".

"Now that we're done harassing the man who hip-fires a heavy machine gun about said gun's name," he said dryly, "it's time. Let's go kick ass."

———

THE INDIVIDUAL BRIEFING files for Operation Sun Net had stayed on the data keys given to the unit Commanders, except for being loaded onto the computers used for displays. Most of those computers had no internet connection.

What Majestic found in ONSET's core database was the complete operation plan. She'd gone digging for details of whatever it was that was causing so much activity across the country, and eventually found it.

She searched for David White in the file, and found a briefing list for "ONSET Strike Team Thirteen". It laid out the details of the building they were moving against and the shell corp—this Solis Niger —that some cult was using to own it.

The name of the cult meant nothing to her, but Solis Niger rang a bell. It had turned up in something she'd handled recently. Majestic was a hacker, and a *lot* of information crossed her computer screen in a given period of time, but she was a *paid* hacker because she could make the connections.

She was curious now. With a practiced hand, she reached across her desk and turned on a computer tower that had been silent till now. It popped up as a link on her computer, as a program confirmed for her that the direct link to it was blocked from all internet access.

This spare tower was her data store, the archive of information that a lot of her employers and most of her targets would have had apoplexy if they realized existed. With a few keystrokes, Majestic loaded up a search program and gave it the company number and name of Solis Niger Corporation.

Then she began setting up audio gear and a direct data feed so she could listen in on this Operation Sun Net.

It looked like it was going to be one hell of a show.

41

WITH A MAN AT THE CONTROLS WHO COULD MAKE THE MACHINE DO whatever he wanted regardless of its physical limitations, the Pendragon flight was even quieter and smoother than David was used to.

The trip was still nerve-wracking, and the joking atmosphere of the armory had slowly faded back to silence. It went unbroken for most of the flight, enforced by the tiny digital clock in everyone's helmet display, ticking down toward zero hour.

Everyone on the chopper, even David now, had flown on a Pendragon into action as an ONSET team member multiple times. No one had ever been involved in this widespread and coordinated an operation. Even the Montana Incursion two of the team members had served in as members of OPSI's High Threat Response teams hadn't been on this large a geographic scale.

"We're here," Pell said softly over the team network. "Salinas River is to the north, our left."

A shudder ran through the helicopter as he touched the gunship down on the soft California loam. David checked the time as he unstrapped himself from his seat. Forty-five minutes left.

"How close are we?" Commander McDermott asked; his voice quiet even in the radio.

"We are two miles inland along the river from the target," the pilot replied.

"All right," the Commander breathed. "All right, people, get your boots on the ground and get moving. We don't have much time."

David finished unstrapping himself and followed the ex-SEAL Commander out of the helicopter into the fading autumn light. His clock informed him it was now ten to six Pacific Standard Time.

"You ready for this, David?" McDermott asked softly, standing next to the former cop. "We can still rearrange things if you don't think you're ready to lead independently."

"We have forty minutes and two miles to travel quietly and on foot," David told his superior crisply. "We don't have time to fix what isn't broken, and in the worst case, the Techno-Mages tell me no power on Earth can break our encryption. Go get wet, sir; we'll see you on the other end."

The Selkie held David's gaze for a long moment, then turned without a word and gestured for Mary to follow him. The pair headed off north toward the river, vanishing surprisingly quickly in the gloom and shadows of twilight.

David looked at his own team. Walsh and Hellet both looked ready but nervous. Stone was running his hand down Becky's crystalline barrel sleeve.

"We good?" he asked them sharply.

"Yup," Stone confirmed, slinging the heavy machine gun out of the way and speaking in a tone that dared the two women to disagree with him.

"Target is on your GPS units," David reminded them. "We've got two miles and barely thirty minutes to be in position. Let's move."

Determined not to show his own discomfort with what was coming, his fear of failure, or his nervousness at being in command, David White set off west, toward the ocean and the Solis Niger building.

———

Majestic's archive search pinged shortly after the helicopters across the country disgorged their troops. With an eye and an ear on the tactical feed she was hijacking, the hacker turned to her results.

A customer list? That was all. A customer list and a bunch of invoices made out to Solis Niger Corporation from the multinational conglomerate she'd been paid to steal the results from. Shipping addresses given across the country, most of them matching up with locations her stolen feed told her teams were at.

Big invoices...tens of thousands of dollars. Majestic was about to dismiss the find as irrelevant, only coming to mind as the place she'd seen the name, and then she saw which *division* the invoices were from.

It was the conglomerate's *arms* division's customer list she'd stolen —and the invoices were for hundreds of heavy machine guns normally only sold to armies and governments!

Majestic looked back at her tactical feed. The purchases had been mere weeks before. The delivery dates were all in the past. At least a third of the sites Omicron was moving against had between thirty and forty Browning M2 machine guns there.

They had to know. Didn't they? Nothing in the plan had said anything about that level of resistance. She needed more information

The woman who was probably the best hacker in the world warmed up her programs and went digging. If there was anything to find, she had less than an hour to find it.

———

It took the ground team, with David in the lead, twenty-seven minutes to cross the forest and reach the edge of the hotel property. At T-minus thirteen minutes, David turned on his radio.

"Thirteen Actual, this is Thirteen Deuce," he reported. "We're at the target, beginning surveillance and preparing to move in."

A small paved parking lot, almost entirely full of midrange cars in the darkening evening, stood between them and the former hotel itself. The hotel was a three-story Victorian-style building, and lights gleamed behind most of its windows. A large set of double doors was directly across the lot from David, and he could see what looked like a side door on the east side of the building along the river.

On the other side of the door, a boxy boathouse was attached to the old hotel building. Dark-stained wood blended into the ground, silhouetted against the light reflected from the river behind the boathouse.

"Roger, Deuce," McDermott replied over the radio. "We are still at least six or seven minutes out. Will infiltrate through boathouse and the back door; you move in through the main entrance, as per the plan. Good luck."

"Luck, sir," David said softly into the radio before allowing it to fall into silence. He looked at his team. "Let's move in," he ordered. "Slowly—use the cars for cover. We have time."

A cold shiver ran down his spine, and David looked back at the building. At this distance, he couldn't See auras or make out heat signatures with his IR goggles, so he couldn't tell how many people were inside or where they were.

Everything looked right for what should be happening. Lights were on; people were there. All the indicators suggested that it was exactly what OSPI's intelligence people had said it would be.

Yet, somehow, as David joined his team in crouching behind the first line of cars, he felt a deep foreboding. He kept looking for what was causing it, as part of him knew that *something* was wrong. With McDermott in seal-shape, though, the only person who could prepare for that something...was him.

———

MAJESTIC STARED at her search results in horror. It wasn't much—not much at all—but it was enough to paint an ugly picture.

First, the invoices for hundreds of machine guns. She was sure now that similar invoices existed for the rest of Omicron's target sites, under other front companies.

Second, she had an esoteric collection of blog entries, mostly by truck drivers but some by commodity distributors, about an odd cult purchasing vast quantities of silver—tons upon tons of the stuff. None of the truckers were so blind to confidentiality to say *where* the cult was, but they dropped enough details.

Third was a similar note by an agent from a California firm specializing in bullet reloading gear. The agent called the cult "rich loonies" and said they'd purchased enough reloading gear to equip a good-sized ammunition factory—cleaning his firm out, in fact. They'd also specifically asked if the equipment could handle making silver bullets. The agent had found the whole thing laughable. Majestic did not.

Equipment to manufacture bullets, vast quantities of silver, and hundreds of heavy machine guns had been delivered to a small number of sites. A pathetically easy hack into the reloading gear company's computers gave Majestic the destination of the gear.

The Solis Niger building. The Cult of the Black Sun had turned the building into a munitions factory and shipped tons of silver into it, and probably *hundreds* of thousands of silver bullets out.

None of this was hard to find, and Majestic couldn't believe that Omicron, with their analysts and experts, hadn't found it. She doubted they were as good as she, but they had more people, more time...and a government sanction to access people's files.

This meant that someone, somewhere along the line, had either messed up or betrayed *everyone*. If there were traitors in OSPI, then they'd told the Black Sun what was coming. *That* meant that David White and the rest of the Omicron strike teams weren't walking into churches full of unsuspecting cultists to arrest.

They were walking into fortresses guarded by fanatics with heavy weapons loaded with the ammunition needed to kill even Omicron's best. Majestic's research in ONSET's files left her with no illusion what those Brownings, loaded with the silver bullets all of that reloading gear would have made, could do to ONSET's supernaturals.

In slightly under two minutes, all hell was going to break loose unless *she*, Majestic, did something. Majestic was not the kind of person who did things. She'd built a life of secrecy, theft, crime, and absolutely no loyalty to anything beyond a contract.

She'd hacked into this whole organization out of curiosity and dug into the Black Sun's operation for the same reason. Now she found herself holding information those men and women out there needed to have. Information she knew had a price, and she'd never *not* asked for a price before.

Majestic looked at the tactical feed and knew her curiosity had driven her into a choice. She'd never had information this immediately relevant—this life-threatening to so many—before. Till this whole mess, she'd rarely put a thought into another's well-being.

She realized she'd already *made* the decision. It wasn't the one she'd expected, and it was surprisingly easy, considering the life she'd lived and all the things she'd done.

With less than sixty seconds to go, Vanessa Loring dove for her microphone.

———

DAVID TOOK another quick glance toward the double doors into the hotel, then ran, still crouched, to conceal himself beside another big SUV. Stone kept pace with him, moving slowly but surely through the parking lot. They were hiding behind the last line of cars; Walsh and Hellet back a row.

Now only a fifteen-foot space of concrete, obstructed only by bushes too low to serve as cover, separated the quartet from their target. David checked the time. Forty seconds.

"Four-oh seconds, people," he breathed into the radio. There was no response, but he saw Stone checking his grip and the safety on his modified M60. The dimming twilight reflected off of the crystal of the gun's enchanted cooling sleeve. David checked his own weapon.

His foreboding had only grown stronger, and David turned on his infrared goggles and swept the building. It was strange. He *knew* there were people in there, but he couldn't see them. The ground-floor windows were all closed and shuttered, and it didn't help his mood.

He was reaching for his Sight, to search again for auras now he was closer, when an unauthorized transmission broke into his radio channel.

"It's a trap!" an unidentified semi-panicked female voice snapped on the channel. It wasn't ONSET Thirteen's channel, though—it was the ops-wide channel, the one they were supposed to use to report mission completion. The channel *everyone* would get.

"They have machine guns and silver rounds," the voice continued, less panicked and firming as she continued to speak. *"They're waiting for you."*

David turned his Sight on the building, but his prescience *clicked* with the voice. He *knew* it was true. Dozens of auras were waiting, just the other side of the wall. They weren't listening to a service. He'd seen auras like that before—men waiting for action. Waiting for the signal to do violence. If he couldn't see them on infrared, it was because the building was shielded against it.

Which meant the stranger on the radio was right. It was a trap.

"Thirteen-Deuce—trap confirmed!" he barked into the ops-wide channel himself. *"They're all traps.* Abort!"

"Abort," confirmed Warner immediately. "Abort and extract if possible. Maximum force authorized!"

It was too late. He *knew* it was too late. With seconds to spare before dozens of simultaneous attacks went in, most would go in regardless. In his own case...if Thirteen tried to pull back, the gunners would open fire across the open concrete.

"Stone," David snapped, unslinging his weapon. "Hose the building. *Now*," he barked, as the big man hesitated.

It was enough. Stone's face turned grim and he lifted the massive weapon. David could See the other man's power flaring as his shoulder and other recoil-absorbing areas turned to granite.

Then the machine gun opened fire with a terrifying crescendo. Bullets smashed into the walls of the hotel as Stone walked his fire across the front of the former hotel. The façade pitted and holes blew through the stucco. For a full twelve seconds, the only sound in the world was the crashing thunder of the modified M60.

Then Stone had to reload, and the Church of the Black Sun unleashed its surprise the moment he stopped shooting. The shuttered windows swung open, and explosives blasted out pre-marked gun ports in the hotel wall. As the debris drove David and Stone back behind the cars and the thunder of explosions rang through the air,

David and his half-team found themselves facing the black muzzles of over a dozen heavy machine guns in a fortified position.

Before they fired, though, David heard the sound of other guns firing and knew even his warning had failed. A terrifying deep sound like a repeated hammerblow echoed across the parking lot, and only David's Empowered hearing allowed him to pinpoint it. The gunfire came from the boathouse and lasted only a few seconds.

David *knew*, with the certainty that came with being a perceiver, that McDermott and Lynch were dead, cut to pieces by the heavy silver bullets they'd probably never even seen coming. In seal form, McDermott probably had never even got the warning about the trap.

The same repeating hammer sound came again, only *much* closer. David dived away from the SUV he was hiding behind as four streams of silver ripped it to pieces, the igniting fuel tank serving merely to illuminate the shattered debris. Other streams of silver bullets ripped apart the rest of the front row, the gasoline flares and explosions only the punctuation to the violence ripping open the California twilight.

"*Stone,*" David bellowed across the radio. He could see the machine gunner taking cover behind a Hummer. The ex-cop didn't think even the military version could stand up to .50 caliber bullets, let alone the civilian version.

"Right," the gunner replied. "Long, wildly uncontrolled bursts, *sah!*"

David barely had time to realize that the younger man thought he was calling for suppressive fire before the big Empowered left his flimsy cover with a new drum in his M60 and began firing. Stone loosed neat, controlled bursts at gun slits. Most of the guns he fired at stopped shooting, at least for a moment.

The unexpectedly promoted team Commander looked back at his other two squad mates. Walsh was showing the use of her talents as a massive weaving web of what appeared to be *weeds* broke through the concrete with a CRACK that echoed even through the gunfire. The weeds grabbed up cars and concrete and bound them into a shield around the two women. Hellet, apparently relying on Walsh to protect her, was throwing bolts of fire from her right hand. Like Stone, the guns she aimed at stopped shooting.

As he thought that, though, one of the guns Stone had silenced opened up again. His people were killing the crews, but the weapons themselves were too sturdy to be damaged indirectly. They couldn't see the guns to damage them, and there didn't seem to be any shortage of gunners in the ex-hotel.

And they were focusing on Stone. David watched in horror as the big man intentionally walked forward, out of the burning inferno of the parking lot. His neat bursts kept hitting gun slits, but the silver streams of bullets now swept toward him. Bullets slammed into him, sparking off flesh turned to stone and driving the big man back and then to the ground as they unbalanced him.

They were out of time. Out of options. Fear flashed through David, and he felt the fire in his stomach again. It was familiar this time, and he reached for it. He forgot his fear of becoming inhuman. He forgot his fear of exposure. He forgot his fear of what he might do. All of it was nothing against his fear for the people he was responsible for.

Silver could kill him. Even *he* could only take one or two of those bullets, but if he *was* the man who killed Marcus Dresden, they wouldn't *hit* him. If the fire in his stomach could make him fast enough, he could do it.

At that moment, he realized he *would* be a monster, if that was what it took to save his people. To fulfill his oath. David White grabbed the flame inside him and dragged it out. He fed it his fear, his rage, his desire to serve and need to protect, and let it erupt.

As Stone fell, even his nigh-invulnerable flesh broken and marred by the heavy bullets, his Commander rose from behind cover.

$$[\ 42 \ ]$$

BULLETS FLICKED ACROSS THE CLEAR AREA IN FRONT OF THE HOTEL DAVID now recognized as a killing zone, speeding over the slumped form of Stone toward him. David had no illusions about his ability to dodge bullets, but prescience made it easy to not be in the same place they would be.

"Pell," he snapped into his radio, bringing up his channel to the pilot as he began to move toward the hotel entrance. "Level the boathouse," he ordered.

"But the Commander—" the pilot objected.

"Is dead," David told him flatly. "Or they'd still be shooting. *Level the boathouse.*"

He then ignored the channel but heard the distinctive *whirr* of a Pendragon's magically quieted rotors as the gunship closed in for an attack run. He had more important things on his mind—like avoiding bullets from over a dozen machine guns.

Prescience and high-tech targeting merged in David's movements, and he tracked his M4 across the right side of the building. Bursts of bullets lanced out, crashing through stucco to impact against the armored inner wall. Guns fell silent, and David drew closer to the front door of the hotel.

Without even checking, David knew the door would be locked, so he found a new use for the M4. He emptied the magazine into the door around the lock, weakening the lock and the wood of the doors. Then he slammed the barrel of the gun into the ground and used it as a vaulting pole to slam a pair of heavy combat boots with one pissed-off supernatural cop behind them into the center of the door.

The doors didn't break open—they *shattered*, spraying wooden and metal shrapnel across the room behind them. Another pair of machine guns had been set up to cover the door, but the high-speed remnants of the door scythed through their gunners, sending both men crumpling against the rear walls in a splatter of blood.

David's ruined assault rifle hit the floor with a clatter as he landed on his feet, dropping beneath the single burst the gunners had fired before dying. He rolled back up to his feet toward the left half of what had been turned into an armored bunker. His caseless pistol was in his hand, though he didn't remember drawing it, and he swung it around.

Six guns faced out of the slots along the half he faced, and a gunner and a loader still manned each. Bodies were scattered by the guns where Stone's bullets and Hellet's fireballs had dropped them—the survivors grabbed for weapons anyway. Even from here, he knew the weapons were loaded with silver, and a few lucky shots would drop David where he stood.

David challenged that fear and channeled it into the fire that moved him. The cultists seemed to move like molasses to David as he swept the Omicron Silver up and across. If they fired, he would die. He never gave them a chance.

Before any of them had raised a weapon, he emptied the Silver. Heads and chests exploded under the heavy rounds as he cleared the side of the bunker, and then dived forward as the gun crews in the *other* half of the bunker found their weapons and fired.

He dropped the empty Silver—he had no time to reload—and drew his mageblade. His dive took him into the sprawl of bodies where he'd been shooting, and he grabbed up an MP5 submachine gun whose owner didn't need it anymore.

More bullets sprayed around him as he rolled over behind the sandbags covering the machine guns in front of the door, hoping the cultists had done *something* to make the defenses hold up against ONSET's weapons. The gunfire followed him and he heard bullets thud into the sandbags and clang off the guns themselves in confirmation of his guess.

David took a deep breath, allowed the gunfire a moment to slow, and then leapt over the sandbags, mageblade in one hand and MP5 in the other. Bullets kept slamming into the sandbags below him as he crashed through the air, returning fire as he went.

A bullet caught him as he landed, a different kind of fire burning through his flesh. A scream of pain escaped David's lips, but he emptied the MP5 along the bunker, dropping the remaining cultists in a hail of silver and flame. They were dead before they realized they'd hit him and he dropped the weapon, clutching the radiating wound in his side.

His prescience gave him a flash of warning, and he ducked under the red blade of what looked like a fire ax. David dove forward and rolled around, coming to his feet in time to block another ax strike with the flat of his mageblade.

The cultist carrying the ax had come through a door from behind and was wrapped in a black robe concealing even his face. The ease with which he carried the heavy ax and the speed with which he reacted suggested he wasn't human under the robe, and David stabbed forward with the knife.

The robed man barely parried, his defense almost enough to match David's speed. The mageblade sliced through the metal handle of the ax like a twig. The strike was still deflected, only tearing off a strip of the black robe.

David bounced back a step and watched the robes unravel, revealing the naked form underneath the black wrappings. Dark red skin, just like Ix's, met David's gaze, and a pair of small horns on the top of the forehead gave an inhuman impression neatly topped by pure black eyes.

The demon snarled, and jet-black claws shot out from the gloves covering its hands. They slashed at David's face, and his silver-inflicted wound burned as he defended himself. The strike flashed toward him in a lightning blow he barely caught with the mageblade, but when enchanted steel met unnaturally grown obsidian, the obsidian gave way.

The claws clattered to the ground, separated from the demon's hand. The demon froze for a moment, and that was enough. As the demon hesitated, David struck again. The mageblade flashed out like dark lightning and drove into the demon's chest. With a grunt of effort, David tore the knife upward, ripping the creature's torso open from sternum to shoulder.

The demon's black gaze met David's for a moment, and then the creature burst, dissolving into black ichor before his eyes. The ONSET Agent stared at the pool of goo for a moment, breathing deeply.

He let the heat go. The flame receded into the hidden part of him it had come from, leaving only the burning fire radiating from the silver round embedded in his hip, and David looked around him at the bodies he'd strewn across the wreckage of the ex-hotel's front room. Machine guns and sandbags lay askew everywhere, toppled onto bodies and covered in blood.

It took the former cop a minute to take it all in, and then he promptly threw up. Clearing his mouth grimly, he stepped further into the building.

The object of his search was the wooden door the demon had come through to attack him. It hung half-open, never closed behind its last user. David stepped carefully across the bloodstained carpet and through the door.

Whatever the inside of the building had once looked like, it didn't look like a hotel now. The interior of the structure had been gutted at some point. The front chunk of the building had been turned into the bunker he'd already fought through, and he could see by glancing back that there were still two floors of rooms behind him, but the rest of the walls and floors had been removed.

Heavy industrial equipment supporting catwalks had replaced them. David recognized a smelter, and a forming press that looked like it was designed for bullets, but much of the equipment eluded him.

He could guess at its purpose from what he could recognize. This was a munitions factory, churning out the hundreds of thousands of silver bullets the Church of the Black Sun had loaded into its heavy machine guns to hurl at officers of the United States Government.

———

As soon as he was sure the building was clear, David checked on Stone. The big man had turned entirely back to flesh at some point after going down, which made it a lot easier for David to find a pulse.

Both of the younger man's legs were shattered, but he was still breathing and his heart was beating—for now. He looked up to see Walsh and Hellet walking toward him and Pell's Pendragon sweeping slowly back toward them from the shattered and burning ruins of the boathouse.

Stone was wounded, but McDermott and Lynch were still dead. That left David in command and responsible for reporting in. With a nod to the two women, he hit his radio.

"This is ONSET Thirteen," he said grimly, taking responsibility for the entire team for the first time. "Target is neutralized. We have three down, two fatalities, one in need of immediate evac."

He cursed under his breath as Hellet decided to take advantage of his distraction to sneak up on him and *cut* the silver bullet out. He gasped in pain, but then the radiating fire from the wound vanished.

"Understood," Major Warner's voice said over the radio, her tone strained. She wasn't supposed to be answering coms, David knew, yet somehow, he wasn't surprised to hear her voice.

"Be advised that our evacuation resources are tied up with teams in worse condition," the Major continued grimly. "You'll have to move your wounded and dead with your own helicopter."

"Understood," David confirmed softly. "Pell, bring the chopper down," he ordered.

Pell slowly brought the gunship down next to David, on the killing field in front of the hotel's shattered front façade. The machine animist made a gesture barely visible in the cockpit, and a hatch popped open, revealing a collapsible stretcher.

"Let's load him up and leave this disaster for a cleanup crew," the pilot suggested.

"Hellet, can you stabilize Stone?"

"I can make sure he stops bleeding and stays asleep, yeah," the Mage replied. "Not much else."

"All right," David said calmly, drawing from some inner source of control he didn't think he had to ignore his fear and rapidly healing wound. "You two load Stone up and see if you can find McDermott's and Lynch's bodies," he ordered, his voice gentle but firm.

"Control, this is Thirteen Deuce," he linked back into the channel to ONSET HQ. "The Solis Niger building was a munitions factory. They were manufacturing silver bullets here in massive quantities."

"That makes sense," the response came after a minute. It was Major Warner again, and ONSET's second-in-command sounded exhausted. "Every team walked into a meat grinder, White. *Every single team.* Even teams that got your abort call in time got nailed before they could pull out. These *bastards* knew we were coming. They knew when, they knew how, and they shouldn't have known *anything*.

"Get your people back here, David. We have bigger problems than where the bullets came from."

"Understood, ma'am," David confirmed.

———

VANESSA SLUMPED in her chair in mixed horror and relief. Unlike David, she'd been in a position to track the progress of Operation Sun Net across the country, and the brutality of the violence had stunned her.

She was no soldier, no cop, but even she suspected that her warning had saved lives. Without it, so many of these brave people would have walked into a trap they didn't even know existed and died before they even knew they'd been trapped.

Even *with* her warning, so *many* had died. Hundreds were dead, thousands injured. She'd blown her own cover, and was more than half-expecting a knock on her door at any minute, but she thought she'd made a difference. She just wasn't sure.

Her phone rang. She looked at it, and it rang again. As it rang a third time, her connection to the ONSET network suddenly terminated, the icon telling her that the connection had shut down.

She answered the phone.

"Vanessa."

"Vanessa, this is Charles," a gravelly voice brogued at her. "Ye've gain a long way and annoyed a lot of people, girl. Not many of those tracking 'Majestic' would have expected this, would they?"

"You know," she said flatly. It wasn't a question.

"Ai run net security for Omicron," the brogue replied. "Ye realize, girl, that one phone call, and you're headed for a cell? The FBI would love to get their paws on ye."

"Why are you calling me and not them?" she asked. The FBI, the Pentagon, a few of her former employers…a *lot* of people would like to see the world's foremost professional black hat hacker behind bars.

"Because we think ye saved a lot of lives, girl," the gravelly voice responded. "So, we're prepared to offer an alternative. Are ye prepared to listen?"

Vanessa Loring, also known at the hacker Majestic, blinked in surprise and considered. She did not doubt that they could be calling the FBI right now, even as this Charles kept her occupied on the phone. Somehow, though, she thought their offer of an alternative was honest.

"I am," she said quietly. She'd see what they had to say.

Besides, it wasn't as if she had any illusions about her ability to *escape* Omicron now.

THE FLIGHT BACK TO CAMPUS WAS DEATHLY SILENT. THE FOUR REMAINING conscious members of ONSET Thirteen said nothing to each other. Pell was focused on getting back as quickly and safely as possible, and Hellet was sitting next to Stone, trying to keep the big gunner alive.

McDermott and Lynch received no such attention. Hellet's magic had succeeded in dredging the two ONSET agents' bodies up from the wreckage of the boathouse, but no one could doubt they'd died long before it had been destroyed. David's momentary glimpse of the massive ugly wounds on his Commander's body had driven that point home.

Part of him knew that he was now in command of these people and should say *something* to these people about their fallen friends, but the thought of speaking was ashes in his mouth.

Three times he had unleashed what was inside him, and he knew now why he'd had so many issues doing it intentionally. He was *afraid*, and only a greater fear had been able to drive past the barriers he'd subconsciously erected around the core of power that dwelled within him.

David was *afraid* of becoming more. He went over his memories of the Solis Niger building, the horror he'd unleashed in there. One man had walked into a building with dozens of armed enemies who knew he was coming, and killed them all.

It sounded like something out of a Greek myth or a dark superhero comic. He was a killing machine, a weapon able to be turned against any enemy. Magic and blood had made him terrifyingly efficient at it, and it scared him.

That fear had solidified inside him somewhere and locked that power away, that ability to be a walking weapon of war. He'd broken through it three times now, and that meant he *knew* what it was.

The helicopter drove on through the night, returning the survivors of the team home, and David White faced down his own demon, the monster inside of him he was so afraid of that he'd locked it away.

———

THE BODIES HAD BARELY BEEN UNLOADED from the helicopter under David's painstaking supervision before a hand tapped his shoulder and a throat cleared behind him. The night mountain air was brisk and cold, and David felt the cold in his bones as he turned to face whoever was trying to get his attention.

The man standing behind ought to have been freezing in the dark and cold but looked completely unbothered by standing out on a Colorado mountain in an unmarked uniform. David recognized the man as one of Major Warner's shadows who seemed to be around whenever she left her office. This one was dark-skinned and -haired, and looked almost Arabic to David's eyes.

"Commander White," the man greeted David flatly. David winced, realizing that, yes, he was now the commanding officer of ONSET Thirteen.

"What is it?" he asked slowly.

"Major Warner sends her apologies for dragging you away from your team, but she needs to see you in her office immediately," the suited agent replied.

David turned helplessly to Hellet and the other two, and the matronly Mage met his gaze firmly.

"I'll get them inside and fed something warm," she said firmly,

taking the other two by the shoulders as if they were her old kindergarten charges. "Go do your part of the job."

"Thank you," David told her, surprised by the degree of gratitude
that welled up inside him. He turned to Warner's messenger. "All
right, let's go."

The agent gestured toward the main administration building. "If
you'll follow me, sir," he said calmly.

———

EVEN WELL INTO the middle of the night, and with two men now well
known to the security on the Campus, both David and Warner's bodyguard were given a full ID check both on the ground floor and when
they reached Warner's floor.

The bodyguard peeled off at the door to Warner's office, joining his
fellow guard, both back in uniform here on the Campus, standing at
the door. David stepped through the unimposing wooden door and
onto the familiar blue carpet in Major Warner's office.

Michael was already in the room, in one of the comfortable stuffed
chairs, looking rather the worse for wear. The werewolf gave David a
nod as he entered but otherwise remained silent.

"Have a seat, David," Warner told him, the tiny Mage gesturing to
the second of the chairs. David took the proffered chair, wondering
what was going on.

"I'm sorry to drag you away from your teams at a time like this,"
she told the two men, "especially you, David. Being an Acting
Commander is hard enough without what I'm about to do to ONSET's
Nine and Thirteen."

"What's that, Traci?" Michael demanded. "One of my people is in
critical condition, and I don't even have a damned chopper
right now."

The Mage raised her hand. "You're both going back out," she said
flatly. "I've already ordered Thirteen's chopper prepped to fly out
again with both Nine and Thirteen's equipment. You don't have a
chopper or a pilot with Akono in critical, but David does—and I'm
afraid that between you, you only have a team's worth of people."

"What happened to Akono?" David demanded of his former Commander.

"Bastards had Stingers at our site," the werewolf said flatly. "Shot down the Pendragon as he came in for a sweep." He turned to Warner. "He's in ICU, and the rest of my team is exhausted and beaten up. You can't be serious."

"Thirteen's in worse shape," David said slowly, less willing than Michael to challenge Warner directly. "We're down almost half our people—two of them dead."

Major Warner stood in a single motion, and somehow, her lack of height didn't rob it of any power to intimidate.

"Both of you shut up," she said harshly, "and listen to me.

"I am fully aware of the state of both of your teams," she continued, "but I am also aware, as you are not, of the state of the *rest* of my teams. The average casualty rate on this goddamn operation was seventy percent—most of our teams and OSPI's teams lost over *two thirds* of their people, wounded or killed. Thirteen and Nine are my most intact teams, and combined, they make the best strike force I have without recalling teams from the Middle East—and we don't have time for that."

David was struck dumb by the number. That meant *hundreds* of people wounded or dead—well over a thousand.

"It could have been worse," the Major continued, "if not for that hacker's warning. We're not sure how the hell she got *into* our systems," she said softly, and David felt a chill run down his spine, "but her warning and our attempted abort probably saved us from losing the entire Sun Net task force."

"That bad?" Michael asked, his voice hoarse.

"We are surprisingly low on fatalities so far," Warner told him grimly, "but that may change as hospital reports roll in. We got walked into a perfectly synchronized series of meat grinders, and we never saw it coming."

"Charles talked to Majestic, the hacker, and got the rundown as how *she* knew it was a trap," ONSET's executive officer told the two team leaders. "There's no way OSPI missed it by accident, so we were forced to consider the theory that OSPI had been compromised. We tested it by using an override access on OPSI HQ's computers."

"And?" David asked, horrified at the thought.

"So far as we can tell, the OSPI Headquarters building has been compromised since before this Operation began being planned," she said flatly. "It may have been compromised as early as forty-eight hours after Ekhmez was delivered to the site."

"He's the source?" Michael demanded. "I *told* them to kill the bastard!"

"We now have evidence that suggests that Black Sun had elements within OSPI to begin with who encouraged the line of thought that Ekhmez should be captured alive," Warner told him, her voice tired. "We are certain, in any case, that Ekhmez has now secured full mental domination of all the mundanes in the building."

"What about supernaturals?" the senior of the two agents asked. "We're generally resistant to that sort of thing."

"Any supernatural Inspector they could justify moving was sent on a mission outside the building within seventy-two hours of Ekhmez arriving," Warner replied. "No one even considered it, as there were other supernaturals in the building."

"Like Stutter," David observed with a sick feeling in his stomach.

The Major nodded. "So far as we can tell, every supernatural that wasn't removed from the building is dead," she told them, her voice very quiet and grim. "We are completely certain that SSTTR, especially, has been exterminated. They attempted to get a message out three days ago advising of the situation and their intent to launch a counteroffensive within the building. We only found the message an hour or so ago when we started looking into this—we've only received communication *about* Stutter from OSPI, no one had spoken to them directly since just after Ekhmez's capture. We have confirmed by scrying that they are all dead."

David winced. Casey was the only SSTTR man he'd known at all, but the others had seemed like good people. Now they were all dead. Wiped from the face of the world, and no one had even *known* for three days.

"What's the plan?" he asked, his objections to his team going back out forgotten in the realization of what had happened.

"Colonel Ardent activated OSPI HQ's Judas Protocol"—Warner checked her watch—"forty-one minutes ago. The building has gone into a complete lockdown that cannot be overridden from within the structure. We are coordinating with the NYPD to evacuate the surrounding area and are moving in Anti-Paranormal Companies."

"You think he's going to open a hole," David said softly, remembering his flash of vision before. "Create an Incursion, like in Montana."

"We can't fight a full supernatural war in downtown Manhattan," Warner said quietly.

"Watch me," Michael replied, and his voice carried a level of cold, ruthless menace David had never heard the other man use before.

"The plan is to avoid needing to, Michael," Warner said firmly, still looking down at the two sitting Commanders.

"Your people are meeting with medical teams right now," the Major continued, "who are patching up their wounds and issuing them stimulants. You'll have an hour or two aboard the Pendragon to sleep if you can, and I suggest you use it."

"Plan?" Michael asked. "Kick in the door and go in shooting?"

"We hope to land you on the roof," Warner told him, "but it may come down to that. But remember"—she surveyed the two men—"the people in there are *ours*—your mission is to kill Ekhmez, which will release them from his control. Don't kill the poor bastards he's taken over."

"If Ekhmez is that strong, it will take more than one Class One Supernatural to take him down," Michael warned, "even me."

"You'll have me," David said quietly, and inside himself, he dared that fear of becoming inhuman to stop him. Thousands—*millions*—of lives could be at stake. Service demanded sacrifice.

Warner and Michael both looked at him.

"Are you sure?" the Major asked.

"I'm sure," David replied firmly. "I can do it."

"We'll need you," Michael told him. "If you and I can go in together, we have a fighting chance against the bastard."

"Good luck," Major Traci Warner told her two team leaders quietly. "I'm afraid you're going to need it."

The pair stood and saluted, and Michael swept out of the room immediately. David hesitated at the open door and then looked outside, glancing at the bodyguards.

"Ma'am, this hacker," he said quietly. "She contacted me before—tried to blackmail me. I reported it."

"I didn't see any report," Traci answered, looking at him.

"The OSPI team swept the computers and didn't find anything," he told her. "I think they thought I was crazy or lying."

"I see," the Major said coldly. "That's water under the bridge now, I'm afraid. It seems she found another way into our systems without blackmailing you...and honestly, I can't say I'm objecting right now. Without her, it could have been worse. *Much* worse."

David nodded, looking at the Base Commander for a long moment.

"What happens if we fail, ma'am?" he finally asked.

"We now know what's going down and are evacuating the city," Warner said unflinchingly. "A B-2 bomber is being prepared as we speak. If you fail, it will be used to deliver an air-to-surface cruise missile carrying a variable-yield nuclear warhead."

"You'll nuke Manhattan?!"

"Given the choice between that and an Incursion, yes," she said flatly. "Now go make it unnecessary, Commander!"

"Yes, ma'am."

[44]

WHEN DAVID RETURNED TO ONSET THIRTEEN'S DORMITORY, HE FOUND A
full medical team had taken over the common room and was running
it as an impromptu first aid station. Walsh and Hellet had both
acquired numerous scrapes and bruises while being shot at, but neither
had actually been shot. Pell had three nurses swarming over him,
checking his blood pressure and probably making sure the pilot was
safe to shoot up with amphetamines.

When the acting team Commander walked in, the medical team
ignored him for a moment, but then Pell cleared his throat loudly and
pointed at David. The team's leader, a dark-haired and -bearded man
perhaps ten years older than David in a white smock, stepped over to
him and gave a snappy salute.

"Commander White, I'm Dr. Varric Corb," he said softly. "Your
team is fit, but they're tired as hell. Whose cockamamie idea was this?"

"Not mine," David replied. "Unfortunately, I understand and agree
with the decision. My understanding is you've been authorized to
issue stimulants?" he asked.

The doctor nodded and removed two small plastic prescription
bottles from his smock. "These," he said, holding up the first bottle,
"are aetherically tailored short-term sedatives. They will take effect in

ten minutes and last for exactly ninety minutes. You'll give them to your people—and take one yourself," he added firmly, meeting David's gaze, "upon boarding the Pendragon."

"Understood," David responded, taking the bottle. "Will they help?"

"It won't be the equivalent of a full night's sleep," the doctor admitted, and proffered the second bottle. "Hence these. They're not a powerful stimulant, but they should be enough to wake you all up completely."

"What about Pell?" David asked, looking over at his pilot, who was submitting to the nurses' ministrations with ill grace and a gaze locked on David.

"We will be giving him a time-release amphetamine injection," Dr. Corb answered. "He will be fully functional for eight hours after the injection."

"And after eight hours?"

"Make damned sure he's out of the helicopter and sitting down, as he will collapse," Corb answered. "He's had the lecture himself, but I'm relying on you to make sure, understand?"

"Yes, sir," David replied. "Are you done otherwise?"

"Yes," the doctor confirmed.

David gave the man a nod and stepped past him, gesturing for his people to join him. Pell was held back by his nurses for a moment as one of them finished swabbing down his arm and injected him. The pilot was rubbing his arm as he came over, but he gave David a firm nod.

"Folks, we're heading out again in a few minutes," he told them bluntly. "We'll rendezvous with ONSET Nine at the pad, where Pell will be piloting the Pendragon. We will be under Commander O'Brien's command."

"Heading out *again*?" Hellet demanded, looking around at the other team members. "David, *none* of us—not even you—are up to that! This is insane."

"Kate," David said softly, blinking at the thought of another Mage named Kate. "The situation right now is extraordinarily dire. We are, as of this moment, one of only two teams on the Campus at over fifty percent strength."

The former kindergarten teacher gasped and looked at him in horror.

"Operation Sun Net was a trap," he told his people quietly. "The entire operation was organized from *inside* OSPI as a trap to wipe out as much of Omicron's field-deployment capability as possible."

None of the team said anything, the three agents simply looking at him in mounting realization of just how accurate "extraordinarily dire" was as a description.

"OSPI HQ has been compromised," he continued into the silence. "We now know that the demon Ekhmez has taken over the minds of everyone left in the building and killed anyone who managed to resist his control. Among others, the entire Special Supernatural Tactics, Technology and Reconnaissance team has been killed."

David paused and met each of his people's gazes in turn. "We have activated the Judas Protocol on OSPI Headquarters, which is an externally activated complete lockdown. Unfortunately, we don't expect the Protocol to hold for long. The decision was made at the highest levels to move *now*.

"I'm sorry," he finished softly, "but we need to do this. The fate of the entire country may hinge upon Ekhmez being destroyed tonight." He saw no need to mention the backup plan if they failed. The silence in the room told him his people had enough pressure on them.

That silence reigned unchecked for a long moment, and then Hellet rose to her feet.

"What are we sitting around for, sir?"

———

ONSET Strike Teams Nine and Thirteen arrived at the helipad at the same time. In full combat gear, they were hard to tell apart. Black body armor and helmets obscured identity, with only size and auras to mark people as different.

Even through the armor, David felt Kate Mason's hug after she spotted him, and he returned the younger Mage's surprise affection with interest. He hadn't realized how much he'd missed being able to talk to Kate until just now.

When Kate released him, David turned to Michael and saluted the werewolf in command of the combined team. He glanced at the members of ONSET Nine, who should have been missing only Akono, and realized there were only three of his old team's five members.

"Where's Ix?" he asked as he exchanged nods and handshakes with his old team members.

"Here," a voice replied from behind him, and he turned to spot the red-skinned and many-horned demon standing by the edge of the heli-pad. The demon was dressed in civvies.

"He's not coming?" David asked Michael, but the werewolf simply gestured the younger team Commander toward the demon.

Ix took David's hand in both of his and bowed over it.

"I am not coming with you and the others tonight," he confirmed. "I cannot fight Ekhmez—he is a higher-court demon than I am. Indeed, were I in his presence, it is possible he could command me to fight *you*. I would be a greater liability than an asset, I am afraid."

"I...understand," David said softly. He wasn't entirely sure he did, but he knew that Ix had not been able to fight the demon before.

"David, Michael," Ix continued, gesturing the werewolf Commander over. "It will fall to you two to fight him; you know this," he said softly. "Kate and the other Mages can get you to him, but he is a high court demon and human magic is not strong enough to challenge him yet."

"When you face him, he will be waiting for you," the demon continued. "You cannot surprise him. Most likely, he will have taken over the security center, as he will like having all the information at his fingertips.

"It will take both of your strengths to fight him, but remember this: only your mageblades can hurt him," Ix told them. "He is too powerful to be bothered by mere silver—it will bounce off of him. Your mage-blades *can* hurt him. Remove his head and his body should fail. Then destroy the head by whatever means you can."

Michael nodded firmly. "Last time, we used a nuke," he said

quietly. "It took four class one supernaturals to do it too. Two of my best friends died that day."

"If you're careful, if you're lucky, and if you aim for the head, no one has to die today but him," Ix told them, and reached out to take both their hands. "As the world endures and stars turn, let those who walk in Light guide your way."

David didn't recognize the blessing, but he bobbed his head in thanks and walked back to his people, his hand on the little bottle of sedatives that they would need for the flight to New York.

———

THE SEDATIVES WORKED EXACTLY AS ADVERTISED. David and Michael made sure everyone on the team took the little blue pills, and then popped their own. Ten minutes later, Pell was the only one awake in the helicopter as it shot across the country.

Ninety minutes later, David awoke, refreshed if still slightly tired, and made his way past the slowly awakening team to the cockpit of the Pendragon, dropping himself into the copilot's seat.

"How're you holding up?" he asked Pell.

"These are wonderful drugs," the pilot replied dryly. "Just *wonderful*. Next time someone suggests I take these, please shoot them."

"That bad?" David asked, worried.

"No. The opposite," Pell answered. "I've been running for almost twenty-four hours straight now, and I feel like I could keep going forever. I feel *wonderful*. I'm scared of addiction, to be honest," the younger man admitted.

"From what they told me, coming off it is going to hurt," David told his team member.

"If it sucks wet dogshit, I might be able to avoid the temptation to talk someone into letting me take this shit again," the machine animist said bluntly. "It's quite the high."

"How much longer?" David asked, forcing himself to put aside his concerns about the time-release amphetamine until the mission was done.

"We're back into highly populated areas," Pell replied slowly, staying focused on his map and GPS transponders in front of him. "When we were flying over sheep and cows, a sonic boom or two wasn't a problem. Now I've had to take us back subsonic."

"So, how long?" David asked. He wasn't afraid to admit he knew almost nothing about aircraft.

"We're about ten minutes out of New York City," the pilot told him. "I'll then make a low approach and try and get an eyeball on the roof before I bring us in to land. We should be in range to bring up the Apes on the ground."

Footsteps behind them in the cockpit announced the arrival of Michael, who stepped up behind David and looked over at Pell.

"Do it," he ordered. "We need to know what's going on down there."

A moment later, a voice crackled across the radio.

"Captain Narita, AP Six," it said calmly. "ONSET Strike, what is your status?"

"This is O'Brien, Narita," Michael said on the channel, relayed to David's helmet as well. All of O'Brien's channels were being mirrored to both David and Kate Mason, actually, just in case something happened to the operations Commander.

"What's the status on the ground?" the operations Commander asked.

"We've managed to find an in-the-know Homeland Security liaison to coordinate between us and the NYPD," Narita, who had helped ONSET Nine and SSTTR capture Ekhmez in the first place, told them. "The NYPD has been told we have a terrorist with a mini-nuke, and have evacuated a rapidly expanding zone around the building."

"Not a bad idea," O'Brien said calmly. "If we fail, this could be *worse* than a nuke. What about the building?"

"Judas Protocol is in complete effect," Narita confirmed. "All windows and doors have been sealed. The outside of the building is now brick and metal. Nobody gets out, but I have no idea how you're getting in."

"Explosives," David suggested. To his mind, the nuke warning was pretty relevant. After all, if they *failed*, a nuke was *exactly* what was going to be hitting the area.

"It may come to that," Michael agreed. "We're going to try the roof, but if you can have one of your demo teams that did so well in Montana on standby, just in case..."

"Consider it done," the Captain confirmed. "We have you on Newark's air traffic control. Homeland Security has cleared you all the way in." The Anti-Paranormal officer paused for a moment. "My demo team will be standing by, but there's not much else for me to do unless it all comes apart. It's up to you boys now. Good luck!"

The channel cut to silence, and David focused out the front window as the helicopter began to drop toward the towering skyscrapers below. Figures and numbers flashed across the screens and dials in front of David, none of which he understood.

"There," Pell said softly, pointing to a brown stone building. They were barely skimming the top of the buildings now, only a mile or so from the target.

Then a light on the board flashed red, and David's enhanced sight spotted a burst of flame and smoke from the roof of the OSPI building.

"Missile!" he snapped, but Pell was already reacting. He did *something*, and the helicopter dropped like a stone.

The missile continued to head directly toward the ONSET helicopter, and David felt Michael grab onto the back of the copilot's chair as Pell, totally focused on the aircraft now, worked the controls.

The helicopter continued to drop, but now it was heading sideways. David's eyes were locked to the closing missile, and then it was gone. A massive metal-and-glass building had swung between them and the missile, and moments later, David's enhanced hearing picked up the sound of an explosion.

"Please tell me that building was evacuated," Michael said quietly.

"It should be. We're inside the AP's secured zone," Pell replied. "I'm bringing us in lower and setting us down by Narita's HQ—I doubt that was the only missile they've got."

The pilot glanced quickly back at the two team leaders.

"The roof is not an option."

45

THE PENDRAGON SET DOWN NEXT TO A NEAT CIRCLE OF GREEN ARMY trucks, lit by headlights and a pair of large ugly halogen floodlights on extendable stands. Four men in urban camouflage met David and Michael as they exited the chopper ahead of the combined team.

Three bore assault rifles identical to those in the ONSET men's hands, and the fourth wore a familiarly styled pistol and long knife on his belt. He was a familiar scarred Asian man with Captain's insignia on his fatigues.

"Michael, David," Narita greeted the two ONSET officers. "We saw the missile and worried that they'd shot you down."

"Not this time," Michael grunted back. "You have that demo team standing by?"

"Yes, sir," the scarred captain replied. He gestured to one of the gray-clad men with him. "Sergeant Buck, you're with these men."

"Yes, sir!" the demolition team Commander, a stocky redheaded man a bit shorter and wider than David himself, replied smartly. "My team has prepped shaped charges for the front doors, but there are issues," he told the ONSET men.

"What's that?" David asked, as he and Michael followed the demo team leader toward his men as their own people exited the chopper behind them.

"We'll need covering fire to get to the doors," Buck replied simply. There's almost certainly snipers up with those missiles launchers.

"Once you're in, the front hallway is a killing zone," he continued. "Silver-loaded claymores, Ag-nitrate gas mines, the works—all of it triggered by infrared lasers. It won't be easy to get through. My boys can clear it, but it will take time."

"We don't have a choice anymore," Michael said grimly, waving the two ONSET teams over to join the Anti-Paranormal demo squad. "We'll spend the time."

"Understood," the sergeant said simply, then turned to his own people. "Load up the shaped charges and the clearing gear," he ordered. "Let's go blow a hole in Federal property."

THE TRIP through the Manhattan streets was eerie. The seven ONSET agents were outnumbered by the ten-man demo team escorting them, driving home the point that the two teams were at barely half strength.

No one spoke except for quiet directions given over the radio, and the streets were empty. The streetlights hadn't been turned off, so they shone over the famous streets most of the small force had only seen in movies.

Even at night, Manhattan tended to be envisaged as full of people, and the complete emptiness of the evacuated skyscrapers was creepy. There were still some cars parked in the street, but the NYPD had been surprisingly successful at evacuating the area.

David recognized the streets from his previous visit to the OSPI headquarters, so he knew when they turned a corner onto the street it was on. Buck told everyone over the radio anyway, though no one had to point out the brick building with all of its windows and doors covered in sheet metal.

The glass front and doors that David recalled had vanished behind a solid plane of steel that had dropped from the slot he'd noticed before. Streetlights shone upon the metal, and the ex-cop understood why they needed a demo team. While the team's Mages could probably get through the barrier, it would drain energy they would need later.

"Lyons, Desmond," Buck snapped. "Set up the charge. Everyone else, watch for snipers!"

Michael moved forward to keep an eye on the shaped charge, while David stayed back with the team.

There wasn't much cover here, but the covering team used what they could find, watching the roofs of the buildings and sweeping the upper floors with thermal goggles.

No one saw *anything*, but before the werewolf Commander and the demolition men had made it within twenty meters of the building, a gunshot rang out across the dead silence of the street and Lyons, the smaller of the two demo men, stopped in his tracks and simply crumpled to the ground.

"Shit! *Find that sniper!*" Michael ordered, and began to move to pull the other demo man down.

Before David could do anything other than start back-tracking the gunfire, another shot rang out and the massive werewolf Commander out front stopped in mid-movement.

David watched as Michael turned back to face him but couldn't see the other man's face through the Plexiglas of the helmet. Somehow, though, he knew he was meeting his old Commander's gaze, and then the werewolf collapsed.

This time the fire inside David rose without searching, without the bone-deep terror that normally triggered it. He reached for it and grabbed it, dragging it out without a moment's hesitation. His enhanced senses told him the shots were coming from above, and he scanned upward, his rifle barrel following his sightline. The team's networked computers were back-tracking the shots,

A third shot rang out, and Desmond, halfway back to the rest of the team, pitching forward as the front of his face exploded outward, gore spraying across the pavement as the sniper took him out.

Then David spotted them. The computers were struggling with distance and vectors, but David's Sight of the future and enhanced senses picked out the men. The snipers—there were two, one likely a spotter—were human, men dressed in the uniforms of OSPI Security.

If they shot him, he was likely as dead as the two Demo men. But a sniper would need time to set up a shot, and they wouldn't be expecting counter-fire at this distance.

With a deep breath, the Empowered police officer stepped out of his cover and fired a burst, relying on his Sight to let him aim quickly. A moment later, he adjusted for recoil and fired again. He knew, without even looking, that he'd just crippled both men. His bullets ripped into their knees and lower legs, disabling them without killing them.

"We need medevac," he said into his radio, and his voice seemed so distant and slow. "On the ground for three, and on the roof for two."

"The roof?!" Pell's voice replied in an achingly slow drawl.

"They're our people too," David reminded him. "Under Ekhmez's control—and they should live if they get medical attention soon."

Mason had already made it to Michael and Lyons' bodies, passing the clearly dead form of Private Desmond.

"Michael's alive," the Mage reported grimly. "They were firing Ag Injector rounds. I don't know if Lyons will make it, and Michael is down for the count. Too much silver in his system for me to do *anything*." Her voice pitched higher with the last sentence, panic cutting into it.

"Understood," David snapped, and turned to Buck. For a long moment, he almost accepted that the mission was doomed, and they'd have to nuke the building.

Unless…it was possible, remotely possible, that he could do it. If he was fast—if he was lucky—he could make it through—but he was the only one.

"Blow the door," he ordered. "I'll worry about the mines."

"You'll *what*?" the demo sergeant demanded.

"Just do it," the ONSET Commander ordered, then turned to his Mages. "Hellet, Mason, Dilsner," he snapped. "Ready your strongest knockout spells and sweep the building with them."

Kate Mason's helmet was frozen as she stared at him, and he returned her gaze levelly as Morgen and Hellet gathered around him.

"Between the three of you, you should be able to knock out everyone in the building from here, correct?" he asked, and his voice sounded slow to him, and he was sure it sounded distant to them. He could feel the fire burning within him, fueling his strength and speed. The demo team stared at him in complete shock until Buck chivvied them into getting the shaped charges back from Lyons and Desmond.

"Yes," Hellet said firmly, her hand now gripping Kate's shoulder. "But it will only affect mundanes, and some strong-willed mundanes may be able to shrug it off."

"Anyone left in that building who can withstand your spell is probably not under Ekhmez's control," David replied. "That means they either won't get in my way or are there voluntarily. That's a very different problem. My problem."

"Your problem?" Mason demanded. "What exactly are you planning to do?!"

"You put the building to sleep, Buck blows the door, and Walsh keeps Michael and Lyons alive," David said quietly as the plant Mage knelt by the wounded AP man and began to examine his wounds in more detail. "I kill Ekhmez."

"We're ready," Buck reported, joining the cluster around David.

The newly blooded ONSET Commander looked at his three Mages.

"Do it," he ordered.

———

BUCK'S shaped charges detonated in a thunder crash of violence that tore apart the inch-thick steel like paper. David moved before the sound of the explosion had faded, charging forward into the debris cloud.

He dove through the door, moving with a speed he'd never used before. Even knowing he was the fastest he'd ever been, David reached for more speed, sending every ounce of the now-familiar heat to his legs.

There would be a delay between his tripping the lasers and the mines detonating. If he was fast *enough*, he could make it through. If he wasn't, he would die. If he died, Manhattan would die.

With his senses, he knew when he hit the first set of laser beams, and moments later felt the explosion behind him as he burst through the second, gaining even more speed as he went.

Then he spotted the desk at the end of the room. A single door beside it, and the reception desk that kept people who had no idea what this building really was out of it.

Behind it was the same grizzled older woman who'd been here before, and she was unconscious—an ugly bruise on her head suggested it had nothing to do with his people's spell. *David* might be able outrun the mines, but she wasn't even awake to know she *needed* to escape.

If he grabbed her, they'd both die. He wasn't sure he could make it out on his own, and yet...

All of this passed through his mind between the fourth and fifth tripwires, and he was halfway across the room when he changed angles. He fired his assault rifle without even thinking about it. The hail of bullets that demolished the wood around the lock on the door with a lethal precision, he barely noticed.

At the eighth beam, he dropped the encumbering rifle, and the fourth line of mines detonated as he crossed the ninth and last set of laser beams and dove over the reception desk.

The fifth line of mines detonated as David stopped, and the sixth as he scooped up the receptionist, cradling her neck carefully to *minimize* the inevitable damage. The seventh detonated as he rolled out from behind the desk with her, and the eighth sprayed ball bearings toward him as he body-checked the shattered door open.

Silver from the stray bearings seared his back as he rolled out of the doorway as the ninth set of mines detonated and a spray of silver mist and ball bearings emerged from the door.

The shock of the explosions bought David enough time to drop the woman whose life he'd saved before a pair of creatures charged toward him. These weren't the mostly human demons he'd seen before. They were vaguely humanoid, but unclothed and green-skinned, they looked more like giant frogs than people.

Human-looking or not, the large swords they were carrying looked perfectly functional, and David sprang sideways, out of their swings.

The toad demons might be slower than him, but they were still far faster than any human, forcing him to dodge away as he drew the silver-loaded caseless automatic from his shoulder holster.

The swords slashed at him again as he flicked the pistol from SAFE to a setting he'd thought he'd never use—BURST. Grabbing the pistol with both hands, he pulled the trigger and emptied three .45 caliber silver rounds into the torso of the closer of the two demons.

The creature barely had time to hiss in pain before it collapsed into a pool of black ichor. Even as it collapsed, the other sliced at David, who ducked under the blade and grabbed the creature by its wrist. A huge tongue shot out with speed astonishing even to David, wrapping around him and yanking him right up to the disgusting demon.

Dragging him allowed him to slam the Omicron Silver pistol into the demon's chest and pull the trigger.

Three more heavy bullets ripped the demon's heart apart, and it collapsed into ichor all over David, its tongue leaving a smeared trail across his clothes. He straightened, ignoring the shining black goo all over him, and looked around the richly decorated interior reception hall.

The two human receptionists at the desk were unconscious, victims of the sleep spell that his Sight told him was still sweeping the building. Other than them, the unconscious woman he'd saved and the two pools of ichor that had been demons, the reception was empty.

"This is Thirteen Actual," he said into his radio, on a channel linked to ONSET Campus as well as Narita and his own teams. "I'm in and secure. I don't think Ekhmez has triggered an Incursion yet," he continued, "but there are definitely demons loose in the building. Two are down."

"David, this is Warner," Major Warner's voice announced over the radio. "We've finally managed to override the security protocols on the building and get into the security cameras."

"Thank you," he said fervently, feeling his heart beat like a wire drum as his body continued to function at several times normal speed. He couldn't release his gift, in case he was surprised...and in case it didn't come back immediately if he let it go. "Where is our demonic bastard?"

"The security control room," his superior told him grimly. "Three floors up, in the center of the building. David..." She trailed off.

"Yes, ma'am?" he asked, already setting off for the stairs.

"It took four Class One Supernaturals to take down the last high court demon we encountered," she said softly. "You're on your own. You *need* backup."

"If there are already demons here, he's well on his way to an Incursion," David replied calmly. "We have, at most, hours. How long would it take to gather three more Class Ones?"

"Days," Warner replied quietly, her voice sad.

"Then I will have to be enough," David told her simply. "Because I'm all that's here. If I fail..." He trailed off and knew that Warner understood. If he failed, there was always the bomber and its deadly cargo. Better a nuke than a supernatural invasion in New York.

The radio was silent as David kicked down the door to the stairwell and started for the third floor.

46

By the time David had reached the third floor, someone at Campus HQ—probably Charles or one of the other computer people—had sent over a floor plan of the OSPI building. His helmet visor had helpfully popped it up in a screen in the corner of his view, hopefully allowing him to find his way to the security center.

When he stepped out onto the third floor, it felt like stepping onto the scene of an action movie after the hero had shot his way through the villain's front entrance. The room the stairs and elevators opened onto *had* been well decorated, with the neat carved pillars and sunburst-marked blue carpet of the rest of OSPI HQ.

Then someone had come through with a machine gun of some kind. The pillars had been shredded, and the carpet was spattered with what David recognized as demonic ichor. No one had bothered to clean up, and three human bodies also lay in the room.

Even through his filtered helmet, he could smell the stench of bodies left dead for several days, and it took him only a moment to identify one of the fallen men—clad in the same black combat gear as David himself now wore—as an SSTTR man he'd seen with Casey in Montana. The other two bodies were in OSPI Security uniforms, and the machine gun had torn them apart beyond recognition.

One wall had been completely blown away by what David's Sight showed had been magic, and the battle had clearly moved into the foyer through the blasted wall. The path of destruction continued down a side corridor away from the foyer. It took only a moment with the floor plan to confirm that that was the fastest route to the security center.

He followed the trail of combat along the corridor and found more bodies waiting for him. Just outside the foyer appeared to have been the heart of a firefight, where whatever had been left of the SSTTR platoon at that point had clashed with a team of OSPI security people.

The SSTTR people hadn't had David's option of stunning the entire building. They'd cut through the security personnel who'd tried to stop them, with deadly force, and David couldn't be sure how many dead there were. No one had tried to clean up the mangled piles of body parts, and it would have taken a forensics team to separate them all for identification.

Seven of the bodies, however, spaced irregularly along the corridor, were Stutters in full combat gear. The last David had heard, the SSTTR force had forty members, which meant he'd now seen a fifth of the platoon dead with his own eyes.

He rounded a corner, expecting to see more bodies, and his prescience screamed a warning. With inhuman grace and speed, David turned his step into a dive as assault-rifle fire cut through the air where he was standing.

A pair of toad demons, like the ones on the main floor, was halfway down the corridor. At the end of the corridor, David's enhanced sight could pick out the armored security door leading to his destination. It was closed and barred. More bodies were strewn along the corridor, and the demons—presumably lacking the human inhibition against such things—had piled a dozen or so of them into an impromptu and effective barricade.

David rolled away as more fire came his way, and found himself kneeling beside the body of another SSTTR soldier, this one a familiar youngish woman. Forcing himself to ignore the smell and sight of her mangled body, he noticed her weapon—a stubby device like an over-sized shotgun that he recognized as a man-portable grenade launcher.

He was going to die here, he knew, but he didn't let that slow him as he picked up the weapon. He was going to die in this building, amongst these dead comrades, because his odds against a greater demon were less than nothing. He *wasn't* going to die to a pair of *flunkies*.

The demons fired again, a continuous burst that followed David as he grabbed the launcher and rolled away again. For a moment, he thought they were going to succeed at walking him into the wall, and then the gunfire stopped as the demons ran out of ammunition.

The Empowered ONSET Agent reacted with deadly speed, coming up onto one knee long before the demons could expect him to. With a cold smile, he raised the launcher and fired.

The grenade blasted down the corridor and hit the ground halfway between the demons and the armored door. David hit the ground as the shrapnel came blasting back toward him, presuming the grenade was probably loaded with silver.

When he rose, the demons had dissolved into ichor, confirming his guess on the grenade's content. David stepped back to the fallen Stutter woman and recognized her. It was Pam Uphoff, who Casey had introduced to him when he'd been here before.

"Thank you, Pam," he muttered softly as he removed her bandolier of grenades and slung it over his own shoulder. "I'm sorry."

He moved over to the demons' macabre barricade, checking that they were definitely dead, and eyed the devastated stretch of corridor between him and the security door. Bodies were everywhere, and he couldn't even separate the security people and the SSTTR men anymore. There couldn't have been much left of Stutter by the time they'd made it through there.

The security door looked intimidatingly intact, and David glanced down at his grenade bandolier. It took a moment to remember the meaning of the markings, and then he extracted an armor-piercing high-explosive grenade and snapped it into the M79's breach.

With another muttered apology to the bodies of the dead in the barricade, he aimed the shotgun-like weapon at the door and fired, ducking behind the pile of bodies as he did.

The explosion hurt his ears, and he slammed another grenade into the launcher as he prepared to assault the security center of his own government's supernatural police headquarters.

———

DAVID CHARGED through the shattered security door into the cool air of an air-conditioned central security room. Video screens covered three out of four walls of the large room, and a circular setup of computer consoles with more screens occupied the middle of the room.

About half of the video screens had been shot out, but the rest still showed parts of the building, many of them blocked or separated by the metal shutters and blast doors that the Judas Protocol had sealed. The source of the bullets that had shattered the screens lay to David's right, where Captain Anderson's body lay slumped against the wall. Texan officer had lost his helmet somewhere, and his bleached white hair was stained with blood. His body was over half-covered by the massive six-barreled minigun he'd brought in with him.

More of his team lay around him, cut down by gunfire from within the room. They were the only corpses within the room, but David spotted several more of the patches of ichor that marked the death throes of a demon.

"You are not the one I expected," said a melodious voice, and David turned to point the grenade launcher at the speaker. A tall man in a black suit and holding a sword stood behind the circle of computer consoles. His hair was black as night and his skin paler than snow.

The sword had a simple hilt and a narrow crossbar, connected to a long leaf-shaped blade with an unsettling red tint to the steel. David's Sight told him the blade was a *lot* more than it seemed, and the man who wielded it...was something else again. However human he looked, he was far from it. This was Ekhmez, a noble of the courts of the Masters Beyond.

"Ekhmez," David said quietly, the grenade launcher pointed unwaveringly at the demon.

"You are David White," the demon replied, equally quietly. "I was expecting Michael O'Brien."

"O'Brien had a messy encounter with a sniper," David replied coldly. "He'll live, but he won't be here today."

"Like I said," Ekhmez told him with a smug smile, "I was expecting O'Brien. You are an unexpected bonus." He shifted slightly, bringing the sword up, and David's finger tightened on the trigger.

"Don't be so hasty," the demon said silkily. "One of us is going to die before dawn, but there's no need to be *rude* about it."

"I've passed a few too many bodies on my way in here to be particularly polite," David told the monster in the suit. "Give me a reason not to pull the trigger on this."

"You have passed thirty-four bodies belonging to your Special Supernatural Tactics, Technology, and Reconnaissance team," Ekhmez said, his voice calm and soft. "Along the way here, they killed seventeen demons I had brought into this world and seventy-six of your security personnel.

"The other seven members of your SSTTR died elsewhere and more productively," he continued, his voice gentle and almost warm as his spare hand caressed the red-tinged blade of his sword. "I was impressed with the manufacturing facilities concealed within this building. Minor, I know, compared to other sites your Omicron possesses, but sufficient unto my needs.

"As for a reason not to shoot me," he said, his gaze locking with David's, "it won't exactly *do* anything." David realized that the creature's eyes were blood-red. No iris, no cornea, just a slightly glowing red.

"Let's test that theory, shall we?" David said calmly, and fired. The high-explosive grenade caught Ekhmez directly in the chest and detonated. The demon was blasted backward, crashing through a set of computers in a cascade of sparks and breaking plastic.

David slammed a second grenade home in the M79 as Ekhmez rose back to his feet, barely even scuffed by the explosion and glaring in anger.

"I told you..." he started, but David shot him again before he could finish. A second silver-tinged explosion blew Ekhmez into the wall with a crash that shattered monitors and dented the concrete.

The demon was up and moving before David could fire again, and the red-tinged blade of his sword sliced through the barrel of the M79. Even David didn't see the creature move, and he dove backward, releasing the destroyed weapon, as Ekhmez slashed at him again.

He dodged the sword a second time and drew the Omicron Silver. The weapon was still on burst mode, and David emptied the nine rounds remaining in it into the demon noble. The sheer kinetic force of the heavy bullets drove Ekhmez back, but none of the bullets penetrated his skin. Splotches of silver on his clothes marked the impacts, but the demon was unharmed.

Dropping the gun, David drew his mageblade. Its seven-inch blade looked pathetic next to the full three-foot length of Ekhmez's sword, but Ix had said it could hurt the demon. It didn't look like anything else could. In the end, even if the demon killed him, all he had to do was take off the thing's head.

His Sight wasn't giving him as much of an edge as it normally did, he realized as he dodged out of the way of another cut. Somehow, he could only See Ekhmez's actions moments into the future, not his usual second or so. Only his unnatural speed was allowing him to keep dodging. The demonic noble was fast, but so was David.

He used that speed. As Ekhmez attacked again, the ONSET Agent ducked under the strike and stabbed forward with the knife. Its enchanted blade sliced through the demon's skin like tissue paper, ripping open a gash that would have disemboweled a mortal.

Ichor oozed from the wound, but no organs spilled out. The demon's form *had* no internal organs anymore; the stolen body had rotted away, and what remained was simply a creation of the monster's will. No wound could really inconvenience the demon. No injury would slow it or distract it.

David had expected being gutted to distract Ekhmez, if only for a moment. In that moment of expected relief, the demon attacked. The long red-tinged sword shot forward in a lunge that David should have been able to dodge—but the demon's power meant he didn't See it coming.

The blade pierced the ex-cop's chest in a burst of searing flame.

47

DAVID OPENED HIS EYES TO A SURPRISING LACK OF PAIN. HE COULDN'T help himself glancing down, and realizing that not only was he lacking a gaping hole in his chest, he was in his old cop uniform, not his ONSET bodysuit.

"This isn't real," a gruff voice said quietly, and David looked up at the speaker. The huge black form of Leonard Casey stood before him, dressed in camouflage fatigues.

David began to take in his surroundings. It wasn't a room, more of a...space. Sharp metal and shining colors, all tinged red, surrounded him. He'd never seen anything like it.

"What do you mean?" he asked his former fellow trainee. "You look pretty solid to me."

"Yeah, I know," Casey replied. "And the issue with that is that I'm *dead*, David. I was captured and ritually sacrificed along with six of my friends to forge the sword that is embedded under your heart right now. Our souls were folded into the metal and the blade was quenched in our blood. The power of our life flows through it."

David blinked. "Am I dead, then?" he asked. He'd hoped to do more. He'd hoped to do *anything* to Ekhmez before the demon killed him.

"Dying," Casey answered bluntly.

"I've survived that before," the ONSET agent replied, looking around. "Where are we?"

"Inside the sword," the black soldier told him. "And inside your head. It's weird—a form of communication we can sustain as long as the blade is inside you. I don't recommend trying to talk to us this way later."

"I see why," David said dryly. "What happens when Ekhmez pulls the sword *out*?"

"This conversation is cut short," Casey admitted with a throwing-away gesture that seemed…un-Casey-like to David. "Subjective time is different. We have an hour or so of time in here."

"Other than giving me an extra hour of subjective time, why are we here?" David asked.

Casey turned away. "The blade Ekhmez wields is forged of souls, blood and magic as much as it's forged of steel," he explained. "The souls are warped—broken. In a very real sense, I am not Leonard Casey. I am the gestalt of the souls trapped in the blade. Casey is the one you knew, so we wear his face."

"And this?" David queried, gesturing at his uniform.

"You are as you see yourself," the sword told him gently. "Even now, you are first and foremost a police officer, sworn to serve and protect. Your own mantra."

"How do you know that?!" David demanded.

"This is a very…intimate form of communication," the Casey-figure reminded him. "Right now, we know you better than you know yourself. This is why we are here."

David watched the figure of his dead friend pace back in the strange confines of his dream.

"This weapon is called a bloodsword," the gestalt finally told him. "Among its many powers is inhibiting regeneration. Any wound that would be fatal to a mortal human, like the one you have taken, will be fatal even to one like you or O'Brien."

"Dammit," David cursed. He'd feared something like this. "So, what? I have an hour of subjective time here and then I go back to my body to die?!"

"No," Casey said firmly. "*Being* the sword, we are relatively certain of its properties. We can also control them. Ekhmez can punish us for defying him," he continued with a strange shudder, "but we *can* make sure your regeneration still functions once he withdraws the sword. We can, in fact, actually enhance your regeneration so you'll be healed almost as soon as the blade is removed."

"Then do it!" David ordered. "What more is there?"

"We will only ever have this one chance to speak to you, David," Casey said quietly. "And only ever to you, we think. We're not sure why, but we don't think we'll ever be able to talk to anyone else."

"What do you need to say?" the cop asked, his voice suddenly quiet. This was a gestalt of seven men and women who had died a horrible death. "I can pass messages on to your families if I live. What more do you want?"

"The sword cannot be unmade with modern magic," the Casey-gestalt said softly. "We are dead, but we are bound into this blade, this weapon. Understand this also: this sword is ancient, powerful magic, stronger than any weapon Omicron can forge. *We can kill Ekhmez.*"

The ONSET Agent looked at them in understanding. "I need you, don't I?"

"And we you," the gestalt replied. "We were soldiers, David White. We died because we chose to fight, to protect others. We...killed so many trying to get Ekhmez." Casey's voice twisted now, becoming more high-pitched and choked.

"And we failed," he continued, his voice now carrying the tones of at least three people saying the same words simultaneously. "But in forging us, he has created a weapon that can kill him—and others like him!

"We died to protect our people, but in death, we can still serve," the strange voice continued as the figure of Casey faded to become simply a glowing humanoid form, speaking with seven voices. "We can give you the chance to defeat Ekhmez, but only you can take it. Only you can destroy him and stand against those that will follow.

"We were forged like this for evil, but we gave our lives to protect," the voices continued, in perfect sync. "If what has been done cannot be undone, then let it serve as we did. Let it protect, as we could not.

"We will give you your chance, David White," the blade gestalt told him. "But we have a price. One price. One command. Remember us! Wield us!"

David looked at the figure before him, formed of souls and loyalty and power. Seven souls, slain in horror to forge a weapon of evil, demanding that he take up that weapon for the very cause they had died to protect. For the very cause he had sacrificed the life he'd known.

To take up the weapon to serve and protect his people.

"I will," he said firmly, and then the confines of the sword were gone, and he was staring once more into Ekhmez's eyes, the length of red steel being slowly withdrawn from his chest.

With a gasp, David stumbled backward, hitting the wall by the door and slumping down. Pain racked his body as his heart tried to beat and failed. He focused on it, willing the warmth of regeneration to surge through it, to give him the chance he needed.

For a moment, he feared that the gestalt had failed, that his regeneration was gone. Blackness dropped over his vision as unconsciousness came for him. Then the sword's parting gift of energy hit him. Warmth surged through him, and the pain faded as his chest healed and his heart beat. Once, twice, and his blood flowed again. Oxygen rushed back to his eyes and brain, and he could see once more.

He saw Ekhmez turned away, the soaked bloodsword casually gripped in his hand as he checked a computer to see if it was still working. He saw a video camera in the corner of the room; it was focused on him as if the team following him through the security cameras was praying for him to get back up.

He saw Anderson's corpse, just out of arm's reach, and the massive minigun with its belt of silver bullets across it. Ekhmez's back was still turned, the demon showing his contempt for his fallen foe.

A volcano of power surged through David, and he lunged from his slumped position to his feet. He scooped the minigun up into his arms and braced it against the wall. The sound of metal thumping on plaster caught the demon noble's attention, and David saw him begin to turn.

The cop never let Ekhmez finish the motion. He pulled the trigger on the minigun and let recoil press it against the wall as he used his prodigious strength to hold the stream of silver on the demon.

No bullet, not even silver, not even the high-velocity minigun rounds, could penetrate the defenses of a high court demon. But not even a high court demon could withstand the kinetic force of so *many* bullets. The bloodsword slipped from Ekhmez's grip as the minigun's last hundred or so rounds picked the monster up and flung him across the room.

David moved before the demon even hit the floor, leaving the gun half-embedded in the wall as he snatched the bloodsword from the ground and charged the creature that had left so many corpses in its wake.

Ekhmez rose from the ground with lightning speed, nearly a match for David's own. The ONSET Commander met the demon's eyes and knew that if he missed, he was dead.

The demon parried with its arms, but the sword sang with willing power and sliced clean through the ichor-forged flesh. David held the monster's eyes for an eternity, and then the demon's head toppled from its shoulders as its body collapsed into black goo.

EPILOGUE

VANESSA LORING WAITED IN THE BACK CORNER OF THE TINY NEW YORK café—on the opposite end of Manhattan from OSPI HQ—wondering when her Omicron contact was going to show up. Charles had told her that someone would meet her in this place, and the time was less than a minute away.

The café was an imitation French affair, with umbrella-topped circular tables separated by low patio fencing. The effect was slightly spoiled by the fact that it was late November and the entire café was inside of an office-building atrium.

The hacker had found herself nervously doing her hair and nails before coming there, something she hadn't bothered with in years. She suspected she knew who Charles would send to meet her. The Omicron personnel had interrogated her about how she'd penetrated their systems, and both her use of David's email to break through and her attempt to blackmail him had come up.

Her suspicion was confirmed when the door to the café swung open at exactly two twenty-five and a stocky man in a long navy blue duster belted tight against the winter chill stepped in. He was dark-haired and unscarred but moved with a grace that sent shivers of fear and desire down Vanessa's spine.

The familiar man stepped over to her table and looked down at her, his eyes unreadable.

"Ms. Loring?" he asked quietly.

"Yes," she replied. "You are?" she asked, though she was almost sure she knew.

"Commander David White, ONSET," the stocky agent said firmly. "May I join you?"

"Certainly," she agreed, gesturing to the chair opposite her. "I presume you are my jailer?"

Vanessa had no illusions about her ability to escape this meeting. While White was her contact, at least two other people in the café were his support, and she was reasonably sure she'd spotted a sniper outside.

"No," the Omicron man told her, his voice drawing out the single syllable. "I am here to discuss the terms of your freedom."

"And they are?" she asked carefully, wondering what the organization that she suspected now knew *everything* about her past would want.

"You saved lives with your warning," White said gently. "One of them was mine. Any personal debt between us is clear."

The hacker known as Majestic nodded in silence. That was far more than she'd ever hoped for.

"And with your employers?" she asked.

"As of this morning," he told her quietly, "your file with the FBI was deactivated. No one will be hunting you. No one will be chasing you. It is a closed book."

"A pardon?"

"No," the government agent told her, his eyes watching her. It was an uncomfortable feeling to have him watch her. She was sure he was seeing more than she wanted him to. "A chance. If you return to your old ways, the file will reopen, and Omicron will lend our considerable aid to the FBI in tracking you down."

Vanessa stared at him. On the one hand, they were offering a clean slate. On the other, they were threatening to destroy her entire life and livelihood.

"It is our opinion," White said, his voice still ever so soft, "that you are perfectly capable of finding a legitimate employment for your talents. While the decision has been made at a higher level that you are too much of a loose cannon for us to hire you, Charles said to suggest working as a security consultant—and to expect him to call you from time to time."

The hacker leaned back in her chair and regarded the cop. They were suggesting she turn white hat—protect the very systems she'd once taken so much pleasure in breaking. Take on the other side of the battle of wits she'd always enjoyed. The side that didn't hurt people.

Oddly enough, the thought had never seriously occurred to her, and she nodded slowly as she regarded the supernatural sitting across the table from her. David White looked like a normal if heavily built human being. She knew better. She'd watched him walk into a fortified bunker and clear it alone. More, Charles had allowed her to see an edited version of the footage from his assault on OSPI HQ.

"Did they let you keep the sword?" she asked softly to buy herself time. At David's questioning look, she shrugged and smiled. "Charles felt I had the right to find out how things had ended."

He nodded slowly and twitched the long coat back. A thick hilt protruded from his belt, but the scabbard looked far too short to be for a sword.

"That looks like a knife," she observed, and he twitched a smile. White quickly glanced around the room to be sure no one was watching, and slid the sword partially out of its sheath. In a moment, there was more steel visible than the scabbard had looked like it could hold. Vanessa could make out some sort of lettering on the blade.

"The scabbard is a pocket dimension," White told her. "The pun is horrible, but I got lost when they tried to explain it beyond that. The blade is Elsewhere until I draw it."

"What does the writing say?" she asked as he resheathed the sword, more curious than buying time now.

"Memoria," David said simply. "Latin for 'remembered.' The rest is the names of the men and women Ekhmez killed to forge it. To make sure I never forget." He shrugged. "We couldn't seriously damage the blade or unmake its magic, but we could at least laser-etch it.

"Now," he said firmly, his gaze meeting hers. "We are here to talk about you. Do you have an answer to our offer?"

Vanessa Loring looked at the man across the table. This man had walked out of a normal life and into something extraordinary. He'd fought and killed a demon lord. Everything he did was to protect people. That desire gave him strength, and she found herself wanting to share it. To, like him, take her gifts and use them to protect others.

"Yes," she said firmly. "I'll take your offer. And Charles's suggestion. Maybe it's time I tried to some good in the world."

"That's all we try for," David White told her. "To do some good. To serve and protect."

———

ABOUT THE AUTHOR

Glynn Stewart is the author of *Starship's Mage*, a bestselling science fiction and fantasy series where faster-than-light travel is possible–but only because of magic. His other works include science fiction series *Duchy of Terra*, *Castle Federation* and *Vigilante*, as well as the urban fantasy series *ONSET* and *Changeling Blood*.

Writing managed to liberate Glynn from a bleak future as an accountant. With his personality and hope for a high-tech future intact, he lives in Kitchener, Ontario with his wife, their cats, and an unstoppable writing habit.

facebook.com/glynnstewartauthor

twitter.com/glynnstewart

OTHER BOOKS BY GLYNN STEWART

For release announcements join the mailing list or visit GlynnStewart.com